THE PHOTOGRAPHER'S WIFE

Nick Alexander grew up in the seaside town of Margate. He has travelled widely and lived in the UK, the USA and France, where he resides today.

Nick's first five novels – the *Fifty Reasons* series – were self-published from 2004 onwards and went on to become some of the UK's best-selling gay literature. His crossover titles, *The Case of the Missing Boyfriend*, *The French House* and *The Half-Life of Hannah* each reached #1 in Amazon's UK chart, jointly selling over 850,000 copies to date. *The Photographer's Wife* is Nick's 11th novel and, as of going to print, has already reached #1 in Amazon's ebook chart and sold over 100,000 copies. For more information please visit the author's website on www.nick-alexander.com

THE PHOTOGRAPHER'S WIFE

Nick Alexander

BLACK & WHITE PUBLISHING

First published 2015
by Black & White Publishing Ltd
29 Ocean Drive, Edinburgh EH6 6JL

1 3 5 7 9 10 8 6 4 2   15 16 17 18

ISBN: 978 1 84502 955 5

A CIP catalogue record for this book is available from the British Library.

ALBA | CHRUTHACHAIL

Typeset by Iolaire Typesetting, Newtonmore
Printed and bound by Nørhaven, Denmark

ACKNOWLEDGEMENTS

Thanks to Rosemary – without your constant encouragement nothing would ever get finished and without your friendship this planet would be a much darker place. Thanks to Sam Javanrouh Photography for the beautiful cover shot and to Allan for his eagle-eyed copy-editing skills. Thanks to all my readers for sticking with me and showing so much enthusiasm about every new project – you make it all worthwhile.

This book is dedicated to our parents who, for all their successes (and all their failures) have lived through more than we, their children, can ever imagine.

"Don't think you know what battles I had to fight to get where I am today. Don't think you can even imagine what suffering we had to go through, what secrets we had to hide. You think you know everything but you know nothing. You don't know me – you don't know anyone. Because that's what life is. It's thinking you know everything, and thinking you know everyone, and finding out, the older you get, that you didn't – that you had it all wrong." – B. Marsden.

1940 – SHOREDITCH, LONDON.

Barbara pushes up onto her toes and grasps the windowsill with her small, pale hands. A flake of green paint breaks away and falls to the floor and momentarily she is distracted by the fact that it is green on top, yet white underneath.

"Look!" her sister says again, squashing a finger against the window pane.

Barbara looks at the finger and notices the way the light shines through it from the other side, then looks at the dirty pane itself. Finally, she shifts her focal point to whatever is beyond the window – whatever has her sister so excited.

In the distance, high above the rooftops, she can see a group of dots floating in the clear September sky. They are still only dots but Barbara can hear a droning sound and already knows, even at six years old, that these dots are warplanes, that these dots are bombers.

The door behind them bursts open and she turns nervously to see her mother. She's not sure if she has done anything wrong but it's best to be prepared these days just in case – it seems to happen a lot.

"And what the hell are you two doing at the window?" Minnie asks crossly, as she pulls off her coat. "And don't tell me you didn't hear the warnin'."

"But look!" Glenda says, still pointing.

"I'll give you, 'look'," Minnie says, but intrigued by something in her eldest daughter's voice, she crosses the kitchen to peer from the window all the same.

Troubled by Minnie's momentary silence, Barbara turns back to the blue sky beyond the window and watches the dots again. They are bigger now; the droning is louder now. She tilts her head towards the ceiling and looks up at her mother, whose upside-down face is shifting from its usual, almost permanent, expression of annoyance, to puzzlement, then concern.

"Bleedin' Krauts," Minnie whispers after a moment, then, with a deep, sad sigh, she drags her regard from the sky outside and, tapping Glenda gently on the side of the head, she says, "Kitchen table, Madam. Now!" She grabs Barbara's left hand and drags her from the room.

Barbara sits with her back against the lathed leg of the table and runs her index finger along the grain of the wood above her. The droning noise from the planes is loud now and a little frightening, and is soon joined by the rattling crackle of the anti-aircraft guns.

"Definitely Germans then," Glenda says, addressing her mother's knees as she moves quickly around the table preparing sandwiches. Barbara can tell from the smells wafting down that these will contain fish paste, her least favourite filling.

"Who else are they gonna be?" Minnie replies, the table resonating strangely with her voice.

"I thought they might be *our* boys," Glenda says. "They're a bit early in the day to be Krauts, aren't they?" The limited air-raids to date have been almost exclusively nocturnal.

A chipped, floral plate appears, floating beneath the edge of the table. It is piled with three doorstop sandwiches rather than the usual triangular bite-sized kind.

Barbara, who in these times of rationing has been told off repeatedly for helping herself, hesitates a moment before delicately taking one.

"Well, take the plate!" Minnie says. "D'you want me to stay out here till a bomb comes or somethin'?"

Glenda reaches past her sister and takes the plate, then snatches the sandwich back from Barbara and returns it with the others. *"Stupid!"* she whispers.

"And I'll have none of that!" Minnie tells her, now crouching down and joining the two girls on the thin mattress beneath the table. She brings with her a pottery jug filled with water and a tin mug which they will share.

"Shouldn't we go to the shelter?" Glenda asks. "Because Mary over the road said—"

"It ain't finished," Minnie tells her. "You know it ain't." The Andersen shelter in the garden needs another full day of spadework and considering it all a bit unnecessary, believing, along with most of the girls at the factory, that the threat to London has been exaggerated, Minnie, exhausted by the end of her working day, has been reluctant to put in the hours.

"Not ours. I mean the proper one. At the youth club," Glenda says, " 'cos Mary over the road – you know, the one whose granddad's an air warden – well *he* said—"

"We'll be fine here," Minnie says loudly, cutting her off. "Now be quiet and eat yer tea or I'll eat it myself."

In the distance, the deep boom of a five-hundred pounder resonates and Barbara postpones the first bite of her sandwich to listen, leaving it hovering before her mouth.

"The docks again," Minnie says. "It's always the docks. Poor buggers. Wouldn't get me working down there."

Barbara bites into the sandwich and, as another round of popping anti-aircraft fire coincides with a second distant bang, thinks, *fish paste. Yuck.* But despite the fish paste, she quite enjoys these hours spent under the table snuggled between her mother and her sister. It's as much fun as ever happens at home these days anyway.

Something whistles overhead and is followed by a new kind of explosion. Barbara sees Minnie frown and look up at the underside of the table as if it has some secret to impart to her about this new sound. Minnie reaches for the three hated gas masks beside her and pulls them within the safety zone provided by the table. And then it happens – another explosion, only this is *much* closer and they not only hear it but feel the thud of it coming through the floor, through the mattress. Minnie inhales sharply and closes her eyes, Glenda's actually widen, and Barbara's sandwich slips from her grasp and falls into her lap.

"Woo!" says Glenda, grinning a little crazily once the moment has passed.

If her mother shared Glenda's excitement, Barbara might have been able to follow her lead – she might have been able to think that this was fun as well. But as another bomb hits and then another, and then another, and as the blasts are ever closer, ever louder, Minnie is realising that this is very different to the old Zeppelin raids of her own childhood, where the Germans simply chucked bombs out of the windows of the airships, different even to the strikes that have hit London to date, and that, solidly built as it undoubtedly is, they may not be as safe as she assumed, here beneath the oak of the old kitchen table.

Barbara studies her mother's face for clues and sees her swallow and lick her lips. She can't know what her mother is thinking but she can sense her feelings almost as if they are her own, and in this case what she senses is fear. A new thought crosses her six-year-old mind, one that she has never had before: that her mother may be fallible, that there may come a time when her decisions are not the right ones. Even sandwiched between her mother and her sister, she suddenly feels unsafe. She starts to cry.

"And you can stop that right away!" Minnie says, threatening a slap by half raising her free hand.

Barbara swallows with difficulty and feels as if her face is swelling, doubling in size as she struggles to contain the next batch of tears.

"Crying never solved nothing," Minnie says, and Glenda shoots her sister a discreet wink and hands her the sandwich again.

"Eat up, Sis'," she says softly. "You'll be alright. We wouldn't let anything happen to you, now would we?"

* * *

Barbara follows her mother out of the newly finished shelter and pauses in the grey dawn light to take in the smog in the air and the sunset-red blaze lighting the horizon in every direction.

Other than the all-pervading smell of smoke and the permanent, multi-directional sunset, everything in their immediate surroundings seems unchanged and this morning, as every morning, this is a surprise. The noise from the night raids is incessant and terrifying and it's hard to imagine, lying there in the dark, that anything beyond the shelter remains.

"Come on," Minnie says. "Let's get you out of those damp clothes," and Barbara touches the sleeve of her nightshirt and senses the all-pervading dampness of the shelter still with her, lingering in the material. She is pulled, with a jerk, forwards past the tiny vegetable patch. "What about Glenda?" she asks, straining to look back at the open door of the shelter.

"Let her sleep," Minnie says. "You two have a big day ahead of you."

Yes, a big day. For today is evacuation day. The 'phoney war' is over; no one is any longer in doubt that the danger is real, and Minnie, under increasing pressure to evacuate the girls since the beginning of the war, has finally caved in. She is dreading letting them go. She's terrified for them, has no idea where they're going, no idea what awaits them in Wales . . . But she's also scared for herself. The air raids are so frightening, they make her feel sick, and her life here now that Seamus has gone (and is he even still alive? There have been no letters . . .) is miserable. With the kids around, she at least has to pull herself together. But what happens once they're gone?

As Barbara eats her bread and marge, Minnie watches her and wonders how this day will pass, wonders even if she herself is really capable of this – capable of separating herself so geographically from her flesh and blood.

"Glenda's a sleepy girl," Barbara says, speaking through a mouthful of bread.

"Let her sleep," Minnie replies. *Yes, let her sleep,* she thinks. *Let her sleep till the last possible moment.* Barbara is too young to understand what evacuation really means but Glenda, Minnie knows, is going to scream blue bloody murder.

* * *

They are at the train station, and Barbara, who has been told a secret, is surprised that her sister is here at all.

There are children everywhere: groups, like cattle, forging their way through moving rivers of other children, being herded by the unlikely association of teachers and fat people and old people and pregnant women that have been assembled to travel with them.

Glenda is sulking, gently kicking her small brown suitcase, but not, Minnie notes, making a fuss as yet.

Barbara, she can tell, is tense, hesitating between seeing this as an adventure or a trauma, watching her sister, her mother, everyone around her for clues as to how to react. Only Minnie herself comprehends just how enormous this rupture will be for them all. Only Minnie is bracing herself for the aftermath.

To the right, a little girl cries out, and is lifted, kicking, into a carriage. Barbara swivels her head and watches and hears the little girl's vibrato voice: "I won't go, I won't go! I *won't!*" Barbara clasps and unclasps her fingers around the rough weave of the shopping basket containing her clothes. The coarse fibres prickle her skin.

A man with a clipboard is heading towards them. "Mrs Doyle!" he says, theatrically.

"Mr Wallace," Minnie replies, emulating his officious tone of voice.

"Glad to see we finally saw sense," he says smugly.

"If you call 'seeing sense' sending your kids to God-knows-where to be brought up by God-knows-who, then yes, Mr Wallace, we've finally seen sense," Minnie retorts, thinking only once she has said it that the girls have overheard. But Minnie just can't help herself in these situations. She is not someone who likes to be told what to do and Grenville Wallace has been doing just that ever since he traded his grubby, overpriced little corner shop for this role as evacuation officer. His attitude alone is almost enough to make her turn around and head home.

A train behind them hoots and puffs and starts, groaningly, to pull out of the station, and Barbara watches the slideshow of passing faces pressed at the grimy windows. Some of them seem happy and excited, while others are red-eyed and tear-stained. It's confusing.

"I don't have all day to discuss the pros and cons of government policy, Mrs Doyle," the man is saying, waving his pen in the air with flourish. "So, it's just this one, is it?" he asks, nodding at Barbara.

"No, it's . . ." Minnie says, turning to where Glenda should be standing. "Where . . .?" she murmurs, reaching to pull Glenda's suitcase closer before scanning the hordes around them. "Where did your sister go?" she asks, frowning heavily.

Barbara shrugs and stares at her feet.

"Did she go looking for the loo?" Minnie asks.

Barbara shakes her head.

"Mary mother of Jesus," Minnie says, now grasping Barbara's chin and forcing her to turn towards her. "Did she say something?"

Barbara nods vaguely.

"Mrs Doyle!" the man says.

"Just wait, won't you?" Minnie tells him, then to Barbara, "What did she say? Tell me what she said."

"It's a secret," Barbara whispers.

"What's a bloody secret?" Minnie asks, and Barbara, who understands this tone of voice only too well, knows better than to obfuscate.

"She said she isn't going to Wales. Not for anything, she said."

"Mrs Doyle!" the man says, and Minnie scans the horizon once more before turning to face him.

"It seems you're having trouble controlling your brood. Perhaps the Welsh will fare better! But in the meantime, there is this slight matter of these forms and what I should inscribe upon them. So just Barbara here, travelling alone is it?"

"I don't know," Minnie says. "Sorry, just . . . just hang on a mo."

Minnie starts to push her way through the crowds, pausing to ask people, "Have you seen a little girl? Have you seen my girl? She's got brown hair and a blue coat. About this tall. Have *you* seen her? Have *you* seen my girl?"

The people around her either ignore her – they're just too busy – or frown at her as if she is mad. Even Barbara can see that expecting anyone to answer this particular question, today, in the middle of this mass of children, is indeed a kind of madness.

The man with the clipboard grabs Barbara's hand and, initially, because it feels reassuring, she lets him do this. But when he starts trying to pull her towards a train carriage, she begins to struggle. "No!" she says, then, "Mum!" But Minnie isn't looking. Minnie is lost in her nightmarish search for her other daughter, running towards girls who look a little like Glenda from behind and pulling them by their shoulders to face her.

"Mum!" Barbara shouts again, then, emulating the little girl she saw before, she says, "I won't go. I won't!" Seeing that this is having precisely zero effect, she begins to scream. Her piercing cry registers on some primeval level and Minnie stops in her tracks and turns to see her youngest, in mid-air, held at arms length, being passed by Grenville Wallace to a bald, greasy-looking man in a three-piece suit. She sees Barbara's legs flailing and runs back through the crowd, knocking a little boy over as she does so; she offers a fumbling apology over her shoulder to the boy, now crying, but continues to run all the same.

Wallace attempts to block her path, saying, "Mrs Doyle! In God's name! This is all most irreg—"

But Minnie pushes him aside, lurches past the bald man, and grabs her daughter's hand just as she is being sucked into the darkness of the train – jerkingly, painfully yanking her back out onto the platform. "She ain't bloody going to Wales on her own!" Minnie says, her voice incredulous. "She ain't going without her sister! What are you thinking of?"

"If she doesn't go today, then she won't be going at all," Mr Wallace says. "I'll make bloody sure of that. Thousands, millions of children to evacuate and you think you can muck us around like this?"

"Don't make me go," Barbara sobs. "Please don't make me go, Mum. I'll be ever so good. I promise I'll be good."

"She's on the list now anyway," the man says, waving his clipboard at her.

"Well, you can bloody well take her *off* the list," Minnie tells him. "Go stand by Glenda's suitcase over there," she instructs, prising Barbara's hand from her own and pushing her across the platform away from the train. "And stop bloody crying!"

Barbara forges her way though a sea of children moving in the other direction and places one hand on the suitcase as she watches the altercation between her mother and the man. She can't hear what she is saying but there is something magnificent about her mother's posture, hands on hips, giving him what-for. She feels proud.

"Right," Minnie says, once the man, with a shrug and a disparaging wave over his shoulder, has turned his attention elsewhere and she has crossed to join Barbara. She picks up the suitcase and heads for the exit.

"Aren't we being 'vacuated, then?" Barbara asks.

Minnie pauses and, uncharacteristically, crouches down in front of her daughter. "Do you *want* to be evacuated? Do you want to get on the bloody train and go to Wales? Because believe me girl, you're one step away from it. Just say the word."

"No!" Barbara says, starting to cry again.

"Then stop your sobbing girl! I'm taking you home."

"And Glenda?" Barbara asks, trying to look over her shoulder as they pass through the echoey madness of the station hall.

"She's twelve. She knows how to make her own way home," Minnie says. "And she'll find a nice hard slap waiting for her when she gets there. The little cow!"

Unexpectedly, Minnie stops walking, so Barbara peers up at her. "Where's your things?"

Barbara looks at her empty hand and tries to remember when she lost track of the basket. "The man," she says, pointing backwards. "He put it in the train."

"Jesus! That's all we need," Minnie says. "We won't be getting that back now. A right bloody waste of time this has all been. And what am I supposed to dress you in now? Honestly! As if times aren't hard enough! You had better behave, girl. You had better be so bloody good. I swear, you cry once, you'll be on that train to Wales and it won't be just for the war, it'll be *forever!*"

Barbara squeezes her eyes shut to prevent more tears, so close now, from leaking out, and she fails as a result to see an uneven paving stone. She trips and is yanked upright again.

"Walk nicely!" Minnie says.

* * *

Barbara sits alone, her legs crossed, on the single bed they have moved into the shelter. She is supposed to be reading but is instead studying the reflection of the candle in a newly formed puddle on the ground. She is listening for the first bombs to arrive. The air-raid siren was five minutes ago.

The door to the shelter opens and Glenda appears. "It's 'orrible out there," she says, starting to pull off her wet coat, hesitating, then finally removing it after all. "It's horrible in here too. Where's Mum, then?"

"Gone to get soup," Barbara says. "She said don't move a muscle."

"Mapledene Road got hit," Glenda announces.

"Really?"

"Fell in someone's back yard. Blew all the windows out. And blew the shelter right out of the ground too. They wasn't in it though."

Barbara blinks at her sister, then looks around at the corrugated iron walls and tries to imagine them being *blown out of the ground.*

11

"Don't worry," Glenda says, sitting on the edge of the bed and removing her shoes. "Lightning never strikes twice."

"Here they come," Barbara says, cocking one ear to the distant whistle of an incendiary bomb.

Glenda nods, waits for the explosion – it's a long way away – then crosses her legs and sits opposite her sister. "Oh Sister," she says, dramatically. "Whatever am I going to do now?"

Barbara folds her book – a tattered copy of *Little Black Sambo* – and looks up at Glenda, her wrinkled brow somehow exaggerated by the candlelight. "What's happened, Sister?" she asks.

"Johnny's being evacuated tomorrow. They got hit three doors down and his mum says it's just too dangerous to stay."

Barbara nods seriously. Johnny is Glenda's boyfriend and though she has never seen him, though, even now, she doubts his existence, she has heard all about him. "Is he going to Wales?"

Glenda shakes her head. "Not everyone goes to Wales, silly."

"I knew that," Barbara lies. "I just wondered."

"Oh, it's the worst thing in the world when they leave you," Glenda says. "I just want to die."

"Oh Sister!" Barbara says, opening her arms and hugging Glenda awkwardly.

"He was the only thing that held me together," Glenda says, a phrase that she overheard her weepy teacher, Mrs Richardson, say that morning.

"Don't cry," Barbara says, rather enjoying her role as confidante in this melodrama.

"I can't help it," Glenda says, leaning back just far enough for Barbara to see that she has managed to produce a real,

12

single tear. The ability to form tears on demand is a gift that Glenda has and this is perhaps one of the reasons why Minnie has so little truck with them.

"You mustn't cry," Barbara tells her. "If Mum catches you, you'll be sent to Wales."

"Maybe I *should* cry," Glenda says. "At least that way I'd see Johnny again."

"But Johnny isn't in Wales," Barbara says, confused now.

Another bomb whistles outside, closely followed by a far-off explosion and then, without warning, there is a stunning, earth-jolting sonic boom that shakes the bed from side to side, makes the flame of the candle flicker, even makes the ground ripple. Afterwards, everything is deathly silent, and it is only after thirty seconds or so when their hearing starts to return that the girls realise that this is not silence because the world has ceased to exist but a silence born of the fact that they have been momentarily deafened.

The girls remain immobile, cross-legged and facing each other, until Glenda – looking genuinely panicked – swings her legs over the edge and starts to pull on her shoes.

"Where are you going?" Barbara asks. "Mum said . . ."

"Mum said, Mum said . . ." Glenda repeats.

"She said to stay put. She said you mustn't."

"It's Mum I'm going to check on," Glenda says. "What if she got hit?"

Barbara bites her bottom lip. She doesn't know what to do. She doesn't know what to say.

When the door to the shelter jerks open and Minnie appears, Barbara releases the breath she has been holding. "Did you hear that?" Minnie says, blustering into the shelter. "I almost spilt the soup. I swear the blast messed up me bleedin' hair."

She puts the pan of soup down on a small stool, then turns and closes the door behind her. "You girls bein' brave?" she asks, and Barbara turns away just long enough to wipe a tear – a genuine tear of relief – from her cheek. "Yes," she says. "We're absolutely fine, aren't we Sis'?"

* * *

The fear is so pervasive, so constant, that it begins to seem normal. But being scared, even all the time, is still being scared, and Barbara wishes she could be harder, like her mother, or even better, like her sister – apparently immune, apparently still thrilled by every bang, still excited by every near-miss.

But the danger is undeniable, the signs are all around them now. The house at the end of the street is gone, the family within all dead; the gasometer around the corner is in flames. Barbara's days at school are spent listening for distant air-raid sirens, which sometimes, if she concentrates, she can hear before anyone else. Sometimes she can hear them whole minutes before the local siren prompts their descent into the cellar where, despite the games and rhymes and distractions the teachers attempt to organise, Barbara listens, still, for clues from above. She's trying to detect a secret sign that might differentiate this bombardment from all of the others; she's trying to detect some dark, non-audible vibration which might reveal that everything has changed, that Glenda and Mum have not, this time, escaped.

Once the air-raids are over, she walks home in the pitch black, past the vague shadows of bombed-out buildings, past smoking, steaming remains, past shadowy figures who might be friends, only it's too dark to see. Sometimes a blazing building provides light and she jumps over vast, snakc-like fire hoses dragged by exhausted, blackened firemen. She tries not to notice the child's toy poking from beneath a collapsed wall, tries not to worry about the origin of the red stain on

14

the pavement. War provides no censorship, so Barbara tries to create her own. And now she must round the final corner – she holds her breath. Will the house still be there? Will it be in flames? Or will it be flattened?

She lets herself in and sits watching the door, waiting for Glenda and her mother to come separately through it, hoping that the siren won't sound before they do so. And here they are, revealing that it has happened again: they have been spared – another daily miracle amidst the mayhem of bombed-out London. But today something is different. Barbara can sense a change. Minnie is holding Glenda's hand, and Glenda is as white as a sheet.

"Come on," Minnie tells her. "Get your things. We're going to the shelter tonight," and Barbara doesn't ask why; she doesn't want to know what has happened, because she has learned that there is enough terror in each day for everyone and that sharing it around is superfluous, that sharing it around just adds to everybody's burden. It's one huge life-lesson that she will never forget.

Last night's raids were local and lethal, and the youth club shelter, in the arched tunnel of the basement, is packed solid. There is sitting room but no more. Minnie tells Barbara to look after her big sister and starts to tiptoe to the far side to fetch soup from the WVS ladies. Everyone around them looks exhausted; no one slept much last night.

"Are you OK, Sister?" Barbara asks, a little unnerved by Glenda's silence. She hasn't said a word yet.

Glenda nods and blinks slowly. "They were asleep," she says quietly. "The whole family. It was an unexploded one from the night before, so they wasn't even in the shelter. Not that it would have done 'em any good. That was flattened too."

Barbara nods and hopes that Glenda won't tell her *who* has died. She doesn't like to put names and faces to these stories,

15

because once fleshed out she knows that they will have the power to haunt her dreams, turning them into nightmares.

"Poor Billy," Glenda says, shaking her head and breathing erratically with the effort she is making not to cry.

Poor Billy, Barbara repeats in her head and then, despite herself, the image of Glenda's schoolfriend Billy Holt comes to mind, closely followed by Mrs Holt sweeping the front porch. She wonders about Billy's sister Harriet – with whom she sometimes played – but decides, quite consciously, not to ask. All the same, she imagines Harriet, whose pretty dresses she was always so jealous of, buried somewhere beneath rubble, the crisp, starched cotton crushed by the weight of fallen brick. She imagines what that would feel like.

Minnie returns with mugs of watery soup and Barbara takes hers, grasps it between both hands, and counts to twenty so as to delay the first sip. Her anticipation of the soup is, she knows from experience, more powerful than its ability to actually satisfy her hunger. She likes to wait as long as possible.

"Eat your soup," Minnie tells Glenda. She crouches down and pushes the hair from her daughter's eyes – a rare display of affection reserved for exceptional circumstances such as these.

Someone at the far end of the cellar tries to start a singalong with a warbling rendition of *Doing The Lambeth Walk* but tonight it fails to catch on – it doesn't always work – and the singer falters at the end of the first verse, then mutters, "Bugger you all then," which at least provokes a few laughs.

"We're all knackered, Annie," someone shouts, and Glenda, who would have found a singalong hard to bear, feels relieved.

Minnie, who claims to be unable to sleep sitting (even if the girls have frequently caught her doing so), heads to the far side to "have a natter" with Mrs Peters.

In the farthest corner from the gas lamp, a couple are discreetly canoodling beneath their coats. Barbara peers at the shifting shapes for a moment and wonders what *that* feels like, then turns her attention to the woman beside them who is knitting what looks like a glove.

Once she has finished her soup, she closes her eyes and, ignoring the rumbling of her tummy, tries to imagine her favourite scene of the moment, a farm in Wales.

"Do *all* farms have cows?" she asks her sister, momentarily opening her eyes, and Glenda, who knows as much about farms as her little sister, says, "Oh yes. They always have lots of cows. Otherwise there wouldn't be any milk, would there?"

Reassured not only about her conjured image of a farm but also that her sister is talking again, Barbara closes her eyes anew and pictures a rosy-faced Welsh woman squirting the cow's milk straight into a bottle. "Take that to the dairy would you, Babs?" the woman says. "And help yourself to some cheese if you fancy it."

2011 – SHOREDITCH, LONDON.

"Sophie, darling!" Genna Wild floats through the dazzlingly bright expanse of the gallery to where Sophie is shrugging off her wet coat. Behind her, rain is falling from a dark October London sky.

"You made it!" Genna says, helping her out of the coat and smiling beatifically, as if Sophie is her very favourite person on the planet. "How marvellous!"

"Are you kidding?" Sophie says. "I wouldn't miss this for anything. Not even on a revolting evening like this one."

Genna wrinkles her nose. "It is horrid, isn't it? Come get yourself a drink. The white is rather special. It sounds German but it's from Alsace, apparently."

As Sophie follows her across the room, she takes in the assembled crowd – forty, perhaps even fifty people who have braved the weather to see Arakis' photographs, or perhaps, like her, bask by association in the glow of his exhibition.

As she reaches the drinks table, she starts to notice the photographs themselves, vast, three-metre black and white prints, mostly of naked women, most of heavily *bound* naked women. To her right, the image is of a woman tied up in an enamel bath, to her left, it shows a nude suspended by rope from a ceiling.

She hates these photos. That is her first reaction, and she tries, as she sips at the wine, to analyse why this is so, tries to decide just how much of her aversion is political and how much is, well, for want of a better word, jealousy. As far as

18

her eye can tell, these are porn shots – technically masterful, beautifully lit porn shots but porn shots all the same.

"Aren't they gorgeous?" Genna says, following her regard, so Sophie wrinkles her nose cutely and nods. There's no point falling out with the owner of one of London's most successful photography galleries – there's no point at all.

"Must circulate," Genna says, turning, then scooting back to the entrance in order to greet a new arrival – a slightly overweight and extraordinarily pale man with round glasses and a very wet, grey-checked suit. "Brett!" she exclaims. "Oh how *wonderful* that you could make it!"

Sophie moves to the right and positions herself in front of a vast photograph of a naked, pregnant woman, bound again with generous quantities of rope.

"Such energy!" a man beside her says as he peers over his half-moon glasses at the photo.

"Yes," Sophie says, thinking, *Really? Where?*

But she must go to these events – she needs to understand what is happening here. She needs, more than anything, to find a way to inject some of this excitement into her own career. But how to do that? How to get people to start randomly eulogising about *her* work? Perhaps one really does need to shock, she thinks. Perhaps she should start tying up men and photographing *them*. That would make a bloody change. But no, too obvious, too derivative. But then, isn't this?

"Sophie, this is Brett," Genna, who has reappeared beside her, says. "I don't think you've met, have you?"

Deciding that Genna is palming Mr Blobby off on her, Sophie conceals a sigh and takes Brett's cold, damp hand in her own, forcing a smile. She's not here to date, she reminds herself. She's here to network and she knows better than to let her disdain – disdain based on mere physical appearance – show. "Sophie Marsden," she says.

19

"Brett Pearson," the man replies, shaking her hand limply, then letting it go.

Sophie resists the desire to wipe her hand on her dress, then squints at him vaguely. "Brett Pearson," she repeats. "Now why do I know that name?"

Brett shrugs. "The *Times*, maybe?"

"Ah, that's right! You're the new arts correspondent."

"*Junior* arts correspondent. Yeah."

"How fabulous," Sophie says, wincing at her choice of superlative. She mustn't overdo it. She mustn't sound like Genna. It's important not to appear sycophantic.

"Marsden," Brett says thoughtfully. "You know, there's a photographer called Marsden. Well, *was*. Anthony Marsden. You know his stuff at all?"

"Vaguely," Sophie lies.

"He died way back," Brett says. "But he was good. A lot of social comment stuff. In the seventies."

Sophie squints and shakes her head vaguely. "I just, you know, know the name really," she says.

"So, what do we think of these?" Brett asks, waving his glass towards the photo before them with such largesse that the wine almost slops out.

"I'm not sure," Sophie says, tracking the sloshing wine from the corner of her eye just in case, and waiting for Brett to provide a cue. "What *do* we think of these?"

"Three words, one letter," Brett says.

"I'm sorry?"

"Oh, it's, you know, a game," Brett explains. "I play it when I'm stuck for an angle for a piece. The first three adjectives that come to mind. But they all have to start with the same letter."

"I'm not sure I follow," Sophie says. "You go first."

"Doleful, dysphoric and dirty," Brett says.

"Ha, OK. I get it."

20

"And yours?"

"Um . . ."

"No hesitation," Brett says. "That's the whole point."

"OK, then . . . enigmatic, exploitative and, um, empty," Sophie says. She scans the room to check that Genna is out of earshot, then pulls a face and raises one hand to her mouth, Japanese style. "Did I really just say that?" she asks. "About the great Arakis?"

Brett grins at her strangely. It's half grin, half sneer, Sophie decides. She's surprised that she finds it such a sexy combination.

"I kinda know what you mean," Brett says. "It's a fine line, I guess."

"I'm overreacting, probably," Sophie says. "I just get a little bored with the abused-women-equals-art thing. It just all seems a bit eighties to me. Do you know what I mean?"

"Madonna? Erotica? Feel the pleasure, feel the pain?"

"Exactly!"

"But very much in vogue now," Brett says. "Ha! Vogue! Did you see what I did there?"

"I did, actually."

"But what with *Fifty Shades of Grey* and all . . ."

"Sorry?"

"*Fifty Shades*. The S&M novel?"

"Sorry. I don't read as much as I should."

"Oh you don't need to read this one. Unless you're into that kind of thing. But it's huge back home and no doubt coming to these shores shortly."

"I'll look out for it."

"Anyway, as far as these are concerned, I'm not sure about exploitative *per se*," Brett says, as they move on to the next, even more shocking photo. "I mean, she's a professional model, presumably. No one made her do that shit. She even looks like she's into it."

21

And suddenly, arts correspondent for the *Times* or not, Sophie can't help herself. "So here we have a woman being paid by a rich *man* to be naked, being paid to be *tied up* naked, being paid, on the photographer's whim, to let him stick the tail of a plastic dinosaur inside her . . . *Inside her!* Oh, and being paid, while we're at it, to look like she's, what was it you said? Oh, 'into it'. That's it. And this is *not* exploitation?"

"You'll have to excuse Sophie," Genna says, moving between them in what looks like a precise damage-control intervention. "She's terribly political. Like father, like daughter."

"Oh, I kinda think she's right," Brett says. "But you know, as long as the press chatters, the buyers buy, the punters get hard and the credit card machine keeps spitting out those little slips of paper (he nods here at the terminal in Genna's hand), then who cares, hey?"

Genna freezes for half a second, clearly unsure how to react, then licks her lips, smiles and laughs. "Brett! You're terrible!" she says. "Just terrible! Now promise me that you won't be saying *that* in your write-up."

"I promise I won't be saying that in my write-up," Brett repeats, sotto voce. "Any chance of another glass of that white?"

"Of course!" Genna says, taking his arm and physically pulling him away from Sophie. "It is rather gorge, isn't it?"

Damn, Sophie thinks. *You screwed that up.*

*   *   *

"So Genna tells me that Anthony Marsden was your father," Brett says. "Were you offended that I didn't know that, or were you just jerking me around?"

"Just . . . winding you up," Sophie says, wondering how she ended up leaving the gallery with Brett. Does she find him attractive now, or was it just that third glass of wine? Or even worse, does this have something to do with the fact that he is the arts correspondent at the *Times*. And what if it was a mixture of all of these things? Would that make it OK?

"The rain has stopped," Brett says, folding his umbrella. "We could walk it instead. If we're going to my place, anyway. I'm in Hoxton, so it's, like, ten minutes from here."

Sophie looks at him and thinks about pretending to be outraged, thinks about saying, "Now why would you even think that I'm coming to yours?" But then he does the smile-cum-sneer thing again – a *leer*, that's the word – and she hears herself say, "Sure, let's walk. I like to walk and I've been cooped up all day."

It's cold and damp but there's something rather lovely about these early winter nights, something about the reflections of the lights on the wet pavement, about the swishing of the passing cars and the clip-clop of her heels on the pavement that Sophie can't resist. London always feels so much more like itself once winter starts to close in, when the streets are shiny with rain.

"And you're a photographer too, I hear," Brett says. "That's some pedigree to live up to, right?"

"Yes," Sophie says. "But I do fashion shoots mainly. So it's, you know, a different world."

"Huh!" Brett says, buttoning the top button of his jacket, folding his collar up against the cold and then yanking on his tie so that it juts out a little more from his collar.

"Huh?"

"Fashion. Just doesn't really fit with the discourse. About Arakis. I would have expected you to be photographing starving kids or lesbians or something."

"Yes, well . . ." Sophie agrees, shocked that Brett has so quickly placed his finger on her weak spot, the one spot that can actually make her want to cry. "We all have to make compromises, don't we?" she continues. "And we're all full of contradictions. It's part of being human."

"I guess," Brett says, doubtfully. "And you don't carry any equipment?"

"I'm sorry?"

"All my photographer pals have their cameras with them at all times."

"Oh, I have this," Sophie says, pulling her Leica compact from her inside pocket, then dropping it back in again. "But I don't carry the big one around unless I'm actually going on a shoot. Why? Did you want me to photograph you?"

"Maybe," Brett says, raising one eyebrow and shooting her another cocky leer.

* * *

His flat is beautiful. They step from a dingy, external walkway that looks like it might feature in a Mike Leigh film into a vast lounge that is so white, so chic, it almost resembles a gallery.

"Wow!" Sophie exclaims, heading straight for the bay windows. "A room with a view!"

"Yes, you can see right down to the river," Brett says.

"I'm impressed."

"It's a rental," Brett says, "and shared. So don't be."

"Right."

"I'm not sure I'm staying yet, so . . ."

"Staying?"

"Yeah. I might be going back home."

"And home is?"

"Manhattan."

"Right. Well, I can understand the appeal of that."

"But London's fine for now," Brett says, hanging his jacket on the back of a chair, loosening his gold tie and undoing his top button. "So, Drink? Food? Kiss? A spot of fiendish rope-work perhaps?"

"Let's start with a drink," Sophie says, "and see where it leads us."

"Sure," Brett says. "Let's do that."

1941 – SHOREDITCH, LONDON.

They can see the blaze from over three streets away and as her mother's hand tightens around her own, Barbara realises that something bad has happened. All three are thinking the same thing: *Is that coming from our house?* But as they trip along in the dingy morning light, no one says a word.

As the corner of their street comes into view, they can smell the smoke and see the fire hoses. Minnie starts to run, dragging her daughter along beside her. Glenda is already in front.

And now they round the corner and, just for a second, it's as if they have made a mistake, as if they have come to the wrong place, because the street is unrecognisable. The house opposite – the Robinson place – is gone, just a pile of rubble. The house to the left of theirs, where the Smiths and the Havershams live, (lived?) is gone as well. And the house to the right of theirs, number twenty-six, is a red ball of licking, crackling flame producing a dark column of smoke which twists and turns as it rises into the sky.

"Oh," Minnie says – more an exhalation than a word. Because language has just failed her.

Five blackened firemen are pointing hoses at the blaze. They have clearly been here for some time now, as there is no apparent urgency – just the noisy rush and hiss of water jets hitting the base of the fire, jets which, though massive, seem entirely insufficient for the job at hand. They might as well be spraying petrol on for all the good it's doing.

After a full minute of paralysis, Minnie says, "My tin!" and unexpectedly breaks free from the girls. "Stay!" she instructs as she starts to sprint towards their house, now skipping over fire hoses, now opening the gate to their front yard, somehow absurd amidst all this destruction. A gate to protect from what exactly?

Imagining the building collapsing, Glenda shouts, "Mum! No!" and lets go of Barbara's hand to run after her.

The nearest fireman now turns to see what the commotion is and drops his hose, which snakes and buckles on the ground, then spins, briefly spraying Barbara with water, before backing up and lodging itself against the wheel of a fire-truck. The fireman jumps over the small dividing wall between the two gardens and seizes Minnie's arms just as she is trying to force the front door open.

A struggle ensues – an actual fight – where Minnie, held from behind by the fireman, buckles and kicks and shrieks about her tin as she tries, hopelessly, to break free. Glenda is pulling on her mother's arm, shouting, crying, "Mum, please, no! It's dangerous! I'm scared. Please, Mum, *please!*"

Barbara stands on the wet pavement watching all of this, smelling the smoke, sensing the heat of the flames on her face, and listening to the crackle of burning wood and the pop of windows exploding with the heat. She sees when the fireman finally loses patience and slaps her mother hard across the side of the face. She sees how everything stops, how Minnie's arms drop to her sides, how she doubles up and cries out a long warbling, "Nooo!" before allowing herself to be led, looking crumpled like an abandoned set of clothes, from the front door, then back into the street, first by Glenda and then by an air-raid warden who has run to them in order to join the fray.

Glenda returns for Barbara, and the fireman, who is still watching Minnie in case she makes a dash for it (he's seen it happen before), crosses the road to address them.

"You'll be able to get your things tomorrow, alright?" he tells the girls. "So just get your mum out of here. She doesn't want to be here tonight. She doesn't want to be seeing this."

"Take her where?" Glenda asks. "Where should we go?"

"But that's our house," Barbara protests angrily, feeling that the nasty man who slapped her mother hasn't understood this simple fact.

"Go to a friend's or something," the fireman says. "Or go to a shelter. And then come back tomorrow once the fire's out."

Glenda nods rigidly. "Thank you," she says, and her sister blinks up at her in confusion.

She starts to lead Barbara along the road, towards where Minnie is now sitting on a wall being spoken to sternly by the air-raid warden, but as they pass the collapsed house – the Robinson place – Barbara freezes.

"Come on!" Glenda prompts, pulling at her hand, then, "What?"

With her free hand, Barbara is pointing, and Glenda now follows her gaze, her features forming a frown in the flickering light. "Oh," she says.

"Look," Barbara says.

"Yes. Um, go to Mum and I'll . . . I'll tell the fireman. He'll know what to do."

Barbara walks robotically on, her head swivelling as she does so, unable to tear her eyes from the horrific sight. Behind her, she hears Glenda shout to the fireman. "Excuse me! Excuse me! Mr Fireman!"

"Yes?" the man replies.

"There's someone stuck under that door," she says, her voice quivering with emotion.

"What?"

"There's a hand sticking out. Over there. Someone's under that door."

"Jesus!" the fireman says, walking backwards so that he can look at the door in question while still pointing his hose at the fire opposite. "Alright love," he says calmly, reasonably, as if this is all quite routine. "Don't worry. We'll get them out. You just go with your mum now. Off you go!"

As Glenda runs to catch up with Barbara and takes her hand again, they hear him shout, "Jack! JACK! They missed one over 'ere. There's another body. Can you come give us a hand?"

Minnie does not go to work that day and the girls do not go to school. For want of a better idea, with Minnie still in a worrying, trance-like state that Glenda has no idea how to deal with, they return to the youth club shelter. Being daytime, and with no warnings having sounded, the shelter is almost empty now.

Minnie lies down on an empty mattress and, as far as the girls can see, sleeps all day.

"What's wrong with Mum?" Barbara asks.

"She's just tired," Glenda tells her. "She didn't get any sleep last night. She can't sleep sitting up. You know that."

But Minnie isn't tired. And she isn't sleeping either. She has simply run out of courage. It's not, as everyone keeps pretending, an unlimited resource.

Because the hours in the shelter are so horrifically slow, Glenda takes Barbara, who has been getting fidgety, for a walk. They ramble aimlessly through the empty streets, some untouched by the bombing, some missing houses or shops, and a few, like their own, so unrecognisable that Glenda worries they are lost.

In Liverpool Street they see a demonstration by communists demanding access to the underground stations for shelter, so they stand and watch and listen to the chanting until the police arrive and things start to get raucous, whereupon Glenda shepherds them back towards Shoreditch.

As the daylight starts to fade, they pass back down their own street. The flames have been extinguished now, and their house, though blackened and windowless, is otherwise undamaged. Sandwiched between the smouldering remains of number twenty-six and the pile of rubble that is number twenty-two, it makes a forlorn sight.

The girls independently cast glances at the collapsed house opposite to check. They both see that the door and the hand have gone.

Looking at their own house, Barbara asks, "Can we go inside?"

"We're not supposed to. It's unsafe, I think."

"Unsafe?"

"It might fall down."

Barbara nods. Seeing that Glenda is furtively checking left and right, she says, "But you're going to go inside anyway and get Mum's tin."

"Yes," Glenda says. "Yes, I think so."

"It's in the cooker."

"I know. If someone hasn't nicked it. I want to get my nice dress, too, before someone nicks *that*."

"Your birthday dress?"

"Yes."

"Can I have Lucy Loop?"

"If I can see her," Glenda says, glancing left and right again, then sprinting past the burned-out building and around to the back of the house.

When they get back to the shelter, Minnie is still lying on her back staring at the ceiling. The place is filling up now and her occupancy of an entire mattress will soon be cause for jealousy.

"I got the tin," Glenda tells her proudly, and Minnie's face starts to animate as if someone has swapped in new batteries.

First her brow wrinkles, then her eyes widen, then she sits up and stares peculiarly at Glenda as if she has perhaps spoken some foreign language that she doesn't quite understand.

"Everything's still in it, I think," Glenda says, proffering the tin and nodding encouragingly.

Minnie swallows, then snatches the rusty Jacob's Cracker tin from her daughter's grasp.

She pulls off the lid and starts to empty the contents: a roll of pound notes with an elastic band around them, a pile of dog-eared photos, the girls' birth certificates, her mother's headband, Seamus' broken watch . . . All of these, she casts aside. They are not her primary concern.

And then she finds her wedding ring. She slips it onto her finger and says, "Thank God for that. That won't be coming off again." She looks up at Glenda and manages a weak smile. "You're a good girl, Glenda," she says. "I don't know what I'd do without you." And Barbara wishes that it had been she who braved the danger of the house to recover the box.

"Can we look at the pictures?" Glenda asks.

Minnie sighs, then nods and pats the mattress beside her. "Course you can," she says, then addressing Barbara and spotting the doll under her arm, "You too. Bring Lucy Loop and come sit on my lap."

Barbara slides between her mother's arms and for the first time today, feels safe again.

"That was our first trip out," Minnie says, pulling the first tatty photo from the pile. "That's Margate pier, that is."

All three stare at the picture, a plain but pretty woman smiling sheepishly, holding hands with a good looking lad all buttoned up in his best Sunday suit.

Barbara reaches out and runs her finger across the image of her father, as if perhaps she might touch him, as if perhaps that might make him seem more real to her.

31

The image is so alien, so detached from everything around them, that none of them can think of a word to say, so they just sit, a little awed, the mother and her two daughters. They stare and wonder, each in her own way, if things will ever be that simple again.

By the time of their return to the house the next morning, someone has painted "Danger!" across the front door in dribbled, red letters.

Mrs Haversham and her son Bertie are next door in what used to be their front room, sifting through the still smouldering remains for intact possessions.

"Alice!" Minnie exclaims, climbing over the burnt remains of the front door and hugging her. "You're alright then. I thought you'd come a cropper."

"We was down the shelter," Alice replies. "Thank God for small mercies."

Minnie nods thoughtfully as the true meaning of the phrase hits her for the first time. She looks around, then up past where the ceiling and roof should be at the sky. "You poor things. And the Smiths?"

"She evacuated the little-uns just last week. So *they're* OK. But . . ." Here she glances at Barbara, pulls her mouth downward and shakes her head.

"Oh those poor babbies," Minnie says. "It's shameful what they're doing to us. Shameful."

"We're off to my mum's place in Dorking," Alice says. "Happy to get out of London, to tell the truth."

Minnie nods.

"You should get out too," Alice says. "Or at least send the kids."

"I can't," Minnie replies. "I've got my job, ain't I? Someone's got to keep coats on our boys' backs."

32

"I found this," Bertie says, holding up a dusty shoe.

"That's good," Alice shouts, then, to Minnie, "Half the stuff's already gone."

"Looters?"

"Just people like us. People with nothing. They took me coat though, the buggers. Only one I had, as well. I chased them out of your place too."

Minnie nods, sighs deeply, then, unable to think what to say that could possibly help Alice, she mutters, "Bloody Hitler," and steps back outside.

Inside her own house, everything is blackened and sooty and she can see that some things have already been taken.

"Can we fix it up?" Glenda asks.

"No," Minnie says. "No, I don't think so."

"What are we going to do, Mum? We can't live here like this, can we?"

"No. No, we can't live here," Minnie agrees.

"We could live in the dugout," Glenda suggests, screwing up her nose.

Minnie shakes her head and scans the room once again, noticing now how all of the wallpaper on the left side of the house is singed. She runs her left hand across the wall and feels that the bricks are still warm.

Glenda picks up a framed photo and rubs the soot from the glass with her finger, revealing their father's face. "Where are we going to live, Mum?" she asks.

"I don't know. I need to talk to that bloke from the council," Minnie says. "See what he says."

"Shall I gather stuff together?"

"Yes," Minnie tells Glenda. "Yes, make a pile on the doorstep. Anything we can carry. Anything we might need. Anything that's worth something. And don't let no one nick nothing."

"I can help," Barbara says.

"Yes, you 'elp your sister. And if there's a raid, go to the shelter."

"The dugout, or . . .?"

"Yes. The dugout's fine. We'll go to the youth club tonight."

Minnie heads to the bedroom and takes her old fur coat from the wardrobe. She sniffs it, then gives it a shake and hangs it over one arm before leaving the house. She peers through the burned-out window next door. "Here, Alice!" she calls out, proffering the coat. "This is for you."

Alice lets go of the sleeve of a jumper she's trying to extract from the rubble. "Your lovely coat?"

Minnie nods. "It was my mum's. But it's yours now."

"You sure, love?" Alice asks, taking the coat and stroking it as if it were still alive.

Minnie nods and blinks slowly.

"I feel like I should be saying 'no'," Alice says, her voice wobbling with emotion. "But I'm gonna just say 'yes'."

"Good," Minnie says. "You two look after each other in Dorking."

"We will."

"I'm off to the council, see if they can fix up somewhere for us to live."

"Right," Alice says, pulling on the coat and frowning as she becomes aware of the inherent contradiction of being a woman in a fur coat standing on a mound of rubble. "Well, I hope they give you somewhere nice."

*   *   *

The accommodation allocated turns out to be a single room above a boarded-up shop on Willow Street. Each bedroom in the large house contains another dispossessed family. Because it's only two streets from Luke Street, they're able to carry on foot what clothes, photos and small items of furniture remain.

Minnie and Glenda are horrified that they're supposed to live in a single room but Barbara – who sees in the kids playing on the stairs, not squalor and poverty, but fun and companionship – struggles to tone down her excitement. She can tell from Minnie's grim expression that it's not appropriate.

Minnie alternates between muttering, "One room. It's not right," and spurious attempts at reassuring the girls. "We'll be alright here, girls, won't we?" she keeps saying, as she moves around the room lifting framed photos from the walls. She is removing the images of the happy Italian family that lived here before internment and replacing them with their own family history from the biscuit tin – it's not a pleasant process.

On the way back to the shelter that night, they walk along Luke Street one last time. The intention is to recover three of the blackened cushions to sit on but really Minnie just needs to see her old house one more time in order to convince herself that their life there really is over. But they are too late for cushions. The house has been stripped bare.

Barbara and Glenda soon come to prefer life in Willow Street. The kitchen downstairs is like a social club for the war weary, and within days they have integrated Mildred's supper club, pooling their ration books and sharing in the communal rabbit stews that Mildred somehow manages to whistle up out of thin air.

The shared bathroom on the first floor has (a little) hot water, which makes the weekly scrub quite delicious compared with the cold outdoor tub they had in Luke Street. Even the air-raid shelter is closer now, and often Barbara runs to it with one of her new friends, little lame Benjamin, or Patty, or ' half-caste' Yasmin.

She's aware that her mother has not taken so well to this transition. She has noticed that it is they now, not Minnie, who clean the room, and she suspects that on the frequent occasions when their mother fails to materialise at the shelter, she isn't as she claims stuck due to poor timing in another shelter elsewhere but at home, in the room, in her bed.

But the harsh truth is that even as her seventh birthday goes by unmarked (except for a hand-drawn card from Glenda), Barbara doesn't care. She feels safer and happier and is undeniably better fed since they moved to Willow Street.

So when, one day – the day in fact before the bombing unexpectedly pauses – Glenda says quietly, "I think Mum's given up. I think it's up to us to look after her now," Barbara just nods.

"That's OK," she says. "I don't mind."

And it's true. She doesn't.

2011 – SHOREDITCH, LONDON.

Sophie straightens her back and stretches her neck from side to side, then grabs the mouse again and peers back at the screen. She selects Photoshop's cloning tool and starts to erase a blackhead to the right of her model's nose. Sportswear Direct uses the cheapest models it can find and it shows, Sophie reckons, by their general lack of skincare. In their raw state, these could be acne-cream ads. The 'before' photos, that is, not the 'after's.

Brett, behind her, folds the newspaper noisily, then slurps the dregs of his coffee and crosses the room to peer over her shoulder.

"Hum. Trailer-trash-wear," he says, dismissively, Sophie thinks, or was that 'hum' meant instead to be *suggestive?*

"I know," she replies with a sigh. "I so need to up my game. I hate all this shite."

"Hate is probably overstating it," Brett says.

"You have no idea how *exhausting* it is to do this rubbish every day," Sophie says.

"It could be worse. You could be delivering people's groceries on minimum wage," Brett says.

"I'd rather be delivering people's groceries."

"You really wouldn't. Has he got a boner?" Brett asks, pointing at the bulge in the man's shiny Adidas joggers.

"Sock," Sophie says. *"Big* sock."

"That's true, then?"

She leans into the screen and zaps another blemish on the

man's right ear before saying, "Socks in the undies? To make them look like they have bigger packets? Of course it's true."

"Always?"

"Nearly always."

"Maybe I should try that," Brett says, stepping closer so that his groin is pressing against her back.

Sophie releases the mouse and swivels to face him. She reaches out and strokes the material of his suit trousers and senses that he is already semi-erect. "I don't think you need to, sweetheart," she says, running her hand down the smoothness of his tie before starting to fumble with his zip.

Brett laughingly pushes her hand away. He glances at his watch, then says, "No time for that, I'm afraid, hon'. I have an appointment with one of your peers."

"Really? Who?"

"Colley."

"*Milly* Colley?"

"Uh-huh."

"You're winding me up!"

"Nope. She has a show coming up at Beetles. We're doing an exclusive."

"Well, give her a slap for me, would you?"

"If it sounds like jealousy and it looks like jealousy—"

"She does the same shit that I do," Sophie interrupts. "She's just prettier, that's all, so she gets better breaks."

"She actually isn't," Brett says, stroking Sophie's cheek with the back of his hand making Sophie feel momentarily better. "But maybe she puts out. Maybe that's it. I'll let you know."

"Bastard."

"She's pretty damned good, Sophie. Have a look at her fine art shots. Even her Top Shop stuff looks like fine art these days. She's where it's at. You should seriously check her out."

"Enough!" Sophie shrieks, raising one hand. "Be gone!"

She turns back to her Sportswear Direct bodybuilder and Brett, behind her, sighs and begins to move around the room, now unplugging his iPhone from her charger, now pulling his jacket on and jingling his keys.

"I hate my life," Sophie says, zooming in on the nasal passages of the on-screen model.

"Thanks," Brett laughs.

"Not you. You know I don't mean you. I mean this."

"Then do something different," Brett says, and Sophie braces herself for one of his American Dream speeches.

When the expected rant fails to materialise, Sophie asks, "If I did, would you help me up my profile?" Her hand freezes over the mouse. The question has been on the tip of her tongue for weeks but now it's out in the open. She holds her breath.

"Up your profile, *how?*" Brett asks.

"You know, get me some publicity. As a kosher arts photographer."

Brett laughs.

"Don't *laugh*," Sophie says. "You're doing it for Colley."

"Take some kosher art shots, babe," he says, "and we'll see. Do the work and I'll try to find an angle."

Do the work, Sophie repeats in her head. *Take some decent shots. Bastard!*

"Are we meeting here *ce soir*?" Brett asks.

Sophie glances over her shoulder and looks at him blankly, her mind still on Milly Colley. "Sorry?"

"Here? Tonight?" Brett repeats.

"Oh, no. I'll come to yours," Sophie says. "I'm removing nasal hair at home all day, so I'll need a change of scenery by then."

"OK. Have a good one. And make sure you zap all those pimples," Brett says.

Sophie turns back to the screen and listens as the flat door opens and then closes and as Brett's hard shoes echo away down the corridor. She bites her lip and thinks about Brett.

Because somehow, without any decision having been taken, they have ended up dating. For a month now, they have seen each other almost every night and she wonders again how this could have happened.

Brett is so far from the image she fostered of her ideal man. She always imagined herself with some dreadlocked artist in paint-spattered clothes, which, let's face it, is about as far from Brett's Republican suityness as anyone could manage. Then again, the paint-splattered artists she *has* dated have all proved to be far from ideal. She had also hoped for someone younger. Someone funnier. Someone fitter.

But the strange truth is that she fancies Brett. Despite herself, she thinks he looks sexy in his suit, almost more than sexy. Seductive. Somehow naughty. Pervy perhaps. And there's something about the way he pulls his cock – his unfeasibly *large* cock – from his suit trousers without even getting undressed, something about the way he expects her to – no, *assumes* that she will – worship it, that despite everything she has ever believed about men, about women, about gender identity, about roles and feminism, she really rather enjoys.

Intellectually, she would rather she didn't but that's just the way it is. She wrinkles her nose and refocuses on the screen where she has switched to Safari and is googling 'Milly Colley'.

Colley's fashion shots aren't that much better than her own, she decides. Yes, Colley has access to better models wearing better gear, because, well, she's hip at the moment, but the photographs themselves are nothing Sophie couldn't manage. Technically, she's just as good.

But then Sophie clicks on 'Fine Art' and her heart sinks. Because Milly Colley has that magical, elusive thing she has been hunting for ever since she went into photography, has the same kind of 'eye' that propelled her father to stardom.

She clicks through a few photos, then, imagining a speech bubble above her own head containing the word 'Grrrrr!', she quits Safari and the screen is filled, anew, by the man in the shiny sportswear.

"So, tracksuit man," she says out loud. She looks at his bulge now, then zooms in on it and nods. "Yeah, OK, that *is* a bit O.T.T," she mumbles.

She wishes she had spotted this during the shoot and removed the sock, or used a smaller sock, because now she will have to spend fifteen minutes massaging his package into a smaller state. She grins at the thought of this and, as she starts to do just that, thinks about doing the same thing to Brett, tonight, only for real.

When Sophie gets to Brett's place, it is his flatmate who opens the door – a permanently stoned satellite-dish installer called Raoul.

"Come in, come in!" Raoul says, grinning sheepishly as if perhaps he doesn't often see women, before hurling himself rather spectacularly over the back of the sofa to continue watching *The Simpsons*.

Sophie checks the kitchen and, finding it empty, heads on to Brett's room where she finds him wearing boxer shorts, lying face-down, typing on his laptop.

"I'm here," she says.

"Yeah, I got that," Brett replies without looking up. "Just let me send this copy and . . ." he mutters.

"You're looking very summery," Sophie says.

"It's the heating in this place," Brett says distractedly. "It's ridiculous."

Sophie pulls off her coat, then sits in the armchair and stares at Brett's back as she listens to the clicking of the keys. She runs her tongue across her lips and tries to decide whether or not to be offended by his lack of welcome. *Are we already at this point?* she wonders. Are we already at the point where one's arrival doesn't even merit a glance? Wasn't that supposed to take just a bit longer than a month?

She stretches and groans as Brett, with a flourish, hits the send button and rolls on to his side so that he can look back at her. "Hard day in Photoshop hell, honey?" he asks.

"It just makes my back hurt," Sophie says, twisting and rubbing her neck. "My desk is too low or something. I think I need one of those weird Swedish chairs. Can you give my back a rub?"

Brett smiles lopsidedly and as usual the result is both creepy and sexy at the same time. "Sure," he says, scooting to the side of the bed.

As he bends to pull open a drawer, Sophie tries not to look at the pale folds of skin around his belly.

First he pulls a little bag of white powder from the drawer and wiggles it at Sophie. "Do you want a hit?" he asks.

Sophie shakes her head. "Maybe later," she replies. She is aware that since meeting Brett she has been taking a *lot* of coke and she's not entirely happy about it. She had decided not to partake tonight but can already sense her resolve weakening.

Brett shrugs, drops the bag and pulls a bottle of Body Shop massage oil from the drawer. "Fully prepared for all eventualities," he says, waving it at her instead. "Impressed?"

But something else has caught Sophie's eye. "What are those?" she asks, rounding the bed and pulling the drawer fully open. Inside, stuffed at the back behind the underwear, are a pair of chrome handcuffs, a dog collar and a large, pink dildo.

"Those," Brett says, pushing the drawer shut again, "are for later, when we get bored."

"When we get bored?" Sophie repeats, hesitating between being offended that he assumes that they *will* get bored and feeling flattered that he thinks there will be a later.

"Look, do you want this back rub or not?" Brett asks.

And Sophie really *does*, so she nods and crawls onto the bed, then because her back hurts, she rolls to her side momentarily so that she can wedge a pillow beneath her belly, effectively lifting up her haunches just enough that the pain stops.

"Hum, nice," Brett says, running a hand up her inner thigh.

"You promised me a *massage*," Sophie comments, speaking through the pillow.

"Yes, right. Sorry Mistress. Massage," Brett says with spoof seriousness as he slathers his hands in massage lotion and starts to work Sophie's shoulder blades.

"Ooh, that's cold," Sophie tells him. "But don't stop. It's good too."

As soon as Brett's bulge presses through his boxer shorts against her bottom, Sophie knows that neither of them is going to be satisfied with a back rub for long. *Well, at least we're not bored yet,* she thinks.

1944 – SHOREDITCH, LONDON.

It is only ten o'clock but Barbara is walking home. Her teacher, Mrs Pritchard, has failed to turn up and the rumour amongst the children is that she is dead.

Above her, in the blue spring sky, Barbara is vaguely aware of the buzzing of a doodlebug, another of the hundreds of daily flying bombs that have been raining destruction on them for months now. The air-raid warning sounded just as Barbara was passing back out of the school gates but she doesn't care. The sirens are almost constant these days and unlike the bombers, which needed the cover of nightfall to do their dirty deeds, the doodlebugs fall day and night. No one seems to care about the air-raid warnings any more because caring about them simply isn't compatible with any other activity. It's impossible to go to the shelter every time and once that pattern has been broken, there doesn't seem to be any point in going there at all.

The buzzing above continues and the frequency of the sound peaks overhead then begins to drop away, which means that the danger is now heading into the distance. Someone else will be listening for the splutter when it runs out of fuel. Someone else will have ten seconds to throw themselves to the ground, hands over ears. Someone else will feel the blast rip overhead and then will stand and carry on walking down the street, perhaps exchanging a raised eyebrow with a passerby at the fluke of having survived yet another near miss. Or they won't. Or they will join the ranks of the dead and maimed.

All of this passes through Barbara's mind but she is barely

even aware of it, because war, which has been going on now for almost half her life, seems normal. She doesn't imagine that it will end because she can't even picture what that might mean.

When she gets to Willow Street, she finds her friend Jean sitting on the wall. Jean never goes to school and Barbara has never thought to ask her why.

"You're back quick," Jean says.

"Teacher didn't come."

"D'you want to play?"

Barbara looks up the staircase and imagines her mother in the darkened interior. She will be sitting in the armchair and Barbara knows exactly what she will be wearing, the position she will be sitting in, and the expression she will have on her face. She knows because since the factory got bombed and Minnie stopped working, none of these things change any more. Minnie's silent presence makes Barbara feel funny these days – sort of queasy. She thinks she should probably do something to help her mum but other than cooking and cleaning and running errands, she doesn't know what. "OK," she says.

"Shall I get my skipping rope?"

"OK."

Jean runs into the dark interior of the house and then reappears with her skipping rope. She is closely followed by Yasmin.

"You not at school either?" Barbara asks Yasmin.

She stares at Barbara with her huge brown eyes and dolefully shakes her head.

"Shall we go to the gap?" Jean asks.

"Why not?" Barbara replies nonchalantly. The gap is the rubble-strewn space left by three bombed-out buildings in the next street where they like to play. It's extra exciting because it's totally forbidden.

"I'm not allowed," Yasmin says.

"Then stay here, chicken," Jean tells her. To Barbara, she says, "Come on."

As they start to walk, Yasmin hesitates, then predictably, runs to catch up with them.

"Benjamin got hit by shrapnel," Jean says. "They took him to the hospital. But he'll be alright, Mum reckons. It's just his leg."

"His funny leg? Or the good one?"

"I don't know," Jean says. "I s'pose it'd be better if it's the funny one."

"Yes, I s'pose it would. Otherwise he'll have two funny legs, won't he?"

* * *

Barbara uses her hip to push open the door.

Minnie, looking up from the sewing machine, exclaims, "Tea! Thank God. I could eat a 'orse." The bombed-out factory has just started sending out piecework and her mood has begun to improve.

"No horses, I'm afraid," Barbara says, "it's corned beef fritters."

"Cheeky," Minnie mutters, releasing the section of uniform that she has been sewing and stretching her arms by linking her hands behind her head. "Where's your sister, then?" she asks.

"She's eating downstairs," Barbara says – a lie. As often these days, Barbara doesn't know *where* Glenda is, and as this will either make Minnie angry or upset depending on her mood, Barbara has got used to covering for her.

Minnie scoops a finished pile of khaki collars from the table to the bed so that Barbara can put the plates down. "No greens?" she mutters when she sees the plates.

"We've got carrots," Barbara offers.

"Since when were carrots green?" Minnie says. "I'm starting to wonder what Mildred is doing with everyone's rations. Because she certainly isn't cooking with them."

"There's nothing in the shops, Mum," Barbara says. "It doesn't matter what rations people've got. These carrots came from someone's garden. A friend of Sylvia."

"It's not right," Minnie says. "No potatoes, no greens, no eggs, no cheese. I don't know how we're supposed to win a war if there ain't any food. It wouldn't surprise me if Mildred is keeping the rest for herself."

"She really isn't, Mum," Barbara says, lifting a slice of fritter to her mouth. "And we're doing better than most."

"Carrots, carrots and more bleedin' carrots," Minnie says. "We won't even need streetlights by the time the war's over."

Once they have eaten, Minnie returns to her piecework and Barbara carries the plates back downstairs. Three women are eating similar plates of food at the kitchen table: two of them, Agnes and Sylvia, are residents of the house whilst the other, sporting a black eye, is no doubt one of Mildred's 'waifs and strays'.

"Are you sure your Glenda's coming back to eat that?" Agnes asks as Barbara moves Glenda's plate to the side and begins to wash her own.

"I'm here," Glenda says breathlessly, from the doorway. "So keep yer hands off!"

Barbara turns and smiles at her sister. "I saved you some."

"And I've got pudding," Glenda says, producing a brown tube of M&M's from her pocket.

"Sweets!" Sylvia exclaims.

"Don't tell us what you had to do to get *those,*" Agnes comments and Sylvia nudges her and mutters, *"Agnes,"* under her breath.

"Well . . ." she says. "It ain't much better than whoring."

"You won't be wanting any then," Glenda says sourly, but with steely self control.

"You're right," Agnes says. "I won't."

"Scoot over," Glenda says, removing her hat, then sliding onto the bench seat behind the table. "Corned beef again, is it?" she asks, as Barbara places the dish before her.

"Don't you start," says Sylvia. "Not unless you want to try shopping yourself."

"Oh, I ain't complaining," Glenda replies. "I don't mind the stuff, I don't."

Once she has eaten, she hands all of the women, Agnes included, a single M&M. Sweets are considered such treasure these days that no one even imagines that they might be given two.

"Ooh, these are good," Sylvia says.

Even Agnes manages a nod.

"Mum sewing?" Glenda asks, once the M&M has finally dissolved in her mouth.

Barbara nods. "She's got a whole pile to do. Collars. I should go and help her, really."

"We both will in a bit," Glenda says. "But first come out back so we can have a natter."

Barbara, keen to hear her sister's adventures, follows her down the steps to the small yard, now transformed, like most yards, into a vegetable patch.

"Our boys took somewhere in Greece," Barbara says. "And the good guy won the elections in America." Minnie leaves the radio on almost twenty-four hours a day, so Barbara unconsciously collects thousands of mini-facts about the war, facts which for the most part mean little to her.

"Roosevelt?" Glenda asks.

"Yes. That's the one."

"Well, that's good then. Harry will be celebrating," Glenda says. Harry is Glenda's latest boyfriend.

"What's he like?"

"He's lovely," Glenda says, pulling an almost empty packet of Target cigarettes from her pocket. In fact, Harry, in his late thirties, is a little old for a fifteen year old – her mother certainly wouldn't approve. But in wartime London where everything, including men, is scarce, she is enjoying the perks.

"He gave you cigarettes, too?"

"No, I nicked these," Glenda replies, sending her sister a wink. "But he won't mind."

"Where did you go?"

"To a dance at the Red Cross club," Glenda tells her, lighting up the cigarette with studied panache.

"Ooh lovely."

"The music was American songs. Jive. And there was hundreds of them doing it. Ever such good dancers, they are."

"Were they all GIs?"

"Yeah. And hardly any girls, so . . ."

"You had your pick."

"I could have. But Harry was the best one there. He's ever so good looking," Glenda says. "Looks lovely in his uniform. He's a sergeant. And then we went down the West End."

"Did you, you know . . ." Barbara says.

"First base," Glenda says.

"First base?"

"That's what they call it. It means just kissing."

"So, you kissed?"

"What do you think?" Glenda says, laughing to cover her embarrassment, because she went far further than first base. In fact she's concerned that she may still have the imprint of the door on her buttocks. She chokes briefly on the cigarette

49

fumes – she has only just started to smoke and it doesn't always seem to go down the right way. But she's determined to get used to it.

Barbara checks over her shoulder that no one is listening, then asks, quietly, "Is he a good kisser, then?"

Glenda nods knowledgeably. "They all are," she says. "Much better than the local boys. I think I might marry myself a GI when the war's over."

"You could marry Harry," Barbara says. "You'd have chocolate every day."

"I might just do that."

Barbara bites her bottom lip and restrains a naughty grin. "Don't let Mum hear you say that though."

"Over-paid, over-sexed and over-'ere," Glenda says, mocking Minnie's voice as she offers Barbara another M&M from the tube.

Barbara takes one and hands back the packet. "These are smashing," she says. "Are they from America?"

"Of course they're from America."

"Save some for Mum," Barbara says. "She said she's still hungry. And you know how she loves chocolate."

"I can't. She'll want to know where it come from, won't she."

"Oh," Barbara says, frowning. "Can't you tell her Maisie got 'em or something?"

Glenda nods vaguely. "I s'pose. But she might not believe me."

Somewhere to the east, they hear the trademark double supersonic boom of one of the new rocket-bombs, followed, almost immediately, by the sound of the explosion.

Over the last few weeks, the doodlebugs have all-but ceased as the allies have overrun the launch-sites in France, but their particular, almost familiar terror has been seamlessly

50

replaced by new bombs arriving from farther afield. Unlike the buzzing, spluttering doodlebugs, the supersonic rockets provide no warning – even the air-raid sirens sound afterwards, not before. Faced with such invincible technical prowess, the government is at a complete loss to even suggest what people should do and so all official channels have been pretending that these explosions, up to ten a day of them, are being caused by exploding gas pipes. But no one is really fooled.

"Bloody flying gas pipes," Glenda says, which has become the most common nickname for the rockets. She drags on the cigarette, then coughs again as she stubs it out on a rock.

"Ben says they're rockets," Barbara says. "New German rockets. The air-raid warden told him."

"Harry told me that too," Glenda says – a lie. "So it must be true."

As they climb the stairs to the room, the air-raid warning belatedly sounds. It's almost certainly a response to the explosion they just heard rather than a warning of anything to come. This lack of warning, this new impossibility, when faced with missiles that travel through space and announce themselves at the moment of explosion, this impossibility of doing anything whatsoever to protect oneself has produced a new kind of terror, so acute, so unmanageable, that there seem to be only two ways left to react. The first, opted for by a few, is to go mad. These people can be seen wandering the streets talking to themselves or sitting in corners rocking gently. But for most people, the V2 attacks have pushed them to adopt a new form of fatalistic determination that these things are beyond control. Enjoy yourself while you can, is the philosophy of the day.

"When are you seeing Har—"

"Shh!" Glenda says. They have almost reached the door behind which Minnie is sewing.

"When are you seeing him again?" Barbara whispers.

"Tonight," Glenda says.

"Tonight?"

Glenda shrugs. "There's another dance on over in Pimlico."

"You don't have to go to *every* dance, do you?"

"My number could be up by tomorrow. Anyway, he promised me some nylons if I go."

"Ooh, nylons!" Barbara says.

"I'll sneak out once Mum conks out."

"You're so lucky, Glenda."

"It'll be your turn soon enough."

1945 – SHOREDITCH, LONDON.

Barbara is walking home from school. Because everyone is abuzz with rumours that the war will end today, they have been sent home early. Though Barbara's tummy feels light and fluttery, as if full of butterflies, beyond the fact that there will be no bombs and beyond the fact that a barely remembered man called 'Dad' should be coming home soon, she doesn't really know what to expect. But the fact that they have been sent home early adds to the feeling that this is an exceptional day.

It's exactly three p.m. when she walks around the corner into Willow Street and a cheer rises up from a house across the way, almost as if timed to greet her. To her left, a window is thrust open and a woman's head and shoulders appear. "It's over!" she shouts, grinning a little madly. "The war's over!"

A man and a woman walking towards her freeze and turn to face the window. "What did you say?" the man asks, sounding perhaps incredulous, perhaps angry at the poor taste of this joke the woman is making.

"Really!" the woman shouts. "Winnie just said it on the wireless. It's over!"

Barbara stops walking and the woman addresses her as well. "It's all over, little one!" she tells her. "You can smile again! We can all smile again."

And though Barbara isn't quite sure why, smile is exactly what she does. She turns to face the couple again. They are staring into each other's eyes.

"Oh Derek!" the woman says. "Can it be true?"

Another round of cheering erupts from another house and the man breaks into a grin. "It sounds like it might be," he says.

The woman's eyes are glistening as he slides one arm around her waist and they start, silently, in the middle of the road, to waltz.

"I have to tell my mum!" Barbara says.

"Yes," the woman at the window replies. "Go quickly! Tell your mum!"

Barbara hikes her satchel over her shoulder and starts to run. As she progresses along Willow Street, people start to appear from doorways, all desperate to share this exceptional moment with others.

"It's over," she hears again and again as she passes by. "The war's over!"

"We beat the bastards," a man pushing a barrow says, then, spotting Barbara, he adds, "Pardon my French, love."

"It's OK!" Barbara laughs, running on.

The door to their building is open and everyone has congregated in the communal spaces. There are at least twenty people crammed onto the lower flight of stairs and the hubbub of excited conversation is deafening.

"Did you hear?" her friend Benjamin asks, when he sees her.

"Yes!" Barbara replies. "Yes, I heard."

As she squeezes between a group of women, Mildred, who cooks for them all, grabs her arm and says, "The war's ovah, darlin'. You should go get yer mum."

"Yes!" Barbara says. "Yes, I'm going!"

When she pushes their door open, she finds Minnie frozen at the sewing machine, seemingly suspended in time.

The radio is on and a news presenter is excitedly listing the successive surrenders of the Axis powers during the last twenty-four hours. Right now he's talking about the Channel Islands. Barbara isn't sure where they are but they sound terribly important.

Minnie has her left hand on the lapel of an unfinished khaki jacket and her right hand on the handle of the sewing machine. She is staring, in apparent shock, at the radio. Tears are slithering down her cheeks.

Barbara has never seen Minnie cry before. "Mum!" she says. "It's over. The war's over. You need to come outside."

Without moving the rest of her body, Minnie swivels her head to face her youngest. As she frowns at her daughter, the tears continue to fall, landing now on the sewing before her.

"Mum!" Barbara prompts, hoping to wake her from her trance.

Minnie's brow wrinkles further. "I don't know what to do," she says.

"Come outside, Mum!"

"But do I need to finish this jacket or not?" she asks, her voice other-worldly. "That's what I can't work out."

Barbara shakes her head. "No, Mum, you don't. It's over," she says. "They won't be needing uniforms any more. It's all finished." Barbara gently prises her hand from the sewing machine. "Come outside," she says again. "Everyone's outside. Come see!"

By the time they get outside, the street is full of people. Three men are dragging a battered upright piano through the front door of a house opposite and a fourth man is already playing a one-fingered version of 'Take me back to dear old Blighty' as they do so.

The couple Barbara saw dancing before are still at it, and two other couples, one mixed, one comprising two women, are now dancing with them as well.

Barbara pulls her mother down the path and into the road, where a group of women from their building have congregated.

"Oh, ain't it marvellous!" Sylvie exclaims, hugging both Barbara and her mother simultaneously albeit awkwardly due to their differing heights.

"It's peculiar," Minnie says quietly. "It's . . . it's hard to believe, really."

Barbara spots her sister in the distance talking to a young man in uniform.

She releases her mother's hand and runs over to her. "Glenda!" she shouts when she gets there. "The war's over!"

"I know!" Glenda says, grasping her hand. "Come on. We're going to Trafalgar Square."

"Trafalgar Square? Why?"

"Everyone's going there," Glenda tells her. "They say it's going to be the biggest party ever."

"The biggest party ever," the young man confirms, nodding seriously.

Barbara turns back to look at their mother. "But what about Mum?" she says.

"She'll be fine," Glenda says. "Nothing's gonna happen to her now, is it? The war's over!" And then Glenda takes the young man's hand as well and they start to walk briskly away.

As they head through the streets, the crowds become ever denser. This May evening, everyone has stepped outside; the whole of London has downed tools. Everywhere Barbara looks, people are laughing and singing, they're dancing and waving flags.

"Everyone's so happy!" she says.

"Of course they bloody are!" Glenda laughs.

"Will Mum be OK?" Barbara asks.

"Of course she bloody will!"

"I'm worried about her."

"She's with Sylvia and Mildred and all that lot, isn't she?" Glenda says.

But that isn't what Barbara meant. She didn't mean, will Mum be OK *now*. She meant, will Mum be OK *in general*.

"Everything's gonna be better now," Glenda tells her. "You'll see."

"Will it?" Barbara asks.

"Yes. Dad'll be home soon and there'll be no more rationing."

"Yes, rationing will stop," the young man says. "I'm looking forward to that!"

"We'll probably get our old house back too!" Glenda says, and Barbara begins, for the first time, to imagine what a future without war might look like. As she runs, she starts to throw an occasional skip into the mix.

By the time they have made their way to Trafalgar Square, the sun is setting behind the buildings, and the crowd is bigger than any Barbara has ever seen. If people weren't so smiley, she'd feel a little scared.

Helped by the man, Glenda climbs up on a pillar box, then points to the east. "Over there," she says, jumping down and taking Barbara by the hand again.

When they get to the far side, the impromptu band of GIs and locals that Glenda spotted has started to play Harry James' *Two-O'Clock Jump,* so, in an ever smaller space in the midst of the swelling throng, led first by her sister and then by an actual (and rather good looking) GI, Barbara jives for the first time in her life. The eighth of May is one date that she'll never forget.

* * *

It's five p.m. and the heat of the day is starting to fade as Barbara reaches Willow Street.

She runs up the stairs, then pauses with her hand on the

doorknob. She takes a deep breath and launches herself into the room, determined that today her mother's sadness will not make *her* feel sad. Today is election day and everyone has been talking excitedly about how much things will change should Clement Atlee be elected to replace Churchill. And even Barbara can sense that something needs to change soon. People are worn out, hungry and poor, and many are getting angry. Revolution is in the air.

Though the fear of invasion and attack has lifted, their lives seem stuck since the war ended. They are still living in a single room and rationing has not come to an end as hoped. In fact, with the influx of returning evacuees, food, if anything, has become even more scarce. Minnie's piecework has ended, so although Glenda has now found a job training in British Home Stores, they seem to be no less poor than before.

Finding the room unexpectedly empty, Barbara drops her bag and runs downstairs in the hope that someone in the kitchen will know where her mother is.

She finds Minnie alone in the kitchen. She's in the process of spreading batter into a cake tin with slow, precise movements, crouching down so that her eyes are level with the tin.

Barbara raises her eyebrows in surprise. Her mother has not so much as boiled an egg since they had to leave their old house.

"Hi Mum. Is that a *cake*?"

Minnie looks up at her but remains level with the cake. "It will be. Hopefully."

"Gosh. Is it somebody's birthday?"

"No," Minnie says. "Not that I know of."

"Did you manage to find some eggs?"

"This is Elsie's Tottenham Cake recipe. It doesn't need eggs."

Barbara nods and watches as her mother continues to

smooth the surface of the batter with a spatula. "Does it need to be *very* smooth?" she asks.

Minnie nods. "It needs to be perfect," she says quietly. She squints at the cake, turns it and smooths a little more. "This cake has to be absolutely perfect."

"Can I lick the bowl out?" Barbara asks.

"I suppose so," Minnie says, her eyes flicking briefly at the bowl and then back at the cake tin.

Barbara pulls the bowl towards her and then runs her finger around the inside. She lifts a blob of the sticky, sweet mixture to her lips. "Umm. Tastes lovely," she says, then, "Everyone says Clement Atlee's going to win the election."

"Good," Minnie says. "Things can't get no worse than they are now."

"Is that what the cake's for? Is it for the election?"

"Maybe it is and maybe it isn't," Minnie says, mysteriously.

"Is it a surprise?"

"Looks that way," Minnie says.

The cake, once iced, is the shiniest, pinkest, most beautifully smooth cake that Barbara has ever seen. She hadn't known that her mother was such a good cook.

When Glenda gets home at six-thirty, Barbara immediately informs her that their mother has baked a cake. But rather than serving up the cake as Barbara had hoped, Minnie crosses the room and lifts the tin to place it on top of the wardrobe. "If either of you touches that, you'll get such a hiding, so help me you will . . ." she says. "That's a special cake for a special event."

It's not until Minnie goes to the toilet that night that Barbara is able to ask Glenda, with whom she still shares a bed, who she thinks the cake might be destined for.

"I think it's for Dad," Glenda whispers back. "I think he's

been demobbed. Mildred said there was a telegram came this morning or something."

Barbara lies awake until the early hours with a strange mixture of excitement and fear elicited by the potential return of her father, but Seamus doesn't return that night and he hasn't returned when Barbara gets home the next day either.

Despite the much celebrated change of government, rationing continues and even worsens, the room on Willow Street remains home, Minnie still spends her days staring out of the window, and the tinned cake sits untouched on top of the wardrobe. Neither Barbara nor Glenda ever dare mention the cake, nor their father for that matter, again.

2012 – PICCADILLY, LONDON.

"Jesus!" Sophie exclaims. They have just set foot in the first hall of the David Hockney exhibition and already Sophie is overwhelmed by the scale of the paintings.

"Not so small, huh?" Brett says.

"The exhibition *is* called A Bigger Picture," Sophie says, "so I suppose we were forewarned."

In front of them is a vast painting of an autumnal forest: fifteen metres by three of purple, orange and red trunks rising from a vibrant, almost fluorescent ferny undergrowth.

"You never saw any big Hockneys before?" Brett asks, glancing at the programme then back at the painting.

"Not for real," Sophie says, leaning in to study the quality of the paint before retreating across the room until she can see the entire scene without turning her head. "I mean, we studied Hockney at college but this is just so . . . vast."

"I saw his Grand Canyon stuff at the Smithsonian," Brett says. "They were kinda CinemaScope too. I think there's one here, somewhere."

Sophie glances left and right and notices again the emptiness of the gallery. Being able to see an exhibition alone is really rather special and she feels a little bubble of warmth towards Brett for having smuggled her in with his journalist's pass.

"So snap each of the biggies," he says. "Maybe one with me standing in front for scale – yeah, I like that. And then we'll see what we use at the end."

Sophie nods and raises the Nikon to her eye, and for a few

seconds she is lost in the technicalities of taking the photo. But when she lowers the camera and sees the autumnal scene again, unframed by the viewfinder, she senses an unusual feeling rising in her chest. Because she can't immediately identify the source, she strokes the camera and thinks about it for a moment: yes, she's actually welling up here and it's a direct emotional response to the picture. "God that's beautiful," she croaks, shaking her head, and Brett, who has already moved on to the next picture, looks back at her and grins wryly.

"Are you actually getting teary there?" he asks.

"Yeah, a bit. It's strange," Sophie says. "I don't think that ever happened to me before. Not with a picture."

Brett nods. "He's one clever dude," he says, then, "Take a shot of these too, will you? The whole wall. I'll be next door."

As Sophie walks towards the wall of smaller (but still large) woodland scenes, she glances over her shoulder at the autumn panorama again. "That's extraordinary," she murmurs. *I wonder how you could do something that awe-inspiring in photography,* she wonders. Only the vast photos of Andreas Gursky come close and they're huge too. So maybe scale has everything to do with it. Perhaps if you blew up a simple photo of a face to thirty square metres, it would suddenly become art.

"Come on!" Brett is poking his head back through the doorway. "We only have half an hour, remember?"

As they continue around the exhibition, the sensation of being moved, of being emotionally destabilised, comes again and again and Sophie is able to analyse it further. It's the same feeling she's had once or twice when, lacking in sleep, she's been up early enough to see a beautiful sunrise. Something about being overwhelmed, just momentarily, by the beauty of existence. Could it really be within the power of these Hockney paintings to do this to her, or is something more happening here? Is it perhaps because she's here with Brett? Is she finally falling in love?

"Wow," she mutters, when in another room, she wobbles on her feet in front of the fifteen metre rendition of the Grand Canyon, as she struggles as if suffering from actual vertigo to remain standing.

As they leave, only half an hour later (Brett has an article to pen before midnight), they cross paths with a posh, frumpy female journalist and her twenty-something bearded photographer. Brett air-kisses them both.

"Any good, Brett, darling?" the woman asks and Brett just shrugs and says, "Enjoy!"

Outside in the crisp, January evening, Sophie asks, "Who were those two?"

"*Telegraph,*" Brett says, buttoning his overcoat.

"So, the enemy?"

"Kind of."

"Why did you shrug when they asked what you thought? You did like it, didn't you?"

Brett shrugs again. "I haven't got an angle yet. And if I did have one, I wouldn't tell those assholes."

"I think it's beautiful," Sophie says. "One of the most beautiful exhibitions I have ever seen."

"Sure. But *beautiful,*" Brett says, in a soppy, mocking voice, "isn't an angle."

"It was too big for me," Sophie says, shaking her head. "I couldn't take it all in. At least not in half an hour."

"Now that," Brett says, "is an angle."

"I'm sorry?"

"*Too Big A Picture,*" he says, with a wiggle of an eyebrow. "Geddit?"

63

Sophie rolls her eyes. "Yeah. I geddit. And I'm freezing out here."

"Food?" Brett asks, glancing at his watch.

"Sure, I'm hungry."

"Dolada?" he asks, nodding across the street. "I don't have too much time."

"Sure," Sophie says, starting to walk. "I could have spent all day in there. You will give it a good write-up, won't you?"

"Maybe. Probably. It's all about working out what people want to read."

"Is it?"

"Of course. Hockney's amazingly lucky as well," Brett says. "That's the first time the Royal Academy has ever given the entire place to a single artist."

"And while he's alive too."

"I'm sorry?"

"Well, retrospectives are usually reserved for dead artists, aren't they? It's pretty rare for it to happen when they're still alive."

"It's not technically a retrospective," Brett says, as they cross the pavement towards the cosy glow of the restaurant. "A lot of that stuff's brand new. But yeah, I guess. Did anyone ever organise one for your father?"

"A retrospective?"

"Uh-huh."

"No," Sophie says thoughtfully. "Maybe we should."

"Yes, maybe you should," Brett repeats, with meaning.

When they enter the restaurant, Brett's glasses steam up so completely that he is rendered momentarily blind, so Sophie grinningly leads him to the table the Maitre d' is indicating.

"It's weird no one ever put together a Marsden retrospective, really," Brett says, once he has polished his glasses and the menus have been handed to them.

Sophie shrugs. "No one even suggested it. And it's hardly Mum or Jon who are going to organise something like that."

"Because?"

"Well, Mum's pretty old now. And she was always a bit of a heathen to be honest."

"A heathen?"

"That's probably not the right word. I just mean that she's not very arty."

"Oh, OK. And your brother?"

"He's a quantity surveyor. So he has no interest in art either."

"Which is weird. Coming from your background."

Sophie nods thoughtfully. "Dad was pretty low-key about it. And they kept Jonathan well away from the art business. Mum wanted him to have a proper reliable career. And so he did. Very sensible, my brother."

"But not you?"

Sophie shrugs. "I was pretty determined," she says. "And I wouldn't say that I *am* in the art business really."

"Not yet."

"Not yet," she agrees.

"Fiorentina," Brett says.

"I'm sorry?"

"Pizza Fiorentina," he explains, folding the menu shut. "Spinach and egg. Can't beat it. Then home to write *Too Big A Picture.*"

During the meal, Brett chatters about his own family: his father the banker, his mother who runs a whole-food store in the East Village, Connie, his sister, now married to an evangelical Christian in Wyoming. But Sophie is only half-listening, because her mind is buzzing with the idea of an Anthony Marsden retrospective.

It's not until the bill has been paid and they are walking home along sparkly, frosted streets that she mentions it again. "How much interest would there be, do you think? In a Marsden retrospective?"

Brett laughs.

"What?"

"I just knew we'd be revisiting that one," he says.

"And?"

"How much media interest, d'ya mean?"

"I suppose."

"Quite a lot, I guess. You'd need some really mega Hockneyesque prints of some of his famous shots."

"The summer of seventy-six, the abortion demo, stuff like that?"

"Yeah."

"I'd have to contact the rights owners. A lot of them belong to the *Mirror* or the *Times*."

"And a batch of stuff people have never seen. You'll still have rights to those."

"That might not be so easy, actually."

"Really?"

"Mum burned them all."

"Really?!"

"Actually, no that's not true. But she did destroy some. All the stuff from the Pentax tour went up in flames. You never heard that story?"

Brett shakes his head.

"Pentax sponsored him to do a big show. In the eighties. But he died halfway through the shoot and Mum lost the plot and burned everything." Sophie slips on the icy pavement and Brett grabs her arm and pulls her upright. "Careful there," he says.

"Thanks."

"That's interesting," Brett says, "about the Pentax tour."

And Sophie can hear in his voice a different tone, the tone of Brett the journalist. "It's not a scoop, Brett," she explains. "The story was all over the papers at the time."

"Oh," Brett says, sounding disappointed.

"But Mum has boxes of other photos and negatives and stuff. Jon has some too. So I'm sure we could find some good stuff."

"I guess you need to start there," Brett says. "See if there's enough material."

"Could we get someone big interested, do you think? The R.A. or the National Portrait Gallery, or the V and A?"

"Possibly," Brett says. "He was a big name. It would help, of course, if you knew someone at a major newspaper who could help you publicise it . . ."

"Like someone at the *Times*?"

"Like someone at the *Times*," Brett says, with a wink. "But again, it depends on the work you can put together. And it would be a big old game to organise it all."

Just in front of them, a cab is dropping someone off. Brett starts to walk faster. "Shall we jump in this one?" he asks.

"Yes," Sophie replies. "This pavement's lethal."

Once they are seated and on the move, Sophie says, "I suppose that's the problem. It's loads of work and there's no money in it."

"You'd have to get a sponsor. Maybe talk to Pentax again."

Sophie snorts. "Pentax wouldn't go near it with a bargepole. He died, remember. The return on their investment was nil once Mum had burned the photos."

"Someone else then. And you'd have to budget in a salary for yourself to cover running the whole thing."

"Right . . ." Sophie says, vaguely.

"Of course," Brett adds, smiling wryly, because he knows

that this is the elephant in the room that Sophie has been pretending to ignore. "Ideally you could find a way to link your own work into the mix, make it a father–daughter thing and use it to launch your new career as an arty-farty Milly Colley lookalike. So that could make it worthwhile."

"You reckon?" Sophie asks, as if the idea is only now crossing her mind.

Brett just laughs and rolls his eyes.

1950 – EASTBOURNE, EAST SUSSEX.

Barbara awakens to the screeching of seagulls and momentarily can't work out where she is. She rubs her eyes and looks up at the unfamiliar, pale-blue ceiling, then across the room at Glenda, sleeping in the single bed beside her.

And then she remembers: she's on holiday. She smiles to herself and stretches with cat-like contentment. It's the first time in her entire sixteen-year life that she has been on holiday and though they only arrived by train late last night, she's already loving the sensation of a different bed with different sounds. She thinks about getting up to look outside but instead falls asleep again. Lie-ins are rarely permitted at home.

When she awakens next, the sun is streaming in through the salt-splattered bay window and Glenda, wrapped in her dressing gown, is silhouetted against the blue sky beyond.

"Morning," Barbara says, through a yawn.

Glenda turns her head to look back at her. She looks puffy and indistinct without her make-up but also a little less severe, a tad more friendly.

"It's a lovely day," Glenda says. "I think I'd like to go swimming. Before breakfast. What do you reckon?"

"Ooh! Yes!" Barbara says, sitting sharply upright. "Let's do that!"

There isn't a single cloud in the sky as they cross the main road from the Sea View (No Vacancies) and descend the few steps to the pebble beach. "Will it be cold, do you think?" Barbara asks.

"Freezing," Glenda says. "But I don't give a damn."

"Me neither."

Barbara swivels her head to take in the vista: the sun rising to the left, the vast, empty pebble beach before them, the pier to the right . . . It's all so crisp, so clean, so refreshing after London. A simple change of vista can, she is discovering, make you feel like a completely different person.

They remove their dresses, revealing the one-piece swimming costumes they wriggled into before leaving, then linking hands, they run shrieking across the painful pebbles and into the murky green water. It is indeed freezing. The morning dip is short-lived but exhilarating.

After a fried breakfast complete with bitter, over-stewed tea and watered-down orange juice, the sisters head back out and walk along the seafront in the direction of the pier.

"I love the seaside," Barbara announces. "I think I'd like to live here one day."

"I know what you mean," Glenda replies. "But I think you'd get bored. There's lots more to do in London that in Eastbourne."

"I suppose," Barbara says, even though she can't think of a single thing that she would prefer to 'do' in London than simply being here today.

Halfway along the pier, just after the candy-floss booth with the organ music, they are approached by a young, blond beach photographer. "Come on girls," he says. "You've got to have a picture to take home to Mum."

And because he's about her age and good looking with it (Barbara loves men with beards and they're pretty rare in 1950s England), she asks, "How much?"

"For you lovely ladies, a shilling," the man says. "And I'll take three for the price and let you choose your favourite. I promise you'll look like film stars."

"A shilling!" Glenda laughs. "We can get lunch for that."

"Oh, come on," Barbara pleads, looking into the photographer's blue eyes. They seem to contain a hidden smile. "It'll be a present for Mum when we get back."

"We can't afford it," Glenda says. "You know we've got just enough for the—"

"Please?" Barbara pleads.

"Sixpence, then," Glenda says, addressing the man. "Not a penny more."

The man's mouth slips into a cute grin.

"And we get to keep all three photos," Glenda adds. "They're of no use to you anyway."

"Alright, alright," he says. "You drive a hard bargain girls but because you're both so gorgeous, I'm gonna let you have what you want."

Once the photos have been taken – two leaning against the railings with the wind blowing Glenda's hair around and one posing with a fake, full-sized bull (thoughtfully provided for this exact purpose) – the man hands the girls his card, then, as an afterthought, tags along as they start to walk along the pier.

"Did anyone ever tell you, you look like Claudette Colbert?" he asks Barbara.

She senses that she is blushing as she replies, "No, no one ever did, actually."

"Don't listen to his smooth talk," Glenda tells her. "He's only after a bit of slap and tickle. They all are."

"I'm not saying I wouldn't mind," the man says, shockingly, making Barbara blush again. "But you really *do* look like Claudette Colbert. It's uncanny."

Barbara glances at Glenda and smiles coyly. "Do I?" she asks, and Glenda just pulls a face.

"Can I take your photo over there?" the man asks, pointing to a bench seat in a small wooden shelter. "The light's lovely over there."

"We're not paying for any more photos," Glenda tells him. "So you can just buzz off, now."

"These are just for me," the man says. "To remember Claudette here by."

"Aren't you worried about all the film?" Barbara asks. She knows that film is expensive.

"My mate's dad's got a shop," the man tells her. "I get them for free. Developing too. Go on. Go sit on that bench there. Just for a couple of shots."

Barbara fiddles with her hair, then crosses the pier to the bench. When Glenda starts to follow her, the photographer says, "Hang on a mo. Just let me get one of Claudette on her own."

"It's Barbara, actually," Barbara says.

"Nice to meet you, Barbara," he replies, bending over the viewfinder of his very professional-looking Rolleiflex. "I'm Tony."

"And I'm Glenda," Glenda tells him, hand on hip. "Not that you care."

"That's lovely," Tony says, and just for a minute Glenda thinks he's referring to her name.

"Turn a bit to the right so that the sun . . . that's it. Lovely! . . . So are you two sisters, then?"

"We are," Barbara replies.

"I knew it. You both have real star quality. And turn the other way now," Tony says, and as Barbara does so, she sees that Glenda is leaving them to it, already heading back along the pier.

"Glenda!" she calls out. "Wait!"

Glenda wiggles her fingers over her shoulder. "Have fun, Sis'," she says. "Just don't do anything I wouldn't. I'll meet you back at the hotel for dinner."

"Gosh," Tony says quietly, his voice smooth and cheeky. "Lucky me!"

"Glenda!" Barbara shouts, but really she's rather glad that her sister ignores her.

The photos taken, Tony and Barbara continue to the end of the pier where they lean over the railings and look into the swirling depths. The air is filled with the iodine smell of seaweed.

"The sea's really cold," Barbara says, digging a fingernail into the thick, pocked paintwork of the railings. "I went for a dip this morning, with Glenda."

"You have to go in the afternoon," Tony says. "Wait till it's warmed up."

"That's what I said too."

"So, are you two on holiday?" Tony asks.

"Yes. We're only here for three days. More's the pity."

"You like it?"

"Yeah. It's lovely. The air's so fresh and it's got the sea and everything," Barbara says. "Do you live here all year round?"

Tony nods. "It's fun in summer but it gets a bit boring in winter. I like it when the waves are all crashing around though."

"Glenda said it'd be boring in winter. She said there's more to do in London. But I'd still rather live here, I reckon."

"Where abouts are you?"

"The East End. Shoreditch."

"You got a boyfriend in Shoreditch, then?"

Barbara looks away, closes her eyes briefly, then takes a deep breath and replies, "No. I haven't. What about you? Have you got a girlfriend?"

"No," Tony says. With a grin, he adds, "Not yet, at any rate."

They walk around the end of the pier and, from a booth, Tony buys a packet of chips, thickly cut and smothered in salt and spicy, tangy vinegar. These they share as they head back to land. "Chips always taste better out of newspaper," Barbara says, licking her fingers.

"You're right. They do."

"So, is that your actual job?" Barbara asks, pointing at Tony's camera.

"No. It's just a hobby, really," Tony says. "I make some pocket money with it though. Especially on bank holiday weekends. As long as I don't cross paths with the proper photographer, I'm OK. He chases me off his patch sometimes. But my real job is a courier. I deliver packages on a motorbike. Things that are too urgent for the postman."

"Gosh, you've got a motorbike?"

Tony shakes his head. "They lend me one for work. A knackered old thing it is. A Royal Enfield from the war. It sounds like a machine gun and it's a bugger to start."

"It must be fun though."

"It's OK when the sun's out," Tony says. "Bleedin' horrible in winter though. I have to go all the way up to London sometimes. Maybe I'll come visit you next time."

Barbara glances at her feet. "Maybe," she says.

"D'you fancy a cuppa?" Tony asks. They are walking past a workman's cafe.

"I had better not," Barbara says. "Glenda's being a bit funny about money. She says we've got a limited holiday budget."

"This is on me," Tony says. "Come on. I'm thirsty."

The air inside the cafe is steamy and laden with the greasy fumes of the fried breakfasts the workmen around them are eating. They buy cups of thick, sickly tea from the counter and slide into two window seats. Tony wipes the condensation from the window with his sleeve so that Barbara can see outside – a generosity of gesture that does not go unnoticed. "There you go," he says.

"Thanks."

"Where are you staying?" Tony asks.

"A bed and breakfast. On the seafront. The Sea View."

"They're all called that."

Barbara laughs. "They are! We knocked at two Sea Views before we found ours."

"My mum runs a guesthouse too. Ours is called Donnybrook," Tony says.

"Why?"

"Why what?"

"Why Donnybrook?"

Tony shrugs. "Search me. I think it's somewhere in Ireland or something, but it was already called that when we moved here."

"And your dad?"

"He drives lorries. Long distances. He's away a lot. Which is alright by me."

"You don't see eye-to-eye with him, then?"

"He's alright, I suppose. When he's sober. A bit handy with his fists when he isn't."

"Oh, that's not so good."

"What about your folks?"

"Mum's a seamstress," Barbara says.

"She does sewing and stuff?"

"Yeah. Sort of."

Tony nods. "And your dad?"

Barbara sighs and swallows.

"Sorry," Tony says. "I didn't think. Was it in the war?"

Barbara clears her throat. "He's not dead," she says. "He just never came back, really."

"He's missing?"

"No. He never came home to us, I mean."

Tony is frowning, so Barbara tries to explain the inexplicable.

"I don't know that much about it, really. Mum never lets anyone talk about it. But I think he met someone else. Someone told Glenda that he was living in Harlow working as a builder or something. He's got a whole new family now."

"And you never go and see him?"

Barbara shakes her head. "No."

"Never?"

Barbara turns to look out at the street. The window is already misting up again, so she wipes it with her hand. "Can we talk about something else, please?" she asks.

"Sorry," Tony says. "Me and my big mouth. Famous for it, I am."

"It's OK," Barbara says. "But I'd rather talk about something else, that's all."

"Sure. So what shall we talk about?"

"Tell me about Eastbourne. Have you got a lot of friends here?"

"Oh yeah. Loads," Tony says, sipping at his tea. "It's a very friendly place, is Eastbourne."

"Do you go dancing and stuff?"

"In summer, sometimes. They have some good ones at the Winter Gardens. D'you like dancing, then?"

"I think so," Barbara says.

"Maybe I could take you," Tony suggests.

"Maybe," Barbara says, daring to wink as she says it.

Though it's naughty, Barbara does not return to the Sea View for lunch that day. She sits with Tony at the water's edge on Eastbourne's (now-crowded) beach and throws pebbles into the water. She rides with Tony on a donkey. It's supposed to be for children only but Tony knows the donkey man so it's alright. And exactly as the clock-tower begins to chime, Tony says, "It's five."

"It is. I should go back and find Glenda. She'll be worried."

"Can I kiss you, then? Before you go, I mean." Tony asks.

Barbara flushes a deep shade of puce as she stops walking, brushes her hair from her eyes, and then summoning all of her courage turns to face him. "Do you really want to?" she asks.

"Of course I do," Tony says. "You're a cracker, you are."

"D'you really think so?" Barbara asks. "Or do you say that to all the girls?"

Tony nods. "I've been waiting my whole life for a girl who looks like Claudette Colbert," he says, dramatically. "Maybe you're the one I was waiting for."

Barbara squints at him. "Maybe just a peck then," she says.

On the train home, Glenda tells her, by way of warning, that she needs to realise it's just a holiday romance. Barbara turns from watching East Sussex slide by to face her sister. "Why would you say that?" she asks.

"Because I don't want you moping around when we get back," Glenda says. "It's just a holiday fling."

"How would *you* know?" Barbara asks. "You've never had a holiday fling. Or a holiday for that matter."

"It's happened to friends of mine, alright? Tony forgot you ever existed the minute you got on this train. And you'll forget all about Tony the—"

"We saw each other every day. He gave me these flowers," Barbara says, nodding at the small bunch of roses lying on the seat beside her. "I think he really likes me."

"He probably stole those from somebody's garden," Glenda says. "And he wanted to get into your knickers, that's all. You don't know what men are like yet. But you'll learn."

"That's a horrid thing to say," Barbara says. "I think you're just jealous!"

Glenda shakes her head knowingly and turns to look out

of the window. They are creaking into a tiny station called Polegate. She doesn't say anything more on the matter because, though she is utterly convinced that Barbara will never hear from Tony again, Barbara has hit the nail on the head. This is the first time in her life that a man has focused his attention on her little sister rather than on her. So yes, she *is* feeling jealous.

The photos arrive that Thursday morning (Tony used the excuse of sending them on to obtain Barbara's address). Enclosed in the envelope with the three rather good holiday snaps is a handwritten page. "I think you're the most cracking girl I've ever met," it says. "I think I'm in love with those melancholy Colbert eyes of yours. Please tell me I can come and visit you soon?"

Barbara stares at herself in the mirror and wonders if she has melancholy eyes and if that's a good thing. But the two-room flat they occupy, above the laundry where her mother works, is squalid and Barbara is too ashamed to let Tony see it. So she borrows the train fare from Glenda and only two weeks later, telling Minnie she's visiting a new girlfriend, Diane, she heads back to Eastbourne.

On the train down she ponders the fact that if she were to marry Tony, she'd have to live in Eastbourne. She'd avoid the three a.m job at the bakery her mother has been pushing her to take, she'd escape the horrible rooms above the laundry, and she'd get to live at the seaside, all in one fell swoop. She feels a bit guilty for being so calculating but nothing ever appealed more.

On arrival, The Donnybrook looks exactly like the bed and breakfast she stayed in with Glenda, all flock wallpaper and winceyette sheets. Being on a side road set back from the sea-front, it doesn't have a sea view, but with Tony's mother, Joan, run off her feet, and his father, Lionel, away driving somewhere,

Tony is able to sneak in and out of her room pretty much at will. Which makes it the best four days and nights that Barbara has ever spent.

By day, they wander along the beaches and hang around in the seafront arcades with Tony's friends Hugh and Diane.

Hugh is a dry, charming, permanently-suited proselytising communist, while Diane (who lives above the photo shop and constantly smells of developer fluid) is a tearaway Tomboy with perfectly straight, floppy, black hair and thick, dark eyebrows that really need plucking.

But what with Hugh constantly trying to steal kisses from Diane, and Diane nonchalantly laughing at his advances, they are great fun to be with. And the air and the light of Eastbourne are as fresh and invigorating as ever.

Barbara worries that Diane might have eyes for Tony but when she asks him about it he says, "Don't be daft. She's a mate. I've known her since I was three or something."

Barbara still thinks that she's right though, and decides that maybe she just needs to nab Tony quickly. Maybe she needs to get there before Diane does.

When Barbara gets home that Sunday evening, she finds Glenda preparing stew on the little Bendix cooker and Minnie repairing the frayed collars of shirts from the laundry.

Barbara drops her bag and pecks her mother on the lips.

"Here, holiday girl," Minnie says. "Take a bunch of these will you? Just the ones from the top of the pile. Missing buttons. Otherwise I'm never gonna get through 'em all."

Barbara nods, slips off her coat and scoops some shirts from the pile before retiring with the sewing box to the armchair. She's tired from the journey home. She would have liked to have had a cup of tea first. But she knows better than to argue.

"How was Eastbourne?" Minnie asks.

"Lovely," Barbara says, already cutting a length of cotton and threading a needle. "Not as hot as when Glen and I was there. But it was sunny."

Minnie nods and tips her head sideways, prompting her to continue.

"Diane's mum was really nice," Barbara continues, launching herself into the lie. "And their guest house was almost exactly the same as the one we stayed in, only farther from the sea."

"And they didn't mind having you to stay, then?" Minnie asks, her voice doubtful.

"No," Barbara says, putting on a thimble, selecting a matching button from the tin and starting to sew it into place. "And we helped making beds and things. I did washing up too."

"You did?" Minnie says, sounding even less convinced.

Barbara senses that she is on the verge of being rumbled. It's hard to pull the wool over Minnie's eyes. She swallows with difficulty and tries to concentrate on the sewing.

"Shall I put *all* of these carrots in, Mum?" Glenda asks, and Barbara knows that this is her attempt at providing a distraction. Glenda too, senses the danger.

"Just use your common sense," Minnie says, then addressing Barbara, "What else did you get up to? Tell me more. Tell me everything."

"We walked along the beach," Barbara says, remembering the feel of Tony's hand in her own. "We listened to the band in the Winter Gardens," she says, remembering the feel of Tony's beard as he kissed her behind the beach huts. Are her lips still red? she wonders. "Only from outside, of course. It cost too much to go in. We walked along the pier as well," she says, when in fact she, Diane, Hugh and Tony had all got tipsy

80

on beer Diane had stolen from her father *beneath* the pier, and once tipsy, she had let Tony slide his hand up her blouse. "Just normal, seaside stuff."

Minnie nods and glances up at her, her expression vaguely troubled.

"Diane's mum said I can go again next weekend if I want," Barbara says.

Minnie snorts. "And how are you going to pay for that, then?"

"Diane's dad said he'd pay for the ticket," Barbara says, and the fact that Glenda, behind her mother, pauses preparing the stew and frowns at her, makes her aware that she has gone too far.

Minnie stops working again. She licks her lips, then lays down the sewing and stares at her hands for a moment as if inspecting her manicure. "Can you go to the shop and get me some matches?" she asks Glenda without looking up.

"I'll go," Barbara offers.

"No. You'll stay here," Minnie instructs. "And no need to hurry, Glenda."

"No, Mum," Glenda replies, already pulling on her coat and heading for the door. She does not want to be present for whatever is about to happen.

The second the door has closed, Minnie asks, "So, what's his name?"

"Who?" Barbara asks, pretending to concentrate on her sewing. "Diane's dad? He's called—"

Minnie's fisted hand smashes against the tabletop. "I will *not* be lied to by my own daughter in my own home," she spits. "What's his bleedin' name?!"

"Tony," Barbara splutters. "His name's Tony."

"Tony," Minnie repeats, her eyes narrowing.

Barbara stares at her sewing and wonders if she's going to cry.

"Well, go on then, girl. Talk!" Minnie says.

Once Barbara has told Minnie everything she can think of about Tony that doesn't involve kissing or beer, Minnie, without a word, resumes her sewing. She is wishing Seamus was here to deal with this. She is trying to decide how she is supposed to react. Things with Glenda were so different – she spun out of control when Minnie wasn't watching and by the time she noticed, she was too independent to even be guided. But Barbara? Barbara is fragile. Barbara needs protecting, Minnie reckons.

Barbara waits for a moment, then opens her mouth to ask if she can continue seeing him. But she changes her mind and says nothing. She too resumes her work.

After a few minutes, Minnie breaks the silence. "Are you serious about him?" she asks. "Do you really like this boy?"

Barbara clears her throat. "I think so," she says.

Minnie nods. "I hope you're not doing nothing a girl your age shouldn't be."

"No, Mum," Barbara says. "He hasn't even tried anything like that. He's a proper, well brought up boy."

"Well, if you're going to start courting, I suppose you'd better get him up here so I can meet him," Minnie says.

"Oh. OK. I'll, um, write and ask when he can come, shall I?"

"A Sunday's best," Minnie tells her. "Tell him to come here next Sunday afternoon. I'll make some scones." She doesn't really know why Sunday is best, nor why she needs to make scones, except that this is how her own parents greeted Seamus all those years ago. She doesn't really know how to do any of this but Sunday and scones is at least a start.

"Couldn't we meet him in town somewhere?" Barbara asks, her eyes flicking around the room.

"Why? There's nothing wrong with here."

"I just thought it might be nice if—"

"Unless you think he's too posh to come here," Minnie says. "In which case you should maybe find yourself a nicer boyfriend. 'Cos I'm not changing anything just because you've found yourself some Little Lord Fauntleroy."

"That's not it, Mum," Barbara lies. "That's not it at all. I just thought it would be nice for you to get out. I thought it would make a change."

"No. He can come here next Sunday afternoon," Minnie says. "Or not at all."

* * *

It's just after three when Barbara hears the motorbike pull up outside. She goes to the window to check, then announcing, "It's him. He's here," she runs to the landing, then downstairs through the laundry to the front door.

She opens the door and the bell clangs and the 'closed' sign swings from side to side. Tony is removing his crash helmet and looking puzzled. "I thought I'd come to the wrong place," he says. "I didn't realise you actually lived *in* the laundry."

"Above it; we live in the flat upstairs," Barbara explains, pointing ashamedly. "It's nothing fancy but it's home to us," she adds, a line she heard in a film somewhere and saved for this very moment.

"OK," Tony says, following her inside the darkened shopfront. "It's just your mum upstairs, is it? Or is Glenda there too?"

"No, Glen's out. It's just us. I'm feeling all shaky."

"Me too."

"Come. It's this way," Barbara says, taking his hand and

pulling him through the laundry, past the racks of clean clothes, past the bags of dirty washing and on behind the counter and through the rear door.

If the laundry itself is shabby, it's as nothing compared to what lies behind that rear door. The Chinese owner hasn't done any work since he bought the place at the end of the war and Barbara reckons it must have been in need of more than a lick of paint before that. But as they don't have the time nor money to paint it themselves, shabby is how it remains. She wonders if Tony will simply turn around and leave. She wouldn't blame him if he did.

When they reach the upstairs landing, Barbara points at the coat-stand. "You can take your coat off and hang it there," she says.

Tony unzips then takes off his waxed-cotton motorcycle jacket revealing a slightly undersized black suit. "Ooh, you look lovely," Barbara says, straightening his skinny black tie.

"It's Hugh's," Tony murmurs. "I loaned it off him."

"I thought so. It looks alright though. So! Ready?"

Tony pulls a scared face and takes a deep breath. "Ready," he says.

Barbara pecks him on the cheek, then puts her hand on the doorknob and pushes the door open, leading Tony into the first of their two rooms, the room which serves as lounge, dining room, kitchen, workroom and Minnie's bedroom, and in which, due to lack of storage, not a single surface has been spared. Around the sink area, pots and pans are piled up. Near the armchair it's books and magazines. Near the single bed are piles of Minnie's clothes. And everywhere else are stacks and stacks of laundry awaiting adjustments or repairs. Barbara imagines seeing the room through Tony's eyes and thinks that she knows that it's all over – is convinced she knows that he will leave her at the end of this.

"Well?" Minnie prompts. "Aren't you going to introduce us?"

"Mum, this is Tony," she announces. "Tony, my mum."

"Hello, Mrs Doyle," Tony says, and Barbara can hear the tremor in his voice. "I'm really pleased to meet you." He steps forward and offers his hand.

"We'll see about that," Minnie says, ignoring his proffered hand, as ferocious as ever. "Just sit yourself there," she adds, nodding at the dining table upon which she has cleared just enough space for the plate of scones and the pot of tea. "And you, Miss," she says, addressing Barbara. "Go make yourself scarce for an hour, would you?"

"Oh," Barbara says. "I thought we were going to have tea together."

"Well, you thought wrong," Minnie says. "Now, off you scoot."

Barbara steps back out onto the landing and pulls the door closed behind her. She pulls on her coat but then hesitates and stands beside the door, listening. "So, *you're* the famous Tony," Minnie is saying.

"Last time I looked I was, Mrs Doyle," Tony replies.

Barbara pulls a face. Her mother won't appreciate being cheeked like that. Not one bit.

"And you came up from Eastbourne on that motorbike of yours, did you?"

"That's right, Mrs Doyle. Quite chilly it was."

Because this is followed by a lull in the conversation, Barbara leans in closer to the door and almost faints in fright when Minnie rips it open. "I thought you were going," Minnie says, her voice surprisingly calm.

85

"Yes, yes. Um, I'm just g-going," Barbara stutters, turning and running downstairs.

Out on the street, she hesitates, then turns towards the high street. It's a coolish September day and the sky is a pale grey, the breeze gentle.

As she walks, she tries to imagine the conversation between her mother and Tony. She imagines them eating scones together and wonders if Tony will dribble jam down his tie – he's a horribly messy eater. She tries to guess what Minnie will say when she gets back. "I'm sorry, he's a nice lad, but he's just not the kind of boy I want you to see," seems a possible formula. Or perhaps, "I've thought about it but you're just a bit young to be courting right now. I think you need to wait a few years." Her mum always says 'courting'. But would Tony wait for her? Of course he wouldn't. Especially not with Diane waiting in the wings. Minnie will surely have noticed his frayed collar and the undersized suit as well. Of that much, Barbara is certain. And will Tony still want to see her now he knows she lives in a slum above a laundry? Most probably not. Her heart is racing and she can't think of any reasonable way to make an hour disappear. "Please?" she prays, silently. "My whole life depends on this."

When, after forlornly wandering the streets for an hour, she gets back, she glances up at the windows as if they might reveal something about the atmosphere inside but all she can see is a reflection of the sky.

She lets herself in, walks through the laundry and pauses at the bottom of the stairs to listen. To her great surprise, she hears Minnie laughing. She can't remember ever having heard her mother laugh. It's a shock to discover that she is actually capable of doing so.

She listens a little longer, then after glancing at the clock to check that exactly an hour has passed, she climbs the stairs, takes off her coat and then hesitantly knocks on the door.

"Come in, love," Minnie says, and after the laughter, even her voice sounds changed and unfamiliar.

Barbara enters the room and finds Minnie wiping a tear from her eye and Tony grinning broadly. "You've got yourself a proper little comedian here," Minnie says. "He's had me in stitches, he has."

Barbara struggles not to frown as she looks at them both. This is such an unexpected result, it feels like some kind of a trick. "Well, come and have a scone then," Minnie says. "Tony's going to have to leave soon, more's the pity."

Tony winks at her and only then does Barbara let her features relax.

Out on the street, half an hour later, as Tony pulls on his crash helmet, Barbara glances up at Minnie watching them from the window and asks, quietly, "What on earth did you say to make her laugh like that?"

Tony shrugs. "I told her some jokes," he says. "My dad's mainly. She's really nice, your mum is."

"Jokes! What jokes?"

"Dunno. The one about the cannibals cooking the clergymen. Stuff like that."

"What, 'Shall we boil him? No this one's a friar'?" Barbara asks, perplexed.

"Yeah."

"But she was in *tears*."

Tony shrugs again. "Maybe nobody bothered to tell her any jokes for a while," he says.

"No," Barbara concedes. "No, maybe nobody did."

"So, when can I see you again?"

"I don't know. I suppose Mum will talk to me now. Once you've gone."

"I had better get going then."

"I'll write. As soon as I know something, I'll write."

"And I'll be back as soon as I can."

And then Tony jumps on the kick-starter of his motorbike, clunks into gear and heads off down the street.

When Barbara gets back inside, Minnie is already sewing.

"Can I have another scone?" she asks.

"As long as you leave some for Glenda."

"So, did you like him?"

"Yes," Minnie says. "Yes, he's a nice enough lad."

"Can I carry on seeing him, then?"

Minnie pauses and looks up at her. "I'm going to write to his parents," she says. "I want assurances you'll be in separate rooms when you stay there."

"We *always* sleep in separate rooms."

"Good," Minnie says. "Because as I told Tony. If he gets you in trouble, he marries you."

Barbara gulps and looks down at the pile of scones.

"Did you hear me?" Minnie asks.

"Yes, Mum," Barbara says. "Yes. I heard you."

2012 – SOUTHWARK, LONDON.

Sophie arrives early for her photo shoot. She surreptitiously stacks her equipment in a corner of the cavernous warehouse structure the studio is located in and pulls her Nikon from the bag.

When she reaches the stage, Ralph, who is gay and ripped (and prettier than most of the models), is busy draping vast white sheets across the backdrop. He hasn't noticed Sophie, so she silently removes the lens cover and raises the camera to her eye.

Ralph is on a too-small stepladder and is stretching to reach the far corner of the frame. His denim shirt has risen up revealing a tantalising stretch of skin above his low-waisted jeans and he actually has stirrups on his cowboy boots. It's going to be a sexy shot, Sophie reckons.

Unfortunately, she has forgotten to silence the camera, so the beep of the auto-focus alerts Ralph to her presence.

"Hey, Sophie," he says, turning and smiling. "What you up to?"

"Shh!" Sophie says. "I'm doing a little photo-réportage."

Ralph raises the staple gun and fires a shot into the top corner of the sheet. "Cool, well make sure you send me copies."

"Of course I will," Sophie says, zooming in on his arse and firing off three more shots. "Nice abs, by the way. I wish *my* boyfriend had a set of those."

"Oh, they're pretty easy to come by," Ralph says, climbing down. "You just have to abandon any idea of having a social life and spend all your free time at the gym."

Sophie laughs and then, switching the camera to silent mode as she does so, heads around the back to peer into the make-up room.

Inside, she finds the three models that *Now* has chosen for today's shoot. There are two women, the ferocious mixed-race Eddi Day, whom she has worked with before, and a new, skinny, slightly green-tinged blonde creature. The guy is of the stunning-but-dumb-looking genre, with thick eyebrows which are so horizontal you could use them as a spirit level. He looks a bit like a young, built Colin Farrell.

Sophie raises the camera and takes a few rear-photos of Butch powdering his nose in the mirror, one of Eddi Day checking her nasal passages, and one of Miss Skinny's boney hand ripping off a tiny chunk of croissant and putting it to her lips. Judging from her lack of body fat, or indeed body, this is the first bit of nourishment to pass those lips this year.

Silently, Sophie edges into the room. She sees that Butch has now noticed her presence – he grins at her but continues to powder his nose. Sophie hopes that *Now* won't be wanting any smiley shots, because his grin is frankly creepy. But he doesn't say anything, which is good because Sophie knows that as soon as Day spots her presence, this session will be over.

"Did they choose you for that Monsoon shoot in the end?" Day is asking Skinny.

"Nah. They chose some anorexic redhead," Skinny replies, and Sophie pulls a face as she tries to imagine what a model who *Skinny* considers anorexic might look like. Auschwitz imagery comes to mind.

Sophie edges along the right-hand wall and manages to take a series of photos of the three models in profile, all peering into their mirrors but with a different face in focus in each shot. If they work, it could make a great triptych.

And then Butch, damn him, says, "So, what are those

for?" and Eddi Day turns to face Sophie with one of the most terrifying scowls she has ever seen. *No one even imagines that models can look like this,* Sophie thinks, managing to snap three more shots as she lowers the camera.

"What the fuck?" Eddi Day snarls.

"They're just for me," Sophie says.

"Fuck that," Eddi Day spits. "That's not in the contract."

"Calm down. This isn't work," Sophie says. "As I said, they're just for me."

"They had better be," Eddi says. "Or I will sue the arse off you."

Skinny turns to look at her now and nods exaggeratedly. "Me too," she says.

Butch shrugs. "I don't mind," he says, sending Sophie a wink. "Shoot away."

* * *

When Brett arrives at Sophie's flat on Saturday morning, the screen of her twenty-seven-inch iMac is filled with the gruesomely curled lip of Eddi Day.

Brett hangs his coat up, then crosses the room and leans in to kiss Sophie's neck. "Gees!" he exclaims, performing a double take. "Who's that?"

"Eddi Day," Sophie says.

"And who might Eddi Day be?"

Sophie laughs. "You know Eddi Day even if you don't realise it. You just never saw her like this before."

She clicks a few times on the mouse and finds an online advert for Noméa anti-ageing cream.

"Oh, the face of Noméa, huh?"

"Yep."

"And she's moving into horror movies or what?"

Sophie snorts and restores her stolen photo. "A bit of a shocker, right?"

"A bit of an understatement. And she has wrinkles!" he says, pointing at the fine lines around her eyes.

"She *is* thirty-five," Sophie says. "I have to Photoshop them out these days."

"But she still does the adverts for anti-wrinkle cream, right?"

"Exactly. That's why I Photoshop them out."

"So, w'happen?" Brett asks, walking over to the kitchen and pouring himself a mug of coffee. "You hit the shutter button by accident?"

"No, I've been mucking around. Looking for an angle, as you would say," Sophie explains.

"And?"

"This is part of an idea I had. The hidden side of the fashion industry. That's my big idea. Well, currently it is anyway."

Brett leans back against the kitchen worktop and smiles. "Nah, that's not a big idea. That's just you being lazy. Thinking you can take a few extra shots while you're at work and call it art."

Sophie leans back in her chair and swivels gently from side to side as she studies the photo. She feels vaguely mesmerised by Eddi Day's scowl, specifically by the blob of saliva in the corner of her curled lip. "Art is all about the explanation you put on it," she says. "If you explain it in the right way, it becomes art."

"Hum," Brett says, sounding sarcastic. "Now let me see. Didn't a certain Anthony Marsden say something different. Wasn't his catchphrase something about—"

"Well, that was Dad being clever," Sophie interrupts. "Saying that art wasn't meant to be explained, that it was just meant to be looked at . . . well, that was Dad's clever deconstructionist explanation of what art is, wasn't it? It was a double bluff."

"If you say so."

"But seriously, Brett, look at this. There's something magnificent here, don't you think? Imagine this blown up to three by three. Metres that is, not feet. Or more. Maybe five by five. You'd be able to see every pore. Every blackhead."

"It would be awesome," Brett says. "And she'd sue the ass off you."

"Her exact words, in fact."

"Uh?"

"That's what she said when I took the photo. That she'd sue the ass off me if I used it. Well, she said 'earse', actually," Sophie says, doing a Liverpool accent. "She's from Runcorn, not New York, so . . ."

"So, you really *can't* use it?"

"Not this one, no. But I could probably get authorisation for some of them. Look at these." She fiddles with the mouse until the screen is displaying the first of her three triple-profile photos, now converted to high contrast black and white. "Well, come on!"

Brett sidles over and crouches down beside her and Sophie clicks through the three almost identical photos of the three models doing their make-up, the focus moving with each click from one face to the next. "I was imagining a huge triptych."

"It's kind of cool when you click through them like that," Brett says. "Video might be the way to go."

"Yes. You're right."

"Is he actually powdering his nose?"

"He is."

"Wow."

"And that's just the first layer. The make-up artist came just after that and plastered them all with foundation. Look." She shows Brett a series of photos with the make-up artist applying foundation from a spray gun.

"Wow!" Brett laughs. "They literally spray it on."

"Literally."

"And the final result?"

Sophie lines up two photos side-by-side, one of Eddi Day in a *Now* black skirt and a sleeveless orange cable-knit jumper, and one of Patrick (Butch's real name turned out to be Patrick Evans) wearing an off-the-peg grey three-piece suit with a white round-collared shirt and a skinny pink tie.

"Huh!" Brett exclaims. "Foundation suits him. Nice suit too. Who's is that?"

"*Now*," Sophie says.

"*Now*?"

"The high-street chain, yeah."

"Their suits don't look like that in the window."

Sophie grins and bites her bottom lip. For once, she is the expert here and she's enjoying it. She's loving being able to reveal the secrets of the fashion world to Brett. "Look at this," she says, selecting a different photo of Patrick taken from behind.

"What *are* those?" Brett asks. "Clothes pegs?"

"Yep," Sophie says. "That's how you get a *Now* suit to look good on a gym built model. Pegs all down the back so that the front hangs right. And if you look closely . . ." She chooses another photo taken from behind. In this one, Patrick is wearing only the trousers and the satin-backed waistcoat. Sophie zooms in on the waistband of the trousers. "You can see that they actually had to unstitch the waistband, yeah?"

"Because it was the wrong size? Or he has exceptionally big buns? What?"

"The fashion is skinnier this year than they'd expected. So to make the suit look skinnier they've pegged the jacket to pull the waist in and used an undersized pair of trousers. But to get him into them, they had to unpick the seams."

"So, if this guy goes into a branch of *Now* and buys this same suit—"

"It will look like shit," Sophie confirms.

"That's crazy."

"Plus of course, I still need to Photoshop it."

"More nasal hair, huh?"

"No. But his left eyebrow is thicker than the right one, see? So I'll even that up. And I'll get rid of some of these creases here . . ." Sophie runs her finger down the inner thigh of Patrick's trousers. "I'll whiten everyone's teeth too."

"And we wonder why we never look like the people in the ads," Brett says.

"I know. And I know I can't use these because they're professional models and everything, but if I did the same thing with some non-professionals . . . paid them for their time and did double shots, you know, before all the trickery and after . . . do a whole series of them showing the pegs and the foundation-from-a-can and the Photoshop stuff, don't you think it could be cool?"

"Hum," Brett says.

"Hum?"

"Yeah. Hum."

"Hum what?"

"Honestly?"

"Honestly."

"OK, I see two problems. The first is that it's a news item, not art. It's a myth buster and it's interesting . . . it's, it's . . . *liberating*, even. But it's not art."

"Surely that depends how good the photos—"

"There's still too much narrative. It's too useful. Too literal."

"Oh."

"Sorry, hon."

"And the second thing? You said you saw two problems."

"Oh yeah. You'd never work in the fashion industry again."

"No," Sophie says. "No, I thought about that."

"So," Brett says.

"So?"

"So, are you gonna suck my dick or aren't you?" he asks, his sexy leer suddenly back.

Sophie sighs, rubs her brow, then tears her eyes away from the screen. "Hum," she says.

"Gee, thanks for the enthusiasm."

"Hey, you can't blow my entire project out of the water and then expect me to—"

"To *blow* me?"

"Exactly."

"OK! Then it's a great idea!" Brett says. "It's so good, I'll bet they give you a one-man show at the Tate Modern."

Sophie frowns at him.

"So, *now* will you suck my dick?" Brett asks.

1951 – EASTBOURNE, EAST SUSSEX.

Tony glances up at Barbara, his brow furrowed. He is crouched beside the motorbike with a soapy sponge in his hand. Barbara has waited until this moment to make her announcement, because, due to the fact that Tony has his hands full and can't run away or strangle her, she somehow feels safer.

"*What?*" he says.

"I think you heard me," Barbara says quietly.

"I *heard* you," Tony says. "But I don't know what that means."

"You know," Barbara says. "My woman's trouble. It happens once a month. Only it didn't this time."

"I still don't know what that's supposed to mean," Tony says. "Are you ill? Do you need to see a quack?"

Barbara covers her mouth with her hand and murmurs, "Oh Tony."

"You're not trying to say . . . you don't mean . . ." Tony coughs. "You're not, you know . . ." he says, nodding at her belly. "Are you?"

Barbara nods vaguely.

"You are?"

"I think so."

"But we haven't even been trying," Tony says.

Barbara clears her throat. "I know. That's what I thought. But I don't think you need to actually try. I think you just need to do . . . you know . . . what we've *been* doing."

"Jesus!" Tony says.

"Please don't swear."

"I know. But . . . blimey. Just like that? Did you do it on purpose? Did you do it to get me to marry you?"

Barbara frowns deeply and licks her lips. She shrugs. "Of course not. Did *you?*"

"Don't be stupid. Bloody hell, Barbara! I can't believe you're telling me this. Not this way."

"So you're upset," Barbara says. "I thought you might be pleased."

"Pleased?!" Tony splutters. "I don't know what I bloody am."

Barbara turns and strides back into Donnybrook, then runs upstairs to her room on the top floor. She pulls the door closed and throws herself upon the bed.

Were she someone who cried, she would cry. But unlike her sister, Barbara isn't someone who cries. Even when she wants to, she can't. Because she's fully expecting Tony to follow her and she wants him to see how upset she is, she wets her finger and rubs it down the crease of her nose. She wants him to take her in his arms and tell her that it's all going to be OK.

Though she understood that she *could* get pregnant, she honestly didn't think it could happen so quickly, so easily. She didn't quite understand what the term, 'trying for a baby' meant, but along with Tony, she did in some way imagine that you had to at least *want* to get pregnant for it to happen. But perhaps secretly she did.

When her period had failed to materialise, she'd been unable to believe it was true, had assumed that there must be some other explanation. But with Glenda holding her hand, she had gone to the local library and together they had read through that well-thumbed pamphlet. Her tiredness, her nausea, her tender breasts . . . the conclusion was unavoidable.

These last two weeks have been horrific. She has alternated

between having thrilling visions of the perfect white wedding she and Tony will now be forced to have (Tony has repeatedly said he's in no hurry but now the hurry has arrived of its own free will) and more often, feelings of sheer terror: the terror of the dark street and the coat-hanger. Or the terror of a trip to a convent somewhere in Wales, as happened to her schoolfriend Valery. For those are the only possible outcomes she can think of.

After almost an hour, Barbara stands and crosses to the window. Outside she can see the motorbike, but Tony is no longer there.

She splashes water on her face and heads down to the kitchen, where she finds Joan washing potatoes.

"Mrs Marsden," she says. "Have you seen Tony?"

Joan pouts and shakes her head. "He went off with Diane, I think. I thought you was with them to be honest. I saw them head off and I thought you was all together or something."

"No. I was upstairs having a snooze," Barbara says.

"You OK, love? You look a bit peaky."

"I think I might be coming down with a cold. I caught a chill when Tony was doing the motorbike, I think," Barbara lies.

"Well, before you take to your deathbed, how about peeling some spuds for me? I've got so much to do today and I've barely even started. I've no idea how I'm going to get it all done."

"Sure," Barbara says, moving to Joan's side. "I'd be happy to."

Tony doesn't return at all that evening, so, to avoid the embarrassment of eating alone with Joan, Barbara walks to the seafront and dines on a bag of chips instead. The pamphlet said she has to eat healthy food full of vitamins if she wants a healthy baby but it can't matter just yet, can it?

When she gets back to the house, Joan asks her if she's seen Tony. "You've not had a row, have you?" she asks.

"I think he said he had to help Diane with some photo developing or something," Barbara fibs. "I think I just forgot. Yes. I'm sure he said something like that."

Joan looks unconvinced but nods all the same. "Do you want some tea? I could knock you something up; can't have you going to bed on an empty stomach."

"I had fish and chips, thank you," Barbara says. "I might go to bed though. I think I need an early night."

Barbara lies staring at the cracked ceiling and listens to the wind whistling under the gaps beneath the sash window of her room.

Her thoughts are a-whirl and she doesn't think she will get a wink of sleep tonight, but as the light fades, her fatigue overtakes her and pulls her into a world of tormented dreams where babies are ripped from their mothers and stacked, on shelves, like jumpers.

She awakens at first light and checks her watch: it's just before six. She rises, washes her face and pulls on her clothes.

On her way downstairs, she peers into Tony's room – the bed has not been slept in – and then continues down to the kitchen where she knows Joan will already be preparing breakfast. She discovers Tony leaning in the doorway talking to Joan, who is in the process of shaping potato cakes on the kitchen worktop.

She touches Tony lightly on the shoulder and he jumps and turns to face her. He looks pale and blotchy. His eyes are red too. He reeks of beer.

"Have you been out all night?" she asks him.

"Go on, go to bed," Joan tells her son.

"But—"

"Go to bed!" she says again, only more sharply this time. "Barbara and I need to have a chat."

100

Tony nods and then, without catching her eye even once, squeezes clumsily past her and on down the hallway.

"Is he drunk?" Barbara asks.

"Never mind him," Joan says. "Come wash these dishes will you?"

Barbara watches Tony swing around the banister and then vanish from view as he clomps his way upstairs in his motorcycle boots, then turns back to Joan. "OK," she says. "Of course."

The countertop to the right of the sink is piled high with dishes from last night's dinner service, so Barbara extracts a pile of plates and begins to wash them as Joan, beside her, continues to shape the potato cakes.

"So Tony thinks you're up the duff," Joan says suddenly and without warning.

Plate and scrubbing brush in hand, Barbara freezes. Her mouth drops. She forces it closed, swallows with difficulty and then resumes washing the dish with slow, circular movements.

"Well, are you?" Joan asks.

Barbara raises her shoulders. "I think I might be," she says quietly.

"You've missed your period?"

Barbara bows her head shamefully. She has never had a conversation about sex in her life. Not with Minnie, not with Glenda and not with anyone else for that matter. The closest she has ever got has been to tell Glenda she hasn't had her troubles this month, upon which Glenda led her to the library.

"Yes," she says. "It just didn't come."

"Any sickness in the mornings?" Joan asks.

Barbara nods. "And I hurt a bit, here," she says, lightly touching her belly with the back of her wet hand.

"Cramping? Like tummy ache?"

"Yes."

"Well . . ." Joan says.

"Is that what it is, then?"

"Probably. Yes," Joan says. She sighs deeply, then continues, "Does your mother know yet?"

Barbara shakes her head.

"Are you scared to tell her?"

Barbara nods.

"I would be too," Joan says, then, "There's a woman in Newhaven. A friend of a friend. She . . . you know . . . deals with this sort of thing."

Barbara stops washing dishes again and turns slowly to look at Joan's face. The two women stare deeply into each other's eyes for a moment, then Joan's features soften and she says, "Oh."

"Oh?"

"You want to keep it then?"

Barbara licks her lips and opens her mouth to speak but her throat feels constricted. Instead she just nods.

"You're just so young, love," Joan says. "You both are. Wouldn't you rather have some fun first?"

Barbara clears her throat. "I'm how old my mum was when she had Glenda," she says, aware that she's sounding vaguely belligerent but unable to help herself.

"You're the same age I was when I had Tony," Joan says. "That's why I'm telling you it's too young. I *know*."

"I thought he'd be glad," Barbara says, her voice wobbling. "But he thinks I did it on purpose."

Joan's face softens again. She drops the tea-towel she has been wringing and crosses the room to take Barbara in her arms. "On purpose?" she says. "As if that was something you could do on your own. Men! They don't get any better. You do your best to bring them up proper but nothing ever changes."

"I thought he'd want to get married," Barbara says, emboldened by Joan's support. "But he just seemed angry."

"Is that what you want?" Joan asks. "To get married?"

Barbara nods and buries her face in Joan's shoulder.

"We had better get Tony back down and talk to him," she says.

Barbara nods. "But I think he's still drunk."

Joan pushes her away and looks into her eyes. "Exactly," she says. "You've still got a lot to learn, girl – a *lot* to learn. Now go fetch him and let's see what he has to say for himself."

2012 – EASTBOURNE, EAST SUSSEX.

Sophie rings the doorbell and, unsure if it is currently working or not, raps on the front door as well. Her mother gave her a key years ago but because she doesn't seem to like Sophie actually using it (she always makes a fuss about *nearly having had a heart attack*), Sophie rarely even brings it with her these days.

Her mother's voice comes from behind the frosted window of the front door. "Who is it?"

"It's me! Sophie!" she says, rolling her eyes and thinking, *who else is it likely to be?* Her mother has few visitors and Sophie forewarned her that she would be here at ten. She checks her watch. She's one minute early.

The door opens a few inches, its movement limited by a flimsy gold chain that any of the ruffians mentioned in her mother's *Daily Mail* could snap with a single kick. Her mother's face peers through the gap and Nut, her ginger cat, looks up at her from ground level. "Oh, it's you," she says, and Sophie can't help but roll her eyes again.

She strokes Nut, then kisses her mother on the cheek and heads into the house. "Yes, it's me. As expected."

"I suppose you'll be wanting some lunch?" her mother says, locking and chaining the door behind her – an invitation to dine disguised as criticism.

"No, I said on the phone that I'd take you out," Sophie says, looking around the room and sensing that inexplicable queasiness she always feels when faced with the floral stasis of her mother's house.

"There's no point wasting money on silly restaurant prices," her mother says. "I've got a fridge full of perfectly good food."

"Oh, come on, Mum. Let's go out. It doesn't have to be expensive."

"It'll still cost the same as my weekly shop," she says, but she twists her mouth sideways indicating that she's prepared to be convinced.

Sophie restrains a sigh. She has never understood her mother's obsession with the cost of everything, particularly because, though she has never been rich per se, she has never, to Sophie's knowledge, been hard up either. As far as she knows her mother has never had to struggle to pay for anything essential. "Look, one it's my treat, and two, it doesn't have to be expensive. I actually quite fancy fish and chips. What d'you reckon?"

"I suppose we could go to Qualisea. That wouldn't cost an arm and a leg."

"Sure. Why not," Sophie concedes. Qualisea is Eastbourne's most popular, most economical, fish and chip restaurant. It also happens to be, for all of these reasons, a firm favourite with the most geriatric section of Eastbourne's population. And in a town where the biggest daily hazard is being run over by a mobility trike, that's really saying something. But Sophie has succeeded in persuading her mum to leave the house and that, these days, is reward enough.

"How have you been?" Sophie asks, once they are outdoors and heading towards the blustery seafront.

"Oh, you know," her mother replies. "*Comme ci, comme ça.*"

"So, what have you been up to?"

"Nothing. The usual. Sleeping, cleaning, eating."

Sophie, despite herself, tuts, prompting her mother to add, "It's called life, dear. It's called retirement. So don't tut at me about it. It'll come to you soon enough."

They pause at a pelican crossing and Sophie pulls a face as she presses the button. Her mother has never really been much fun to hang out with. In fact Sophie's not even sure if she understands the concept of 'fun'. But she worries about her all the same. Her father's many friends faded from view at a shocking rate after his death and the only time her mother's friends seem to get a mention nowadays is when they're ill or, more and more frequently, have died. Her social life seems to have contracted to such a ridiculous degree that Sophie suspects that eating, sleeping and watching television really is about as exciting as it gets most of the time, and she can't help but feel bad about that.

"I spoke to Jonathan," Sophie offers – an attempt at lightening the conversation. "He seems well."

"Lucky you."

"Lucky?"

"Well, he certainly never calls *me.*"

"*I* called *him,* actually," Sophie says. She knows for a fact that what her mum is saying isn't true. Jonathan is the perfect doting son. She knows, also, that her mum says exactly the same thing to Jon about her. But she lets it ride. "I shall give him a good telling off the next time I speak to him," she says, "and I'll make sure he calls you."

Her mother simply snorts.

During the train journey this morning, Sophie had debated, yet again, whether or not to tell her mother about Brett. She suspects that secretly (because her mother would never admit as much) this news, that her daughter finally has a boyfriend, would cheer her up no end. But as she never asks Sophie about her life, she also makes it incredibly easy *not* to tell her, so easy in fact that Sophie is now six months into the relationship and her mother has no inkling that anything has changed. And this is now the problem. Because if she *does* tell her mother the truth, she will be opening the door to a whole lorryload of *well you kept that one quiet* reproach. Of course, she could lie and say that she met Brett a few weeks ago but then her mother would assume that it's just a passing romance of no importance, which really *wouldn't* cheer her up. Which is why she didn't tell her at the start. So, she's a bit stuck.

As they move beyond the shelter provided by the Redoubt Fortress, they are hit by the full force of the salt-laden wind. "Gosh," Sophie exclaims.

"Gosh indeed," her mother shouts back, leaning into the wind and, rather sweetly, taking Sophie's hand. Sophie remembers when it was to anchor *her,* not her fragile mother, that they held hands.

As they step into Qualisea, the change of temperature is so shocking that both mother and daughter flush red. "Well, that was bracing," Sophie says.

"You're the one who wanted to go out," her mother replies.

A Polish waitress crosses to greet them. "Hello," she says, nodding at her mother, then turning and smiling at Sophie too. "You want usual table?"

Her mother nods. "That would be nice," she says.

They cross to a corner table, take their seats and place orders: cod and chips twice, a side order of mushy peas and two cups of tea. Sophie looks around at the blue rinses and trembling hands surrounding them and wonders again why they can't ever go and sit in a nice restaurant. She has never been able to see, really, what such working class pretension has to do with her mother.

They shrug off their coats and hang them over the backs of the chairs and then Sophie's mother interlinks her fingers and looks her straight in the eye. It's something that she has always done and it's a gesture that has always set Sophie's nerves on edge. It's as if her mother is peering into her soul in search of hidden secrets, which Sophie reckons, is probably precisely what she *is* doing.

"Jonathan's working lots," Sophie says, more because she feels she has to say something than because it's any more true than usual.

"He always was a hard worker," her mother replies, and Sophie struggles not to take this as a criticism of her own supposedly dissolute lifestyle.

"And Judy's still churning out hundreds of those horrible paintings of hers," Sophie adds, subconsciously pointing out that even if she isn't particularly productive herself, at least she doesn't produce shit.

"You're a harsh one," her mother tells her. "Just because you went to art college doesn't give you the right to decide what everyone else has to like."

"I don't," Sophie says. "I just know that poor old Judy couldn't paint a white wall white."

"I like them."

"Yes, I know you do," Sophie replies, struggling to keep the exasperation from her voice. She wonders for the hundredth time quite how her mother and brother managed to spend so much time with the artist that her father undoubtedly was without absorbing even a smidgin of his good taste. And nowhere is their failure to learn from her father's gift more evident than in their awed appreciation of Jon's wife's badly painted, nauseatingly bucolic landscapes.

"So come on," Sophie prompts. "What *have* you been up to since I was down last?"

"I told you," her mother replies.

"Have you seen Patti?" Sophie asks. Patti Smith (not *the* Patti Smith, sadly) is her mother's neighbour.

"Her hip's playing up again."

"Oh, that's a shame," Sophie says.

"They're talking about operating again," she continues, finally finding her rhythm. "Patti reckons one of those superbugs slipped in when they operated. It's because the hospitals are so dirty these days."

The monologue about Patti's hip condition lasts through the entire main course. It's only when they reach dessert, an obscenely large slab of pappy lemon meringue pie, that her mother pauses for breath.

"I met the new arts correspondent for the *Time* the other day," Sophie says, having decided that, for multiple reasons, she needs to bite this particular bullet (or at least nibble at it) "He's ever so nice."

"That's nice dear."

"He asked me if anyone had ever thought of doing a retrospective of Dad's work."

Her mother stops eating for a second and looks Sophie directly in the eye. She shakes her head sharply. "No," she says looking concerned. "Never." It sounds not only like a response but like an interdiction too.

"It's funny that, isn't it?" Sophie says. "I mean, he was such a big figure in British photography. You'd think someone would have thought of it."

"I don't think they do them for photographers."

"Do what?"

"Retrospectives. It's more of a painter's thing, isn't it?"

"Sometimes they do. For big names. I went to the Mapplethorpe one. And Dad was a pretty big name. I thought it would be quite cool to organise one."

Her mother raises one eyebrow.

"What?" Sophie asks.

"Well," she says. "It's just one of those crazy ideas of yours, isn't it. You'll be on to something else within a week."

Sophie runs her tongue across her teeth, then, to avoid saying the harsh words on the tip of her tongue, she forks another lump of oozing pie to her mouth. For this has always been Sophie's reputation. Jon is the hardworking, serious son and Sophie is the inconstant, airhead daughter. And never shall those myths be challenged. She frowns at the mouthful of sugar she has just swallowed and then pulls a face as she pushes the plate away.

"I hope you're not dieting again," her mother says.

"Mum! I just ate a billion calories of fish and chips," Sophie laughs. "I'm not sure what diet you think I'm on."

"Well, good. You're too skinny."

"I *wish*. If anyone is too skinny, you are."

Sophie doesn't bring up the idea of a retrospective again until they get back to the house. While her mother makes a pot of coffee, Sophie leans on the kitchen counter and takes a deep breath before asking as casually as possible, "So, are all Dad's photos still up in the loft?"

"Probably," her mother replies. "If they haven't all turned to dust." It's only when she has said this that she realises that she has just provided her daughter with a perfect justification for checking on them. "But I'm sure they're fine," she adds.

"I should probably check," Sophie says, pouncing on the opportunity.

Her mother pulls a pained expression. "It's horrible up there, Sophie," she says. "It's full of junk and dust and bird-poo and—"

"I bet there are photos of you when you were younger too, aren't there?"

"I'm *not* having you rooting around in the loft."

"Oh, go on Mum," Sophie pleads. "I'd love to spend the afternoon looking at old photos with you. Just a few."

110

"Oh *Sophie!* It means getting the ladder from out the back and everything," her mother whines. But she is twisting her mouth sideways again, so Sophie knows that she has won.

In the loft – which is indeed filthy – Sophie finds the photos, perfectly preserved in a pile of stackable wooden boxes. She doesn't know who stored them thus, but each box contains a series of plastic sleeves, each of which contains a tiny sachet of damp-absorbing silica gel.

She takes a selection of the packages and hands them one by one to her mother.

"Is it all dry up there?" she calls up. "There aren't any leaks, are there?"

"No, it's fine," Sophie replies. "It's absolutely dry."

Once her mother has declared that, "that's enough now," Sophie closes the box, then, before she climbs back down, she looks around at the rest of the junk in the attic.

Behind the photography boxes are a pile of old suitcases. She lifts one to check the weight, then, sensing that it's not empty, she pulls it towards her and, with difficulty, opens the rusty clasp.

"What are you doing up there?" her mother asks.

"Just a second," Sophie says, lifting the lid on the suit-case.

Inside, she finds her father's old overcoat and a lump forms in her throat. The sensation of being wrapped in his arms, of being wrapped in the texture of this coat, fills her memories. She sniffs it in the hope of detecting some trace of him but thirty years have passed. It smells of nothing these days but musty, dusty loft.

She folds the coat, strokes it gently, swallows with difficulty, then puts it to one side and peers back into the suitcase. It contains a man's hat, a trilby, she thinks, though she doesn't know how she knows this and doesn't remember ever having seen her father wear it. There are, God knows why, some old, nylon net curtains, a blanket, a pair of children's slippers and a funny old doll in a sailor dress. She frowns at the doll, then, when her mother says, "Sophie! You're letting all the heat out," she returns to the trap door and climbs down the ladder.

"I found this," she says, handing the doll to her mother, who smiles and strokes the doll's hair.

"Was that mine?" Sophie asks. "I don't remember it at all."

"No, it was mine. When I was little," her mother says.

"Wow. How old is she?" Sophie asks, scooping the packages of photos from the telephone table where her mother has piled them.

"Thirties," she replies. "Late thirties. She's supposed to be Shirley Temple."

"Really?"

Her mother nods. "It's a Shirley Temple doll. They were all the rage. She used to have a Shirley Temple badge too but that got lost pretty early on."

"Hello Shirley," Sophie laughs, peering in at the doll's shiny, surprised face.

"Actually, I always called her Lucy Loop," her mother says.

"Lucy Loop?"

Her mother nods. "Don't ask me why. I don't remember any more. But yes. We always called her Lucy Loop. I dragged her around my whole childhood."

They sit, side by side, at the dining room table, the pile of plastic packages before them. Sophie sips her coffee and notices that her mother is wringing her hands.

"Does this make you nervous, Mum?" she asks her.

Barbara wrinkles her nose. "A bit. There's a lot of past in there."

"I can do them on my own if you want."

"No, no, I want to look at them. It's just . . . well, it's been a long time."

Sophie pulls the first of the folders from the pile and slides it towards her, opens it, then pulls the contents onto the table. "Did you pack all of these up like this?"

"Yes. When I moved."

"You did a good job."

"Jonathan helped me."

Sophie starts to leaf through the photos. The first twenty are rather dull black and white images of landscapes but then suddenly there is a scene change and the images are of people in London. "Wow!" Sophie says, sliding a photo of a woman in a mini skirt and knee-high boots towards her mother. "The sixties!"

"Huh," her mother says, studying the photo and then pushing it back.

"Isn't that Aunty Diane?"

"Yes."

"She was pretty."

"Yes, she was."

Sophie flicks through another series of dull images: a house-front, a motorcycle, some kids playing football in the street, and then, coming upon a photo of her father in a dark checked suit holding her mother's hand, she pauses. "Dad looked good in a suit," she comments.

Barbara laughs. "He did. I could never get him to wear one, though. He reckoned wearing a tie strangled him."

"You look good too. You look really happy."

"I was. We were on holiday in Scotland. That's Edinburgh, I think."

"Who took the photo?"

"Phil, your father's friend."

Sophie continues to leaf through the photos, but other than three or four images of her father, the first package is something of a disappointment. For the most part, these are faded, often poorly developed photos of dull buildings and unexceptional landscapes.

Sophie sighs softly and hands the pile to her mother who repackages them while she opens the next batch.

"Gosh, Dad in a suit *again*," Sophie says. "And look at those flares."

The photo shows her father wearing the same suit. He has long hair, a beard and a huge kipper tie.

"That was Phil's wedding," Barbara says. "There should be some more with all of us."

Sophie skips through the pile until she comes to a photo showing her mother and father standing behind the bride and groom. Her mother is wearing a long tie-dye dress and a floppy orange hat.

"That's Phil and Jean," her mother says pointing. "You loved Phil. Do you remember?"

Sophie nods. "Was I at the wedding? I don't remember it."

"You were. You ate half the cake. You were covered in it."

"That's a great dress."

"I was so proud of that dress," Barbara says. "It was the most daring thing I ever wore. But I only ever put it on twice, I think. Maybe three times."

"Because?"

"I don't know. It made me feel self-conscious, I suppose. People always commented on it. It was a copy of something I had seen in London."

"You *made* it?"

114

"I did. I made lots of clothes."

"I didn't know that," Sophie says. "I mean, I remember you making curtains and stuff. But not clothes."

"I stopped. About then. It got cheaper to buy things than make them."

Sophie pushes the photo to one side and continues to work her way through the pile.

"Ooh, the summer of seventy-six," she says, pausing to study a picture of a woman in a bikini, sunbathing on a beach that is so sunbaked, it has fractured into a crazy-paving pattern. "That's not *the* photo though is it?"

"No, that's not the one that won a prize. It was the same day though. The same beach."

"This is actually really interesting," Sophie says. "People would love to see some of these. You know, the photos *around* the photo. All the ones that never made it into the public eye."

"I'm not so sure," Barbara says. "I think people like the myth."

"The myth?"

"That the famous photographer only ever took a few tens of really memorable pictures. I'm not sure people want to see all these other ones."

Sophie looks up at her mother in surprise.

"But what would I know?" her mother adds.

Sophie frowns. Her mother has always had this ability to surprise her with a sudden pertinent remark. It's almost as if she has learned to dumb down her conversation but occasionally forgets and lets out some razor-sharp comment.

"That's very true, actually," Sophie says. "I suppose it depends on whether there are enough good ones for an exhibition. Enough good ones that people haven't already seen, I mean."

"I think you'll find that there aren't that many," Barbara says.

"Gosh, this is an old one," Sophie says, pulling a tattered image from the pack.

"Huh," Barbara says. "I don't know how that got in there. That's your grandmother."

Sophie leans in and peers at the picture. A scowling woman in an apron, standing in front of a laundry and holding a bag of washing. "She looks like a tough old thing," Sophie says.

"People had to be tougher back then."

"Because of the war?"

Barbara shrugs. "In part. But everything was harder in those days. There was no hot water, or central heating, or even proper cooking facilities. Lots of people in the East End didn't even have a tap. There were no refrigerators, no washing machines . . . You have no idea how lucky you were to be born when you were."

Sophie groans and points at the laundry behind her grandmother. "Looks like Gran used to take her stuff to the laundry," she says. "So things can't have been that bad."

"No," Barbara says. "No, I suppose they can't have been."

1951 – EASTBOURNE, EAST SUSSEX.

Barbara holds out her hand and Tony fumblingly slips the thin gold band over her ring finger. He looks nervous and sweaty in his rented suit, but in Barbara's mind's eye he is as smooth and as suavely dressed as a prince.

"You may kiss the bride," the aged official says, and Tony grins and leans in to peck her on the lips.

When they turn to face the room, just for a second, the reality of the pale green walls (slightly shiny), of the seven people sitting on stackable chairs (slightly rusty) and the dim grey light filtering through the dirty windows, pierces Barbara's mental bubble.

Minnie, mistaking her daughter's expression, dabs at the corner of one eye and nods at her encouragingly, and Barbara forces herself to smile back, *has* to force herself because in this instant, this is all so very far from how she thought her wedding day would look that she can barely bear *to* look. But then the Wedding March begins to belt out of the gramophone and Barbara finds her inner princess all over again and starts to drag her imaginary train across the cold noble floors of Canterbury Cathedral, nodding at the gathered gentry as she does so.

Back at Donnybrook, Tony's parents have organised a reception party. The dining room table is covered with triangular sandwiches (crusts cut off) and pigs in blankets and cheese balls on sticks. It looks, Barbara can't help but notice, a lot like the food their neighbour laid on when her husband died. "What a lovely spread," Minnie comments.

"Yes, you've done us proud, Mum," Tony agrees. "Would you like a drink, Mrs Doyle? A glass of punch perhaps?"

Barbara blushes as her mother leans over the punch and sniffs it. She actually sniffs it and Barbara can sense the whole room watching her do so. "What kind of punch is that, then?" Minnie asks, causing Barbara's teeth to ache with embarrassment.

"It's strawberry tea punch," Tony's mother replies using her special posh voice, the one she usually uses when guests arrive.

"Strawberry tea, is it?" Minnie says, doubtfully, and Barbara prays silently for her to just drink it and like it.

"But if you fancy something a little stronger we've got sherry or egg nog, or I can even mix you up a gin fizz," Tony offers, sensing the tension and trying to avoid a diplomatic incident.

"Ooh yes, I think a little glass of sherry might hit the spot better, thank you, Tony," she says, and Barbara sees that Joan, who doesn't drink and doesn't much like people who do (her husband included), raises one eyebrow.

"Can I put a record on, Mrs Marsden?" best man Hugh asks.

"Are you asking me or Barbara?" Joan laughs. "Because there are two Mrs Marsdens now."

"Oh, of course there are! Well you of course," Hugh says. "You being the lady of the house."

"Please . . . go ahead," Joan says, waving one arm regally at the curved wooden radiogram in the corner of the room. "Tony brought all his records down *especially*."

Hugh crosses the room and lifts the lid on the radiogram and Barbara, who has been feeling self-conscious, moves to his side, happy for the distraction of helping with the music.

"You switch it on there," she tells him, pointing at the chunky Bakelite knob. "But it takes a while to warm up." She runs the tip of her finger across the radio dial, over Paris, Luxembourg and Oslo, before letting it settle on Hilversum. "I want to go to all of the places on the dial," she says.

"Really?"

"Not immediately but, you know, before I die."

"Ah, well, in that case, you've got plenty of time."

"Where is Hilversum anyway?"

"In Holland, I think," Hugh says.

"Oh, put that on," Barbara tells him, as he slides *Hop Scotch Polka* from the rack.

"This one?"

"Yes, I really like that," Barbara says, wrinkling her nose. "It's really, sort of, *happy*."

"So, are *you* happy now, Mrs Marsden?" Hugh asks her, and Barbara, wondering what the word *now* is doing in that phrase, smiles and nods enthusiastically.

"Of course I am," she says.

"Is this everything you wanted it to be?" Hugh asks, and because of something strange in his voice, Barbara turns to study his face. "I mean the wedding and the party," Hugh explains, and his voice, which sounds falsely flippant, doesn't match his regard which looks soulful, regretful almost, and Barbara has no idea why.

"Of course it is," Barbara says, frowning now and wondering momentarily if perhaps Hugh alone understands the yawning gulf between this cheap, rushed, working class wedding and the fairytale ceremony that every girl dreams of. But then she realises that with Hugh being a communist, the opposite is more likely true. He probably sees this marriage as some obscene expression of capitalist excess.

"I hope Tony will live up to your expectations," Hugh says.

"I don't really have any," Barbara replies.

"Then he probably will," Hugh says darkly, then changing tone, "You look lovely anyway." He lightly touches her shoulder. "That's a lovely wedding dress."

Barbara looks down at her simple ivory dress. "I made this myself," she says. "With a bit of help from Mum."

"I know," Hugh says. "Tony told me. That's very impressive. It looks like the dresses you see in films."

The radiogram pops, buzzes and then pops again. "That means it's ready," Barbara says, moving gently to one side so that Hugh's hand can but fall away.

"Are you ready to dance?" he asks, lifting the stacking-arm to one side and lowering the record over the spindle.

"I think I need a drink of something first," Barbara says. "But yes. Nearly ready."

Still attempting to analyse her strange conversation with Hugh, Barbara crosses to the drinks cabinet where Tony's father Lionel is mixing gin fizzes. "Can I have one of those?" she asks.

"Sure," Lionel says, grinning at her. "Have this one. I'm just churnin' 'em out for anyone and everyone."

A group of Tony's friends appear in the doorway just as the needle hits the record and, as *Hop Scotch Polka* starts to play, it begins to feel a little more like a party.

Barbara downs her gin fizz quickly, then, suddenly tipsy, accepts Tony's offer to dance and soon Diane and Hugh and Glenda and James join them, jiving around in the corner behind the dining table.

After a few songs, Barbara breaks free and crosses the room to join Minnie, who she has noticed is standing alone, staring out of the window at the street beyond. "Are you alright, Mum?" she asks.

Minnie turns and distractedly replies, "Sorry dear?"

120

"Are you OK? Are you having a nice time?"

Minnie nods and smiles unconvincingly. "I'm fine," she says. "Anyway, today's not about me. It's about you. Are *you* having a nice time?"

"I am," Barbara says.

"The best day of your life," Minnie says flatly. "That's what they say." And Barbara feels suddenly sad and isn't sure quite why.

"You're not OK, are you, Mum?" she says. "Is it because Dad's not here?"

"Is *what* because your dad's not here?"

"Is that why you're sad?"

"Ha!" Minnie laughs. "No, that's a blessing, believe me," she says. "Anyway, I'm not sad. I'm proud. You look lovely."

Barbara nods. "Good," she says. "Come over and talk to Joan or something. Don't stand by yourself. It's supposed to be a party."

"Yes," Minnie says. "Yes, I will. Now you go and enjoy your wedding day with that husband of yours."

Barbara strokes her mother's arm tenderly, then resigning herself to the fact that she has never much understood, let alone been able to influence her mother's moods, she returns to the rear of the room where Hugh is now swinging Glenda around to the "Chatanooga Choo Choo".

"Is Mum alright?" Glenda asks, pausing breathlessly in front of her. Barbara smiles tightly and shrugs.

"Just make sure you enjoy *your*self," she says, throwing herself back into the dance.

By seven, Tony's father has fallen asleep on the sofa, visibly drunk and audibly snoring. According to Tony, this is by far the better of the two possible outcomes but then Tony himself is already swaying on his feet, already slurring his words. A

121

sobriety gap is fast opening up between Barbara, who stopped drinking two hours ago, and her new husband.

Barbara, who has been watching Tony from the corner of her eye whilst talking to Minnie, now stands and heads through to the kitchen, where, on her mother's advice, she intends to make Tony a "good, strong cup of coffee".

In the kitchen, she finds Glenda and Diane talking to James. Both, it would appear, judging by all the eyelash fluttering and hip-jutting going on, are flirting with him. With his impeccable blue suit, his immaculate blond hair and his bright blue eyes, Barbara can see the appeal. He has to be the most eligible bachelor present, if not actually in town.

Barbara lights the gas ring and puts the kettle on to boil, then turns to see James leaving the room, closely followed by Diane.

"Come outside, Sister," Glenda says, reaching for her hand. "I need to talk to you."

Barbara follows Glenda outside, thinking that Glenda, too, is going to comment on Tony's inebriated state. "I think Tony's had too much to drink," she says, attempting to head her off at the pass.

"Of course he has," Glenda says. "It's his wedding day."

"I'm making him coffee to sober him up a bit."

Glenda raises one eyebrow. "Well, good luck with that," she says, then, "Now, tell me about James."

"I don't know him any better than you," Barbara says. "I only met him yesterday. Tony has so many friends buzzing around, it's hard to keep track."

"He's handsome," Glenda says.

"He is."

"You're not having regrets, are you?" Glenda asks, smirking.

Barbara laughs. "You're terrible," she says.

"Then you are!"

122

"Of course I'm not!"

Glenda pulls out a packet of Target and points it at Barbara.

"I *still* don't smoke," Barbara replies.

"You should. The boys think it's sexy," Glenda tells her.

"I don't and neither does Tony. Which is just as well."

Glenda lights up and takes a drag, then blows the smoke up into the cooling evening air. "Can you help me with James?"

"Help you with what?"

"Help me snag him," Glenda says. "I'm in competition with Diane."

"I saw that," Barbara says. "Maybe you should just let her have him."

"Now why would I want to do that?"

Barbara glances back at the house to check that they are alone. "To start with, they both live here in Eastbourne."

"What's that got to do with anything?"

"You live in London, Glen."

Glenda laughs and coughs out cigarette smoke. "I don't want to *marry* him, Sis. I just want to kiss him! He has the loveliest lips."

Barbara checks the back door again. "You're awful! If Mum heard you . . ."

"Do you know what he does? For a job, I mean?"

Barbara shrugs. "Sorry," she says. "I think he works in a bank or something but I'm not even sure of that. But seriously, I wish you would let Diane have him."

"Absolutely not."

"For me?" Barbara whines.

"For you? Why?"

Barbara shrugs and feels a wave of heat wash over her.

"You don't think Diane's after Tony, do you? You do! Oh Barbara. They're childhood friends. They virtually grew up together."

"I know that. It's just . . . I don't know. She makes me nervous."

"He married *you*, Barbara. If he liked Diane, he's had plenty of opportunity."

"I suppose so."

The whistling sound of the kettle starts to rise from the open doorway so Barbara sighs and turns towards the house. "I'd better sort that coffee out," she says. "Or he'll be too drunk to know *who* he's married to."

"And I had better go sort that James out," Glenda says, saucily.

By the time Barbara has returned to the lounge with the cup of coffee, all of the older guests have vanished to other parts of the house leaving Diane and Glenda dancing a little madly with James, while Tony and Hugh argue drunkenly about politics.

Barbara stands patiently beside Tony for a while, waiting for the right moment to interrupt him but he is being animated and annoyed, bombastic and loud. She has never seen him like this before and spends a few moments debating with herself the age old question: does drink make them more themselves, or less themselves?

Whichever it is, she decides that she doesn't much like it. She gives up on there ever being a pause in their argument and holds the coffee cup out in front of him. "Here, Tony," she says, loudly. "I made you this."

Tony falters momentarily but quickly returns to his monologue, saying, "And . . . and . . . anyway, Atlee isn't a communist, so whether things got better or worse when he got in is neither here nor there. You're comparing oranges and lemons, Hugh."

"Apples and oranges," Hugh says. "It's apples and oranges, my friend."

"Is it?" Tony asks, finally turning to face Barbara.

"I don't think it matters," she says. "Here." She waves the coffee cup in front of his nose again.

Tony wobbles his head slightly and then, with apparent difficulty, focuses on the cup. "I don't want coffee, woman," he says. "Why would I want coffee?"

"I thought it might sober you up a bit," Barbara says softly. "I think you've maybe had enough to drink, sweetheart."

Tony raises his eyebrows almost to his hairline in an exaggerated grimace of surprise, then turns to face Hugh, who grins broadly in reply. "She thinks I've had too much to drink," Tony slurrs.

Hugh pulls a funny, confused face and looks at Barbara. "But your husband's *never* had too much to drink," he laughs. "Didn't you know that?"

"That's right!" Tony says, now pointing an oscillating finger at Hugh. "Now take that horrid stuff away," he tells Barbara, "and bring me a beer!"

As he says this, he gives her a push. The gesture, she understands, is meant to be comic, but because he is so very drunk, he miscalculates and his hand collides with her elbow. Coffee slops out of the cup and down the front of her dress. "Oh!" Barbara gasps. "No!"

She runs through to the kitchen, places the dripping cup on the drainer and grabs a tea-towel and then a dish-cloth as she attempts to remove the coffee stain from her chest. But the stain just seems to deepen and spread. "Oh God, no! Please, not now, not today," she mutters.

"Is that wool or synthetic?"

Barbara turns to see Tony's mother standing in the doorway. "Yes," she replies. "Yes, it's brushed wool."

"Then you need to rinse it out right now if you don't want it to stain."

"It's only coffee," Barbara says.

125

"Yes. It'll stain if you don't wash it right now."

"But it's my wedding dress."

"Wedding dress or not, it'll still stain, love," Joan tells her. "I had a woollen dress like that once and I spilt wine on it. I never got to wear it again. And I always wished I had been quick—"

"But it's my wedding day," Barbara interrupts.

"I can lend you a cardie or a shawl to hide it, or you can take it off and wash it. But it'll stain. Believe me. I know, because, as I said, I had a woollen top like that once, and once the stain dries in, you'll never get it out."

Barbara bites her tongue and squeezes her eyes to hold back a sudden and unexpected urge to cry. This is the nicest item of clothing she has ever had. It's made from the most expensive material she has ever bought.

"Wash it quickly is my advice," Joan repeats.

"Perhaps . . . Can you lend me something?"

Joan nods. "Of course I can, love. Come upstairs and—"

"Something nice? Can we find something nice? I can't look awful, not today."

"Yes. Come upstairs," she says. "We'll see what we can find."

Joan is not a wealthy woman and neither is she of a frivolous or a spendthrift nature. Nowhere is this more evident than in her wardrobe which contains a series of sturdy, practical dresses, a number of easy-to-launder housecoats, and a few once-pretty, now hopelessly outdated, forties frocks.

Barbara's heart sinks the second Joan opens the door. "They're lovely," she lies, fingering a pink, floral frock, "But maybe I will just keep this on after all."

"Don't be silly, love," Joan says. 'You're family now. There's no need to be shy. Just choose whichever one suits you best.

What about this?" She grabs the hem of a vamp-cuffed Rayon crepe dress and pulls it forwards so that Barbara can see it in all its splendour.

"No . . . really . . ."

"Or that?" Joan says, pointing at a flouncy number with a yoked bodice and a pleated skirt. "That's lovely, that is. It's made of parachute silk." She starts to reach for the hanger.

"No . . . um . . . how about that one?" Barbara splutters, desperately pointing at the only non-floral, non-lacy, non-pleated item visible.

"This?" Joan says, sliding hangers along the rail until she can get to the blue trimmed white dress in the corner.

And only now, only as she pulls it from the rack, does Barbara understand what she has chosen; only now does she understand the full horror of an outfit that is more fancy dress than fashion statement.

"I haven't worn this since I was a girl," Joan says. "But you're right, it's younger. It's probably more your size too." She thrusts the sailor dress against Barbara and it fills the air with the scent of naphthalene mothballs.

"Oh, maybe not," Barbara says softly, turning back to the wardrobe disconsolately.

"Try it on," Joan insists. "Come on. I bet you'll look smashing." She pushes the dress into Barbara's arms. "I've got the matching sailor hat somewhere too," she says.

"I don't want it," Barbara says.

"I'm sure it's here."

"I *don't want it!*" Barbara repeats more loudly, shocking even herself with her abrupt tone. "I'll ask Glenda for something."

Joan freezes and glares at her. "If you don't like my clothes, then . . ." She looks wounded. She looks upset. She looks angry, in fact.

Barbara capitulates. "Actually this is fine," she says. "This is, um, lovely. I just meant that I don't want the hat. That's all. I never wear hats."

Joan chews the inside of her mouth and looks at Barbara doubtfully.

"I'm sorry, I'm just a bit upset about this coffee stain," Barbara offers.

"Of course you are," Joan says, her features softening. "Your lovely dress. You poor thing. So slip it off quick and I'll get it soaking for you."

The sailor dress, to Barbara's horror, *fits*. It's rigid and scratchy and a tiny bit too short. She's not actually showing yet but she's been thinner, so it's a little tight across the chest too. But basically, undeniably, sadly, it fits. Dressed as a sailor girl, Barbara feels absurd, but with her own dress whisked away and, within seconds, soaking in a bucket of water, there's truly no going back.

As she edges to the bottom of the stairs in her new outfit, she sees that Tony, Diane, James and Hugh are now dancing the Conga around the dining room table. The room seems somehow to be too full of noise and music and drunken laughter to still contain any air and she fears, irrationally, that she will suffocate if she enters, so she heads through to the kitchen instead, where Glenda is as ever smoking, whilst picking at the remains of the food.

"What on *earth* are you wearing?" Glenda says the second she looks up.

"Please don't," Barbara says. "This is all I could find. You haven't got a spare dress with you, have you? Tony spilt coffee over me."

Glenda shakes her head. "Sorry Sis," she says. "I haven't. But that's *really* not a good look for you. You look like a port-side tart. She *must* have something better than *that*."

128

Finding herself unable to breathe even here in the kitchen, Barbara turns and runs for the front door. Scrunching up her features to avoid tears, she steps outside and slams the door behind her. A woman and child, walking past, turn to look at her (of course, there are people outside the house too, of course there are!) and she feels so self-conscious, here, now, in Eastbourne, in this stupid sailor dress, that she can barely walk. She reaches down to pull the hem lower and begins to march down the street, watched, she can sense it, by the woman and the child behind her.

It is dusk, and seagulls are circling overhead. The air is fresh and smells of iodine and she suddenly remembers that she is at the seaside and, despite it all, her panic lifts a little, due to the simple fact that at least she now knows where to go. She turns into Beach Road and heads towards the seafront.

A man, busy squeegeeing the windows of a pub, whistles at her as she approaches and calls out, "Hello Sailor!"

"Oh . . . sod off!" Barbara mutters, her voice wobbling. The man freezes and his squeegee drips, and his cheeky grin fades and is replaced by an expression of concern. "You alright, darlin'?" he asks as she stomps on by.

When she reaches the beach, the sun is setting, shifting orange, then red, as it slides into the sea. A young man gives her the once-over as he walks past and she thinks about the fact that there will be even more people on the pier than anywhere else, that on the pier she'll look like some kind of prop – like some kind of tourist attraction – so she turns to walk the other way instead. But then realising that the young man might think she's following him, she stops and sits on a bench instead. She wrings her hands, stares at her feet and tries to calm her racing heart – tries, quite simply, to breathe.

"Babs?"

She looks up to see Minnie standing over her.

"What are you doing here on your own?" her mother asks, concernedly.

"Oh Mum!" Barbara says. Never has she been so happy to see her mother.

As Barbara's features crumple, her mother hitches up her coat and slides onto the bench beside her. "Oh love," Minnie says, putting her arm around her. "Whatever has happened? And what on *earth* are you wearing?"

Barbara takes a deep gulp of the sea air and then the words come tumbling out. "Tony's drunk and dancing with Diane and he spilt coffee all down my dress and so now I have to wear this awful thing and I feel utterly, utterly stupid in it and I wish I'd never . . ." She stops short. She can hear herself sounding like a five year old and she knows Minnie doesn't react well to such displays of immaturity.

Minnie tips her head from side to side as she appraises her. "You don't look *ridiculous*, love," she tells her. "It's just a bit surprising, is all."

Barbara looks at her mother from the corner of one eye. "I look *ridiculous*," she repeats.

Minnie sighs. "Actually, you know who you do look like? Lucy Loop!"

Barbara smiles a little despite herself.

"You do! Really," Minnie says, encouraged.

"But I don't want to spend my wedding day looking like Lucy Loop," Barbara moans.

"No, I'm sure. I had a bloody *awful* old thing on *my* wedding day," Minnie tells her daughter, a confession specifically designed to calm her down. "It was my aunt's old wedding dress, horrid old-fashioned thing it was. Looked like it was from a museum or something, all lace and frills. And, you know, yellow. You know the way lace goes yellow with age? Well it was yellow like that. I hated that bleedin' dress."

130

Barbara sniffs and wipes her nose with the back of her hand, prompting Minnie to pull a handkerchief from her pocket. "I didn't know that," Barbara says. "You never told me about your wedding day."

"It was rotten, really," Minnie says. "That's the trouble with weddings. All that expectation, ain't it? It rained like in the Bible and that horrid dress went all see-through and I was convinced everyone could see me knickerbockers underneath. And then Dad had a bust up with Pop – that's Seamus' father – and then Seamus punched him out."

"Really?"

Minnie nods. "Even though he was a boxer, he just punched him out."

"He hit your dad?"

"No, he hit Pop. His *own* father. Knocked him out cold."

"God, Mum. That must have been awful."

"Pop was too drunk to stand anyway. He didn't even hurt himself I don't think. Fell over like a feather. They never hurt themselves when they're drunk. More's the pity."

"Tony's drunk too," Barbara confides. "I tried to make him coffee like you said but he didn't want it."

Minnie sighs again and squeezes her daughter's shoulder. "It's what men do. It's what they do at weddings, love. He'll pay for it tomorrow. Just be really chirpy in the morning. It drives them mad, that does."

"Why didn't Dad come back?" Barbara suddenly asks, aware only once the words have left her lips that she has spoken the forbidden question.

"You don't want to be talking about that today," Minnie says quietly.

"But he's OK, isn't he? He didn't get hurt or anything?"

Minnie shakes her head. "He met some strumpet, love," she says. "A nurse, I heard. An RAF nurse."

"And he just set up home with her instead?" Barbara asks.

Minnie pinches the bridge of her nose, closes her eyes, takes a deep breath and then opens them again before saying, "Look, you *really* don't wanna be thinking about that on yer wedding day."

Barbara nods thoughtfully. "No. I suppose not. But you'll tell me another time?"

"I'll tell you another time," Minnie says.

"Do you think *we'll* be alright?"

"You and Tony?"

Barbara nods.

"I should bloody hope so," Minnie says. "Of course you will. You just have to get those fairy tales out of that dreamy head of yours. Dreams are like butterflies, love. If you catch 'em, they die. And a marriage is hard work. It's not like in the films. It's not all flowers and chocolates. It's more like . . . like a job of work maybe, or, no, maybe more like a roller coaster. You just have to hold on tight. You have to hold on really tight through all the ups and downs. But you'll be alright. You've got the Blitz spirit, girl."

Barbara smiles weakly and Minnie squeezes her shoulder again, then says, "Now, you'd better get back to your new husband. He'll be wondering where you are."

"Are you going to walk back with me?"

Minnie shakes her head. "I'm too old for all that drinkin' and jumpin' about," she says. "I'm gonna walk once around that pier and buy myself an ice cream, is what I'm gonna do. And then I'm going to go back and turn in."

"Can I walk with you around the pier?"

Minnie stands and holds out one hand to her daughter. "Of course you can."

Barbara takes her mother's hand and stands, then, as Minnie's eyes scan her from head to toe, Barbara says, "You see. I *do* look ridiculous."

"Not *ridiculous*," Minnie says. "But you'd better put this on." She wriggles out of her overcoat, then holds it out for Barbara to step into.

"I'm not cold at all, Mum," Barbara says. "Keep it."

"It's not the cold I'm worried about," Minnie says. "It's all the wanton attentions you're going to get if you walk round the pier in that dress."

"Wanton attentions?" Barbara laughs.

Minnie nods seriously. "Trust me," she says. "Put this on."

Between the coconut shy and the tarot-card clairvoyant, Minnie buys them both 99 ice creams, then mother and daughter begin to head along the pier.

The daylight has almost vanished now and the sea beneath them has shifted from a powdery green colour to a seething, vaguely sinister blackness. In stark contrast, the lights of the pier make the bold colours of the kiosks shimmer and shine.

"I love the seaside," Barbara says, unexpectedly euphoric to find herself enjoying a moment of leisure with her mother – a surprisingly novel experience. "I love all the fresh air and the seagulls, and the lights and the smell of doughnuts, I love all of it."

"I do too," Minnie says. "I always wanted to live by the sea."

"Why didn't you?"

"Seamus' job was in London," Minnie says. "And nowadays, my job's in London, ain't it?"

"You could still move," Barbara says. "If you wanted to."

"I can't afford to. You know that," Minnie says, licking away a dribble from the cone of her ice cream.

"Maybe one day we'll have a big place like Donnybrook," Barbara says. "Then you could come and stay with us any time you wanted."

"Maybe," Minnie says. "With Tony being an only child, you might end up *in* Donnybrook if you play yer cards right. Just make sure you hang onto him."

"Of course I'll hang onto him," Barbara says.

"Marriage ain't easy," Minnie tells her, again. "But even at its worst, it's the better of two evils. And you can trust me on that one."

The tour of the pier completed, Barbara accompanies Minnie to Donnybrook. By the time they get there, the party is over. Everyone has left and only Joan, who is clearing up, is visible.

"Hello," Joan says, looking up from the plate upon which she is uniting all the uneaten food. "I thought you was with Tony."

"No, Mum and me walked round the pier," Barbara tells her. "Do you know where he is?"

Joan shakes her head. "They all left together," she says. "Like I say, I thought you was with 'em. Have you had enough to eat? Because I'm in the process of putting all this away."

"Yes thanks," Barbara says. "I'm fine."

"Me too," Minnie agrees. "It was a lovely 'do', Joan. As for Tony, I expect he's at Beach Cottage, ain't he? I expect he's waiting for her there."

Joan nods. "Yes," she says. "Yes, I expect that's where he is."

Still wearing Minnie's coat (so large, so cosy, so reassuring, like being *wrapped* in mother), Barbara heads back through the dimly lit streets towards Beach Cottage, where they will be spending their wedding night. Joan knows Mrs Pie, the owner. Mrs Pie owes her a favour, apparently.

On the seafront, couples are walking hand in hand, exuding that special kind of contentment that only couples on a sea-front promenade at nightfall can. Barbara wonders if she is like them now. And if she is, where is her husband? Where is the arm she is supposed to be clinging on to?

Mrs Pie is outside watering the window boxes when Barbara arrives. "Hello love," she says. "Everything go to plan?"

Barbara nods and, worrying that Mrs Pie will catch a glimpse of the sailor dress, pulls the coat more tightly around herself. "Yes," she says. "Yes, it did. Is T—"

"So congratulations are in order," Mrs Pie says, pointing the spout of her watering can at the next window box, the one beneath the 'Vacancies' sign.

"Yes," Barbara says. "Yes, thank you. Is Tony here?"

"You haven't lost track of him already?" Mrs Pie says, pinching off a dead branch from a geranium with her free hand and tossing it over her shoulder.

"Sort of," Barbara admits. "Is it possible he's already in the room?"

"It's not im-possible. I was out till half an hour ago."

"Is it OK if I go check?"

"Of course it is. It's your room."

"Which room is it, please?"

"The top one. You don't need a key or nothing. We only have a nice class of guest here at Beach Cottage."

Barbara thanks her and heads upstairs, pausing at the bathroom on the first floor to wee before climbing the three flights of stairs to their attic room. On the way, she pauses to peer at the many royal photographs adorning the walls of the staircase.

The final photo on their landing (and can this really be an accident?) is of the Royal Wedding of 1947. Elizabeth and Philip, spotless, beautiful, opulent; Elizabeth's train tumbling down the stairs before them, both smiling genteelly. And in their position, who wouldn't be smiling?

135

Inside the room, the bed has been scattered with petals. Not rose petals, but geranium petals. Bunches of garden flowers occupy the nightstand and the mantelpiece. Barbara switches on the light and sees that Mrs Pie has draped a crocheted pink placemat over the lampshade. It throws pretty patterns on the wall above the bed.

Barbara crosses to the window and looks out at the sea – glassy, undulating. The moon is rising now, making the broken waves of the shallows sparkle and shine as they hit the pebble beach.

Barbara looks around the room again, then sits and bounces on the bed before standing, removing her coat and shoes and lying down.

She drapes herself elegantly (did she see this in a film?), then props herself up on the pillows and imagines Tony arriving and seeing her lying thus. Which would be more flattering? The subdued patterns from the lamp, or the moonlight? She switches off the lamp, shivers involuntarily, then switches it back on again. The moonlight makes the room feel cold. The lamp is definitely better.

She moves to the edge of the bed and props herself up so that she can track the progression of the moon. The sailor dress is tight around her middle, so she stands anew and moves to the chest of drawers. Inside, as promised, she finds her nighty and Tony's pyjamas. She imagines Glenda here, earlier, folding them and closing the drawer – imagining the night of passion that her younger sister would be enjoying later that day.

She crosses to the window again and looks outside. A solitary man is walking along the seafront with a small dog on a leash. "Where are you, Tony?" she murmurs, sliding one hand across her belly and imagining his baby, which everyone tells her is growing inside.

She crosses to the door and after peeping through the

136

keyhole, steps out onto the landing. She pauses and listens to the sounds of the house. A shrieking seagull above, a radio playing dancehall music somewhere downstairs, an elderly couple talking in one of the other guest rooms . . . But there is no sign of Tony.

She crosses to the photograph again and then, glancing nervously downstairs, she reaches out and lifts it from the hook, then returns with it to their room.

She crosses to the chest of drawers and lays it on the dresser so that she can see it as she changes from the horrific dress into her nighty.

Then she props the photo on the nightstand so that she can see both it and the door simultaneously and drapes herself, film-star style, across the bed. "He'll be here soon," she tells herself quietly and repeatedly, until she finally falls asleep.

The next morning, it's not Tony but the sunlight that wakes her.

2012 – HOXTON, LONDON.

Sophie watches as Brett's bald head bobs up and down between her knees. She notices a bead of sweat and watches as it forms, then trickles down to his eyebrow. They have been dating for just over a year and the sex between them now follows a well established pattern. It's not that Sophie is bored with the sex she has with Brett and it's not that he's in any way a bad lover. Her friend Ralph once told her that he realised he was gay when he found out that going down on women made him gag. Sophie remembers telling him that if not being keen on oral sex was a definition of 'gay', then half of the men she had ever dated were gay. Brett, now grazing her inner thigh as he attempts to lick and slurp her to ecstasy, is, Sophie admits, an extremely generous lover. It's just that, like a pop song on the radio you've heard a hundred times before, sex with Brett no longer has the capacity to surprise her. It starts like this, which leads to that, which leads in turn to the other. In a minute, Brett will start to move upwards, kissing her breasts, nuzzling her neck, kissing her deeply. She knows where and when and how this will all happen. She can even conjure up, in her mind's eye, or perhaps in her mind's taste-buds, the memory (and premonition) of Brett's kiss – that unique mixture of Brett and Sophie and massage oil, re-served to her via mouth-to-mouth.

Despite the fact that she is edging towards orgasm, Sophie thinks about this and she thinks about her ability to think about this, even here, even now, in the middle of sex. And as Brett moves ever upwards, shifting his attention to her nipples, she wonders what this detachment might mean.

But Sophie is distracted today and she knows that this isn't in any way Brett's fault. She woke up this morning far more excited about the idea of a retrospective of her father's work than she is about anything else currently happening in her life. She thinks, again, that she needs another ally if this project is to have any chance of ever seeing the light of day. She needs someone to bounce ideas off, someone less cynical than Brett, someone more enthusiastic than her mother or her brother, and someone who knew her father better than she did, or at the very least, knew his work better.

Brett pauses, snapping Sophie back into the here and now, and she realises that his hardness, today, isn't so hard, and understands suddenly that what always happens next, isn't, today, going to happen next at all. So Brett still *does* have the power to surprise.

"You OK?" Brett asks her now. "You seem distracted."

"Sorry. I am a bit unfocused today. Maybe we can have a coffee break and then reconvene? Would that be OK?"

Brett nods, rolls away, and bounces good-naturedly off to the kitchen, where, finding no coffee, he shouts back that he's heading out: the hunter-gatherer selflessly braving the 7-Eleven for supplies.

Sophie stretches out across the bed, then reaches for her phone and checks the time. It's almost four p.m. And then, without thinking, as if this is what she was doing before Brett so rudely interrupted her, she phones her mother.

"Hi Mum, it's Sophie."

"Hello love. I was just thinking about you."

"You were?"

"Yes. I'm about to make a pineapple upside-down cake. You always used to love that when you were little."

139

"I still do. Who are you making that for, then?"

"Jon. He's coming over in a bit."

"Actually, I phoned because I thought that *I* might come down next weekend."

"Really? Why?"

"To *see* you of course. But if you don't want me to come, Mum, then don't, you know, beat around the bush or anything. Just spit it out."

"Don't be silly. You know I do."

"Well, good then. Sunday maybe?"

"Yes. Sunday's good. Are you coming for something *specific*?"

"Not really. But, um, I did think that I might have another look at the photos in the attic."

"Oh, no, Sophie. We're not back onto that silly idea, are we? I don't want you tramping muck through the house all day."

"Oh come on, Mum. It's fair enough that I want to look at Dad's photos. I *am* a photographer and all."

"Is this still to do with that crazy exhibition you mentioned before?"

"There's nothing crazy about it, Mum."

"So, it is?"

"Not specifically."

"Hum."

"And Mum?"

"Yes?"

"I was wondering. You know Aunty Diane. Is she still alive?"

"Diane?"

"Yes. Dad's friend."

"I know who Diane is, dear. I'm not completely senile. But why on earth . . .?"

"I thought she might be able to help me."

"With what, exactly?"

"With, you know . . . ideas. What to show, how to show it . . . She was a photographer, right? She helped him sometimes, didn't she?"

Barbara doesn't reply to this but Sophie hears her sigh deeply.

"Can you think of any way of contacting her?"

"Not really."

"Really? You have no idea?"

"No. None, actually."

"Mum!"

"I haven't spoken to Diane since he died."

"Really?"

"Really."

"Why?"

"I don't know, dear. Presumably because I've had no reason to."

"Ah. So you *do* know how to contact her? If you had reason to."

"No. I don't. I told you. Now, I'd love to spend all day on the phone to you but Jon's coming and I need to get this cake in the oven."

"Was her name Darbott?"

"You know it was."

"Is that with two Ts?"

"Sophie. Please tell me that you're not going to go on some wild goose chase to find Diane?"

"Why not?"

"Because . . . Because . . ."

"Yes?"

"Because I expect that she's dead anyway."

"Dead?"

"Yes."

"Why would she be dead, Mum?"

"Because there's only so much abuse that a liver can take, dear."

"A liver?"

"Yes. Now I have to go, love. Let me know next Saturday if you're still coming. But I'm not having you traipsing through the loft again. So if that *is* why you're coming, then there's no point at all."

"Mum, hang on a minute. What about Dad's friend Hugh. Or Phil?"

"Oh Sophie, stop it. Stop it now."

"Stop what?"

"I have a cake to cook! Bye, dear."

Sophie has just pulled on her dressing gown when Brett returns with the coffee. "I got croissants too," he announces, dropping the bag on the worktop.

"You have to stop buying croissants," Sophie says. "I'm getting fat." What she really means is that Brett has to stop buying croissants because Brett is getting fat – no, fatter – but Brett doesn't get it.

"You look pretty good to me," he says, with a wink. He rips open the pack of coffee and pours some into the filter machine, then flicks the switch. "So, what are you so distracted about?" he asks.

Sophie is looking out over the London skyline. It's a beautiful day outside with blue skies and fast-moving clouds casting even faster moving shadows. "I'm sorry?" she says.

Brett laughs. "I rest my case!" he says, triumphantly.

"Oh, nothing really," Sophie says, managing to pull Brett's missed comment from some ten-second reality-buffer in her mind. "I've been thinking about that exhibition of Dad's stuff again. Mum's being really weird about it. That's all."

"Weird?"

"Plain unhelpful, really."

"You said she wouldn't be into it from the get-go."

"I know. But this is more than that. She doesn't want me getting the pictures down from the loft. She can't tell me how to get in touch with anyone from his past. It's more like wilful obstruction."

"Who d'you want to get in touch with?" Brett asks.

"Dad's friend, Diane Darbott. His best mate Phil as well. Mum says she has no idea where Diane is, which is pretty unlikely. She actually said that she's probably dead. I think she was implying that she had a drink problem, but I never saw any sign of that."

"You knew her then, this Diane?"

"Uh-huh. She was fun. I really liked her."

"Have you googled her?"

"Not yet. I'm going to. But she's not really the Facebook generation, so . . ."

Brett peers in at the slowly filling coffee pot then straightens again. "Maybe it just makes her uncomfortable."

"What makes who uncomfortable?"

"Your mother. The whole art thing. You said she was . . . what was that word you used?"

"A heathen. But I was being unfair."

"Sure. But maybe it just all reminds her of the past too much. It would make sense."

"Oh absolutely! I'm *sure* that's what it is. But it was all years ago. She needs to get over it, because I need to see what work he left behind."

"So, coffee?" Brett asks, brandishing the glass jug at her.

"Sure."

Brett pours two mugs of coffee and puts them on the small kitchen table. He then sits and rips open the paper bag containing the croissants.

143

Sophie pulls her gown around her, then slides into a seat and tears off a tiny piece of croissant and feeds it into her mouth. Because this solicits the memory of the skinny model doing the same thing, she reaches for the whole croissant and bites into it with gusto.

"Horrible croissants," Brett says, pulling a face.

"It's the 7-Eleven," Sophie points out. "Not the Sept-Onze."

"Meaning?"

"Meaning this is England. You're safer with crumpets than croissants round here."

"Crumpets?"

"They're an English thing. Like muffins. Or bagels. Actually, they're not really like anything."

"Crumpets, huh?"

"I'll get you some. You know, I keep thinking . . . Dad could have been so great."

Brett slurps at his coffee before replying. "He *was* pretty great, Sophie."

"Sure. But he could have been *really* great, I reckon. If he'd just been with someone who understood his art. Mum was a good wife and mother and everything but as far as his work was concerned . . . well . . ."

"Well?"

"Suffice to say that she was more motivated by taking him shopping than going on a photo shoot. That's why he used to hang out with Diane so much. And he never really travelled anywhere. That will have been because of Mum. He could have done so much more."

"He was up there. Don't diss the guy, babe. He's gotten a bit forgotten now, is all."

"Gotten forgotten. I like it. And whose fault is that? That he's gotten forgotten?"

144

"That's a lot of responsibility to pin on your ma. I'm sure she did her best."

"Are you?"

Brett shrugs.

"OK, maybe I'm being a bit mean. But you see my point?"

"Yes, I see your point."

They drink the rest of their coffee in silence, then Brett asks, "D'you want to finish what we started before?"

"I'm sorry? Oh. I'm not sure to be honest."

Brett reaches for a tin box on the shelf beside him. "Perhaps this will get you in the mood?" he says, pulling a tiny bag of cocaine from the tin.

Because Sophie knows that what he's saying is true and because it's the weekend and she has no other plans, and because she's feeling guilty about before, she agrees. "Just a small one then," she says. "I don't want to be feeling wired all day."

Brett lifts a framed photograph from the wall behind him and uses it, along with a business card, to lay out the lines, and as soon as they have snorted them, Sophie does feel different: enthusiastic, euphoric, confident and, yes, aroused.

"Come!" Brett says, standing, rubbing his nose, then taking her hand and leading her through to the bedroom. He heads straight for the 'naughty' drawer and Sophie stands in the doorway, her expression one of wry amusement, as Brett retrieves the two pairs of handcuffs and the dog collar. "Time to ring the changes, babe," he says.

"Does this mean we're now *officially* bored?" Sophie asks.

"Bored?"

"When I asked you about those, you said that they were for when we got bored."

Brett pouts and shakes his head. "I'm not bored at all here, babe," he says. He pulls off his sweatshirt, then adds. "Maybe

145

it's just that now I trust you enough to share this with you. You could choose to feel flattered."

"But do I trust *you* enough?" Sophie asks, picturing herself tied up and at Brett's mercy and surprising herself by not finding the image displeasing.

"I can't see you need to, really," Brett says, now fiddling with the handcuffs and then clipping the end of one pair to his right wrist, then one end of the second pair to his left wrist.

Sophie frowns at him, naked from the waist up, handcuffs dangling from each arm. "I don't get it," she says. "What am I supposed to do now?"

"Whatever you want," Brett says, now climbing onto the bed and spreading his arms so that the handcuffs clank against the iron of the bed-head. "I'm at your mercy, mistress."

"Oh," Sophie says, suddenly embarrassed that the penny has taken so long to drop. "Oh, I see!"

"I'm not suggesting anything," Brett says, "But there are various torture devices in that next drawer down. So if you did feel like I'd been a *bad* Brett, well, you could take it out on me. Get your own back, so to speak."

Sophie sighs and crosses the room to peer in the drawer. Thinking that this isn't what she expected, she lifts a small chain connected to metal clamps from the drawer, pokes, slightly disgustedly, at a set of love balls, then at a ball-gag. "Is this meant to be for you?" she asks, lifting the pink dildo and flopping it from side to side, comically.

"If that is your wish, Mistress," Brett says, for some reason speaking in a strange, science-fiction, robot voice.

"Hum," Sophie says, as she wonders if, even if it *isn't* her wish, if it could be if she tried hard enough. But she's not at all sure she wants to. What she *wants* here, what she *feels like* here, is simply a good, long shag. That's what she really needs.

She turns to face Brett, about to pierce his bubble, about

to explain, gently, that dominatrix isn't really her bag. But then she sees his dick, throbbing, jumping, begging inside his jogging trousers and realises that just because Brett is tied up, just because he has a dog collar on, clamps on his nipples and a gag in his mouth, it doesn't mean that she can't get what she wants too. It doesn't mean that at all.

She walks around the bed and attaches the handcuffs, one after the other, to the extremities of the bed-head. "OK, you little slut," she says, yanking down his jogging trousers and watching his dick spring forth. "You've asked for it."

"Please, mercy!" Brett says.

"*No* mercy," Sophie says, straddling him. "You're going to bloody well get what's coming to you."

1951 – EASTBOURNE, EAST SUSSEX.

Barbara loves living in Eastbourne. She has walked all the way to Holywell this morning (she thinks the spot where the cliffs meet the sea is the prettiest place she has ever seen) and is now on her way home. But this thought, that she *loves* living here, has filled her mind since the second she got up and opened the curtains.

For a moment there, specifically for the first week of her marriage, it was hit and miss – she really did think that everything might fall apart. The worst moment of all had been her return, alone, to Donnybrook the morning after the wedding – having to face her mother, her sister, her new in-laws, and explain to them all, one after the other, that she had no idea *whatsoever* where her new husband was, nor where he had spent the night. Everyone was outraged on her behalf, so outraged in fact, that her own indignation became of little importance when compared to the obvious necessity of calming everyone down before Tony got back, which he did eventually, just before two p.m. He had passed out drunk at Hugh's, he claimed. He looked poorly enough that this might be true.

It was unforgivable, everyone agreed. 'Unforgivable' – that was the word they all kept using. But given the choice between packing her bags and returning to London (an option that Glenda kept repeating would be, under the circumstances, perfectly justifiable) and forgiving and forgetting, Barbara has chosen to forgive and forget. Happiness is a relative concept and after having lived through a world war in the East End of London, Tony's absence registered as a mere blip on her personal Richter scale. And today, as she wanders along South Downs Way with the waves crashing to her right, with the taste of sea-salt on her lips and with Tony's baby just starting to demonstrate her presence (Minnie has swung a ring over her belly and declared that it will be a girl and Barbara believes her), she just *knows* that she has made the right choice.

Of course, Tony's behaviour at the wedding has concerned her, and having now met and spent time with his father, Lionel, she's worried, more profoundly, that she may have married into some kind of genetic fault-line as far as alcohol is concerned. So she watches Lionel and tries to understand. Like a keen botany student, she's observing the world around her and making mental notes about what works and what doesn't. Already, she has identified that Lionel gets grumpy just before he starts to drink. She knows, too, that the first beer makes him normal, the second funny, and the third, euphoric and overbearing. The fourth quietens him down, the fifth leaves him maudlin and then either he falls asleep or carries on to the sixth and the seventh in which case it's time to escape, because it can only end in an explosion of anger or, if you're lucky, vomiting.

She watches Joan, too, to see if she has developed any coping strategies, but other than an inexplicable need to talk all the time (is it the silence that scares her, or the thoughts that might manifest if she shut up for a moment?) she just seems to hunker down and brave her way through each storm as if it were the first and hopefully the last.

But while Lionel hasn't spent a single night sober since the wedding, now two weeks ago, Tony, for his part, hasn't had a single drink. In fact, Tony has been as funny and helpful, as sweet and doting, as he ever has. Glenda told her that she must insist Tony apologise for his disgraceful behaviour but Barbara has never understood Glenda's need for a clean-cut victory in these things. Tony's efforts to redeem himself, his constant attentions towards her, are as much apology as Barbara needs.

When she reaches Donnybrook, the front door is open. Barbara climbs the steps and sees that Joan is in the process of mopping the black and white checkered floor-tiles.

"Hello. I'm back to give you a hand," she announces, and Joan stops mopping and turns, fag-in-mouth to face her. "Hello love," she says. "Nice walk?"

Barbara nods and smiles sweetly. "I went all the way to Helen Gardens again."

"You'll walk yourself out," Joan admonishes. "A woman in your state should be resting. When I was pregnant with Tony—"

"The doctor said walking was good," Barbara interrupts. Joan has already told her how she spent three months in bed before Tony was born. Repeatedly.

"Yes, well. I'm sure he didn't mean you to be running a marathon every day either. In my day—"

"Should I go round the back?" Barbara asks, cutting short another dreaded 'in my day' speech. "I don't want to spoil your nice clean floor."

Joan shakes her head and a small clump of ash from her cigarette falls to the floor and is instantly removed with a swipe of the mop. "No, you can come through on one condition."

"Yes?"

"That you go straight to your room and rest up."

Barbara nods. "OK," she says. "I'll help you this afternoon though."

Joan dries her fingertips on her pinny, then seizes the cigarette and takes a long, visibly satisfying, final drag before stubbing it out in the ashtray on the hall table. "You can peel the spuds and carrots for me," she says. "You can do that sitting down."

As Barbara crosses the hall to the staircase, Joan re-mops the floor in her wake. "Sorry," Barbara says, glancing back.

"It's fine, go on, go on! It's fine!" she insists.

Once inside Tony's bedroom (her old single room has been commandeered for paying guests now the season has started) Barbara unlaces her saddle shoes and kicks them off. She massages one foot, then the other, then crosses the room to open the window. There is no sea view at Donnybrook but she can still hear the gulls, she can still sense the waves crashing against the beach not two hundred yards away and, just occasionally, when the wind is in the right direction, she can hear them too, rushing up the beach, then sinking into the pebbles. It sounds like the sleepy wheezing of some vast, distant giant.

She sits down and holds her breath and listens for a moment, then throws herself back onto the bed. She stares at the ceiling, then slides one hand over her belly. It feels somehow tighter than usual. Perhaps she *has* overdone it a bit.

"Sorry about that," she says, gently rubbing herself. "You can rest now, baby."

By the time Barbara wakes up, the sun has moved around far enough that it is shining onto the bed. A glance at the clock reveals that she has been asleep for almost two hours. She should get up but she feels woozy and strange, feverish and crampy. She closes her eyes and lifts her knees to see if this position will ease the pain, then, when it doesn't, she slides one hand down to her belly, then further down until it reaches the dampness. She swallows with difficulty, then wrinkles her brow, bites her bottom lip, and sits up to look. Her knickers are spotted with red, just like when her time of the month used to arrive. But that shouldn't be happening today. She knows this much.

She tries to imagine herself asking Joan about what's

151

happening – a toe-curlingly embarrassing thought. She pulls open her knickers and peers inside. There is very little blood. Perhaps this is normal. Perhaps she'll be OK.

She feels overly full though, almost like indigestion. She feels a sudden need to 'spend a penny' too. Yes, perhaps that's it. Perhaps she simply needs to pee.

She stands, feels dizzy, and has to reach out to steady herself against the wall before she manages to cross to the dresser, where she retrieves a fresh pair of undies and a clean flannel mitt she can use as a pad. She crosses to the sink, cleans herself up, then changes. Once the blood is all gone, she feels better. She feels, for a moment, like the scare is over.

She'll mention it to Joan later, but at least there's no hurry now.

She opens the door and steps out onto the landing. Downstairs she can hear the upright vacuum cleaner being driven, beating and screaming, around the dining room.

When she reaches the lavatory, she sits down and notes with dismay that the flannel is already spotted with bright, almost fluorescent blood. She'll have to talk to Joan, after all.

She reads, for the umpteenth time, the framed embroidery above the toilet roll holder. Who waits outside the door / One may never know / So tarry not my friend / He too may need to go. She wishes it wasn't there, because, for some reason, she's incapable of ever sitting here *without* reading it, and she didn't find it funny the first time around. By now, she has read it so many times that reading it again makes her feel a little bit sick.

She's just about to stand up when she feels a fresh cramping sensation, strong enough to make her gasp. She sits back down, then wipes her forehead, upon which beads of sweat are forming. "That's not right," she says quietly. She wishes Glenda was here. Glenda would know what to do.

A fresh, even stronger wave of cramping rolls through her

152

body, followed by a weird, sickening push that originates from deep within. A new batch of more-viscous liquid gushes out and she is torn between the alarmed instinct to look and see what's happening down there and a new terror of what she will discover if she does. She is sweating heavily now. She's crying too, she realises in surprise – tears are rolling down her cheeks, snot is dribbling from her nose. It feels as if her body is turning to liquid, melting like an ice cube. "Water, water, everywhere," she thinks. Perhaps Joan will come upstairs and simply find a puddle on the floor and no one will ever know where Barbara vanished to.

She knows what is happening now, and on top of the fear and the cramps, and the sweat and the tears, she feels as if her heart is breaking as well; her sobs become real, become tortured. "Oh baby, not yet," she gasps, screwing up her features.

And then, as if in reply, a vast, stabbing cramp wracks her innards, making her double over and gasp loudly as something slides from within her – something of consequence, something big enough that she hears it slap against the porcelain of the toilet bowl.

"Joan!" she starts to scream. "Joan! Joan! Joan!!" But Joan can't hear her. The damned vacuum cleaner continues to throb and moan below, the vibrations travelling through the walls of the house.

Yet another round of cramping seizes her body but she's empty now, so terrifyingly empty, as empty as she has ever felt. She needs to look. She doesn't think the baby can be alive this early on, but in truth she doesn't know. She doesn't think anyone has ever told her how many months would be needed before the baby is actually alive. But whatever came out felt big; it felt terrifyingly, traumatically big. So she needs to look. Just in case.

153

She moves back as far as she can and peers into the bowl. And there it is. A bloody, translucent bag, a misshapen foetus.

Paralysed, she stares at it. She stares at the tiny arms, at the outsized, alien head. She wonders if it's dead or if it was never, in fact, alive. She wonders if it's deformed because there's something wrong with it, or because it's simply too early. The unborn babies in the book certainly looked nothing like this. And then she wonders, with a fresh batch of tears, if it's alive and slowly suffocating inside the bag.

She reaches out and prods it with a trembling finger. It's warm and surprisingly solid. She had expected it to feel, somehow, less real. She can barely see through the tears now, so she wipes her eyes with her wrist and then reaches out again and tries to turn the head towards her, tries to see if this thing (and could something this ugly really be her baby?) is alive or dead. It unexpectedly slides an inch down the porcelain, making her jump. The movement makes her scream and once she starts screaming, she can't stop. She screams as loudly as she has ever screamed. And below her, finally, the vacuum cleaner stops and over her own screams she hears Joan's voice rising from below. "Barbara? Barbara? Are you alright, love?"

* * *

Barbara opens her eyes and looks at the green curtains surrounding the bed. Her memories of the trip to the hospital are patchy. A neighbour brought her, she thinks. Yes, a neighbour who is a taxi driver, that's right.

She looks to the left at the jug of rehydration salts and remembers both that she is supposed to drink the liquid within and that it tastes horrible.

Behind the curtain, she can hear Joan whispering to someone.

Joan, talking, always talking. "She lost a lot of blood," she is saying now and Barbara remembers that too.

She dozes off again for a while and when she awakens, Joan is still talking. "That's what they said. That it was nature being kind."

"What a thing to say!" It's Tony's voice and Barbara is torn between calling out to him and keeping quiet so that she can hear Joan's reply.

"The baby wasn't right, love," Joan is telling him, now. "I brought the poor thing in so they could look at it and the doctor said it had stopped growing a while back and that even if it hadn't, that it was better this way."

"Tony?" Barbara calls out, as much to interrupt the flow of uncensored information as anything else.

"Sounds like she's awake," Joan says.

Like a Punch and Judy puppet, Tony's face appears between the curtains. "I just got here," he says, moving around the bed now and taking her hand. "I came as soon as I heard."

"I'm so sorry," Barbara says.

"Hey, it wasn't your fault, was it?"

"At least she's OK," another woman's voice says from behind the curtain.

"Is that Diane?" Barbara asks.

Tony nods. "She wanted to come see you. Is that OK?"

"I don't want to see anyone else," Barbara says. "Just you."

"OK."

"I'm so sorry, Tony," Barbara says again. "I think I walked too far."

"That's not the reason," Tony tells her. "They said he'd stopped growing already."

"He?"

Tony nods. "That's what Mum said."

"A boy!" Barbara gasps, an actual future discovered only once it has been cancelled; her loss, suddenly made real.

"You're going to be alright," Tony says, now patting her hand. "That's the main thing."

"It was a boy though."

"Yes, well, we can always try again."

Try again! Barbara can't think what to say to that. Because right now she never wanted anything less. Tony's expectant face is just too much to bear so she closes her eyes and then decides that the best strategy is, in fact, to keep them closed.

Eventually, he releases her hand and she hears the rattle of the curtain runners as he steps outside. "She's fallen asleep again," he says.

"She's exhausted, poor thing," Joan says. "It's the worst thing that can happen to a woman."

"Yes. Of course."

"Such a shock," Diane says.

"I just wish we'd known before, you know . . ." Tony whispers.

"Well, quite," Joan says. "But life's like that, love. You never know what's around the corner."

"Should I stay d'you think?" Diane asks.

"Nah. Go," Tony tells her. "You can both go, actually. I don't think she's going to be in the mood for visits today."

During Barbara's week in hospital, there are three things, three obsessions, that she finds herself unable to push from her mind. The first is the image of the baby – huge head, tiny hands – so human and yet so very wrong. The second is the phrase, "Nature being kind." It's the cruellest thing she has ever heard. And the third is Tony declaring, "I just wish we'd known before."

It's not until they are being driven away from the hospital

that she dares to ask him what he meant by it. Tony asks her to repeat herself twice before looking shifty and saying, "No. I wouldn't have said that. I definitely wouldn't have said that."

But she knows that he did. She knows that beyond doubt.

*　　*　　*

Barbara opens her eyes to find Joan bustling into the bedroom. "I've never seen such a mess . . ." she is saying, and Barbara struggles to focus on the room around her. She tries to see what might be wrong with it, then realises that Joan is talking about a guest's room. "They only came for two nights, but there's shopping bags and underwear all over the floor, knickers hanging on the door-knob, dirty cups they've brung up from downstairs. I dread to think what it's like in their own homes. And I say *homes* advisedly. I'm pretty sure they're not married, even if they *did* introduce themselves as Mr and Mrs Grady. I wonder what the real Mrs Grady would have to say about their little trip to Eastbourne? Then again, she's probably glad of the break. From the cleaning, like."

Barbara blinks and struggles to situate herself in the here and now of this moment, this bedroom, this bed, bathed in the afternoon light. She tries to wrench herself from the woozy afternoon dream she was having where she had been so very pleasantly . . . Where had she been? Damn. It's gone. Only the pleasant afterglow of whatever it was remains.

She tries to concentrate on Joan's stream-of-consciousness monologue as she folds and piles and dusts and collects plates from around the room. ". . . over at Beach Cottage . . ." she is saying now. ". . . actually managed to break a window . . ."

Barbara knows that she needs to concentrate because from time to time Joan throws a curve-ball and actually asks her a question. Much of the time she manages to get away with a noncommittal "hum", or a vague, mumbled, "I suppose so," but not always. Sometimes the questions require specific answers, typically answers that Joan already knows, often answers to questions that have been asked previously, and repeatedly.

Like now. Joan is sitting on the edge of the bed, touching Barbara's forehead and waiting for a reply. From some vapour trail left by the passing of Joan's words, Barbara drags up, 'iron pill' and answers, hopefully, "Yes, I took it with lunch."

Joan nods, apparently satisfied. "Good," she says. "Mrs Davis was anaemic after she had the twins but she won't take pills, says the devil's in them. Ended up with *terrible* jaundice, she did! She was yellow as a daffodil, I swear to God. Had palpitations too. All kinds of horrors. They ended up taking her in just so they could force the pills down her. So you need to take them like the doctor said."

"I took it," Barbara says again, even though she is now beginning to doubt herself. These days and nights of bed-rest merge together so seamlessly, so endlessly, that who's to say if the pill she remembers was yesterday or today?

Tony was here when she took it, she remembers. He had been about to go to London on a delivery. "Where's Tony?" she asks, more to clarify the taking of the pill in her own mind than to ascertain his whereabouts.

"Tony? He's in London today. You know that. But he'll be back in time for tea. For a late tea, he said," Joan replies. "Now, though I'd love to sit and chat to you all afternoon, I've got to get down to the fishmongers. Lionel wants a kipper for his tea and if I don't get there soon there won't be any left. I'll probably get us a bit of cod, maybe make a fish pie for the rest of us. How do you feel about fish pie for tea? Not so keen on the kippers myself. I wouldn't mind so much if it weren't for the smell. Has half the guests complaining and the other half wanting kippers themselves. But Lionel likes 'em so . . ."

Barbara yawns and listens to Joan's voice fading as she retreats downstairs. She will wait until she hears the front door close and then she'll see how well she manages the standing position today. Two weeks of bed rest, the doctor said, and though she's already halfway through, she still can't stand up without feeling dizzy. And she wants to get up. With each day that passes, her need to get up grows exponentially. She needs to escape the house before Joan drives her, quite literally, insane.

On days like today, with the weekend approaching and Lionel and Tony home for tea, it's not so bad. Joan has other ears to bend, other fish to buy and fry. It's the weekdays Barbara fears – endless yawning empty days when the guesthouse is as empty as a church. Tony and Lionel are absent and Joan, with nothing else to do, sits and talks at her. It's surprisingly torturous.

Barbara hears the front door close and swings her legs to the edge of the bed. She needs to be up and about, specifically up and *elsewhere* by the time the weekend is over. She must talk to Tony about moving to a place of their own too. She needs to escape Donnybrook and, as a couple, now the momentum and trajectory the baby had imposed has vanished, they require some new destination, some fresh objective of their own.

She grabs the brass knob on the foot of the bed and levers herself upright and waits for the nausea to hit. After twenty seconds, when it has passed, she murmurs, "Not bad." She's desperately trying to convince herself that she's getting better. Her legs still have that jelly feeling but the nausea is less marked, more easily defeated, isn't it?

She pulls on her dressing gown and heads down to the next landing where the toilet is situated. She's supposed to use the potty but she must make herself progress, even though the toilet is the very same toilet where the terrible thing happened.

She sits on the seat and reads the awful toilet tapestry again and tries not to remember the sensation – the push and the rush; tries not to remember the sound and her scream; tries not to sense the void inside her, a void that says so definitively, so inescapably that she is a failure at the one thing that made Tony want to marry her. Perhaps not even 'want' in fact. The one thing that made Tony marry her, then. *If only he had known,* he had said. And Barbara is pretty certain that she knows what he meant by that. *If only they had known, they would never have had to bother with any of this silly marriage business.* But married they are, so she needs to get up and about and somehow make him proud of that fact.

The next time Barbara wakes up, the daylight has faded and Diane is entering the bedroom. Tony will be home soon. She knows this instinctively, because Diane's arrival precedes Tony's arrival as night precedes day.

"Hello. How are you feeling?" Diane asks, sitting on the edge of the bed and taking Barbara's hand in her own. Her touch is soft, her skin powdery and smooth – a surprising contrast to her tomboy haircut and bushy eyebrows, to her brusk, no-nonsense nature.

"I'm OK," Barbara says, stifling a yawn. "I feel a bit better each day. What are you doing here?"

"I came to check up on you," Diane says. "I thought you might need the company."

Something flutters within Barbara's chest, a convoluted, conflicted flutter caused by a feeling that somehow this would be lovely were it to be true, that this would be a little *too* lovely – abnormally, perhaps *dangerously,* lovely. But it isn't true. It isn't true at all. So the lie is cause for both pain and pleasure.

160

"What time's Tony back?" Barbara asks, pointing as distinctly as she dares at the truth here.

"I don't know," Diane replies, but even as she is saying this, the sound of Tony's motorbike spluttering up the street outside provides a backdrop of irony to her words.

Barbara sees Diane take note of the sound and sees the effort that she expends in order *not* to take note of the sound. She sees the willpower required for Diane to stay interested, in this moment, in Barbara. "Are the pills working?" she asks.

Barbara nods. "A bit. I think. I made it downstairs today. Just for a cup of tea. But don't tell Joan."

"Of course not," Diane says, now winking and squeezing Barbara's hand, and whatever it is that fluttered before now flutters again, only this time Barbara pulls her hand away. "That sounds like Tony now," she says, and they both pause to listen to the front door, then to Joan's voice greeting him. They struggle to capture the content of his reply but he is too distant and the sound waves are too jumbled by the stairwell for them to make out anything more than the excited lilt of his voice.

As if to confirm this excitement, Tony is already bounding up the stairs as fast as his clompy motorcycle boots will allow. "Hello!" he shouts, bustling into the room and bringing with him a rush of cold air drifting off his clothes in waves. Tony often shouts when he gets home – the motorcycle, he claims, makes him deaf. He's wearing his leather motorbike trousers and a vast waxed-cotton jacket. Barbara thinks he looks unreasonably sexy when he's in his work clobber. She wishes secretly that she could sleep with him while he's still dressed that way but there's no way to say that to him and she knows that there never will be a way.

Diane stands and pecks Tony on the cheek which means that she gets to him before Barbara can. "Good trip to London?" she asks.

"Yes, I . . . Actually, I need to have a word with Babs," Tony tells her, and Barbara watches and sees Diane's smile maintained even as her eyes fast forward through a whole set of calculations, a whole batch of emotions. "Sure," she says, breezily. "I'll leave you to it."

Tony closes the door behind her and turns to face Barbara. His eyes look as blue as they ever have, a cold-enhanced, crazed kind of blue.

Barbara props herself up on pillows and smiles and frowns simultaneously. "What's happened?" she asks. "Has something happened?"

Tony licks his lips and sits on the bed exactly where Diane had been sitting only seconds before. Tony too, takes her hand in his own and the contact is so very different. Tony's hands are as cold and heavy as steaks from the butcher's refrigerator. "Something *has* happened," he says. "And I need to talk to you about it."

"OK," Barbara replies, noting that he *still* hasn't kissed her and fearing the worst.

"Now, we don't have to make a decision immediately. So I don't want you worrying, especially not at the moment, not with you being tired and everything . . ."

"Right."

"But I got offered a job today."

"Really?"

"I had to take a package up to London. Film rolls, it was. To the *Daily Mirror*. And the boss there took me aside and offered me a job. Just like that."

"The *Mirror* newspaper?"

"Yes. They do the *Sunday Pictorial* too. Same place. Now it's just delivering packages. Same as now. But it's double the pay."

"Double?"

162

Tony nods. "*Almost* double. Give or take some small change."

"And delivering packages the same as now?"

"Yes. On a motorbike. A better one, I reckon. I saw some parked outside and they had some nice BSAs. A couple of them were those new Golden Flashes I like."

"Tell me about the job though."

"Like I say, it's just deliveries, really . . . going and getting rolls of film from journalists and rushing 'em back to the paper. Stuff like that."

"That's great news, isn't it?"

Tony nods and shrugs. "I think so."

"We could rent our own place," Barbara says. "Specially if I get a job as well."

"I don't reckon you'd have to. Not with all I'd be earning. He said it was nine quid a week."

"Is there a catch though?" Barbara asks. "I'm sensing a catch."

"Not really," Tony says. "Maybe. Sort of. I suppose. It depends."

"Yes?"

"It's in London."

"Yes, you said."

"*All* the trips are to or from London. So I'd need to be in London all the time."

"Oh."

"So we'd need to move."

Once Tony has (finally) kissed her and left, Barbara starts to weigh up the pros and cons of moving back to London. A place of their own. More money. Escape from Joan. Safety from Diane. But *London!* No seafront, no seagulls, no sea air, no sea anything . . . Just smog and grime and the same gritty, grim, determined people she grew up with. She feels miserable even imagining it.

Downstairs she can hear Diane, apparently now in on the news as well, raising her voice. She stands, then, despite the dizziness, moves out to the landing to listen. Both Joan and Diane are talking at once. "Double money's not to be sneezed at," Joan is saying. "Not that I'm pushing you out or nothing but it's not to be sneezed at is all, and we could always use the extra room, you know that. But talk to your father first, he . . ."

Alongside this, is Diane's voice. ". . . what you want . . ." she is saying. "But think about all your mates here. Think about the fact you won't know anyone in London. Think about all the summers on the beach you'll miss. It's all very well earning more but being happy is what counts, I reckon. And my guess is that you'll be lonely as hell in London."

"I'll be with Barbara, won't I?" Tony tells her. "And she knows people in London as well."

"Barbara?" Diane says. "Do you really think that would be enough for you?"

And Barbara realises that she already knows, has known even before the question was raised, what needs to be done here.

2012 – EASTBOURNE, EAST SUSSEX.

Sophie sits on the tiny landing, her back against the banisters, and pulls a sleeve of photographs from the first of the five boxes she has lugged down the ladder.

The landing is hardly ideal for the job of curating her father's work but Barbara has made such a fuss about her 'tramping dust' over the new carpet that she has had to cave in. Her mother has never been 'easy', but as she gets older, the rules and limits she imposes seem to Sophie to be ever more arbitrary, ever more random, and more and more irritating to comply with. But yes, Sophie will look through the photos here on the landing and then she will put the boxes back in the loft *and* vacuum the floor. And perhaps successful completion of these stages as dictated will bring authorisation for her to go through another five boxes next weekend, and another five the weekend after that. And hopefully, by the time all twenty-five boxes have been done, enough gems will have been unearthed for an exhibition.

The first sleeve contains a thoroughly disappointing batch of mundane imagery. Some are interesting as historical relics: a nineteen-fifties corner shop with vegetables piled outside, a man on an old motorbike, a baby in puffed, striped knickerbockers (did babies still look like this in the fifties?) but these photos have no art to them. They are snaps. They are not in any way photographer's photographs. She shuffles quickly through the pile, then returns them to the plastic sleeve and selects another package containing larger prints.

These are more hopeful, indeed a few images almost make the grade. One, of a small group of farmhouses in the midst of a vast field of wheat, looks more like the American midwest than England. The sky above the farmhouse is complex and really rather beautiful, but the print has a missing corner and, damaged, its value to Sophie will depend on whether she can find the corresponding negative for a reprint.

The next pack contains a series of what look to Sophie like failed attempts at art photography. A detail of some bricks in a wall, a rusting bath overgrown with weeds, a close up of somebody's elbow . . . They remind her of the photos she took herself when she was about ten. Perhaps they *are* photos she took when she was about ten. This memory, of going out with her father to take photos on a Sunday morning, takes her by surprise. Some muscle deep within, near her heart (perhaps her heart itself), spasms, and she winces and struggles to push her memories of her father from her mind and to blink back the resulting tears, suddenly, surprisingly present in her eyes.

In the next pack she strikes lucky. These are stark, aggressively architectural shots from the early sixties and she feels a little pride that her father took these. One senses the excitement of a new era: men in sharp suits, women dressed in simple tube-shaped dresses with lopped-off sleeves. One particular photo in the pack reminds her of a film. It's of a woman with a beehive, silhouetted in the window of a new-build home, with sharp angles throwing shadows across an immaculate lawn. She stares at it for a few minutes before the title comes to mind. "*Stepford Wives*," she murmurs, putting the photo to one side. The next image actually makes her break into a grin. "Yesss!" she says. "Now that's more like it, Dad." The photo shows two overweight women in floral dresses – sisters perhaps – on deck chairs on a pebble beach.

166

Next to each is an old-fashioned, sprung pram complete with floral parasol and behind all of this, a pier. *"Not Eastbourne,"* she thinks. *"Hastings perhaps?"*

"Some of these are gorgeous, Mum!" she calls out excitedly.

There is no reply. Barbara may have gone out.

By the time Sophie has rooted through all five boxes the light is fading. She is feeling demotivated by the limited flecks of gold she has been able to sift from the mud and a little depressed from the unavoidable melancholy of spending a rainy day looking through her dead father's work. She hauls the boxes back up into the loft, folds the ladder away and then searches through the house until she finds Barbara in the rain-spotted veranda. "Gosh, you're knitting," she says.

"I am," Barbara replies without looking up.

"I don't think I've ever seen you knit."

"It's for the baby," Barbara says, and Sophie hears accusation in her voice, the accusation of her failure, as a daughter, to produce grandchildren. She quickly analyses this and decides that she's imagining things. *"It's for the baby,"* Sophie repeats in her head. *"That's all she said."*

"It's pink," she comments.

"Yes."

"Do they know the sex now, or something? Because the last time I spoke to Jon . . ."

"It's going to be striped," Barbara says, nodding at the knitting pattern on the coffee table.

Sophie looks and sees the image of a boy and a girl wearing identical blue and pink striped jumpers. "I hope it doesn't get gender confused," she says. "I hope the jumper doesn't make the baby gay or transsexual or something." But she knows as soon as she has said it that it's not the kind of humour that her mother is capable of even recognising as such.

"What a silly thing to say," Barbara replies.

"Joke, Mum."

"Did you find anything?"

"Not much," Sophie admits with a sigh. "Six images."

"I thought as much."

"I've only done the first five boxes though. But to be honest, most of these are going to be unusable unless I find the negatives."

"Show me."

Sophie drags the pouffe next to her mother and sits down. Barbara lays down her knitting, fumbles for her bifocals on the chain around her neck and places them on her nose, then takes the photos from Sophie's grasp.

"Ah, I remember that," she says immediately. "I was with him."

"Really?"

"It was in Harlow. It was a new town back then. It didn't even exist before the war. We went there to see if we could find my father. Tony thought we should tell him about the wedding and Harlow was the last address we could find for him."

"And?"

"And what?"

"Did you find him?"

Barbara shakes her head. "The house had changed hands a few times and they had no forwarding address. People moved around a lot after the war, especially builders. They went where the work was."

"And the woman? In the window?"

"I've no idea. She was just a woman in a house. I spotted her and your father took a photo."

"Right. I like the backstory though. The hunt for Granddad."

Barbara wrinkles her nose at some memory, then hands the photo to Sophie revealing the next image, a row of pop-eyed

168

policemen with lopsided helmets, struggling to hold back a crowd of women.

"A Beatles concert," Barbara says.

"Really? I *thought* they all looked a bit hysterical."

"That one's crying," Barbara says, pointing. "Look. They used to get themselves in such a state. I never really understood it myself. I mean, Ringo was cute but . . ."

"So, this was when, mid sixties?"

"Sixty-three, I think."

"The year Jon was born then."

"Yes."

"Was Dad sent to cover the concert? Do you think I'll find more?"

Barbara shakes her head. "He was still riding packages around back then. He will have been sent there to pick up some rolls of film, I expect. From the proper photographer. But he always had his camera with him."

"If this was sixty-three, you were at home with the baby, right?"

"I'm not sure if this was before or after. But it was around that time."

"Well, either way, you would have been at home with the baby. Either within or without . . ."

"I suppose so," Barbara says as she moves onto the next image.

"Do you think I'll find a box of negatives at some point?"

"I don't know. Can't you use these?"

"Not if I want to do really big prints," Sophie says. "Or at least, not without specialist scanning and restoration work."

"I would assume that they're up there somewhere."

"Oh, you know Diane?" Sophie says. "I found her on the web. She's in Portland in America apparently. She has a photography site. I sent her an email but she never answered."

"No, well . . ."

"The last update to the web page was in 2009 though."

"Are these the only ones you liked?" Barbara asks, definitively refusing the Diane detour.

"They were pretty mundane for the most part."

"As I say, I'm not surprised."

"But I only looked in the first five boxes. There's another twenty to go. I'm just assuming that all the good ones are grouped together somewhere."

"I think you may be disappointed."

"*Mum* . . ." Sophie whines.

"He didn't take as many good shots as you perhaps think he did. That's all I'm saying. And the good ones got used. You already *know* about the good ones. Everyone does."

"Can't you be even a tiny bit enthusiastic, here? Would that really be too much to ask?"

"I'm just being realistic, love."

"And what about the Pentax tour? If I could find those . . ."

"You *won't* find those."

"But if I could, there must be hundreds. He was away for months, wasn't he?"

"Three weeks. But you won't find any photos from that tour."

"How do you know that?"

"I just do."

"Because you burned them?"

"You *know* what happened."

"But I might find the *negatives.*"

"You won't."

"Because you burned those as well?"

"I really don't remember, dear," Barbara says, handing back the pictures. "It *was* thirty years ago."

"How can you *not* remember something like that?"

170

"Because it was *thirty years ago!*"

"I think you remember perfectly well," Sophie says, aware that she's getting carried away, aware now that she's saying the one thing she promised herself she must not say but unable to stop herself lobbing the grenade into the room. "I think you're just too ashamed to admit that you burned the largest volume of work that one of Britain's best photographers ever took."

"Yes!" Barbara says angrily. "Yes, you're right. I probably am. And yes, I probably did!"

"But how, Mum? How could you have done that? I mean, I know that you were—"

Barbara stands.

"Mum. Don't go off in a huff. I didn't *mean* anything."

Barbara walks to the doorway, then pauses, her hand on the door-jamb. "He wasn't a photographer to me, Sophie," she says. "He was my *husband!* And he had just *died!* He went to France to take photos and came back in a coffin. Now I don't expect you to have *any* idea what that feels like but . . .'"

"I'm sorry," Sophie says, finally wrestling her voice under control and actually managing to *sound* sorry. "I just want to understand. Surely losing him should have made you want to *keep* his photos all the more?"

"Should? How dare you tell me how I should have felt when my husband had just died."

"*Would* then," Sophie says.

"I think you *should* leave now," Barbara says, already turning and vanishing into the shadows of the house.

Sophie blows out through pursed lips, then stands, slides the six photos into an envelope and follows her mother indoors. She finds Barbara wrestling the upright Dyson to the top of the stairs. "Here. I'll do that, Mum. I said I would."

"Just go home, please."

"Mum, I wasn't—"

171

"I find you very hurtful today. It's bad enough having you digging through all this stuff but when you then start having a go at me about things that happened thirty years ago, things you know nothing about . . ."

"Mum, I know exactly what you went through but . . ."

"You youngsters, you think you know everything, but you know nothing, Sophie, nothing."

"Mum, I think you're being a bit—"

"Don't think you know what battles I had to fight to get where I am today."

"*Battles?* Now you're definitely slipping into melodrama, Mum."

"Don't think you can even imagine what suffering we had to go through, what secrets we had to hide . . . You think you know everything, but you know nothing."

"I know *you* Mum. And I know when you're making yourself a self-pity sandwich."

"How dare you! You don't know me. You don't know anyone. Because that's what life is. It's thinking you know everything and thinking you know everyone, and finding out, the older you get, that you didn't – that you had it all wrong. Ah, you'll find out one day!"

"Mum, just calm down. All I was saying . . ."

"And don't tell me to calm down. Just go, please. Go!"

"But Mum, I . . ."

"GO!" Barbara shouts. She kicks at the Dyson and it roars into action, and Sophie, knowing when she's beaten, returns to the hallway and reaches for her coat.

Sophie sits on the train and watches as Eastbourne station slides from the window. There's something dream-like about train travel, she reckons. She feels like she's dreaming about herself sitting on a train.

Two overweight girls in pink tracksuits with visibly pierced navels burst into the carriage chewing gum and talking loudly, talking *spectacularly*, determined that everyone should benefit from their wit.

". . . jus' fucking tell 'im," one is saying. "Jus' fuckin' tell 'im that you don't fuckin' fancy 'im."

"Haha," her friend/sister/cousin says. "I might just do 'im first. I 'aven't 'ad a shag since Wayne went off with that slag Denise."

Sophie prays that the girls will continue their way along the carriage, but instead, one of them points at the seats across the aisle from her and says, "'ere?"

Sophie waits until they reach a station called Polegate where she has seen many girls like these two get on and off, but when, with Polegate receding behind them, one of the girls starts playing music on her phone (Rihanna maybe?) Sophie gives up. Her dream of Sophie on a train has been pierced. It has been turned into a nightmare. So she waits until the train reaches Lewes (she must not let the girls know they have won) and then moves through to the next carriage and seats herself opposite an incredibly fit looking man in a crisp, white shirt and tie. Unfortunately, he barely glances at her before returning to his crossword.

Finally seated in silence, she allows herself to think about her mother. Of course, she shouldn't have mentioned the Pentax tour. The Pentax tour, along with a few other subjects (namely her grandfather vanishing after the war) must *never* be mentioned. It's an unspoken rule, something they grew up simply *knowing*. Perhaps that knowledge is inscribed in their DNA.

And she had foreseen the danger, had promised herself that she wouldn't mention it, not at least until she had finished searching the archives. So why, she wonders now, as she glances at the young man's suited thigh, did she do that? Why does she always have to run her tongue over the most sensitive tooth until it screams?

Of course, she's right in a way. If the Pentax photos *did* exist in some form, then they alone could provide the justification for the entire exhibition.

Just think! An entire new body of never-before-seen work. The first (and last) continental photos ever taken by one of Britain's most famous photographers, some of them perhaps even taken on the day of his death. Not to be morbid, but they could end up defining the exhibition. *Hidden Marsden,* she thinks. *The Missing Marsdens,* perhaps. *Marsden: The Final Farewell.*

But what if her mother is telling the truth? What if no trace of the tour exists? What if she really did burn all of the negatives? But even then she owes it to her to at least be up-front about it, Sophie reckons. She could at least tell Sophie, once and for all, what happened.

And now Sophie has upset her and that's something that could last until she apologises, until she repents, until she grovels on hands and knees. She will pay for today and she knows it. Barbara can sulk for years if need be. It could even prevent her accessing the rest of the boxes. She needs to get Jon on her side. Her mother listens to Jon. Jon will talk her down.

God! Jon! Her mother will try to phone Jon immediately and if Sophie doesn't get there first . . . She pulls her phone from her pocket and chooses Jon's name from the contacts list.

"Hi Sophie," Jon says, answering almost immediately. "I'm on the other line. I'll call you back."

"Is it Mum?"

"Yes, it's Mum."

"But I need to talk to you, Jon."

"I can imagine. I'll call you back."

174

Damn! Sophie runs a hand across her face and groans, soliciting a peek from the guy with the newspaper. "Sorry," she murmurs.

He smiles vaguely and shrugs, then lowers his gaze to the newspaper again, and Sophie allows herself a longer glimpse. There's something incredibly sexy about the starched whiteness of his shirt, the silky grey tie . . . something about the way his clothes envelope his body, the way his wrist appears from thick double cuffs. He's gym built underneath, Sophie thinks. That's why he looks so good. He'd make a good model.

Sophie remembers guiltily that she's dating Brett, and forces herself to look away, forces herself instead to think about her mother talking to Jon, right now.

He spoke to her in his special, older brother voice, a voice that says, "I find you trying, sister. I find our mother trying too, but I find you more so. But I shall deign, as ever, to be reasonable in the midst of your unnecessary, self-inflicted drama because I am the older brother. I am the sensible one." All of this was contained in his tone of voice and Sophie is pretty sure that she's not imagining it.

Jon was different when they were younger. As a kid, he had been a cheeky daredevil. No one ever roller-skated faster than Jon. No one ever climbed higher or grazed his knees more often. As an adolescent, no one could cheek you more wittily – so wittily and so subtly, that you didn't realise what had happened until it was over. And even then you didn't know whether to laugh or cry.

But all of that changed when he met Judy. Smiling, shallow, manipulative, artless Judy.

It's not that Sophie has any reason to dislike Judy, she has never been anything except polite to her. It's what Judy has done to Jon that Sophie can't stand, the way she winds him around her little finger, the way she never says what she wants (and thus always passes for a wholesome queen of cool) while simultaneously always getting exactly what she wants all the same, through low level, discreet, grinding warfare. "Do you think it's a good idea to be eating so much dairy?" Judy would say. "Another yoghurt? Really? OK . . . Well, go ahead!" "Are you sure you don't want to try soya in your tea?" she would ask. And just six months down the line, Jonathan announced that he was vegan, and Sophie knew that this was not because he *wanted* to be vegan and it wasn't in any way because he believed in veganism either. It was simply because being vegan was so much less tiring than having to hear Judy bang on about dairy products all day long.

And then there was Judy's 'art'. Jon had reasonable taste until he met Judy. Sophie knows that he hated Judy's horrific paintings at first sight. She knows this because Jon told her so after his first ever date with her. "The only thing that might be difficult," he had said, "is that she thinks she's a painter. And she really *isn't*."

And Judy *did* think that she was a painter and, as ever, Jon's belief system proved to be the most malleable thing around. Now he claims to 'believe in her' as an artist and denies ever having said otherwise. "Nope," he says. "Nope, her art was one of the things that attracted me to her. Definitely." He believes in her to the point of having let her give up work so that she can 'paint'. To the point of subbing her exhibitions and paying for her framing. And to the point of expecting his friends *and family* to turn up to Judy's toe-curlingly amateur private views (the horror!), expecting Sophie to look at what amounts to shit-on-canvas and be full of praise.

Sophie isn't sure if the real Jon is still hiding somewhere deep within, waiting for the thought police to vanish in order to show himself, or if Judy has managed to definitively obliterate him. Perhaps she will never see Jon again. Perhaps she just needs to get used to that idea.

Her phone rings, so she glances at the cute guy, sends him an apologetic shrug, and answers.

"Oh, well done," Jon says. "You've done yourself proud this time."

"I . . ."

"I thought you wanted Mum's help with the exhibition."

"Help? Now that would be a fine thing."

"All the work is in her loft. How do you think you'll get to it unless you keep her on-side? I know it's a challenge for you, but you have to actually be nice to her."

"I wasn't being un-nice, Jon. You know what she's like. I was just trying to find out if she thought any of the Pentax photos were—"

"Do you ever think of anyone but yourself?" Jon interrupts.

"That's unfair. I'm doing this for all of us. And for Dad."

"No you're not. You're doing it for you. But that's not my point, Sophie. My point is that he *died* on that tour. He died, so just try to think how that must have felt for Mum. Try to imagine how she felt about the fact that that tour took the last three weeks of his life away from her."

"But I—"

"I haven't finished," Jon says. Not having finished is one of his specialities. Sophie rolls her eyes.

"How do you think Mum felt about never being able to say goodbye to him? This is painful stuff, Sophie. It's painful for Mum and it's painful for me. Those boxes are all we have left of him and you're lugging them down from the attic and spreading them all over the floor higgledy-piggledy and leaving everything in a state when you leave."

"I did not leave the house in a state and if that's what Mum's saying . . ."

"Mum didn't say anything. I'm just imagining."

"Oh, come on, Jon. Higgledy-piggledy? And that's supposed to not be Mum?"

"She didn't say anything."

"She so did."

"Whatever, it doesn't matter," Jon says. "The point is . . ."

"It does matter. Because she's lying to turn you against me. I'm going to phone her and . . ."

"You're *not* going to phone her," Jon says. The older brother voice is back and it's a voice Sophie finds surprisingly difficult to resist. "You're going to chill out and then you're going to come to dinner here next month so we can smooth everything out."

"I'm sorry, Jon, but I don't *want* to come to dinner and I don't want to wait a month. I *want* to go through my father's photographs and they're in our mother's attic."

"Trust me. The best way to ensure that happens is for you to come here and for us to have a nice family dinner together like civilised adults. You know how this works, Soph. You know how *Mum* works."

Sophie sighs deeply. "If I do, will you back me up? Will you be on my side?"

"Your side? This isn't a war. And if that's how you feel then you need to . . ."

"About the exhibition. Will you back me up. About it being a good idea? Will you tell her you think she should help me?"

"Maybe."

"Maybe?"

"I'm not sure if it *is* a good idea to be honest."

"Really?"

"Really."

"Why?"

"I don't know."

"No, come on. Why wouldn't it be a good idea?"

"I don't know. It's just a feeling. An intuition."

"An *intuition?*" Sophie repeats. Because if the words *higgledy-piggledy* had her mother's footprints all over them, *intuition* can *only* be something Judy has said, a suspicion confirmed by Jonathan's next phrase.

"We just feel that you're setting yourself up for a fall," he says. "We just feel that some things are better left as they are."

"*What* things are better left as they are?"

"I don't know."

"You don't know?"

"No."

"Right," Sophie says, now almost as angry as when she left her mother's. "And who's 'we' anyway?" She has always hated Jon's 'we'. It has always seemed so much less personal, so much less honest than 'I'.

"We?"

"You said, '*we feel*'."

"Oh, Jude and I."

"And Jude has an opinion on this because . . .?"

"She *is* in the art world, Sophie," Jonathan says. "She knows about this stuff."

Sophie's mouth drops. She pulls an astonished face, safe in the knowledge that Jonathan can't see her.

"Sophie?" he prompts.

But Sophie is speechless. Or rather, nothing that she can think of to say would be acceptable here, and for once she manages to hold her tongue.

"Sophie?" Jonathan says. "Can you hear me?"

And this gives Sophie an idea. She is in a train, after all.

"Jonathan?" she fakes.

"Yes?"

"Jonathan?"

"Yes, I'm here."

"Jonathan. Oh, look, I'm on the train. I don't know if you can hear me but I can't hear you. I'll call you back from a landline."

She switches her phone off and glances back at the guy opposite. He is running a beautifully manicured finger around the contour of his lips as he studies his crossword.

As the train rounds a bend, a brief ray of sunlight sweeps through the carriage and the blond hairs on the back of his hand shine in the sunlight and his diamante cufflink sends out little morse signals of rainbow colour. Sophie imagines sitting on his lap and running her hands across his chest, slipping her arms around that crisp collar. She imagines his beautiful hands undoing her blouse. She wonders if Brett will be home. She could do with a shag. Yes, that's what she needs.

1954 – PECKHAM, LONDON.

"Oh, hello," Barbara says, fumbling with a lock of hair that keeps falling into her eyes. "Gosh. I was working so . . . Come in, come in!"

Diane is standing on the threshold of their tiny two-room flat looking pretty and relaxed and summery in a pleated halter-neck dress. Barbara, in skirt and pullover, with her hair tied back, feels dowdy and unattractive and flustered.

"Sorry about the mess," she says, glancing nervously around the room at the piles of clothing in various stages of assembly. "But as I say . . ."

"It's fine," Diane says. "You should see my place!"

"And I've no idea when Tony will be home."

"That doesn't matter either," Diane says. "It's you I came to see!"

Barbara senses that she blushes at this and hates herself for it.

"How have you been?" Diane asks. "How's London been treating you?"

Barbara is scooting around the room, reuniting all of the various piles of textiles into one single, unstable pile that she will have to re-divide once Diane has gone. "I'm fine," she says. "I feel a bit like I've become my mother, but other than that . . ."

"Because?"

"Oh, just all of this," Barbara says, waving her arm in a gesture that is meant to encompass the small dingy room, the piles of cloth, the sewing machine, the tiny flecks of thread that stick to everything like dog hair.

Diane brushes the fluff from the velvet of the armchair before asking, "May I?"

"Of course! Of course! Please. Sit down."

"It must be nice to be able to work from home though?" Diane says, but from the perspective of someone at college, someone who doesn't appear to have to work *at all*, Barbara is unable to see how this can be a genuinely held opinion.

Diane spreads out her dress and sits and crosses her legs. She has lost a lot of weight this last year, Barbara reckons, and she wears more make-up these days too. If she just did something with those eyebrows, she'd look a lot like Suzy Parker. "That's a lovely dress," Barbara tells her. "Quite a change for you though, isn't it?"

"I know!" Diane says. "It's gorgeous, isn't it? It's my room-mate's. Her folks have a dress shop in Oxford and she has more outfits than she knows what to do with. Luckily we're exactly the same size."

"That *is* lucky," Barbara says. "So, how *is* art college? Are you enjoying it?"

"It's a lot more work than I expected," Diane says. "That's for sure."

"Really?"

Diane nods. "Coursework, reading assignments, life drawing classes, essays . . ."

"You're brave," Barbara says. "I wouldn't know where to begin."

"My room-mate is a help. She's a second year, so when I get stuck I can ask her."

"She sounds like the *perfect* room-mate," Barbara says.

"She is. Marie is great." Diane smiles broadly at Barbara now, then scans the room, and Barbara imagines seeing the scene through Diane's eyes and feels a little embarrassed, then a little angry that, for no reason she can identify, Diane ends up floating around art college in designer dresses while she sits in what is little more than a bedsit sewing shirt sleeves all day. She wonders how that came to pass. She wonders where she went wrong.

"And how's Tony?" Diane asks.

"He's fine. He's a bit tired and grumpy at the moment to be honest, but don't tell him I said so."

"He can be like that. I know."

"He's had a lot of long trips recently. He was in Manchester on Monday and Dorset yesterday, then Manchester again today. I think he expected shorter ones, more around London."

"What's he in Manchester for?"

Barbara shrugs. "To get a package, I expect. Or drop one off. I don't really know what's in them. I'm not even sure Tony knows. But it's newspaper stuff. Films and prints and things. Actually, that sounds like him now. That's lucky."

The door to the flat squeaks open and Tony stomps into the room, downs his crash helmet, then pulls off his gloves. He looks from Barbara to Diane and back again, then says, "This is a surprise. What are you doing here, Diane?"

There's something fake in his tone, something specifically about the way he said her name that makes Barbara wonder, just for an instant, if this wasn't pre-arranged.

"I just thought I'd drop in. How was Manchester?" Diane asks. If they *are* lying, she's much better at it than Tony.

"Raining," Tony says. "It's always raining in Manchester. Luckily I got sun all the way home, so I dried out."

"Shall I make tea?" Barbara asks. "Are you staying to eat with us?"

"Of course she is," Tony says. "And then we're going to go out for a drink, aren't we? There's a lovely little boozer down the road."

"Are you sure, Barbara?" Diane asks. "Are you sure it's no trouble?"

183

And Barbara wants to reply that staying for tea is no trouble at all, but that she'd really rather not go out for a drink afterwards. She's tired. And she resents the fact that all it takes is Diane's appearance and suddenly Tony has the money and time to go out on the town. He hasn't taken *her* for a drink in months. "It's just omelette and chips," she says.

"Have you got enough?"

She nods. "I got half a dozen eggs this morning."

"OK then," Diane says, beaming at her. "Thanks. Mum says they're really hard to come by in Eastbourne."

"Eggs?"

"My mum said that too," Tony agrees.

"It's because they came off ration," Barbara explains. "So everyone's going a bit mad with them. But you can get them in London just about anywhere. You just have to go first thing."

She removes the final pile of sleeves from the dining table and adds it to the tottering heap in the corner, then heads to the kitchen end of the room and switches on the Baby Belling. As she starts to peel and chop the potatoes, she listens to Tony and Diane talking behind her and feels a little jealous at their instant intimacy and at the way the tone of their conversation shifts as soon as she leaves it.

"I've just been to an exhibition," Diane is telling Tony now. A case in point. Because Diane could perfectly well have told *her* about the exhibition if she had wanted to.

"Canaletto," she continues. "He was Venetian, so there were all these beautiful paintings of Venice and the canals – incredible skies and reflections on the water."

"I saw a photo-reportage on Venice in the *Sunday Post*," Barbara offers, over her shoulder. "It looks beautiful. I'd love to go there."

"Yes," Diane says, "I'm sure it's great." Then, to Tony, she continues, "He liked to paint outdoors, whereas most of

184

the masters did their work in a studio. They say that's why his work feels so much more real. Why there's so much *light* in them."

"Sounds really interesting," Tony says.

"It is. You should take Barbara. It's at the British Museum."

"We don't have much time for exhibitions, do we Babs?"

"No," Barbara laughs. "Not much."

"I don't have much time for day trips to Manchester," Diane says. "At least you're getting around. And least you're seeing the country. I've never even been up north."

"I suppose so," Tony says, doubtfully.

"And I have to write five thousand words on Canaletto by Friday," Diane says, "so . . ."

"Five thousand?" Barbara asks. "How many pages is that?"

"About twenty, I think," Diane says.

"What will you say?"

"I don't know yet. I'll probably get a book from the library and see what they say first and then take it from there."

"But you're enjoying college, then?" Tony asks, groaning now as he strains to pull off his boots. "Sorry if my feet smell."

"They don't," Diane says. "And yes. College is great. It's completely different from school."

"That's good."

"They treat you much more like adults. And the people there are more fun, more interesting than at school. But it's hard work too. I have to do a lot of things I'm not very good at."

"Such as?"

"Such as drawing and—"

"Your drawings are OK," Tony says.

"Well, I thought so too until I saw everyone else's. And landscape painting. I *hate* oil paints. They're impossible to do anything with. And writing. Which I'm useless at. And being a girl, I feel a bit like all eyes are on me."

"Are you the only girl, then?"

"No. There are two of us in my class. And twenty men."

"What about photography?" Tony asks.

"St Martin's isn't big on photography," Diane says. "They don't consider it proper art, I don't think."

"No one does, really. It's a shame."

"In America they do, apparently. A bit anyway. And what about you? Are you still taking pictures?"

"Yes," Tony says. "Yes, quite a lot."

Barbara frowns and wonders how it could be possible that she doesn't know this, or if perhaps it isn't true – if perhaps it's an invention that reveals that Tony feels as insecure in the face of Diane's art-college evolution as she does. "I'll show you some," Tony says. Barbara pauses peeling potatoes and looks over her shoulder to see where Tony keeps these pictures she has never even heard of. He pulls a folder from behind the sideboard. "I'm having trouble with the camera though," he says. "It keeps getting stuck."

"Stuck?"

"Yes. So you can't turn the knob to move the film on."

"Show me," Diane says, so Tony reaches in his saddle bag and pulls the old Rolleiflex out.

"Oh, yes, that *is* stuck," Diane says. "You need a darkroom, really. How thick are these curtains?"

"Not very," Tony says. "In the bedroom maybe."

Barbara glances back and watches as they disappear from view. Feeling more and more angry but not quite sure why, she continues to peel potatoes, dropping them ever more violently into the strainer, but when she hears giggles coming from the bedroom, she can take it no more. She dries her hands on a tea-towel and moves to the arch between the bedroom and the lounge. The bedroom curtains have been closed but just enough light remains to see what is happening. Tony and

186

Diane are on their knees beside the bed, their heads beneath the quilted bedspread.

"There," Diane is saying, softly. "Feel there. It's a bit of paper or film or something stuck in the cog."

"I can't feel anything."

"There. To the left of the roller. Give me your hand."

Tony snorts with laughter.

"There, see?" Diane says.

"Oh yes . . . I think . . . yes."

"Gosh, your hands are really cold," Diane says.

"It's because of being on the bike."

"Anyway, you need a pin or something. Or a needle. So we can fish that out."

"Perhaps you'd like me to get you one!" Barbara says loudly, and she sees with satisfaction that both Diane and Tony jump at the proximity of her voice.

Tony withdraws from beneath the bedspread looking flushed.

"Um, yes. That would be good, um, sweetheart," he says.

The camera fixed and dinner eaten, Tony shows Diane (and incidentally, Barbara) his photos. They are shots of brick buildings and rusty railings, of anonymous strangers queuing for buses, of men with sandwich boards advertising the *Evening Standard*, of stray dogs digging through dustbins in Salford . . . The truth of the matter is that Barbara doesn't understand these photos. She can't see what the point of taking such photos might be, nor can she imagine who would want to look at them. She certainly wouldn't want any of them on *her* walls.

Diane, for her part, declares them "not bad" if lacking a little "heft or drama" whatever that might mean. She promises to bring Tony some books from the library that she says will "inspire" him.

And then Tony asks Barbara if she is "coming to the pub" with them and she replies that, no, she doesn't think so, and just like that, without a struggle, they are gone.

Barbara watches from the window as they head down the dimly lit street until they vanish beyond the puddle of light cast by the street lamp. She wonders why she declined to go with them. It was something to do with the fact that Tony asked her, to do with the fact that he didn't *assume* that she was coming. That seemed to make her presence optional in a way that she hadn't even imagined possible and she had felt insulted by that and somehow obliged to refuse in order to mark her disapproval. Not that she's sure anyone even noticed.

They left less than five minutes ago but she is already regretting her decision, in fact, she's coming to think that it's one of the most stupid decisions that she has ever made, that she was perhaps manipulated to react in exactly the way she did. If she had any idea which pub they were heading to, she would run and join them right now. But she doesn't know and, in some strange way, she's enjoying feeling righteous, enjoying feeling angry.

She starts (furiously) to do the washing up and, once this is done, she will tidy the flat and once *that* is done, she will sit and wait until closing time, upon which she will watch from the window as various drunks stumble along the street. And she will try to decide if she hopes that one of them is Tony, or if she hopes one of them *isn't* Tony.

2012 – GUILDFORD, SURREY.

"Please don't sigh like that. You know how guilty I feel about this."

Jonathan, who is in the process of pulling fishbones from salmon with tweezers, straightens, then turns to face Judy who has appeared (looking pained) in the doorway.

"I didn't know I did sigh," he says.

"Well, you did. It was your special big *oh-it's-such-a-drag-having-to-do-this-all-on-my-own* sigh."

"It actually wasn't," Jonathan replies. "It was a special *whoever-wrote-this-recipe-has-never-attempted-to-remove-bones-from-uncooked-salmon* kind of sigh." Virtually all of his discussions with Judy revolve around intent. She's a great believer that every throwaway remark must have been designed with intent, as if phrases were cruise missiles, as if sighs were attack drones.

"It still made me feel guilty," Judy says.

"Then I'm sorry," Jonathan says, now downing the tweezers and crossing the room to his wife. "That was not my intention." He's making extra special efforts, now that she's pregnant, to avoid conflict.

Judy rears away from him as if repulsed. "Don't touch me with your fishy fingers," she says. "I've just changed my clothes."

"Sorry," Jonathan says again, now putting his hands behind his back and pulling a face as he leans in for a kiss.

Judy pecks him chastely on the lips, a kiss limited in scope by her ongoing reproach. "And I still don't see why we have to have fish," she says.

Jonathan restrains another sigh and turns back to the chopping board so that Judy won't see his eyes rolling. "Because Mum doesn't think a meal is a meal unless multiple deaths have occurred," Jonathan says. "You know this. We've been through this."

"It's time your mother learned a little more about nutrition."

"She's nearly eighty," Jonathan says, running his finger along the top of the salmon steak, then leaning down close to tweezer out another bone. "The woman's not going to learn anything new now, so we just have to fit around her ticks."

"Ageist, or sexist? Hum. I'm not sure . . ." Judy says. "Maybe both."

"Realist maybe?"

"People can learn at any age, Jon. Even women like your mother. You know that as well as I do. Some just choose not to."

"Well, she's been choosing not to for almost eighty years. So all I'm saying is that the probabilities of the situation as regards my mother favour stasis as opposed to revolutionary transformation."

"I still don't see why—"

"Judy! It's meat or fish or half-an-hour attempting to explain why there isn't a 'main' course. So a bit of fish is the lesser of two evils here, OK?"

"Not for the fish it isn't," Judy says, a smidgin of humour in her voice.

"No," Jonathan says with a grin. "No, I suppose not."

"Anyway, it's her karma, not mine," Judy says. "I'm not eating it."

"I know you're not," Jonathan agrees, reaching for his glass of chardonnay.

"And don't get drunk before the meal. Please don't get drunk before they arrive."

"I won't."

"It's unfair. Especially when you know I can't drink."

"I'm not getting drunk," Jonathan says flatly. "This is my first glass and that was my second sip."

"Sure," Judy says, her voice full of doubt.

"You can check the bottle if you want," Jon offers. "It's in the fridge."

"God, Jon! You make me sound like the wine police or something."

Jonathan chuckles. "The wine police. I like that."

"I'm just saying, don't get drunk before they even get here. Is that too much to ask?"

"No sweetheart," Jonathan says, lifting the wine and placing it on the farthest corner of the windowsill, out of temptation's way. "So, I'm wondering. If I feed Mum fish, whose karma gets fucked the most?" he asks, feeling suddenly devil-may-care and vaguely feisty, perhaps due to the now out-of-reach glass of wine.

"You're being silly," Judy replies. And it's true. He is being silly. But all the same, the question seems like a good one. Whose karma does get butchered the most here? The fisherman for fishing it? Him, for pulling the poor thing's bones out? His mother for eating it? Judy perhaps, for not stopping him – for letting him buy it with money from their joint account? Where do the chains of cause and effect and responsibility end here?

"Anyway," Jon says, momentarily forgetting and starting to reach for the wine before reigning in his erring hand. He reaches for the pepper instead: an alibi. "Maybe it's the salmon's karma that was stuffed. Maybe he was a really bad salmon in a previous life. Maybe that's why he ended up on this chopping board in the first place."

"Your grasp of karma is about as good as your mother's grasp of nutrition," Judy says.

"Yes. You're probably right."

"Just don't let them gang up on me like last time, OK?"

"Of course not."

"I'm your wife. And they're your family. So I'm not allowed to fight back. So I need you to stand up for me."

"I didn't let anyone gang up on you last time," Jonathan says.

"Well, they did."

And this is true.

Sophie had launched a minor attack against Judy, breaking into sacred ground via one of the weaker portals – homeopathy. It had been nothing initially but a border skirmish, but egged on by their mother (who loves her pills) and a little too much chardonnay, and backed up, seemingly, by the whole of western cartesian logic, and sensing Judy's vulnerability on the subject, Sophie had gone in for the kill. And Jon, despite believing vaguely that homeopathy probably did work (because Judy said it worked for her and why would she lie?) had found himself mechanically unable to take position in defence of his wife, had found himself unable, when faced with Sophie's mathematical explanations of the absence of any active compound in homeopathic remedies, to defend Judy's floundering theories about water having memory of having once had a molecule of Thuja near it but not apparently of having passed, since time began, through hundreds of mammals' stinky bowels. Judy had gone to bed early and made his life hell for almost a week after that one. And Jon had secretly stopped taking the Thuja 10ch pills her naturopath had prescribed (without any noticeable change to his health). And there had not been another family meal since.

"I promise I won't let them gang up on you," he says. "Now go and put your feet up."

"You want me out of the kitchen?"

"No. You've been saying you're tired all day. So I'm saying you should make the most of the calm before the storm. That is all."

"I *am* tired. Pregnancy is exhausting."

"I know. Just don't say it when Mum's here or you'll have the whole diet thing to deal with."

"What diet thing?"

"Oh come on. You know this. If you say you're tired, she'll say you're anaemic and that it's because you're vegan and then . . ."

"Jon, I'm sure your mother knows how tiring it is being pregnant."

"Yes. I'm sure she does. But that's still what she'll say. And you know how she's the world's expert on pregnancy. And nutrition."

"She's the world's expert on everything."

"You're right. She is."

"What was she like with Sophie?"

"I'm sorry?"

"When she was pregnant."

"Oh, I don't remember much."

"But you were old enough. You were five or six, right?"

"Six, yes. But I was too busy hiding in tree houses, I think."

"Tree houses? You had a garden?"

"No, we went to Wales. For three months. We came back after Sophie was born."

"Wales? I never knew that. Why on earth did you go to Wales?"

"Mum was tired or something. I think the doctor prescribed lots of fresh air."

"Huh!" Judy says.

"Huh?"

"You see, even with her half-cow per day, she was still so

tired you had to retreat to Wales. It's called being pregnant. It's exhausting, Jon."

"I know," Jonathan says. "So please go and sit down!"

"OK, OK! I'm going. Just shout if you need me, alright?"

"Alright."

Jonathan waits until he hears the sound of the television (a game show) and then sidles over to the glass of wine. He glances guiltily at the doorway, then lifts it and downs the contents in one. "Family dinners," he thinks. "Ugh!"

Jonathan straightens from the delicate operation of folding over the aluminium foil seam of his third fish parcel and sips the final dregs of his second glass of wine. He wonders if Judy will do a wine bottle audit. He wonders if she'll give him hell. *She really is the wine police,* he thinks.

The doorbell chimes, so he calls out, "Can you get that, Jude? I still have fishy fingers."

"OK," Judy calls back. "But if it's your family, they're a bit early."

Jonathan imagines the one or other members of 'his family' beyond the front door hearing Judy's shrieked words and winces, then heads to the sink and begins to wash his hands.

". . . no, she's not here yet," he can hear Judy saying. "But then we did say seven-thirty and it's not even seven."

"You look well," Barbara replies, ignoring Judy's barb about the early hour. Barbara is good at bulldozing through difficulty, at not taking umbrage, which is one of the reasons she 'gets on' so well with Judy where so many other people don't. It's a trait Jonathan has inherited, *thank God.* "Pregnancy is making you bloom, dear!" Barbara tells Judy.

"So people keep telling me," Judy replies. "Yes, just hang it there. Come through. Jon's in the kitchen wrestling with dead things."

"Dead things?" Barbara says, her voice now loud as she enters the kitchen.

"It's just fish, Mum," Jonathan says, drying his hands on a tea-towel.

"Hello dear," Barbara says, crossing the room and kissing him on the cheek.

"Hi Mum."

Judy appears in the doorway behind her, raising her eyebrows comically. "Your *mum's* already here," she says.

"Yes," Jonathan replies. "Yes, I spotted that."

"I was just saying how *well* Judy looks," Barbara says, blustering through the strained atmosphere. "She looks positively ruddy."

"She does."

"I'm *actually* feeling . . ." Judy starts, but Jonathan catches her eye and despite her annoyance that no one is actually *asking* her how she feels, she wrestles her sentence under control before it escapes her mouth. ". . . quite well," she says, wide-eyeing Jonathan and tilting her head sideways.

"Well, it's still early days but that's good," Barbara says.

"Jon was just telling me how you got so tired when you were pregnant with Sophie that you went off to Wales," Judy says.

"I didn't *exactly* say that," Jonathan says. "I didn't say it was because you were tired."

"Was there another reason?" Judy asks.

"Wales? I . . . No . . ." Barbara stumbles. "I wasn't *tired* as such. We just needed a break."

"Sounds quite luxurious," Judy says. "I wish Jon would whisk *me* off somewhere for three months."

"It was just a little cottage," Barbara says. "A little damp cottage. It was hardly luxurious."

"All the same."

"You didn't go out much, did you Mum?" Jonathan asks. "Or have I got that wrong?"

"No, not much. It rained a lot."

"But even when it wasn't raining, you never went out. I remember going to the shop with Dad."

"Yes, there was a tiny shop in the village."

"Gosh, were you laid up in bed?" Judy asks.

"No, I . . . I went a bit mad, to be honest," Barbara says. "A sort of agoraphobia thing. It happens to a lot of women during pregnancy."

"So that's something to be grateful for, at least," Judy says, nodding at Jonathan. "I don't have agoraphobia."

"We used to get stuff for Diane, too," Jonathan says. "We used to do two boxes of food. I remember that."

"Diane?" Judy asks.

"She was Dad's friend," Jonathan says.

"And she went with you to Wales?"

"It was actually Diane who found the cottages," Barbara explains. "They belonged to some distant aunt of hers or something. And she worked as his assistant sometimes."

"Drink, Mum? There's some rather nice white open," Jonathan says, pulling the bottle from the fridge.

"What happened there, Jon?" Judy asks, nodding at the bottle.

"I used quite a lot in the fish parcels," Jonathan lies.

"I'm OK for the moment," Barbara says.

"I'm not drinking either, obviously," Judy says, patting her belly.

"Oh, actually, go on then," Barbara says, soliciting daggers from Judy. "Can't have him drinking alone, can we?"

"Did Sophie manage to track her down then?" Jonathan asks, as he pours two glasses of wine.

"Diane?"

"Yes. I know she wanted to get in touch with her."

"No. I don't think she did. And please don't bring it up in front of her. She's been driving me insane about Diane."

"What did this Diane *do* exactly?" Judy asks.

"She developed and printed some of his films. He was never very good at it," Barbara says. "He never had the patience."

"He must have been doing *very* well to have a travelling assistant."

"No, not really. Not at all, in fact. As I say, the cottages were free of charge. Because they were in her family. And she was sort of a family friend more than an assistant."

"Shall we go through to the lounge?" Jon asks.

Barbara leads the way and Jonathan follows her.

"I'll just serve myself a drink then, shall I?" Judy asks, but Jon and Barbara are too busy talking to hear her, so she sighs, pours herself a glass of Perrier and follows on into the lounge.

"What time did Sophie say?" Jon asks her when she joins them.

"Seven-thirty," Judy says. "I told everyone seven-thirty."

"Everyone?" Barbara asks. "Gosh. Who's coming?"

Jonathan laughs. "No one else," he says. "Unless Judy's invited Manchester United as a surprise treat?"

"I haven't," Judy says with a fake smile.

A silence falls across the room, born of the simple fact that all three people present, including Judy herself, are attempting to analyse why she said, *'everyone'*. Jonathan solves the riddle first and quickly attempts to change the subject before his mother decodes yet another disguised barb. "So . . . tell me more about Wales," he says. "Other than the fact there was a tree house, I don't remember much."

"There were two, actually," Barbara says. "You loved those tree houses."

"And did you actually *have* Sophie in Wales?" Judy asks, as if Wales were the Sahara, as if Wales might not have midwives or hospitals.

"To be honest, I'd rather talk about something else," Barbara says, in a flat, controlled tone of voice. "It was a horrible time for me. I've been doing my best to forget it all."

"Horrible? Because?"

"Mum *said* she doesn't want to talk about it," Jonathan points out.

"OK, OK. I just wondered what was so horrible. The holiday in Wales, or having a baby? Sorry."

"The house was tiny and damp, and impossible to heat," Barbara says, her tone a little exasperated. "The wood-pile was all soaked through because it had a leaky roof, so we could never get the fire to light. It rained almost constantly and, as I said, I wasn't well."

"Right," Judy says. "Not good then."

"And *please* don't bring it up once Sophie's here."

"Why does Sophie want to contact Diane anyway?" Judy asks.

"For this silly exhibition of hers," Barbara says. "But it's utterly likely that she's passed away."

"Oh that would upset Sophie," Jonathan says. "She really liked Diane."

"Yes."

"Sounds like her now," Judy comments, detecting some subsonic vibration from the direction of the porch and, sure enough, the doorbell chimes a moment afterwards.

"I'll go," Jonathan offers, already standing.

"Well, *thank you!*" Judy says.

"Anyway, you *do* look well," Barbara repeats, once Jonathan has left the room.

"Yes," Judy says. "You said. Thanks."

It is just after midnight by the time Sophie gets home. Brett, who promised he'd wait up for her, clearly has not done so.

198

Sophie can hear his snoring the second she opens the front door.

She's disappointed about this. She's feeling upset – a hard-to-define mixture of various unsettling emotions: insecurity, aloneness, inadequacy, irritation – a familiar set of feelings that only family dinners have ever managed to conjure up. She had been hoping, on her return, for a friendly ear and a supportive hug, something to allow her to feel that even if *that* family didn't work too well, at least *this one* did.

She steps out of her shoes and hangs up her coat, then pads barefoot to the lounge where she's surprised to discover Brett asleep in an armchair. He has an art book on his lap and his glasses are cutely skewed. He apparently *tried* to stay up, bless him.

She pours herself a slug of Brett's whisky, downs it in one and then serves herself a second shot. She spent most of the evening gagging for more alcohol to soften the pain of listening to Judy but like Jonathan with his dairy products, she found it easier to forego getting sloshed than to tolerate any additional sniping about her alcohol intake.

She passes behind Brett and gently lifts away his glasses, folds them and places them on the coffee table feeling a little surge of love for him as she does so. She moves across the room and takes a seat opposite him. She sips at the whisky and studies Brett's features, spooky in the light from the reading lamp.

Some muscle he must contract when awake has relaxed now, and his belly has expanded even beyond its normal generous dimensions. He looks fatter and older. But softer too. He always looks a little crafty when awake: sly and perhaps a little too pleased with himself. Asleep he looks innocent, childlike and geriatric all at once.

Sophie imagines him waking up and asking her how her

evening went and she sighs. She wouldn't know what to say if he *were* awake to talk to.

In the morning, when she wakes up, she finds herself enlaced in Brett's hot arms. His body temperature seems to be a couple of degrees higher than hers which is a source of added ecstasy during sex, a supplier of comfort in winter and a sweaty irritation in summer. She yawns and stretches her legs and Brett says, "Awake?"

"Uh-huh."

"You survived then?"

"Umh . . ."

It's not until Brett has showered and dressed that they discuss Sophie's evening and when Brett asks her, "So, how did it go?" she realises that some unconscious mechanism has been operating during her sleep which has allowed her to process the events of the night before. "It was awful and fine, both at once," she says.

"Right . . ."

"Awful because I hated almost every second of it, and fine because it was successful."

"Successful? You got them on board for the exhibition, then?"

Sophie laughs. "No. I didn't mention it once. I was under strict instructions from Jonathan not to mention it and he was right. As official favourite child he knows much better how to handle Mum than I do."

"How was it successful then?" Brett asks, now lifting his collar and pulling his tie around his neck.

Sophie sips her coffee before replying. "The thing with Mum, as Jon correctly identified, is not to let her realise that you need something from her. As long as you don't need it, she'll give it freely."

"Because?"

Sophie shrugs. "Because there's no power to be gained by denying it, I suppose."

"Sure," Brett says. "That makes sense. A sort of Woody Allen sense but sense all the same. So what did you talk about?"

"Jon's job, the human rights – or fishy rights or whatever – of fish . . ."

"The rights of fish?"

"Yeah. Jon cooked salmon for the three of us and I don't think Judy was thrilled about it. So she regaled us with tales of the environmental horrors of salmon farming whilst we ate."

"Nice."

"She's probably right to be honest but she's just so annoying, you can't really help but play devil's advocate."

"My sister's like that," Brett says. "Except that unlike Judy she's invariably wrong."

"Oh Judy's *generally* wrong about most things," Sophie says. "I just meant she was probably right about salmon. But I'm not sure what you *can* eat these days. It's all a bit fucked-up, isn't it?"

"Brown rice maybe?"

"Well, quite. She showed us her latest paintings of course."

"Of course. And?"

"'Ugh' pretty much sums it up."

"It doesn't sound like a very fun evening."

"No. Well, it was never going to be fun. But it smoothed things over with Mum, so I can go down next weekend and carry on as if nothing happened. So in that, at least, it was mission accomplished."

"Good," Brett says, pulling on his jacket. "Sorry, but—"

"I know, you have to run."

"I have to run."

Sophie puts down her coffee cup, stands, pulls her dressing

gown more tightly around her and crosses the room. She smooths out a crinkle in Brett's collar. "I was hoping for a shag," she says.

"No can do. Editorial meeting at nine."

"OK. See you tonight."

"See you *tomorrow*."

"Damn, I forgot, you've got that private view thing to go to in Liverpool."

"I have."

Sophie follows Brett to the front door, hands him his satchel, then kisses him goodbye and closes the door after him.

She turns back to face her silent flat then stands, with Brett's footsteps receding behind her, and stares at the interior. It looks somehow alien. It looks odd like a film set, odd perhaps, like a Kubrick film set. The emptiness of last night has returned, only this morning it is clearer to her where it comes from. Spending time with her family makes her feel like a child . . . No, not like a child but like an *impostor* – perhaps a child pretending to be an adult. Why doesn't she feel as grown up as Jon and Judy, or her mother, or Brett even? She's a pretend artist, in a pretend artist's flat, with a pretend boyfriend. She sighs deeply, then frowns as she struggles to remember first what day it is, and next what her pretend artist's schedule is for today.

"Monday," she mutters, then, "Shit!" She strides through to the kitchen and checks the clock: 8:04. "Shit, shit, shit!" she spits. She's supposed to be on the other side of London; she has a photo shoot at nine. She has a very *real* photo shoot at a very specific time.

1962 – PECKHAM, LONDON.

"How many months is it now?" Phil asks. Phil is Tony's best friend from work, a news photographer at the *Mirror,* and this being Barbara's fourth pregnancy in the ten years he has known them, he knows better than to ask when it's 'due'. Because like Barbara and like Tony, he knows the sad truth is that it probably isn't due at all.

"This is four months," Barbara says, then, to answer some unspoken question lingering in the air, she adds, "So yes, this is the longest I've ever carried term. We're keeping everything crossed."

"Keeping everything crossed" – that oft repeated mantra, a mantra that doesn't even begin to describe the hope and the fear, the terror and the yearning surrounding each pregnancy.

This time, her fourth attempt, Barbara feels ready for anything. She feels ready even for the heartbreak of another miscarriage. She knows the horror now, is familiar, even intimate with it, the way one is intimate with a devious, despicable relative. And though even a *familiar* horror remains horrific, the knowledge that she *can* survive this makes it at least possible to face up to the future; it makes it possible to go through all this hoping.

She is ready to be told that she can never try again as well. The doctors seemed doubtful that she would even be able to get pregnant again after last time. Her womb, they say, is 'under-developed'; it is 'damaged'. But when she asked the (rather abrupt) doctor if it was OK to keep trying, he said, "there's never any harm in *trying*, dear. Just don't get your hopes up."

So try, they did. And now, getting their hopes up, they are.

She's ready for Tony to leave her if it all goes wrong too. She has sensed his growing desperation for children, his growing impatience with her for failing to provide them; she has measured the way her failure to do so has gradually belittled her in his regard. She senses how Joan and Lionel have come to see their son's marriage as a mistake, for the simple reason that it is 'fruitless'. A fruitless marriage to a 'barren' woman. She's certain that this is what people say behind her back. Why would Tony choose to stay?

So yes, this fourth time feels like the last time. She can see it in people's eyes, she can hear it in their sighs. She can sense it deep within – can detect it in the vibration of the space between matter, in an emptiness that longs to be filled. The last time. Her last chance. She's keeping everything crossed.

"You make sure you take things easy," Phil is saying.

"Oh, I'm taking things *very* easy," Barbara replies. "Tony won't let me do anything. I hardly even leave the flat these days."

The front door opens and Tony returns, a clinking bag hanging from his hand.

Barbara eyes the bag. She mentally estimates the weight and deduces the number of bottles within – perhaps five or six. She sighs with relief. The boys really *are* just going to 'have a couple' as Tony said they would. It's been months since his last binge and this makes her feel nervous. A binge is overdue and Phil could well have been, as he has been so many times before, the catalyst that sets Tony off. But she's guessing from the weight of the bag that they're safe this evening.

"I got you this," Tony says, pulling a bottle from the bag and handing it to Barbara.

"What's that?" Phil asks.

"Irn-Bru," Barbara explains, taking the bottle. "It's got iron in it, so it's good for pregnant lassies like myself, or so they say."

"That's what Mum reckons anyway," Tony says. "Swears by it, she does."

"And the fish and chips?" Barbara asks.

"He said to come back in half an hour," Tony says, glancing at the clock on the mantelpiece. "They've got a backlog to get through. It *is* Friday, after all."

"Why *do* people eat fish and chips on a Friday?" Phil asks, taking a bottle of pale ale from Tony's outstretched hand.

Tony shrugs. "Because it's the end of the week?" he says. "Because they're too knackered to cook?"

"I think it's a Catholic thing," Barbara ventures. "I think it's something to do with Lent."

"We have fish and chips every night," Tony says. "I hope it's not a sin."

"Not *every* night."

"Third time this week . . . ."

Barbara pulls a guilty face. "Cravings," she tells Phil in a confidential tone of voice. "And they say it's best to go with what you fancy. They say it's the baby asking for whatever it needs to grow big and strong. And what this one seems to want is fish and chips. And tartar sauce. Particularly the tartar sauce."

"Well, I'll drink to a big strong baby," Phil says.

Tony heads to the kitchen area and returns with a bottle opener.

"Oh, get glasses," Barbara protests.

"Phil doesn't mind, do you?"

Phil shakes his head solemnly and levers off the bottle cap.

"I do!" Barbara says.

"I'll go," Phil says, standing.

"Girls!" Tony laughs.

"So, are you moving?" Phil asks when he returns with Barbara's glass. "Have you decided?"

"We're waiting to see what happens, aren't we?" Tony says.

"What happens with . . .?"

"We're waiting to see if Babs can keep this one in till the end," Tony says.

Though Barbara knows he's just making light of their heartache, she hears the accusation inherent in his choice of words. Because after all, how difficult could it possibly be to *keep it in*?

"If I get to six months, we'll move," Barbara explains. "That's what we decided."

"But you'll stay around here?"

"Babs wants to move back to Shoreditch," Tony says. "She wants her mummy, don't you?"

"I think we'll need Mum to babysit," Barbara explains. "If we ever get that far," she adds, tagging a conditional onto the end of her sentence like a good luck charm.

"So come on," Tony says, addressing Phil. "Show me these pictures of yours."

Phil retrieves a green marbled folder from beside his chair and snaps back the elastic straps. Within are twenty or so glossy colour photographs which he begins to hand around.

"I love that smell," Barbara says, lifting a photograph of a yellow cornfield to her nose.

She hands it to Tony and takes the next one from Phil's grasp. The image is of a little girl in a bright blue dress stroking a cat on a deep red letterbox. "Gosh," Barbara says. "The colours!"

"These are nice," Tony says.

They leaf through the images of windswept fields, fluorescent green lawns and orange autumn leaves, passing them around the circle until they return to Phil and the folder.

"They're beautiful, Phil," Barbara comments.

Tony frowns at her.

"Well, they are!" she insists.

"She never says that about mine," Tony says with laughter in his voice, but beyond the laughter, she can see he is hurt.

"I just wish you'd take colour pictures," she says. "They're so pretty."

"Pretty . . ." Tony repeats dismissively. "Anyway, it's too expensive and I'm saving up for other things at the moment like cots and prams."

"It *is* an expensive business," Phil agrees.

"Plus the colours are all wrong," Tony says. "I'll do colour once they manage to get the colours right."

"They're getting better," Phil says. "These were taken with that new Kodacolor X film and it's a lot nicer than before. I rather like it, to be honest. I like the way everything's just slightly off-key. It makes it a bit surreal."

"Like a dream," Barbara says, fingering a photo of a deep blue sky, streaked through with red from the setting sun. "I like it too. It's like real life but, you know, *more*."

"She's good," Phil says, nodding at Barbara and then winking at Tony.

"Yeah," Tony says, swigging his beer. "I still prefer black and white. I think it's more artistic. I think it's more dramatic."

And because Barbara can hear a slight edge in his voice, an edge that she knows and fears, she backtracks. "Well, you're probably right, Tony," she says, handing the photos back to Phil. "After all, what do I know?" Tony has recently sold a few photos to the *Mirror* instead of just delivering packages, so it's important not to undermine his confidence.

"Lucky for you that's all the *Mirror* wants anyway," Phil says, apparently having decided the same thing. "And those photos you took of that demonstration were good. They were very real. Very gritty."

"Thanks," Tony says, looking as sullen as a two year old.

1963 – HACKNEY, LONDON.

Barbara lies and stares at the ceiling and waits for whatever comes next to come next.

Beside her the drip drip-drips into the tube leading into her arm. The entry point is sore now from when, using her final reserves of fury, she had ripped it out. But it was to no avail. She hadn't known her way around, so they had caught her, they had stopped her, and with an orderly on one side and a nurse on the other, they had marched her back to bed. They said that if she tried it again, they would strap her down but she's too exhausted to fight now anyway. And so she just lies here, distraught, waiting for whatever happens next to happen.

It's three days since they rushed her into hospital, three days since they cut her open and removed whatever was inside. They say it was a baby – they *say* it was a boy. But she doesn't believe them. They won't let her see it. They won't let her hold it. So how can she believe them? But something was removed, this much is sure. Behind the angry scar bisecting her abdomen, she can sense the familiar emptiness, that sad absence which says that this pregnancy is over.

The scar hurts. It's a source of a constant, throbbing pain, which during her breakout attempt, became downright crippling agony. It will heal, they say. The baby's fine, they say.

Footsteps are approaching along the centre of the ward now – hard women's heels clip-clopping against the tiles. Another tough, war-trained nurse, no doubt ready to inflict some new act of malevolence upon her. Barbara stares at the ceiling hoping that she'll simply walk on by.

Glenda's face appears above her. "Hello," she says. "Guess who I've just been to see."

Barbara swallows hard then says, "Not you as well . . ."

"Not me?"

"Even you won't tell me the truth."

Glenda laughs. She actually laughs, then says the same thing the nurses have been saying, the same thing Tony has been saying, the same thing her mother has told her. "He's fine," she says.

They're all in this together.

"He's small," she continues. "He's tiny and wrinkled like a little old man but he's fine. He's still in an incubator thing but soon he'll be out. Soon they'll bring him up to you."

But Barbara knows that this isn't true, because of the simple fact that if it *were* true, they would have let her see him. No one would put her through this agony of not knowing, this trauma of not-bonding, if it wasn't to spare her from some terrible, terrible truth.

She imagines various versions of that truth now. A baby with a huge head like the one she miscarried. A baby with one arm, with no arms. A baby that's a cretin, a baby that's mongoloid, a baby that's already dead . . .

"He's beautiful," Glenda says, patting her hand, and the cruelty of these lies, the treachery of her sister, is such that Barbara can't bear to look at her.

"I don't believe you," she breathes, allowing her head to roll away so that Glenda won't see the tears which have begun to form.

Barbara couldn't say how long Glenda stays at her bedside. These hours, these days waiting for the truth to be revealed, stretch out like chewing gum, so it's hard to count them properly. But eventually Barbara notes her absence and once the nurse has given her a pill, she drifts into sleep, her only refuge from the anguish of here and now, her only escape from this living nightmare.

When she awakens, the daylight has faded (is it still the same day?) and Tony is sitting beside her. "Barbara," he is saying. "Barbara!"

She opens her eyes and struggles against the drugs as she tries to focus on him. He looks hazy and blurred but surprisingly handsome.

"Barbara," he says again, "He's here," and for a moment she thinks he means her father. Which must surely be proof that the end of the world is nigh. She manages to raise one hand to her face; she succeeds in rubbing her eyes.

"Look," Tony says, and now she sees his face, smiling, beaming, radiant. She traces the arc of his arm to the pointing finger and beyond that, to the cot beside him.

Still struggling with her eyesight, she rolls a little towards him and peers at the cot. Inside it is a white bundle. The moment of truth has arrived. Barbara's heart begins to race. She attempts to sit up but is held back by her severed abdominal muscles. She rolls back, grimaces at the pain and then tries again.

Tony says, "Wait." He stands and pushes the wheeled cot until it touches the bed beside her so that from her new, semi-propped up position, she can see.

Swaddled in hospital blankets, she can't see much – only the baby's red, wrinkled features are visible. But it has two eyes, a nose and a mouth. Barbara gasps. It's a start.

Wincing at the pain from her stitches, she reaches out and tries to fumble with the blankets. She's sure the blankets are hiding something.

"What are you doing?" Tony asks, frowning now. "You'll wake him."

211

"I need to see," Barbara says, her voice coming out as an absurd squeak.

"Barbara!"

"Let me see. I need to see what's wrong," she gasps.

"Nothing's wrong," Tony says.

"Show me! Let me see!"

Tony stares deeply into Barbara's eyes and his own features start to collapse. He can see madness here today. Madness but also almost unbearable suffering. "OK, OK," he says. "Look."

As Barbara holds her breath, he leans over the cot and gently pulls back the blankets. As Tony, glancing guiltily over his shoulder, lifts the baby, he stirs. He kicks his legs. He has two of them. He moves his arms. Two of those as well. The legs have feet. The arms have hands. Barbara stares at him and counts toes and fingers. Five and five and five and five . . . She holds her arms out.

"You can't hold him. He has to stay—"

"Give him to me."

"They said . . ."

"Give him to me."

Tony pulls a face – resigned, compassionate. "Here. Look," he says, handing the tiny bundle over. "He's OK, Barbara." His eyes are now tearing as well as he watches her pull the child towards her breast. "He really is. Just be careful—"

"He's very red."

Tony sniffs. "They said it's normal. It's because he's early. It will go away."

"He's all blotchy."

"That too."

"He's so tiny."

"I told you. Four pounds, six ounces," Tony says. "But he's going to be fine, Babs."

"Is this one mine?" Barbara asks, almost unable to believe,

after three days with her fears, that this is her baby – suspecting that she is failing to experience some profound maternal tug that would occur were this truly her child.

Tony nods. "He's *ours*. And he's *fine.*"

Barbara bites her bottom lip and turns the baby to face her.

"I've been telling you for days," Tony says. He moves to the bed and, with difficulty, positions himself sideways so that he can enfold Barbara and the baby within his arms. His face screws up with pride and joy and a hundred other emotions that he can't even identify. "You're fine aren't you, Jonathan," he says, reaching out to stroke the baby's cheek, and the baby gurgles briefly, then begins to cry. "We've got a son, Barbara," Tony says, squeezing her hand. "We've got a baby boy."

*   *   *

The baby comes and the baby goes. Sometimes they tell her it's because she needs to rest and other times they say it's because the *baby* is overtired. But as daylight waxes or wanes, the baby and the visitors come and go and, with each arrival and each departure, Barbara feels a new set of emotions but never, she fears, quite the *right* emotions.

"*You'll see,*" Glenda had said, before the birth, "*Seeing your baby is the most amazing thing that ever happens to a girl. Everyone says so.*"

But what to do if it *doesn't* feel that way? Barbara wasn't there for the birth. Well, she was present but she was not conscious. And the baby wasn't with her when she came-to either, wasn't visible, in fact, for days. And now everything seems wrong. She can't put her finger on exactly why, but everything just seems *wrong*.

She feels anxious when they take the baby away from her and, yes, terrified whenever anyone else holds him – this much is true. But she also feels anxious when they bring the baby *to* her, she also feels terrified when *she* is holding him. She's worried, no, *convinced*, that this isn't really her baby and that if he is, then she should be feeling something more here, something much more. Yes, everyone keeps telling her that this is Jonathan Michael Marsden, but well . . .

So the baby comes and the baby goes and Barbara's overriding experience of childbirth is one of anxiety and confusion and pain. And this in turn feeds into her cycle of anxiety and confusion and pain all over again because everything around her is saying that these are not the emotions she's supposed to be feeling at all.

Of course, there is no way to reasonably express any of this, not without appearing to be the worst, most selfish mother who ever gave birth. And would that not be the truth? So on top of everything else, on top of her exhaustion, which is so dramatic that she feels as if she has been drugged, and on top of her physical pain and her anxiety attacks, so devastating that she fears that she will suffocate, Barbara finds herself having to play-act.

She jiggles the baby against her breast and smiles at Tony, emulating the kind of motherly contentment she has seen other women in the ward exhibit. She calls Glenda 'aunty Glenda' and Minnie 'granny' and the baby 'Jonathan' even though all of these things make her feel like a liar, despite the fact that all of these words make her feel like a fraud.

And somehow, day in, day out, she manages to not say the only sentences that might make any sense here. She does not collapse in a corner. She does not weep. She does not say, "Help me!" She does not say, "I cannot do this." In this, at least, she is strong.

*　*　*

214

Back home, two weeks later, she lies in bed and listens to the baby screaming.

Tony has gone to work and Minnie will not come by until her lunch break, so for the first time since the birth, there are no witnesses. For the first time there is nobody present to see what a terrible person she really is. And so she lies in bed and listens to the baby alone and crying and, as if she has split in two, watches herself to see if she cares.

The milk-van is clinking past in the street outside and the baby is screaming louder, louder now than she has ever heard any baby scream. She wonders if the milkman can hear it. She thinks he probably can.

A neighbour upstairs bangs on the floor, so in a way the witnesses are back. Someone somewhere now knows what a bad mother she is. She sighs and rolls from the bed.

She groans, lifts her nighty, and as every morning before pulling on her dressing gown, she inspects her scar. Registering a brief, unexpected lull in the noise level, she pauses in the bathroom to pee and wash her face. She stares at herself in the pocked mirror of the bathroom cabinet. She looks terrible. People keep telling her that she looks well but she doesn't. She looks truly *awful*.

The baby catches his second wind and starts howling in a new ear-piercing tone that quite simply *requires* intervention, not through maternal instinct but as a pain avoidance strategy. This specific sound must have been designed by God, Barbara thinks, to be simply *impossible* to ignore.

She runs a hand through her hair, inexplicably greasy since her return home, and then pads through to the nursery where she stands in the doorway for a moment. She closes her eyes and lets the ground-glass noise of screams, of the child's gasps as it hyperventilates, wash over her. She asks herself again if she cares. She is definitely a terrible person.

She opens her eyes again and crosses to the cot. The child is

215

red – shockingly, terrifyingly beetroot coloured. His nose is snotty and his chin is glossy with dribble. But he is still tiny – how can something this tiny make this much noise? How is it possible?

"Oh Jonathan," Barbara breathes, her voice hopeless.

And then something miraculous happens: the baby stops crying. Instantly. Just like that. His tiny blue eyes swivel in her direction.

A shudder runs down her spine, a shudder indistinguishable from a shiver of cold, only it isn't cold at all.

Frowning at the queer feeling, she reaches out and gently touches the baby's cheek and he blows a spitty bubble and gurgles vaguely. Something in Barbara creaks and splutters, like water making its way through a rusty pipe; some emotion that seems to have been locked away for so long that it's only barely familiar to her starts to rise up.

She bends over the cot (the pain of the stitches makes her grimace) and lifts the baby out. He is soaked and stinky but she lifts him and pulls him towards her; she holds his cheek to her own and begins to sob uncontrollably.

"I'm so sorry, Jonathan," she says.

When her tears subside, she is able to carry him through to the bathroom, where she removes the disgusting nappy before cleaning and talcing him. As she dresses him in fresh clothes, he stares at her wide-eyed – accusing or loving, she's not sure which. But he does not cry once.

Finally, she carries him through to the dining room where she sits and pulls him to her breast. "I'm so sorry, Jonathan," she says, as he starts to suckle. "Mum's been away. But she's back now. She's back for good."

The emotions Barbara feels towards her newborn are novel, unexpected and (even she realises) entirely unreasonable in their intensity.

When the child is asleep, she's overwhelmed by the fragility of the silken cord that attaches him to this life, to her life. She can tremble with fear at the mere thought that he might not wake up. She has heard of such things happening.

When he's awake and unhappy, she's overwhelmed by feelings of guilt at her inability to calm him, as insecure in her own capacities as she has ever been. But when he's happy, which is just over half the time, she feels a kind of ecstasy that she can't even begin to communicate to anyone else. She watches his every gesture, yearning for recognition, almost crying when he seemingly looks her in the eye, gasping when he smiles and swooning with love when he grasps a finger.

She has never known anything like this, and the whirlpool of emotions she suddenly finds herself in seems to encompass every possible combination: exhaustion, joy, fear, hope . . . There's nothing left out.

For the first three nights, they struggle to sleep three abreast in the double bed. Jonathan wakes them constantly, unremittingly. Often the lapse of time between Barbara managing to get back to sleep and the baby waking her anew is less than an hour. Tony – who claims not to be sleeping at all – heads off to work in the morning looking grey and forlorn. By the time he returns in the evening, he looks like a dead-man walking.

By day five, Barbara and Tony are arguing about the baby, about where he should sleep, about sleep itself, and by day seven, Tony has moved, grumpily, to a camp bed in the nursery. Because Barbara will not, *can* not, leave the child alone in the next room.

It's not that she doesn't want to, it's that it's a physical impossibility. The effect of his wailing on her nerves makes ignoring it out of the question. Trying not to go to him when he is crying is like trying not to breathe. And when he's *not* crying, it takes less than five minutes for the terror of not knowing if he is still breathing for beads of sweat to appear on her forehead.

So no, there are no options here. She has to be with him at all times.

By week three, it has been universally agreed, even admitted by her, that she's hysterical about the child. But Tony and Glenda have at least declared this hysteria a 'normal' reaction to her previous miscarriages. Minnie, on the other hand – no-nonsense, practical Minnie – finding herself unable to visit without arguing about Barbara's parenting techniques (she should leave the child to cry himself out, she insists) has started, simply, to stay away. And the surprising thing is that Barbara doesn't care.

In fact, Barbara finds herself unable to even think about anything other than the baby these days. Tony can sleep in the camp bed or he can stay over at Phil's or he can come home drunk or not drunk . . . He can be in a good mood, or not in a good mood and it has about as much effect on Barbara as a drop of rain on the back of her hand.

All of these aspects to her day, aspects that used to fill her world, things that made a day a good day or a bad day, have become as irrelevant to her as the weather.

It's as if an entirely new reality has been revealed to her, one that is so powerful, so absorbing, so exhausting, that anything that happened to her before Jonathan has no more bearing on her now than a story she perhaps heard on the radio, then half-forgot.

Her world is here and now. Her world is Jonathan. Nothing else matters one jot.

Logically, she can see how this is hard for Tony; she can sense that his nose has been well and truly put out of joint. But she thinks that if Tony can't feel the same gasp-inducing bond of responsibility that she feels, if he can't get over his petty feelings of jealousy, then there's little she can do about that. And the same goes for Minnie.

She worries, vaguely, the way one worries about something one has forgotten to add to a shopping list, that Tony is drifting away, that Tony is being perhaps pushed away, that Tony, even, might leave them. Occasionally she thinks back to the grinding poverty of her own fatherless childhood and understands, on a rational level, that this would be a catastrophe, and that she should probably be doing something differently here. But even these anxious imaginings can't find traction in the sea of hormones swirling around her body.

It's as if every spot of fertile land where thought processes might take root has been taken. It's all occupied. For now, inexplicably, there is no outside world. There is only Barbara and Jonathan, Jonathan and Barbara.

Sometimes she's consumed with loving him and sometimes she's consumed with fear but everything else and every*one* else will just have to wait for normal service to resume.

2012 – TRAFALGAR SQUARE, LONDON.

Sophie wipes her sweaty palms on her black trousers and glances again at the door at the end of the room. Brett had to pull serious strings to get her this meeting and she only has one chance here. She needs to not blow it.

She pulls the folder of her father's work towards her because, rather stupidly, sensing its presence (reminding herself that it's still there beside her, within reach) reassures her.

Dr. Nicholas Penny. The curator of the National Gallery, no less. She can barely believe that she's about to meet him. She checks her watch. She checks her phone. She checks her email. She checks her watch again. A single minute has gone by.

She thinks about the folder within the folder – ten of her best shots. She wonders again if she's going to have the nerve to show them. In her mind's eye, she can see herself leaving with the second folder still unopened. She can see herself chickening out.

Brett hasn't helped by remaining uncharacteristically non-committal about whether she should show them or not. "They *might* find the whole father-daughter thing interesting," he had said, the implication clearly being that, then again, they *might not*.

The door finally bursts open and someone who is not Dr Nicholas Penny appears – a young, bob-cut woman with a broad, professional smile on her face. She crosses to Sophie, who stands and shakes her hand.

"Sophie Marsden, right?"

"Yes, that's me."

"Claire Freeman," the woman says. "Please! Come through."

Sophie follows her through the door, down a long corridor and into a small, cluttered office. Sophie expects her to leave; she expects her to fetch Dr. Penny. But instead she sits down behind the desk. "Please," she says. "Take a seat."

Damn, Sophie thinks. *I'm being fobbed off with his secretary.*

"You're Anthony Marsden's daughter, right?"

"Yes. Do you know his work?"

"A little."

You so don't, Sophie thinks.

"So, what can I do for you?" Claire asks.

"I . . ." *was expecting to meet Dr. Penny,* Sophie thinks. She runs the phrase through her mind but decides against it. She just wishes she knew who this Claire Freeman was but there's no polite way to ask that. She should have researched the staff list at the National more thoroughly but the meeting was supposed to be with Penny, so she only swatted up on him. "I . . . wanted to chat with you about your thoughts on organising a retrospective of my father's work," Sophie says.

"Of course."

"We've been going through all of the archives and there's a whole body of work that people have never seen. We thought it would make an amazing show."

"Yes, I'm sure," Claire says. She's still smiling, which Sophie takes to be a good sign.

"I brought some along," Sophie says. "Would you like to have a look?"

"Um, OK . . ." Claire says. Looking confused, she stands and rounds the desk to Sophie's side.

Sophie takes a deep breath and flips the folder open. She has

221

spent weeks choosing, changing, ordering and reordering these photos. But now she's swamped by doubt, convinced that she's chosen the wrong ones.

"Gosh, what a lovely shot," Claire says, sliding the first print towards her – a photo of a group of kids in their underwear playing beneath the spray from a ruptured water pipe. "You must be very proud."

"Yes, a bit," Sophie admits. "That's 1964."

"These days, they'd all be at home on their Playstations," Claire says.

"They would!" Sophie slides the second print over the first and Claire sighs. It's a fabulous picture of a punk complete with safety-pin piercings and pointy hair, climbing onto a 'brand new' Intercity 125 train sometime in the seventies.

"That's great," Claire says. "He certainly had a good eye."

Emboldened, Sophie continues to hand her the photos one by one, and Claire considers them and makes appropriate appreciative noises. She does, however, spend a little less time on each shot than the last. When finally she reaches the sub-folder at the back, she strokes it and glances up at Sophie. "And in here?"

"Oh, those are just some of mine," Sophie says in as casual a manner as she can manage.

"You're a photographer as well? Of course you are!" Claire says, slipping a fingernail beneath the elastic. "May I?"

Sophie swallows hard and nods, happy at least that Claire has asked, happy at least that she's not having to *force* her to look at them. Claire flips open the folder to reveal the first image, Sophie's triptych: three photos of the three models, still her favourite work of the last twelve months. "That's great," Claire says, then with a fingernail on Eddi Day's chin, "She seems familiar."

"Yes, she's a fairly well-known fashion model."

Claire nods and flips quickly through the remaining shots. "Yes," she says, when she reaches the end. "Yes, they're nice. Really nice."

"Thanks," Sophie says. *Nice. Ouch!*

"So!" Claire says, returning to her own side of the desk. "I had a look at our database and as far as I can see we only have one photograph of your father's. Does that sound about right to you?"

"I actually didn't know you had *any*," Sophie admits. "Do you know what it's of?"

"A demonstration – an abortion demonstration, I believe. If that means anything to you?"

"Sure. It's quite a famous one; it won the best photo-journalism prize that year."

Claire nods and her smile fades and is replaced with something similar to concern. She opens her mouth to speak, then closes it again and works her jaw a little before saying, "I'm sorry, Sophie. But if you didn't know we had any of your father's work, then I'm a little confused about why you're here today."

"I'm sorry?"

"I assumed you wanted to organise a loan."

"A loan?"

"Of your father's work. For your retrospective. But as we only have the one . . ."

"Oh God, no!" Sophie says. "As I say, I didn't know . . . so it didn't cross my mind."

"Right."

"No, I . . ." Sophie clears her throat, a little mortified that she is going to have to spell out the reason for her visit. She had hoped that it was obvious. "I thought the concept might interest the National Gallery," she says.

"Interest us?"

223

"I thought you, the National, might want to host the retrospective."

Claire's eyebrows have risen almost to her hairline, but they now fall as recognition slides across her features. "Oh, I *see* . . ." she says.

"He would have been eighty next year, so I . . . we thought that it was a perfect opportunity. And we thought the National was the perfect venue."

Claire nods slowly. "Um," she says. "Yes. Of course."

Sophie fiddles with the folder to fill a few seconds of uncomfortable silence.

"Then that would be, 2013?" Claire finally says. "The anniversary?"

"Yes."

She pulls a strange face as if constraining a grin and then shrugs as she explains, "I'm afraid to tell you, Sophie, that we schedule our exhibitions at the National many years in advance. So if your father's work *was* something we wanted to show, I'm afraid we'd need two or three years notice. At least."

"Oh," Sophie says. "Well, there's no reason it would *have* to be 2013. 2014, or 2015 would be fine. Perhaps even later."

"Yes . . . Look, Sophie." And Sophie knows that tone of voice. And she knows that this isn't going to work. "To be perfectly honest here, I can't see the trustees going for it," Claire says.

"OK. Fair enough. Why would that be?" Sophie asks, trying to sound neither hurt, nor belligerent.

"If he had been an art photographer . . ." Claire says. "But he wasn't, Sophie, was he? He was a journalist. A very good one but a photojournalist all the same."

Sophie runs her tongue across her teeth, but no, she can't help herself. "Claire," she says. "Look, I'm not sure how well you know the photography world. But perhaps I could chat to Dr. Penny about this? It was him I was expecting to meet today."

"I'm afraid Dr. Penny delegated this to me," Claire says. "I'm so sorry we've been talking at crossed purposes. If I had known, I could have spared you the time." She glances at the clock on the wall. "And now I'm afraid that *I'm* running out of time."

"The thing is," Sophie says, aware that she's sounding desperate now but unable to leave without a final push, "there *were* no art photographers in the fifties and sixties. It wasn't recognised as an art form by any of the art schools until the seventies. So . . ."

"I'm actually quite aware of that," Claire says, smiling tightly. "My art history's not too rusty. Now, I'm really sorry but I'm going to have to go. If I can help you in any other way, please don't hesitate to ask."

Claire slides a business card across the desk and by the time Sophie has slipped it into her pocket, picked up her folder and stood up, Claire is holding her office door open.

"Oh well, thanks for your time anyway," Sophie says.

"You're welcome. Any time. You remember the way out, right?"

"I do."

"Goodbye then," Claire says. "And good luck with your retrospective."

Once Sophie reaches the street, she pauses to catch her breath. She has, she realises, broken out in a cold sweat. She wonders if Claire spotted that. As she reaches into her pocket for a tissue, the business card falls to the floor. She wipes her brow, then stoops to pick it up. 'Claire Freeman M.A. FRPS,' it reads. 'Curator of Photography, National Gallery'.

FRPS. Fellowship of the Royal Photographic Society! M.A. A Masters in art! Curator of photography!

Sophie hears her own voice saying, *I'm not sure how well you know the photography world* and breaks out in a cold sweat all over again. "Oh God!" she mutters. "Oh Sophie!"

* * *

Sophie heaves the carrier bags onto the kitchen worktop and exhales sharply. Brett appears in the doorway behind her looking, for some reason, pleased with himself. He stretches his arms and hangs there on the door-jamb grinning at her. "Food," he says. "Great! I'm starving."

Sophie glances sideways at him, raises one eyebrow and begins unpacking. When Brett sidles to her side and peers into one of the bags, Sophie slaps his hand away.

"Someone's in a bossy mood," Brett says. "I like."

"I don't," Sophie mumbles, ripping the packaging from a stack of yoghurts and adding them to the refrigerator.

"Did I do something bad, Mistress?" Brett says, which is so, *so* the wrong reply, right here, right now, that Sophie wonders if Brett has any idea who she is at all.

"You . . ." Sophie pauses and sighs. "You *could* actually help me here," she continues once she has wrestled her voice under control. "And you could even do some shopping of your own from time to time instead of waiting at home with your tongue hanging out like some untrained puppy."

"Hum," Brett says, now starting to ineffectually lift things from a bag and place them in a even less practical pile on the counter. "Someone's not in the best of moods."

"No," Sophie says. "Someone isn't."

"I can take you out to dinner if you want," Brett offers. "But shopping's not really in my DNA."

Sophie pauses, a tube of toothpaste in one hand. "It's not in your DNA?"

226

Brett shakes his head forlornly.

"And how about cleaning?" Sophie asks, brandishing the tube at him. "Is cleaning in your DNA?"

"No, not really. Which is why I pay a cleaner, I suppose."

"Right," Sophie says. "I *don't* have a cleaner. So if you could just pick up some of your shit from time to time, that would be great."

"Yes, Mistress," Brett says.

"And stop with the bloody Mistress business, OK?"

"Yes, Mistress," Brett mugs.

Sophie groans and shakes her head in despair. When Brett delicately reaches out to touch her shoulder, she shrugs so that his hand falls away.

"Did you not have a good day, sweetheart?" Brett asks, in a more genuine tone of voice.

"No, Brett. I did *not* have a good day."

"The National?"

"It was appalling. It makes my teeth hurt to even think about it."

"OK . . ." Brett says, now folding his arms defensively. When faced with one of Sophie's occasional bad moods, Brett moves quickly from concern, through compassion, to irritation. The crossed arms signal his intermediary stage. "So, how about I take you to dinner and you tell me all about it," he says.

"I have no desire whatsoever to talk about it," Sophie says. "And I don't want to go out to dinner either."

"Would you like me to leave?" Brett asks. "Is that it?"

Sophie shrugs and shakes her head. "I'm not sure what I want, to be honest," she admits.

"How about a hug?" Brett asks, uncrossing his arms and scratching his ear. "Sometimes hugs are good at times like this."

And because Sophie can tell from his voice that this is the

last chance before he moves into combat mode, before he says something like, "Well, if you're going to be like that, fuck you," and because that really isn't what she wants, she drags herself back from the brink. "OK," she says. "Let's try a hug."

Later, as the tuna fries and as she prepares a salad, Sophie thinks about her mood and attempts to decode her harshness towards Brett. The problem is that her meeting at the National has spilled over and tainted everything else. Her moods have always been this way, so she has some understanding of her own processes, even if she still struggles to control them.

On a good day, *everything* seems good. On a good day, she knows that eventually she'll break into the world of art-house photography, that her father's retrospective will be an unqualified success, and that suited, naughty Brett with his spicy bedroom tastes, his never-ending list of wonderful restaurants, and his almost unlimited connections in the art world, is the perfect man for her. But on a *bad* day, like today, she knows just as surely that the retrospective will never happen, that she's a rubbish photographer who just happened to have a famous father and that blobby, overweight, conceited Brett is too lazy around the house and too pervy in bed for her to ever build a proper relationship with him. And that none of it really matters because in forty years they will both be dead anyway.

Maybe she's bipolar and she's on a downswing. Can one be a 'bit' bipolar? It's not the first time the thought has crossed her mind. Then again, maybe she's just immature. Perhaps a calm sense of wisdom will manage to catch up with her one day, just before she finally turns to dust.

Once dinner is served, Sophie does tell Brett about the meeting.

"You should always research the staff list before meetings like that," Brett comments. "It's ever so important to understand who you're meeting."

"Thanks, Brett," Sophie says, sarcastically. "I think I got that."

"Anyway, cheer up," Brett says. "There are other galleries."

"Such as?"

"We went through this. There's the V and A . . ."

"They said 'no'."

"They did?"

Sophie nods as she picks up her fork and starts to draw circles in the raspberry vinaigrette remaining on her plate. "They replied by post. Polite. But no."

"Brett wrinkles his nose. "There's the Wapping project."

"They said no too. I spoke to what's-her-name?"

"Jules Wright?"

"That's her. She was lovely. But definitive. It's a 'no'."

"You should have let me phone her, maybe."

"I *waited* for you to phone her. You didn't."

"I was going to but . . . anyway . . . Oh, and I spoke to my contact at the Tate. But he doesn't think they'll go for it either."

"You see? It's a disaster."

"It'll just have to be a private gallery then," Brett says. "But that's OK, isn't it?"

"I suppose it'll have to be."

"The work would need to be on sale to make it worth their while. Would that be a problem for your folks?"

Sophie shakes her head. "It might even boost Mum's interest in the whole thing a bit."

"You reckon?"

"There's really no telling with Mum. But she's never shown any signs of being allergic to money."

"Well then," Brett says. "I'll have a word with my friend Mike Rowes. He knows Jean Jopling."

"And who might Jean Jopling be, dare I ask?"

"Um, she's a bit of a nobody. She just owns White Cube."

"Oh. Wow! Oh Brett! That would be great."

"See, I'm not entirely useless," Brett says.

"No, I know that," Sophie replies, forcing a smile, her first today. "And I was grateful for that meeting today. Even if I did fuck it up."

"It probably made no difference," Brett says, generously. "It probably would have been a 'no' anyway. It was always gonna be a long shot."

"I wish you'd said that before I went. I wouldn't have been so disappointed."

"I didn't want to put you off before you even got there."

"That's fair enough, I suppose," Sophie says.

"And I'm sorry about the cleaning and shopping," Brett says. "I can pay for a cleaner for here if you want."

"No, thanks. And I was being a bit unfair there. I don't do much at your place either. So I'm sorry too. I'm just having a bad day."

"All the same," Brett says. "I'd fully understand if you wanted to punish me."

Sophie is flooded anew with negative thoughts. Because the sex with Brett has been getting weirder and weirder, the scenarios more and more complex, and the hardware required to get *him* hard, ever more extensive. It's like owning a car with an ever-evolving ignition procedure. And Sophie can't help but think that she will inevitably reach a point where she takes the car back and says, "I can't be bothered with this. Can you give me something simpler? Can you give me something that just starts at the turn of a key?"

"Do you think we'll ever just have plain old sex again?" she asks.

Brett looks surprised. He actually leans towards her as if he has misheard. "I'm sorry?" he says.

"I mean, you know . . . without all the accoutrements," Sophie says. "Or is normal sex off the menu forever more?"

Brett frowns, swallows, then licks his lips. "You *are* in a weird mood tonight," he says.

"I know I am. But the question stands."

"Then the answer is, of course we can. We can have any kind of sex you want."

"Good," Sophie says.

"I'm your sex slave. I'm entirely at your command. All you have to do is say."

Sophie stares into Brett's eyes and exhales slowly. She feels like she has just had a revelation. She thinks she has just seen the future and it is Brett-less. She wonders if she should just give in to her instinct to blow it all up right here, right now. It would be so easy.

Brett, however, has sensed the danger of the moment. "OK, sorry," he says, determined to defuse the situation. "That was a stupid thing to say. You're tired. You're cranky. And you've had a bad day."

Sophie nods vaguely.

"And you just want a kiss and a cuddle and a nice, gentle, everyday bang. Am I right?"

Sophie thinks, *Wow, that was close.* She clears her throat. "Yes. That's about the sum of it," she says.

Brett stands. "Come," he says, holding out one hand.

And more because she lacks the energy for a fight than anything else, Sophie, lets herself take it and allows herself to be led from the room.

231

1968 – HACKNEY, LONDON.

Barbara is making fish pie. She leans in to smooth the potato topping with a fork and struggles to lose herself in the task. For today there is something strange going on, something she can't quite put her finger on and doesn't want to think too deeply about.

Diane is coming to dinner tonight, bringing her new boyfriend to meet them – a first – and there is a sense of anticipation hanging in the air which seems, somehow, out of proportion to the event, which ultimately is nothing more than a simple meal of fish pie shared with friends. Even Jonathan, unusually, inexplicably clinging to her knees as she works, appears to sense it.

Tony, who has nipped out for 'some booze', seems both excited and irritated in equal measure and Barbara's suspicion that he's going to get blind drunk adds to her feelings of apprehension. She's noticed in the past a certain nervousness which manifests just before he starts a bender, as if the alcohol were a safety valve that stops him imploding. And it's been a while since the last time . . . Tonight could be one of those nights.

"I need to get butter from the fridge," she tells Jonathan, ruffling his hair. He giggles and positions one foot on each of hers, clasps her thighs and says, "Go on then." Together, they toddle to the fridge, then back across the kitchen with Jonathan making robot noises throughout.

Barbara cuts tiny chunks of butter and distributes them

across the top of the sculpted potato topping and wonders if Tony will still get drunk once neither Phil (who has moved to Scotland) nor Diane are available. She can't help but sense that Diane's finding a boyfriend is a new beginning for her and Tony as well. And she doesn't want to make a false move. She doesn't want to miss that boat.

* * *

They arrive at six-thirty. Richard is a tall, skinny, nervous-looking man. His eyes dart across their faces as if searching for something, then continue around the room as if collecting details for a police report. But he's a good looking guy. He reminds Barbara of Dirk Bogarde in *Doctor at Sea*. Her eyes flick across his crisp, white shirt and his neatly knotted tie, and she wishes, briefly, that Tony dressed better.

Richard isn't the kind of person she expected Diane to end up with at all, but then again – and she notices this now – Diane's transformation from arty tomboy to elegant damsel is no longer a work in progress. Even the eyebrows have been plucked into submission. Tonight she's wearing an expensive if simple V-neck black dress over a white, large-collared blouse, with white heeled sandals. Next to impeccably suited Richard/Dirk, they look like they have just fallen out of the latest Hollywood movie. Barbara feels distinctly frumpy in comparison and vows to make some new, more fashionable clothes for herself.

Tony is shaking Richard's hand now, patting him awkwardly on the shoulder. "So you're the famous Richard we've heard so much about!" he is saying, which is strange, because Barbara hasn't heard anything about Richard at all.

They moved to this new, larger, rented flat three weeks ago, and the dining room, which smells of paint, is still very much

233

under construction. Barbara painted the walls a turquoise blue less than forty-eight hours ago and found the floral lampshade in a second-hand shop just this morning. Tony says he doesn't like the tone of blue and he *hates* the lampshade, and in truth, Barbara isn't that keen on the overall result herself. It's not as she imagined it in her mind's eye but then so few things in life ever really are. Still, it's better than entertaining surrounded by peeling wallpaper beneath a bare lightbulb. The camping table, borrowed from next door, has been covered with a tablecloth and looks fine, and they have three chairs now, so only Tony has to sit on a crate.

"So you're an architect, I hear," Tony says, revealing that he really has heard things about Richard. "That must be interesting."

"Yes," Richard replies. "And you're another photographer, so Diane tells me."

"Not really," Tony says. "Not like Diane. Just amateur stuff, really."

Diane laughs. "That's not true," she says. "He's had photos published in the *Mirror*. He's good, isn't he Barbara?"

"Yes. Absolutely."

"I only had a few published," Tony says. "I'm just a delivery guy, really."

"Delivery!" Richard says, attempting to make his voice sound enthusiastic. "At least you're out and about! I spend all day in an office. It's dreadful."

His valiant attempt at making Tony's humble employment sound interesting has the opposite effect to that intended, and hangs in the air, momentarily embarrassing everyone. "I'm going to give it up though," Tony says, after an awkward silence. "I'm going to move into photography full time. That's the plan. I'm going to do an evening class."

Barbara feels his pain and despite the fact that this has never

234

been mentioned before, and despite the fact that she doubts his ability to do what he's suggesting, she says, "You should. I *keep* saying it. You're easily good enough."

Tony glances at her in surprise. "Well, thank you!" he says.

Barbara serves halved grapefruits with glacé cherry hearts, followed by the fish pie. Tony, Diane and Richard devour the food as if they have never eaten before; they wash all of this down with numerous bottles of pale ale, yet despite the food hitting the spot and despite the alcohol, the atmosphere at the table remains chilled. Barbara can't quite put her finger on what's wrong, but the conversation remains stilted, the silences frequent and painful. By the time she serves the apple crumble, she's exhausted from the simple effort of trying to find things to say, so when Jonathan, next door, cries out, it's with a genuine sense of relief that she scuttles off to tend to him.

Diane and Richard do not stay late. By ten, unconvincingly feigning early starts the next morning, they are pulling on their coats and waving goodbyes and, arm in arm, heading down the path.

"Well, that was nice," Barbara says, once the front door has closed behind them.

"Was it?" Tony, who is barely on the right side of sober, replies.

Barbara shrugs. So they're playing this honestly. "No, not really," she admits. "It was awful."

"I can't stand those Fancy Nancy types," Tony says.

"I thought you liked him," Barbara says. After watching Tony attempt to ingratiate himself to Richard all night, she's a little confused.

"Bloody architects," Tony says. "Did you see what he was like when I said I do deliveries? Oh it must be *so* interesting being out and about like that."

"I think he was just trying to be nice," Barbara says.

"Thinks he's the bees knees, that's his trouble."

"Oh, he's OK, I think."

"I think that Diane could do much better than tricky Dicky there."

"She seems to like him," Barbara says. She almost adds, *"and he's a good looking man,"* but luckily restrains herself. That wouldn't have gone down well. She has to tread carefully when the beer has been flowing. "They sort of look right together," she says instead, her tone of voice thoughtful.

"Huh," Tony says, cracking open another beer and heading through to the lounge.

"You're jealous," Barbara whispers, behind him.

"You what?" Tony calls back.

"Nothing," Barbara says. "I just said I might turn in. Jonathan had me awake early this morning."

"Sure," Tony replies. "I'm just going to finish off these beers."

* * *

Barbara is sitting on a cushion in the corner of the room. Cold air from the draughty sash windows is drifting down her back but she won't move just yet. She's determined not to make a sound. Between her legs, her son is playing with a bright yellow submarine, driving it along the lines of the rug making spluttering, farty engine noises through pursed lips.

The purple sofa, a recent (second-hand) acquisition via a work colleague of Tony's, is occupied by four tightly packed friends from his new photography class. They are, from left to right, dark-haired Dave – in a thick, off-white, Arran jumper – pretty, hippy Alison, quiet-as-a-mouse Wendy, and sensible Malcolm.

Tony is offering them nibbles on sticks – cocktail sausages and pineapple and cheese cubes – which Barbara prepared earlier.

"The thing about cameras," Dave is saying, "is the way they make people look at things they wouldn't otherwise notice. All the little details."

"A camera is kind of like a butter knife," Alison says, wide-eyed.

"A butter knife?"

"Yeah," she says. "A hot butter knife just, you know, slicing through reality and saving it for later."

"Gosh, I like that," Malcolm says. "A hot knife through reality."

"How do you feel about the still-lives next week?" Alison asks. She always looks a little astonished at the sound of her own voice. Barbara wonders if it's because she's surprised that suddenly, unexpectedly, a woman is allowed to express such complex thoughts. None of them really expected that, and some, through luck, are better prepared than others.

"I think I prefer photographing people and places," Tony says. "I'm not so sure about bowls of fruit."

"Do you really think that's what it will be?" Dave asks, picking at his teeth with the now-empty toothpick. "Bowls of fruit?"

Tony shrugs. "That's what still-lives usually are, aren't they?"

"Hey, bowls of fruit have rights too," Alison says.

"Fruits have rights too!" Malcolm agrees, and everyone laughs, and though she doesn't get it, Barbara fakes a smile too and turns her attention to her son. "Are you pleased with your new submarine?" she whispers.

Jonathan looks up at her and beams and nods ecstatically, and momentarily there is just Barbara and Jonathan, Jonathan and Barbara, and all is right with the world. "That's Ringo," he says, pointing at one of the people in the submarine and emulating her whispered tone.

"That's right," Barbara says. "Well done."

". . . looking forward to the darkroom sessions," Tony is saying when she tunes in again. "I've mucked around developing with a friend of mine – her dad has a photo shop. But it will be good to learn all the techniques properly."

Malcolm is studying a duplicated sheet of paper covered in purple text. "It says we're studying dodging and burning," he says. "Whatever that means."

"It's about changing the exposure for different parts of the print," Tony tells him. "Dodging is when you use something opaque to reduce the exposure, and burning is the other way around. I think that's it anyway."

Jonathan crashes the submarine into Barbara's foot and makes a loud 'pow' noise and everyone turns to face them.

"How are you over there, Barbara?" Alison asks, now the submarine explosion has pierced Barbara's cloak of invisibility. "Are you sure you don't want your turn on the settee?"

Barbara smiles and shakes her head. "I'm fine here with Jonathan," she says, her heart starting to speed up as the attention of the room turns on her.

"Tony told me that you make your own clothes," Alison says earnestly.

Barbara nods and swallows. Her throat is dry. "Yes," she croaks. "Sometimes."

"That's really cool," Alison declares. "I'd love to know how to do something practical like that. I can't even sew a button on. I have to get my mum to do it."

"I . . . I think I'll go see how that quiche is going," Barbara says, now standing and pulling down her very-ordinary, shop-bought skirt.

"She cooks too, then!" Malcolm comments.

"She sure does," Tony says. "Barbara's a great cook, aren't you?"

Barbara runs her hand over Jonathan's head and the gesture calms her nerves momentarily, and allows her to take one almost normal breath which she uses, smiling demurely, to sidle past Tony's clever friends. Alone in the kitchen, she grips the cold hard edge of the sink and stares out at the yard, damp from recent rain. She tries to take deep breaths. She struggles to still her racing heart. She's having one of her 'turns' but she got away with it. She doesn't think anyone noticed.

As the conversation next door continues, she takes a tea-towel, dampens it beneath the tap and dabs at her forehead. Tony is changing before her eyes and she can sense herself being left behind, can hear him learning to have new kinds of conversations. Right now, she can hear him saying, "The thing about the camera is the way it democratises image-making. And that's going to change the way we record history."

She runs the phrase through her head repeatedly, until, on the fourth pass, she works out what it actually means. And then she manages a series of jerky, difficult breaths and crouches down to pull the quiche from the oven. It's so perfect, so symmetrical, so smooth and glossy, that it looks like a quiche from a recipe book. "I can do this," she says out loud. "I'm fine."

2012 – BRIGHTON, EAST SUSSEX.

As the restaurant comes into view, Sophie releases Brett's hand. She's nervous about presenting him to her mother and wants to be able to carefully choose the moment when she'll explain just who he is. Had Brett's editor not told her that it was 'essential' to have 'the wife' – her mother – on-board, she would have been happy to put this meeting off forever. But essential, it is. So here, they are.

Brett, who has been watching the waves, now turns and spots the Regency. "Gee, Soph!" he exclaims. "Is that it?"

"It is, I'm afraid," Sophie says. "It's supposed to be good though. It's got great reviews on TripAdvisor."

"Huh?" Brett says.

"Huh! Don't get snobby on me now."

"I just thought you might wanna take your ma somewhere a bit special, is all."

"Mum's weird about restaurants," Sophie says. "She'll like this. This is perfect. You'll see."

"And you're sure she's gonna be OK travelling all the way here on her own?" Brett asks.

Sophie nods towards the restaurant, where, seated in the window, her mother is waving. "Look. She's already there," she says, waving back.

"Nice!" Brett says, as he pushes against the door.

"Just shhh!" Sophie admonishes, following him in and crossing the spartan interior to her mother. "Hi Mum! You made it!"

"Of course I made it!"

"This is my journalist friend, Brett."

Barbara looks up at Brett and Sophie sees her give him the once-over. Her regard gives nothing away. "Hello Brett," she says flatly.

"Hello Mrs Marsden."

"You'd better tell me *your* surname if we're going that way," Barbara says.

"I'm sorry?" Brett asks, as he slides into a chair, then wriggles out of his jacket and hangs it over the seat-back.

"Mum just means you should call her Barbara," Sophie explains, sitting herself. "Brett's American, Mum. They don't do sarcasm."

"Um, *hello?*" Brett says. "We *so* do."

"Well, that *wasn't* sarcasm," Barbara says.

"OK. It wasn't. So how was the trip to Brighton, Mum?"

"Slow."

"Slow?"

"I never understood why old people have to be so *old*," she says. "That bus stopped every one hundred yards and at every single stop some pensioner got on, and not one of them had thought to fish out their purse or their travel-card before the conductor asked for it. So every stop took ten minutes and the whole trip, just over two hours."

"I said we could come to Eastbourne. I did offer, Mum."

"No," Barbara says, now picking up the menu. "This is good. I don't come to Brighton enough these days. It's a change. And you know what they say . . ."

"What do they say?" Brett asks, looking vaguely distracted as he searches his pockets for a handkerchief with which to clean his glasses.

Barbara glances at Sophie and pulls a face – a suppressed smile. It looks like, *is this the best you could do, dear?*

"He's American, Mum," Sophie says again. "And what *they* say," she tells Brett, "is that a change is as good as a rest."

"Oh, OK then," Brett says, nodding blankly. Sophie's pretty sure he has no idea what's going on here at all.

"This is much more expensive than Qualisea," Barbara announces, peering over the menu.

Sophie struggles to repress a smile. "Six quid? For cod and chips? Are you joking? We pay that for coffee in London."

"It's four-fifty in Qualisea. That's . . . um . . ."

"Twenty-five per cent less," Brett says, clearly having decided to demonstrate that he's not so stupid. "Or a third more, depending on how you wanna look at it."

"Yes, exactly," Barbara says. "A third more."

"This *is* Brighton. And we do have a sea view."

"I suppose," Barbara concedes, and Sophie watches the effort it takes her to be positive. She sees the struggle taking place behind her frozen features until finally she vanquishes the demon, licks her lips and says, "Yes, well, it's lovely. It's worth a bit extra to be able to sit and watch the ships, don't you think?"

The meal is nice enough – simple fare, competently cooked – but the conversation does not go to plan. Barbara seems happy enough to discuss Brett's American origins, or his job at the *Time*s, or his taste in clothes (she approves and wishes more men would dress appropriately, she tells him). But every attempt at guiding the conversation towards Sophie's father, or his work, or the retrospective, is quickly closed down, either through a discreet change of subject, or, when that fails, by a downright refusal to discuss the matter.

"I don't know, now let's talk about something else," Barbara says, when asked which images she'd personally like to see included.

"I'd really rather not think about it," she says, when asked

242

who, from Tony's entourage, they could invite to a potential private view. "So many of them have passed away. That's the thing."

After a walk through the centre of town and a coffee at Costa, they walk Barbara back to the seafront and wave as the departing number twelve bus forces its way into the weekend traffic.

"Huh!" Brett says, his universal exclamation.

"I told you she wasn't keen," Sophie says.

"Not keen?" Brett laughs. "That, babe, is what they call *stonewalling*."

"I thought she'd be better with you, but if anything she was worse."

"Sometimes even *my* charms fail to sway the ladies. What can I say?" Brett says, taking Sophie's arm and giving it a squeeze. They turn and start to walk back towards the Lanes, where their chic little hotel is situated. Sophie blows through her lips and asks, doubtfully, "I *can* do it without her, can't I?"

Brett shrugs. "It's like my editor said. You *can*. But at least half of the PR opportunities come through exploiting the '*Woman Who Knew Him Best*'." Brett raises his fingers to indicate the quotes around the headline.

"Exploiting . . ." Sophie repeats, pulling a face.

"Babe, you know what I mean."

"Yes. I do. So anyway, what now?"

"What now, as in . . .?"

"What now. As in *today*. More coffee? Back to the hotel?"

"I saw a store I'd like to go back to," Brett says. "Just off the Lanes."

"OK. What sort of store?"

Brett takes Sophie's hand. "You'll see."

"Oh, do tell me it's not that sordid little sex shop with all the dildos in the window?"

243

"I said," Brett tells her. "You'll see!"

Sophie hardens her features but then a few minutes later softens them again as Brett pauses outside a tiny jewellery shop. "Oh!" she says.

"Don't be disappointed," Brett mugs. "We can still do the sex shop afterwards."

Once Brett has bought Sophie an inexpensive-yet-pretty turquoise necklace and a pair of cufflinks for himself, and has teased Sophie a little with empty threats of oversized dildos, they head back to the hotel. Because they are unable to pick up the WiFi in their room, Brett heads downstairs with his laptop to check his email, while Sophie lies on the bed and attempts to think about strategies for motivating her mother but instead falls asleep.

When she wakes up, the laptop has returned but Brett is still elsewhere, so she sends him a text asking where he is and then phones her mother.

"Hello Sophie," Barbara answers. "I've only just got in. Are you missing me already?"

"I just wanted to check that you got home alright."

"I did. As you can see."

"Did you have an OK time today?"

"I did. It was a lovely change, actually. I always liked Brighton."

"And what about Brett? Did you like him?"

A ghastly silence ensues until eventually Sophie says, "God! I'll take that as a 'no' then, shall I?" She can hear her mother working her mouth at the other end of the line, almost literally mincing her words. "Come on then, spit it out."

"It's just . . ." Barbara says. "Look . . . He seems nice enough."

"But?"

"But I think you should keep him at arm's length."

Sophie pulls the phone from her ear and frowns at it before resuming the conversation by asking, "What do you mean, *keep him at arm's length?*"

"Why do you need a journalist anyway?"

"I'm sorry?"

"You know what they're like. They're only ever interested in digging up dirt. And if you *are* going to do this silly retrospective thing, then I think you need to keep Brett away from it. That's all I'm saying."

Various thoughts compete for Sophie's attention, including but not limited to: *What dirt?* and, *My mother doesn't trust Brett* and, *Do I trust Brett?* And, with a little rush of adrenaline, she also realises that most importantly of all, her mother has for the first time admitted that the exhibition might actually take place. And that's one hell of a victory.

"Brett's not really got anything to do with the exhibition," she finally says, a comment chosen to cement this new acceptance that the exhibition is a reality. "I mean, other than the fact that he's put me in touch with a few people in the business . . . But that's about it."

"That's not what it sounded like," Barbara says. "He sounded like he was running the whole caboodle."

"He really isn't."

Another silence.

"Mum?"

"Then I don't see why you brought him along."

"I'm sorry?"

"Why bring a journalist to meet me if he's got nothing to do with it all?"

"Oh!" Sophie laughs. "God, I'm sorry."

"What's so funny?"

"He's my *boyfriend*, Mum. I'm sorry. I should have said . . . I just thought you'd got it."

"Brett's your boyfriend?"

"Yes."

"Since when?"

"Since . . . a while now. That's why I brought him to meet you."

"I see," Barbara says. "Actually, I have to go now," she adds, sounding embarrassed.

"I'm ever so sorry Mum," Sophie says. "It's not your fault. I should have explained."

"Of course it's not my fault. But there's someone at the door. I have to go."

"Really?"

"Yes. Really. Talk soon. Bye bye."

And just like that, the line goes dead.

Sophie lowers the phone and grimaces at it again. "That was weird," she says, to nobody in particular.

Just at that moment, the door to their hotel room creaks open and a head-height, plastic, purple penis edges its way through the gap. It is attached, it transpires, to a horrific rubber mask that Brett is wearing.

"Ew!" Sophie exclaims. "That's even weirder."

"I'm sorry?" Brett asks, his voice muffled by the mask.

"God, no wonder she didn't trust you," Sophie says. "What *is* that?"

Brett closes the door behind him and slides the mask up onto the top of his head so that the attachment is pointing skywards like some absurd party hat. He is wiggling his eyebrows and grinning and looking generally pleased with himself. "It's called the *Vulcan Driller!*" he announces, theatrically. "So tell me, are you ready to be drilled, Babe?"

1968 – HACKNEY, LONDON.

Barbara is kneeling before the grate, folding newspaper in the special concertina fashion her mother taught her. Minnie is coming round this afternoon (the laundry is closed for repairs to the hot water system) and Barbara is vaguely conscious of the fact that she will be pleased if she arrives and sees her folding the firelighters properly. The desire to please your parents never quite seems to go away, not even once you have a child of your own.

Below, through the floorboards, she can hear Tony swearing about 'bloody coal dust'. They have just had three bags of coal (the minimum) delivered to the cellar, which is also Tony's new darkroom. Jonathan, who has been grumpy all morning, is momentarily lost in a world of Lego and she's making the most of it. He starts school next week, and though she still loves him with unreasonable intensity, and though she fears the emptiness of the house once he does start school, she is also rather guiltily looking forward to it. She's intending to use the first few weeks to finish decorating the lounge and dining room, and then she's going to look for some part-time work. She would have loved to produce a brother or sister for Jonathan but she's been forced by circumstances to make other plans. Plus, unless she can manage to bring in a little more money, they won't be redecorating the bedrooms or buying carpet for many years, if ever.

"Useless! Bloody useless!" Tony shrieks, and Barbara glances over to watch the effect of his angry voice on Jonathan, who pauses, wrinkles his brow, but then thankfully resumes play.

Barbara fills the fire with her pleated firelighters, lays a few pieces of hard-to-come-by kindling over the top of them, adds a few lumps of coal on top of that and then, with a little regret that Minnie will never see just how well folded the newspapers were, she strikes a match. "It'll be nice and warm in here soon," she murmurs.

Tony will no doubt complain about the cost. He has already said that lighting fires in September is a waste of money, but after three days of drizzle, Barbara doesn't just fancy a fire. She *needs* one.

She can hear Tony's feet now, stomping up the wooden steps. The door to the cellar bursts open with enough force that it slams back against the wall and, as she glances up from the gently rising flames, he appears in the doorway, red-faced and angry looking. "I've had enough," he says. "I'm going down the Ladywell for a pint."

"Did it not work, sweetheart?" she asks.

"No, it bloody didn't. And how I'm supposed to work in a load of coal dust, God only knows." And with that, he vanishes from view, slamming the front door behind him.

Barbara holds her breath for a moment and then, with a sense of relief, releases it. It's strange really, because she always misses Tony when he's at work, yet the truth is that she likes the idea of him more than the reality of his presence. He's always so tense, always on the verge of anger if not actually angry. So she always feels a great sense of relief when he leaves the house, as if some looming danger has passed. He has never hit her. He has never, for that matter, so much as raised a hand to her or Jonathan. But it always feels like it might be on the cards. It always seems like it could happen at any moment.

Barbara puts the fireguard in front of the hearth, then heads through to the kitchen to make herself a cup of tea. By the time she gets back to the lounge with it, Jonathan has fallen asleep, his face pressed against the strewn multi-coloured Lego bricks. She should probably move him to a more comfortable position but he's had a difficult morning and this moment of quiet – just the dripping of the gutter outside and the crackle of the fire – is heavenly. So she leaves Jonathan be, sips her tea, and stares at the flames.

Later on, once Minnie has been and gone – with an umbrella under one arm and Jonathan under the other – Barbara heads down to the cellar. There is indeed coal dust everywhere. It's in the developing trays, it's on the workbench, it's all over the borrowed photographic enlarger. "Of course it didn't work," she tuts, wondering why Tony couldn't just clean it up before he started. She has never been able to understand her husband's lack of patience, his constant need to race to the finish line. He's a good provider and the fastest DIY hand she has ever met. Other men's wives are jealous of the speed at which he can nail up a shelf – many of them wait months for such things. But ask him to sand down a window-frame before repainting it, or to clean a brush after using it, or indeed to clean up coal-dust before attempting to develop expensive photographic film, and there's just no hope. He talks more and more frequently these days about becoming a professional photographer but unless he learns a little patience, Barbara just can't see it working. Racing up and down the country on a motorbike seems to her to suit him much better.

She pulls a strip of negative hanging on a wire towards her. It contains ghostly images of people's faces but because they're so vague, she can't see who they might be.

She picks up a sheet of instructions. It says, 'Ilford Photographic Developer Solution'. She reads the text from top to bottom. It reads like a cake recipe: add so much of this to so much of that. Mix it up. Check the temperature. Wait so many minutes. How hard can it be?

She decides to clean the cellar. Yes, she'll clean up all the dust and then maybe, if he's sober, and if he'll let her (and neither of these are overly likely), she'll attempt to help him try again. Perhaps together they can master it.

* * *

Barbara has had an idea, a crazy, ingenious, slightly dangerous kind of idea that would need authorisation from someone who knows about these things in order to be put into practice, if only someone out there existed who *could* authorise such a thing. But the only people for whose advice Barbara could ask would deter her – this she knows. And she suspects that they would very probably be right to do so.

There's nothing *inherently* wrong about her plan and she can't even put a finger on what it is about this idea that makes it seem so naughty. But even before the plan has been put into action, naughty is how she feels. Naughty and excited, like a second class ticket holder who spots the opportunity to sneak into the first class carriage.

And now, here, ringing the doorbell, is Diane, who is dangerous in her own right.

Sometimes Barbara thinks about Diane and wishes they saw more of her. And sometimes Barbara thinks that she wants to *be* Diane, for there is a vibrancy about her, something edgy and risky and seductive. But other times, most of the time in fact, she wants to keep Diane as far away from her family as she possibly can. Right now, despite Barbara's misgivings, Diane is standing on the doorstep as requested, because when push comes to shove, Diane is the only person she knows with the power to make her plan happen.

"Hello!" Barbara says, wrenching open the front door – it has swollen with all the rain. "Come in! Come in! You look frozen!"

Diane, who is wearing a grey trouser suit over a roll-neck sweater and a purple beret over her new bob haircut, looks amazing. Once upon a time, Barbara was able to reassure herself that she might not be as *clever* as Diane and she might not be as funny either, but at least she was prettier. But that ceased to be true some years ago – proof, if any were needed, of what fashion and a good hairdresser can do.

"I *am* frozen," Diane says.

"Where's your coat?" Barbara asks, ushering her into the lounge. "Don't you have one?"

"I couldn't find one to go with this outfit," Diane admits, pulling an embarrassed face. "Stupid, I know! I regretted it the second I left the house. I'm bound to catch that cold everyone's getting now."

"Well, it *is* November."

"I saw a nice trench coat in British Home Stores, actually. I should have bought it. It's just that . . . well . . . British Home Stores . . . Anyway . . . This is nice," she says, nodding at the fire and then glancing around the room. "It's looking cozy here now you've redecorated."

"Thanks. Well, you warm yourself up there," Barbara says, feeling suddenly nervous, convinced, at this moment, that it is all a mistake. Desperate to escape the cosy proximity of the lounge, she says, "I'll make you a nice hot cup of tea. Don't move!"

"Sure," Diane says, even as she is following Barbara to the kitchen. "So, what's this all about?" she asks, removing her beret and shaking her hair loose. "It all seems very cloak and dagger, wanting me to come around when Tony's out at work and everything."

"Not really," Barbara says. "I just wanted to talk to you about something."

"Talk?"

"Yes." Barbara clears her throat then concentrates her energies on rinsing out the teapot, on spooning in the tea . . . She senses one of her breathless crises coming on. If she can just concentrate on some mechanical action, she'll be alright. If she just executes some simple task until it passes, she knows from experience that she can keep breathing.

"So, what's it about?" Diane asks. "What's the secret?"

"It's probably silly. I mean, it's probably not possible."

"Go on."

"Well, I want to talk to you about photos. About developing them. And printing and all that." Barbara peers into the pot and gathers her courage before, fixing a neutral expression, she glances up at Diane. She's half expecting her to laugh at her.

Diane just looks confused. "I don't understand," she says.

Barbara takes a deep gulp of air, then launches herself. "Tony's been having a hard time since your Dad closed the shop," she explains.

"I thought he would."

"We can't really afford the prices they charge for developing and printing elsewhere," Barbara explains.

Diane nods. "It's an expensive business. But I thought Tony had set up his own darkroom. In the cellar or something?"

"He did. But he isn't getting on with it. They're all too dark or too light or too scratched or too *something*. He's just wasting money on paper and chemicals and not getting *anything* to show for it."

"That's Tony, I'm afraid," Diane says. "There's nothing difficult about it, but he just can't – or won't – follow instructions."

"That's exactly it," Barbara says, now filling the teapot from the kettle.

"But I don't see how I can help," Diane says. "He's always been like that. He's not likely to change."

"I wondered if . . ."

"Yes?"

"Could you . . . do you think it would be possible . . . I mean, I'm not sure if you think I'm up to it but . . ."

"Oh!" Realisation sweeps across Diane's face. "You want me to teach *you*?"

Barbara squints at her. "I'm being silly, aren't I?" she says, tentatively.

"No! Of course not."

"And you probably don't have the time anyway . . ."

"Barbara," Diane says. "I—"

"You know what? Just forget I ever said anything."

"I'd *love* to show you how," Diane says.

"Really? You would?"

Diane nods energetically.

"I might not be any good at it."

"You'll be fine."

"I mean, I'm no photographer or anything, but I can follow instructions. I can follow a recipe and I can follow a knitting pattern. That sounds silly . . . I just mean, if someone tells me how, I can do most things. So I thought maybe . . ."

Diane is suppressing a grin. "You'll be great, Barbara," she says. "Really." She visibly notices something now and frowns as she scans the room.

"He's at school," Barbara says.

"God, of course!" Diane exclaims, as if some mystery has just been revealed. "So you have all the time in the world."

"For the moment, I do. Though I doubt it will last. Here."

She hands Diane a mug of tea which Diane cups in her hands and raises to her lips.

"Mmm. Thanks," she says. "So. Show me this darkroom."

Wednesdays and Fridays become photography days. Film processing is more complex than Barbara imagined. She has to learn to mix chemicals, to read temperature charts, to calculate developing times . . . She has to load film into a canister in the pitch black with her hands inside a bag and learn about overexposing and underexposing on both camera and enlarger.

But she enjoys the process, loves it, in fact, as much as anything she has ever done. After the brain deadening years of child-rearing, she feels like she is waking up, feels as if her mind is stirring after a long sleep, spluttering and juddering into motion.

She enjoys the hours spent in the red light of the darkroom too, thrills (more than she cares to admit) to her one-on-one time with pretty, clever, funny Diane, enjoys feeling, for once, as if she is her friend, not Tony's.

Despite Diane bringing her own papers and products, and even though they take great care to leave the cellar exactly as they find it every time, Tony almost catches them twice. Once, because Barbara forgets to switch off the little electric heater. "I was cleaning down there," she says, "and I was cold." And once when, arriving home early, he catches Diane in the kitchen, a box of photographic paper in one hand. "Perfect timing," Diane declares, seamlessly offering it to him. "I brought you some paper to practise with."

Barbara isn't quite sure why she doesn't tell her husband what she's doing. To Diane, she justifies it by saying that she wants to surprise him. But that's not the truth, or at least, it's not the whole truth. She's scared that Tony will somehow put an end to her new adventure. She's not sure why he would

254

do such a thing but she senses that it's a possibility. And she feels strangely guilty about her time alone with one of Tony's oldest friends. And so they manage to keep it a secret. Just. And one Wednesday in December, as they peer, hips pressed together, at the image slowly revealing itself in the developing bath, Diane says, "I think my work is done here."

"I'm sorry?"

"You've got it," Diane says. "That's perfect. The last three have all been perfect. You just need to practise lots of dodging and burning and do some double exposures now. But you're already way better than Tony at all of it. And I mean that."

Barbara stares at the developing picture to avoid looking at Diane. Because if she looks at her right now, she will need to hug her. And if she hugs her, she will need to kiss her. Surprisingly, she no longer feels conflicted about these desires. She's had time, here in the darkroom, to come to terms with it. She doesn't know where the desire comes from and she's decided that she doesn't really care. She loves Diane, really, but in a different way to the way she loves Tony, in a way a woman can only love another woman. It's something about feeling as if they are in-league together, and she has bonded with her these last weeks in a way that has never happened to her before. But she knows the limits of what's possible and what's not. She knows where the train tracks of her life are leading, and kissing Diane simply isn't on the itinerary. "Don't tell Tony that," she says.

"I wouldn't dream of it," Diane laughs.

"I might tell him this weekend," Barbara says, prodding at the sheet of paper in the chemical bath. "About all of this, I mean."

"Don't *tell* him," Diane says. "Just wait till he's nearly finished a film and then take it out and develop it. He won't believe his eyes."

"But what if I get it wrong?"

Diane bumps Barbara with her hip. "You won't," she says. "You're fine."

"And if he's angry?"

"You should take that out and fix it now," Diane prompts, pointing at the print.

"Yes. I was just about to."

"And if he's angry, then he's stupid," Diane says.

Barbara slides the sheet into the stop bath, then into the fixer. "Hum," she says. "No comment."

"Because you're not allowed to comment. But I am. Anyway, I think he'll be annoyed at first. But then it will be just a huge relief."

"I hope so."

They dry Barbara's print and then tidy the darkroom carefully before moving upstairs to the lounge. "I'm glad you got the hang of it so quickly," Diane says. "Because I'm going to have to vanish for a while and I won't be able to help you till I get back."

"I can't thank you enough," Barbara says, feeling suddenly tearful. "I've really enjoyed our afternoons together."

"So have I. And it's the least I could do. Really," Diane says.

"I'm kind of sad that—" Belatedly, Barbara's mind processes Diane's phrase. "What do you mean, you'll have to vanish for a while?" she asks.

"Just that," Diane says, now pulling on her coat.

"But why?"

"It's just something I need to do," Diane says, her hand fluttering towards her mouth before being wrested under control.

"If I can help, then you should tell me," Barbara says concernedly.

"I don't think anyone can, really."

Barbara reaches out to touch her shoulder now. "Diane," she says. "Just tell me what's wrong."

"I really can't."

"We're friends aren't we?"

"Of course we're friends."

"Then?"

Diane sighs unhappily, then wrinkles her nose. She swallows with visible difficulty and her eyes start to water. "Oh Barbara!" she says, her voice wavering. "Richard split up with me and I'm in such a mess . . ."

"Oh you poor thing!" Barbara says, taking Diane in her arms. She rubs her back as she begins to cry freely onto her shoulder. Barbara can feel the wet tears sliding down her neck.

"Aw, there, there. Don't cry," she says. "You'll get over it. Women have been getting over men since time began. We always get through this. And you're not alone. You have us."

"You're so brave, Barbara," Diane sobs, moving her head from side to side so that her nose gently rubs the underneath of Barbara's cheekbone. "I admire you so much. I wish I was strong like you."

"Strong?" Barbara says. "Me?"

"Yes," Diane sniffs. "You're amazing."

Barbara laughs and pushes Diane just far enough away that she can look into her eyes. "You're far more amazing than I am," she says. "And you know it."

Diane looks up into her eyes and then, before she even realises what's happening, Diane lurches in and kisses her on the lips.

Barbara laughs again but more awkwardly this time. "What was that for?" she asks.

"Because I wanted to," Diane says. "Because I think you're incredible."

The kiss was so unexpected, Barbara feels momentarily paralysed. She frowns and licks her lips and Diane, opposite, still staring into her eyes, does the same.

"Now," Barbara says, gently pushing Diane away. "How about a nice cup of tea?"

"But there's something else I need to tell you. Something important."

"Well, there's no reason you can't do that over a cup of tea, is there?" Barbara asks, suddenly abrupt and business-like.

"No," Diane says, doubtfully. "No, I suppose not."

* * *

Barbara waits excitedly for exactly the right time. She waits for the positions of various heavenly bodies to coincide. She waits, specifically, for the film in Tony's camera to be finished, or at least, nearly finished. She waits for him to be in a good mood. She waits for an intuition that her new life plan – to be Tony's wife *and sometime-assistant* – might be well received. This could be just the new direction their marriage needs.

Her moment comes four days before Christmas. She gets up early to check the Rolleiflex, and seeing that there are only two exposures left, she swaps the film with a fresh roll before advancing it to the same position. It's wasteful but at least that way Tony won't notice.

She can barely wait for him to leave for work that morning and readies Jonathan in such a panic that he starts to whimper and cry as she bundles him up and marches him across town to the laundry.

"I'm rushed off my feet," Minnie tells her. "I don't have time for baby-sitting."

"Please Mum. I've got something important to do," Barbara pleads. "It's a surprise for Tony."

258

Minnie twists her mouth. "OK, but not the whole day," she says.

Back in the house, alone in the chilly cellar, Barbara instructs herself to breathe. "You can do this," she says. "Just don't muck it up."

* * *

It is nine a.m. on Christmas day and Barbara has been up since five, officially awoken by Jonathan but in truth so excited that she couldn't have stayed in bed much longer anyway.

Tony, exhausted after a particularly bad week at work and a series of long, icy trips, is in bed nursing a cold. Jonathan has opened the last of his presents and is now, rather annoyingly, playing with the lurid boxes they came in rather than the budget-exploding toys themselves.

Tony's flat, rectangular gift is still beneath the sparsely decorated tree and Barbara keeps glancing at it as if to check that it's still there, to check that she didn't dream it.

It's almost lunchtime when Tony finally surfaces, his nose red, his eyes watery. He's more interested in breakfast than Christmas, so Barbara fries eggs and bacon before heading through to the lounge and returning with the package.

"For me?" Tony asks, smiling gently and sniffing.

Barbara nods.

"You're a treasure," he tells her. "Whatever would I do without you?"

"I hope you like it," Barbara says, with meaning.

"There's one for you under there too."

"I saw. I'll get it afterwards."

Tony weighs the box in one hand. "Hum. Photographic paper?"

"Almost," Barbara breathes.

Tony smiles wryly, sips at his tea and then begins to rip open the pretty holly-printed paper, revealing a standard, Ilford paper box. He winks at Barbara – who is holding her breath – and lifts the lid to the box.

"Oh!" he says in surprise, rotating the box by ninety degrees. He stares at the print, a sweep of hard, concrete architecture beneath a grey sky, made even more menacing by the fact that Barbara has dodged out the upper edges to make it look like storm clouds are approaching. "That's Birmingham Bull Ring," Tony says.

Barbara nods. "If you say so," she says.

Tony frowns and lifts the print aside, revealing another image of two women in modern dresses leaving the shopping complex with arms full of bags. "But these are—"

"Your photos, yes," Barbara says. "Don't they look great?"

Tony nods but continues to frown. "I don't get it," he says, with a tiny shake of the head.

"It's your Christmas surprise."

"You got my photos printed?" Tony asks, now leafing through the remaining eight images.

Barbara reseats herself opposite and can't quite stop herself from wringing her hands together. "Not quite," she says.

"Not quite what?" Tony asks, sounding a little irritated. He reaches into his dressing gown pocket, pulls out a handkerchief, and blows his nose.

"I actually developed them *for* you," Barbara says. "I printed them too."

Tony snorts. "What d'you mean?"

"Well, as you can't take them to Darbott's shop any more, I thought—"

"Ah, you got Diane to do them?" Tony says, his face lighting up.

Barbara shakes her head. "No. I got her to teach *me* how to do them."

"You got Diane to teach you," Tony repeats, flatly.

Barbara nods and chews the edge of her mouth. "I did them here. Downstairs. In your darkroom."

Tony pushes his bottom lip out unhappily as he leafs through the photos. "They're good," he says. "And you did them on your own? No help?"

Barbara nods again. "I thought I could help you now," she says. "Now Jon's at school and you're going to be doing more and more photography and everything . . ."

But Tony's smile has faded entirely.

"You don't look happy. Don't you like the idea?"

"I just don't get why you think I need *your* help," Tony says.

"I didn't, I—"

"I'm perfectly capable of doing my own developing."

"Of course you are, but—"

"So quite why you and Diane have decided to stick your noses into my darkroom is a little beyond me."

"Right," Barbara says, beads of sweat now sprouting on her top lip.

"And you've been using all my stuff? All my equipment? That's expensive stuff, you know."

"I know. But Diane brought her own chemicals and paper, so—"

"How *nice* of her," Tony says.

"I . . . I think I'll get this washing up done," Barbara says, standing, desperate for some point of focus beyond this sad little catastrophe. Because she's starting to feel a trembling anger that scares her. "Mum will be here soon," she mutters. "I need to get dinner on."

Tony nods. His expression is hard. "I think I'll—"

". . . pop down to the Ladywood for a pint?" Barbara offers, completing his phrase.

"You should give up doing other people's stuff and become a bloody mind reader," Tony says angrily. And then he stands up so quickly that his chair falls over.

When Minnie arrives, half an hour later, she tells her daughter, "Oh, he just needs time to get used to the idea. Men aren't as quick as we are, love."

And in the end, Minnie will turn out to be right. It will take Tony a month to stop sniping at Barbara about it and it will take him six before he'll be able to ask her, begrudgingly, for some advice. And finally, one full year after she handed him that ill-fated gift, he'll actually apologise and tell her that he was wrong. But by then, she'll have her hands far too full to give a damn.

2012 – OLD HOLBORN, LONDON.

Peter Dawkins, the chief editor of Thames and Hudson's *World Of Art* series, is leafing through the prints. Sophie glances at Brett, who she has brought along for support, and he winks at her discreetly.

"Yes, they're very, *very* nice," Dawkins says again. "And the overall package, your father's images, some biographical texts, and a solid ally at the *Times* to plug the whole thing, is more than appealing, I must admit."

"And his daughter's images as well," Brett adds, and Sophie loves him for sticking up for her at the precise moment that her own voice fails her.

"Yes," Dawkins says, scratching his head.

"It's a package," Brett reminds him. "That's what we're offering you. The father, the daughter, words of wisdom from those who knew the man, and some favourable publicity at the *Times*."

"I understand that," Peter Dawkins says. "Of course I do." He scratches his head again and closes the folder containing Tony's photos, then returns to the one holding Sophie's. "Hum," he says.

"So what's on your mind?" Brett asks, fiddling with his cuffs and leaning forward in his seat earnestly. "Tell me where you're at right now."

"Can I be perfectly honest here?" Dawkins says.

"Of course."

"These are good," he says, tapping the top print from Sophie's pile. It is one of her new series of fine-art photos, all taken through rain-stained, misty, or dirty windows. The image currently beneath his finger is of a woman with an umbrella on a rain-swept Eastbourne seafront, photographed through the splattered window of a bus shelter. "I like them, Sophie. I really do."

"That's great news, isn't it Sophie?" Brett says.

Sophie nods. She's waiting for the 'but'. She knows there's a 'but' coming.

"But here's the thing," Dawkins says, confirming her fears. He reopens the first folder and chooses a heavily-contrasted black and white image of a muddy CND protester lying down in front of the caterpillar track of a Cruise missile convoy. Next to this he places the softest of Sophie's images, a wild-flower peppered prairie pictured through a heart shaped gap, drawn, with a finger, in the heavily misted windscreen of a car. Sophie hates him for choosing that specific image. She's particularly attached to that photo, the first of the new series, the moment she had the idea for the series, in fact. She and Brett had just made love in that car, which was why the window was so misty in the first place.

Peter Dawkins spins the two images to face them. "Do you see what I'm saying?" he asks.

"No," Brett says. "Not really. What are you saying?"

"It's OK, Brett," Sophie says, finally finding her voice. "I get it. Come on. Let's get out of here. There's no point."

Brett raises one hand. "No. Hang on," he says, now standing and rounding Dawkins' desk. "I'm afraid I must accuse you of being just a tiny bit disingenuous," Brett tells him, and Sophie marvels at his ability to say such a thing without sounding angry, or rude, or even vaguely aggressive.

"Just let me choose a couple of different images . . ." Brett

264

says, rifling through the two piles. He chooses one of Tony's softer images – a woman in hot-pants riding a Chopper pushbike sometime in the seventies – and puts it next to Sophie's photograph of an aged, visibly lonely widow hugging a mug of tea, pictured through the misty window of a fish-and-chip restaurant.

"OK," Peter Dawkins says. "Yes, I get your point."

"All I'm saying," Brett says. "All *we're* saying, is that we feel these images *can* fit together if chosen with enough flair."

"Yes, I suppose they *could*. But—"

"And what *we're* looking for is a publisher who knows how to do that in the best way possible. Because that's our project. And because Sophie here controls the rights to Anthony Marsden's images."

Peter Dawkins clears his throat. "Right," he says. "I think I understand your proposition better now."

"Good," Brett says.

"I'll, um, need a few days to discuss it. There are other people here who will have input to make."

"That's absolutely fine, isn't it Sophie?" Brett says. "We could do with some time ourselves. We have, of course, other editors to meet."

Dawkins looks up at them. "You do?"

"Of course."

"Might I ask who?"

Hum, Sophie thinks. *Get out of that one, Brett.*

"You *might*," Brett says. "But I don't think we'd be inclined to tell you at this point. Anyway, I'm sure you know the main players in the art-book market as well as we do."

"Yes. Yes, I suppose I do," Peter Dawkins says. "I'll, um, try to get back to you as soon as I possibly can then."

"That would be great," Brett says. "Did *you* have any other questions for Peter here, Sophie?"

265

Sophie, who is a little numb from watching this particular boxing match, just shakes her head.

"Then let's go," Brett says.

Outside in the street, Sophie rests the folders between her legs while she buttons her coat. It's a sunny, crisp, November day. Her coat buttoned, she lurches at Brett and pecks him on the cheek.

"What was that for?" he asks.

"For being brilliant," Sophie says. "For being amazing. For stopping that arsehole trampling my ego underfoot."

She suddenly becomes aware of someone behind them and turns to see Peter Dawkins, who has just descended the stone staircase as well, in the process of buttoning his own coat. "Oh, how awkward," he says smugly. "I can assure you, my dear, that I had no intention whatsoever of trampling anyone's ego underfoot." Then muttering, "Good day to you both," he strides off down Old Holborn.

Sophie exhales slowly, then folds into Brett's arms.

"Huh!" Brett exclaims. "Nice one, Sophie. Very, very, *very* nice."

1969 – LLANELWEDD, WALES.

Jonathan turns from pressing his nose against the steamy window and asks, "Mum? Why's it so rainy in Wales?"

Barbara, who is busy knitting gender-neutral baby clothes, laughs, and that laughter feels good. The cottage is cold and damp and uncomfortable and she has a lot on her mind. At a guess, it's been three weeks since she even smiled.

"You're right," she says. "It is *very* rainy in Wales. You know, when I was a girl, we used to pretend that being sent to Wales was some kind of a punishment." She often talks to Jonathan about concepts that she knows he can't yet fully understand.

Minnie, her mother, mocks her. "The way you talk to that boy!" she says. "He's not your bleedin' husband."

But Barbara thinks it's good for him. And the proof of the pudding is in the eating. People are already saying how clever Jonathan is.

"It was during the war," she continues. "And all the children in London were sent to Wales to escape the bombs. We was – we *were* – ever so happy not to be sent away. And then a friend of mine got herself sent to Wales as well because she had done something a bit naughty. So it became almost like a joke in our family. Aunty Glenda used to tell me, 'Buck your ideas up, Sister, or it'll be The Wales for you'. We always called it *The* Wales. I don't know why."

Jonathan, who has been watching and apparently listening attentively, stares at her blankly now. "I think I prefer London," he says.

"You didn't say that yesterday."

"I did."

Barbara shakes her head. "No you didn't. You said the tree house was the nicest place in the whole wide world."

Jonathan considers this. "The tree house *is* very nice," he admits. "Can I go and sit in it?"

"Not until it stops raining. It doesn't have a proper roof."

"Can we get one from the shop?"

"One what?"

"A proper roof?"

Barbara smiles. "We'll ask Dad when he gets home if he knows how we can fix it."

Jonathan frowns. "Until Dad gets a roof for the tree, I think I like London," he says.

"Why don't you play with some toys? Why don't you build something with the Lego?"

"OK," Jonathan says, climbing down. "What can I make?"

"Make me . . . a bird!" Barbara tells him.

"A *bird?*"

"Go on. I bet you can do it. You're ever so good with Lego."

Jonathan twists his mouth sideways, a facial expression he has learned from Minnie. "A bird is hard," he says. "But I'll try."

Barbara glances up at him between stitches until he settles on the rug with his Lego, and then loses herself in the sound of the rain and the clicking of her knitting needles – in the vague, swirly thoughts that occupy her mind at times like this. She tries to imagine the baby wearing the garment that she's knitting. It seems barely possible that in a month's time he or she will be here. She wonders, for the thousandth time, if it will be a boy or a girl. She'll love either, but she'd secretly like a girl. It seems absurd to want one of each, as if it were a stamp collection not a family. But want one of each, she does.

She wonders how her mother is doing. She wonders if there's news from the hospital. She's too scared to think about her mother so she thinks about the baby again. She wonders if the baby will be cute. She wonders if she'll love her, or *him*, as much as she loves Jonathan. She wonders who the baby will resemble. Jonathan is so much *her* child. Everybody says so. Even now, even here, with her knitting baby clothes and Jonathan making a bird that looks like a train, this is visible. He has none of Tony's uncontrollable energy. She loves that Jonathan looks like her, *is* like her. But sometimes she wishes someone would tell Tony that he looks like him, *is* like him, just for the purpose of reassuring him.

The rain strengthens – it comes and goes in waves – and it lashes now against the window-pane. Both she and Jonathan look up at the sound. "Dad will be rained on," Jonathan says.

"You're right. He'll be drenched."

"What's drench?"

"He'll be very, very wet. Like when you get out of the bath."

"Can I play with his camera?" Jonathan asks, apparently bored with the admittedly challenging task of making a bird from Lego.

"You know you can't," Barbara replies. But of course, he doesn't know. Tony has let him peer through the viewfinder at the upside-down world within a few times recently. She thinks this is a mistake. For various reasons, she's sure this is a mistake. For one thing, it's an expensive, fragile camera – one they can't afford to replace. And for two (not that she could ever tell Tony this) she doesn't want Jonathan 'polluted' with any of this photography nonsense. She wants him to grow up learning a proper trade that pays proper money. She doesn't want him to have to scrabble around for the rent money the way they do. She doesn't want him peering into an almost empty refrigerator, wondering what he can possibly cook with two potatoes, five green beans, an egg and a slice of bacon (the answer is potato fritters).

Tony doesn't have the same relationship with money that Barbara has. He has never been bombed out of his house or had to work all night to finish piecework just to put money in the electricity meter. He has never walked to school in shoes so worn that he could sense the temperature of the pavement beneath them. So he doesn't have her fear of going without. He doesn't have her terror of being hungry, or cold, or wet. And he's able, in a perfectly relaxed manner, to suggest that it might be 'fun' to take a 'gamble' on a new career path.

Barbara sighs and glances at Jonathan who is already dismantling the bird. A gamble. A new career. Just as the family is about to expand. Just as another mouth will need feeding. Minnie told Barbara to just say, 'no', but Minnie overestimates the influence her daughter has on her husband. And she underestimates her daughter's desire to remain married as well. For that is Barbara's gamble. That's her career path.

Yes, as long as they stay together, they'll be OK. As long as he doesn't leave them, Jonathan will never have to know the poverty that she grew up in, will never even have to know that such poverty exists. And isn't doing a little better, from generation to generation, ambition enough?

The front door bursts open and the hunched, glistening form of Tony in a sou-wester (they found it in the woodshed) appears in the doorway. "Bloody hell," he says, kicking the door closed behind him and dumping a half-full crate of vegetables onto the rough wooden table. "It's raining like bloody Noah's Ark out there."

Barbara raises one eyebrow at the expletive and the other at the failed metaphor. She tries to be careful what she says around Jonathan. He soaks everything up like a sponge and a part of her great plan for him includes the fact that, not only

270

will he never go hungry and not only will he never be cold, but he'll grow up speaking better too. All the posh jobs go to people who speak properly.

Changing the way she speaks herself hasn't been easy but she's getting there for Jonathan's sake. Putting on 'airs and graces', Minnie calls it, but Barbara doesn't care, because someone has to do it and, let's face it, it's not going to be Minnie or Tony who will make the effort.

"Still no bloody one-twenty film," Tony says, now hanging his dripping coat on the back of the door. "He said it should come tomorrow though."

"You can't really do photography in this weather anyway," Barbara points out.

"That's true enough."

"So, how is she?" Barbara asks. By common accord, *she* doesn't even get referred to by name any more. Though that's strange, Barbara doesn't want to think about the nature of that strangeness any more than she wants to think about *her* in any great detail. Which is probably selfish of her.

Tony shrugs. "She's fine," he says. "Tired. And a bit cold. She couldn't get the fire going but she's fine now. Oh, this came for you." He pulls a soggy envelope from his pocket and crosses to Barbara, who stops knitting to take the letter from his still-wet hand. It's addressed with her mother's unique mixture of upper and lower-case handwriting. She places it on the mantelpiece, then resumes her knitting.

"Open it then," Tony says, crouching in front of their wood-burner, then opening the little door and poking it around.

"Not yet," Barbara says. "I need to prepare myself."

"Prepare yourself for what?"

"I don't know."

"Don't be such a misery guts. It might be good news. It might be nothing."

271

"I know that," Barbara says flatly. "I'll open it in a bit. Once *You-Know-Who* has gone to bed."

Jonathan, who currently believes that he has two names, Jonathan Marsden and *You-Know-Who*, looks up expectantly.

When his mother fails to address him despite having used his nickname, he asks, "Mum, can we ask Dad about the roof?"

Barbara smiles weakly. "Jonathan here wants to know if there's any way to fix the roof in the tree house."

"It rains inside," Jonathan explains. "If it didn't, I could play in it."

"You really like that treehouse, yeah?"

The boy nods. "I could live there all the time perhaps," he says, hopefully.

"You can't live there *all* the time," Tony tells him. "But when the rain stops, we'll see what we can do. We'll see if we can fix something up."

Jonathan wrinkles his nose as if Tony has just said the daftest thing that he has ever heard. "If the rain stops, we won't *need* a roof, stupid," he says, and Barbara wonders if Tony will get angry at his son for cheeking him like that. But Tony just smirks. "He's a quick one alright," he says, proudly.

After dinner, Barbara puts Jonathan to bed, then retrieves the letter, now dry, from the mantelpiece. Tony, who is reading a book about darkroom techniques, has forgotten about the letter, which somehow gives her the space to brave its contents.

When eventually he looks up, he finds Barbara staring at the flames behind the window of the stove, the letter on her lap.

"So what's the old bird got to say for herself?" he asks.

Barbara takes a deep breath before replying, "I'll have to go see her."

"What?"

"It's cancer, Tony."

"Don't be daft."

"I'm not being daft. It's what the hospital said. They told her it's cancer."

"I mean, you can't go see her," Tony says softly.

"I have to."

Tony puts down the book and crosses the room. He crouches beside his wife and takes her hand. "You *can't*, Barbara. We talked about this."

"She didn't have cancer then."

Tony sighs and kisses the back of her hand. "What does she say. Is it bad?"

"I don't know. That's why I have to go."

"But if you go, you'll have to tell her."

"Obviously."

"So you can't. Just wait a month and . . ."

"I can't wait a month."

"Bloody hell, Barbara," Tony says. "What if she tells everyone?"

"She won't," Barbara says. "She won't tell a soul."

2012 – SHOREDITCH, LONDON.

Sophie wiggles the fingers of her outstretched hand. "Give me that," she says.

Opposite, Brett is waving a letter around above his right shoulder. "I want to talk to you first," he says.

"Give it to me!" Sophie repeats, sharply.

"Just calm *down,*" Brett tells her. "We need to have a brief chat and then—"

"That letter is addressed to me. It was just delivered through *my* letterbox. So bloody well hand it over. Afterwards we can talk about whatever you want."

Brett rolls his eyes and, with a gasp of despair, as if caving in to a three year old, he lowers his arm and proffers the letter. "You're impossible," he says as Sophie snatches it from his grasp and crosses to the far side of the room. She throws herself onto the sofa and caresses the envelope. It bears the elegant monicker of *Thames and Hudson Publishing.*

She blows gently through pursed lips, then rips it open and pulls out the letter (top quality, bonded paper – a good sign?). She closes her eyes briefly, then flips open the sheet of paper. "Following our *interesting* meeting . . ." she mumbles, scanning the dense print. "Blah, blah . . . offer . . . Oh!" She turns to Brett now. "Bloody hell! It's a yes!"

Brett nods serenely and smiles. "Yes," he says. "I know."

"*How* do you know?"

He shrugs. "I rock, is all."

Sophie frowns, then turns her attention back to the letter.

"Contract to follow . . . blah blah . . . standard terms . . . six per cent of cover price, plus, um, reproduction fees to individual rights holders . . ." Sophie glances up at Brett again. "Six per cent. Is that good? It sounds a bit rubbish."

Brett shrugs again. "It's at the low end. But it depends what they pay for the image rights. Most of those are yours, so . . ."

"Mum's," Sophie corrects.

"Yes," Brett says. He clears his throat. "Which brings us rather nicely to the thing we need to talk about."

"It's fine," Sophie says dismissively. "I'll talk to her."

"You'll talk to her," Brett repeats.

"I'll explain to her that it's my project and that she can have a cut, or whatever, of the exhibition proceeds but that the book royalties are mine."

"Yes. I think you're forgetting something though," Brett says.

"Yes?"

"I think you're forgetting *me*."

"You?"

"I got you that book deal, Sophie."

"*We* got that book deal."

"You almost lost it, in fact," Brett reminds her. "If I hadn't called him afterwards to apologise for you—"

"You *what?*"

"I phoned him. I blamed it on your highly-strung, artistic temperament. He was very nice about it considering you called him a wanker."

"Arsehole," Sophie says.

"What?"

"I called him an arsehole, not a wanker."

"Oh, that's fine then," Brett says.

Sophie can feel the heat of anger mixed with a dash of

embarrassment rising from within. She shakes her head and stands and crosses the room to face Brett. "Anyway, how *dare* you contact him!" she says. "You didn't even tell me about it. Let alone ask me."

"It was necessary, Soph. And I knew you wouldn't like it. What matters here is that I saved the god-darn deal, donchathink?"

Sophie opens her mouth to say something insulting but momentarily regains control of herself and closes it again. "So, how much do you want?" she finally asks. "What's the going rate for a *sorry about my girlfriend but she's a hysterical bitch* call these days?"

"And now you're being disingenuous," Brett says.

"Disingenuous. That's your word of the month."

"You're right. It is. I like it. I like how it rolls off the tongue. Though if people stopped being it, then I'd be happy to stop *using* it. Now, if you'll calm down a second, I have some more cool news for you. I've gotten you a gallery. A really rocking gallery. And the owner has already agreed in principle to host the exhibition."

Sophie freezes. She's stuck halfway between outrage and excitement and she doesn't know which way to swing. "You have?" she says.

"Uh huh."

She bites her bottom lip – the excitement is winning out. "Is it White Cube?"

"I'm not telling you."

"It is, isn't it! It's White Cube. Tell me it's White Cube?"

Brett laughs lightly. "I'm not saying until—"

"God, I *love* White Cube. You're a genius, Brett."

"OK, look. It is *not* White Cube."

"Really?"

"Really."

"Then where? Is it—"

"We need to talk first. We need to talk about my involvement in this project, Sophie. I've been spending a lot of time on this. I've lined up meeting upon meeting for you. I got you that darned book deal (he nods at the envelope in her hand, here) by offering to push it in the *Times*. And I got the gallery by telling them we had the book deal lined up. None of this would be happening without me."

"OK, OK, Brett. So you want to be paid. I get it. And here was I, thinking that you were doing this for love."

"No, Sophie," Brett says. "This isn't love. In *there* is love," he points to her bedroom. "This bit, here, is work. So yes, I *do* want paying. And I want a written, signed contract before I go any further."

"A contract?"

"I want exclusive interview rights to you, your mother and Jonathan. And I want the exclusive right to negotiate image rights to the *Sunday Times*. You'll get paid for that if I can make it happen. Minus my cut, of course."

"Of course!"

"And I want twenty-five per cent of all other proceeds."

Sophie blinks exaggeratedly and feigns outrage by dropping her jaw. She takes a step back. "You're out of your mind," she says.

"It's a very fair—"

"Fair?!" Sophie gasps. "Twenty-five per cent? That's not fair, that's daylight robbery."

Brett snorts. "It's actually *not*, Sophie. I feel that it's fairly generous consider–."

"No. The answer is no."

"No?"

Sophie nods. "Yes. I'm saying *no* to your offer. So how do you *feel* about *that?*"

Brett shrugs. "That's OK," he says. "I can cancel the gallery easily enough."

"You wouldn't dare."

"Sure. If that's what you want. And cancelling the gallery will cancel the book deal. You can always rebuild this whole shebang from scratch on your own. You'll end up with a few photocopied pages and some shitty little gallery in some place no-one can even find, but hey, what do I care?"

"Maybe I will."

"Good. Go ahead."

"OK. I think you should leave now."

"I'm sorry?"

"Seeing as this – what I thought was a relationship – is actually a *business* relationship, and seeing as our business meeting is over, I think you should leave."

"I don't understand."

"Then I'll make it simple. Fuck off to your own place, Brett."

"Oh," Brett says, pedantically. "I *see*. Personally, I was thinking more in terms of a quick *bang* followed by a celebration meal somewhere but if that's how you want to play it . . ."

Momentarily, Sophie struggles with herself. One part of her watches two other seemingly independent parts slugging it out in the wrestling wring of her ego. It's like this sometimes. It's as if her body, specifically her mouth, becomes possessed by some alien force whose only desire is to push every argument to the ultimate, destructive limit. What she *really* wants now is exactly what Brett is suggesting. Sex, celebration, happiness. But that part of her loses the battle and she hears her mouth say, "Just fuck off, Brett, will you? Just take your huge, stinky ego as far away from me as possible before I throw up, will you?"

"My huge, stinky ego, huh?" Brett repeats, his mouth still smiling, *just,* even as his eyes burn with anger. He picks up his bag, pulls a stapled document from within and places it on Sophie's desk. "The draft contract," he says. "Call me when you've come to your senses."

He strides across the flat then, embarrassingly, has to return, first for his keys and then for his phone, and then again for his coat, before finally making it to the front door. "You know what, Sophie?" he says, his hand on the latch.

"Oh, just shut up and *go*, will you?"

Brett groans and vanishes from view. He does *not* slam the door behind him.

Barbara is standing at the Embankment end of Waterloo Bridge. She is rocking Sophie's pram back and forth as she waits for Tony to arrive.

She can see Big Ben in the distance, her daughter is smiling as she sleeps and she's meeting her husband for a picnic on a beautiful June day . . . And yet all that she can think of is her mother. They (she, Glenda and Minnie) have a meeting with the cancer surgeon tomorrow and Barbara already knows, just from looking at her mother, that it's going to be bad news. She can tell from the pallor of Minnie's complexion that despite the radical surgery her mother has undergone (and there is no surgery more radical for a woman than this, after all) they did not "manage to get it all".

She's been expecting bad news since the operation and now, today, she's struggling to think of anything other than the fact that she'll have more bad news by this time tomorrow.

She hears Tony calling her name and turns to see him crossing the road towards her. "Hello!" he says, a little breathlessly. "And how are my girls today?"

Barbara forces a smile. Her sorrow at her mother's failing health has been making Tony irritable. He has never said so, but she can tell that he believes her joy over Sophie's birth should somehow outweigh the illness of her mother. She can hear it in the way he insists that Minnie will "probably be fine". She can sense it in the way he shuts off any discussion of Minnie's cancer with a diametrically opposed discussion of

Sophie's loveliness. Tony can't deal with death or illness. Or rather, ignoring it *is* Tony's way of dealing with death or illness. So, "We're fine," is the reply Barbara gives. "She's been asleep since I got on the train."

"I thought we worked out that the bus was better?"

"It was packed, Tony. I couldn't get the pram on. I waited for three buses and then gave up. So we got the train to Charing Cross."

"Is that a picnic?" he asks, pointing at the basket beneath the pram.

"It is. Cheese and pickle sandwiches, and scones and jam."

"Nice," Tony says, "But you didn't have to. I told you not to bother."

Tony had said this morning, in his usual financially irresponsible way, that he would buy them lunch today. But it's cheaper this way. And they avoid the risk of ending up in a pub. "I thought a picnic would be nicer," Barbara says. "It's such a lovely day."

"How about the gardens?" Tony asks, pointing over the road.

"What about St James' Park?" Barbara asks. "We've got time, haven't we?"

Tony glances at his watch. "Sure," he says.

It's a week before the general election, just about the busiest that Fleet Street can be but he'll take an hour today to do this. He'll just have to make up for it this evening. Barbara's right. It is a beautiful day. They start to walk.

When they reach Trafalgar Square, they find a rag-tag band of protestors demonstrating in support of a Labour vote. Various groups are chanting and waving banners but their messages are diverse and confused and their hearts don't really seem to be in it.

"Can we go look?" Tony asks, patting his camera bag.

281

"Of course," Barbara says, turning the pram and steering it towards Nelson's Column.

As they reach the protest, Tony bends over his camera and starts snapping. "There don't seem to be any other press people here," he says, photographing a hippy with a placard which reads, "Labour, Yes. Vietnam, No."

"It's all a bit old news, isn't it?" Barbara says. "I think everyone's bored stiff with the election. Plus, we all know Labour are going to win again."

"They reckon it's not as certain as everyone says. That's what the guys are saying at work."

They walk around the edges of the demonstration and Tony takes a photo of a pretty girl with a "VAT at 20%? No thanks!" poster.

"Look," Barbara says, pointing at a small group of feminists to their right. Tony follows her regard and sees a woman with long blonde hair and a baby strapped to her chest. Stacked at her feet are a pile of placards awaiting distribution, the top one of which reads, "Keep Religion Out of My Womb. Yes to Women's Rights. Yes to Abortion. Vote Labour."

"Some of us will do anything for a baby and others just want the right to get rid of them," Barbara says. "It's strange when you think about it."

"It is," Tony says, now turning to take a photograph of a group of policemen climbing out of a van.

Sophie, awoken by the chanting, starts to cry. "We need to get out of here," Barbara says. "It's too noisy for her."

"Sure," Tony agrees. "Just one second."

"I'll head off that way," Barbara says, pointing west. "You can follow on."

"OK. I won't be long."

"Before you leave, I think you should photograph *her*," Barbara says, nodding.

"The chick with the kid?"

"Yes."

"Why?"

"There's just something funny about a woman holding a baby while fighting for abortion," Barbara says. "It would make a good photo. That's all."

"You reckon, do you?" Tony says, sounding only half amused. He's still a little up-tight about the photography thing, still hesitates between macho annoyance and gentle encouragement any time Barbara has an opinion. "Here," he says, handing her the camera. "Take it."

Barbara takes the camera from his outstretched hand. She's not sure whether he's challenging her or encouraging her, or perhaps a little of both. "I do know how to," she says.

"I know you do. So take it."

She raises one hand to shade her eyes from the sunlight and frowns at him. She's still not sure what she's supposed to do here. He seems to be in a good mood today but that, she knows, can change suddenly.

"Well, go on then," Tony says, and so she gives up trying to work it out, shrugs and, kicking the lock on the pram wheel, crosses towards the group of women.

2012 – EASTBOURNE, EAST SUSSEX.

Barbara stirs her tea and steels herself before returning to the dining room, mug in hand. Pensive, she sits before the pale blue folder. It glares at her; it *dares* at her.

She sips her tea. Another minute can't hurt, can it? There's no one here to witness how much time she takes to find the courage to plunge into the past. It is her past, after all.

She takes a deep breath and almost moves her hand towards the folder but fails. She surprises herself with the thought, *Why couldn't she just wait until I was dead?* And then, in a rush, before that other part of her can interfere, she flips the cover open.

So these are the ones you chose, she thinks, addressing Sophie in her mind. *Tell me which photos you like best, and I'll tell you who you are.* Someone said that once. Phil perhaps?

The first image: A woman in hot-pants on a pushbike.

Images flash up: *A grazed knee. A kite. Another, different bike. Those bikes . . . Jonathan wanted one so badly. All the boys did. What was it called again?* The brand escapes her. Pretty girls on bikes baring flesh – the seventies in a nutshell. She smiles to herself and, feeling momentarily braver, flips to the next image.

A man this time – a man in a sports car. He's wearing a white shirt, a tie and braces. *Braces.* Her mother had a photo of her father wearing braces. Nobody wears braces any more. What was the point of them? Why didn't they just use a belt? The man in the photo is smoking a cigar – he looks smug and wealthy and really rather horrid. What was it they called them? *Yuppies!* Yes, that's it. Yuppies. Young, upwardly mobile something-or-others. The eighties then. The Thatcher years. She and Tony did alright in the eighties, but it was a terrible time for most.

She flips another page. A couple of punks with mohican haircuts, kissing on Brighton pier. She had been beside him when he took it and some sweet, sickly sensual memory, the smell of candy-floss perhaps, comes back to her now. Yes, she had been there. Sophie was begging to go on the Waltzer and in the end, they had caved in. Big mistake. She had vomited all over the pushchair.

She flips another page and inhales sharply. This one has caught her by surprise. She had forgotten, momentarily, why she was nervous about this. And here it is. The past rushing at her like a freight train. 1969 or 1970? She's not sure. Election year anyway. The year of Edward Heath's surprise victory for the Conservatives. One of the worst governments in history, wasn't that what people used to say about Heath? If only they had known what was to come, they might have gone easier on him.

She remembers Tony taking this one. Or did *she* take it? Yes, she suspects that she did. She thinks (but isn't sure) that she did it to spite him over some slight, real or imagined. For who, forty years later, can recall which moods were justified and which moods weren't?

She studies the photo and feels vaguely sick. Yes, she took it. And she developed it too. Tony had been run off his feet whizzing up and down the country picking up rolls of film and typed news stories from journalists covering the election rallies. So she had developed it herself in the cellar, the first time he had ever asked her to do so. Sophie, who was upstairs in a cot, cried throughout. Yes, it's *all* coming back to her now.

She remembers Tony excitedly announcing that he had sold a photo, remembers buying the *Mirror* and thrilling to see her photo in print. She hid that newspaper. She wonders when she lost it. It probably got used to light a fire at some point.

Her throat feels dry, so she sips her tea. She can sense, again, the strange atmosphere around the flat at the time, born of the fact that they would not, *could* not discuss that photo. They both knew who had pressed the shutter release and they both knew that the other person knew the truth as well. It was the only photo in the whole batch that she had taken and it was the only one the *Mirror* chose to publish. *Women Voters Fear Roll-Back of Rights*. She can still picture the headline in her mind's eye. She spent hours looking proudly at that page of newsprint. She would get it out and sit and stare at it – her guilty pleasure.

Tony had vanished after that, in theory to celebrate, but in reality it was a truth he needed to drown, a truth that came back to haunt them almost seven months later when that same photo won the damned prize. But by then they were pretending, even in private, even between husband and wife, that Tony had taken it himself. She can't remember when the decision to lie to each other, to lie to *themselves*, was taken. It felt like it just *happened*. It was required, that was all. Rewriting history turned out to be a surprisingly easy thing to do and within a couple of years, she had struggled to remember quite *who* had taken the photo. But that must have been a choice because she certainly remembers now.

At the time of course (so it was 1970 then), she had far more important things to worry about. Who actually pressed the lever was neither here nor there in the grand scheme of things.

She inhales sharply. She wasn't expecting *that*. She wasn't expecting the physical sensation of Minnie's boney hand to suddenly leap out of her memory at her. Her last physical contact with her mother. She remembers begging the nurses for more morphine, remembers laughing hysterically (in the true sense of that word) when the ward sister informed her that any more morphine than Minnie was already taking would kill her. Her eyes are wet now, her eyesight unfocused, her mind's eye projecting above the soft, grey blur of Trafalgar Square, the full horror of Minnie's slow death.

She swipes at a tear and even this provokes a memory, the physical sensation of crying at the time, not from sorrow but from a profound sense of relief that it was all finally over.

She realises that she has been holding her breath and forces herself to exhale. It's just too hard. This whole thing is just too hard for her heart to bear. It truly *would* have been better if Sophie had waited until she was gone but how could Sophie even begin to understand that? Barbara has made it her life's work, after all, to protect her from all of this.

She had braced herself, yes. She had known that certain images would bring up specific memories of particular moments in time. That's why it has taken her a week to sit down and do this. But no, she had not prepared herself for *this*. She had not imagined the way each image would lead to every other image and lead in turn to wholesale submersion in the most powerful sensations – the smells, the sounds, the *feelings* – of the harshest most dreadful highlights (or lowlights perhaps) of her eighty years on this planet. She hadn't expected to find herself transported back in time.

There's no way around it now, though. That train has left the station and she certainly can't stop it. The exhibition is undoubtedly going to happen. She closes her eyes for a moment and stretches her neck from side to side before continuing rapidly through a few more images.

She pauses next on an image of Sophie, perhaps five years old, on the beach. She's holding a plastic spade and staring directly into the camera lens. She grew up with cameras, was entirely relaxed around them, and here her expression is completely neutral – her innocence still complete. Such a beautiful child. She still is. Barbara sighs.

Perhaps the time has come for her to tell Sophie part of the truth. Not all of it, of course. They all agreed a long time ago that that would never happen, that it *could* never happen. But just enough to warn her off? Just enough to avoid Brett sniffing around? Just enough to make sure that the rest, the important stuff, the stuff with the power to harm the lives of the living, remains buried?

The trouble is, Barbara realises, still staring into those big, dark eyes, that never mind Brett, Sophie herself is like a sniffer dog. Give her even a whiff of intrigue and she won't stop digging until she's unearthed everything. Best, without a doubt, to say nought.

1971 – HACKNEY, LONDON.

Barbara is feeding Sophie at the kitchen table. She has a snotty nose and the beginning of a cold. She looks pink and angry and ready to burst into a tantrum – it's just a matter of time. Jonathan, beside her, at the end of *his* cold, is making dams and rivers amidst the peaks of his mashed potato.

"If you keep playing with that, it'll get cold," Barbara reminds him. It amazes Barbara how many times you have to tell children things before they remember them. Even things about danger – warnings about hotness or sharpness – she has to tell them over and over again. Sometimes she tires of telling *before* they learn and resigns herself instead to watching them burn or cut themselves just so that they can find out on their own.

"It's the Thames," Jonathan says. "Look."

"Yes," Barbara tells him. "Lovely. Now eat it!"

The door to the cellar opens. Tony, unusually, is home for lunch, not to see Barbara or to spend time with the kids but to use the darkroom. There's a postal strike on and he's hoping to sell some pictures he has taken.

"Yours is in the oven," Barbara tells him. "But be careful. The plate is hot." And how many times has she said *that*? And how many times has he burned himself all the same?

Tony crosses the kitchen, touches the plate and gives an unconvincing 'ouch', before using a tea-towel to carry it to the dinner table. He places a contact sheet next to his plate then, while studying the rows of photos on it, begins to eat.

"So how did it go?" Barbara asks.

"Not good, I'm afraid. They're all misty," Tony says, through a mouth of steak and kidney pie.

Barbara swipes the spoon across Sophie's mouth to remove the excess, then leans in to study the photos herself.

"Isn't that b—" Barbara says, then, "Never mind."

"Yes?" Tony asks.

"No, nothing. I'm really not sure."

"Go on," Tony says. "Really."

"Um, is the fogging on the negatives? Or just the contact sheet?"

"Both."

"Then you didn't fix it long enough."

"I did a full six minutes," Tony says. "A bit more maybe."

Barbara wonders at that use of the word *maybe*. Minutes are real things. There were six of them or there weren't. If she had done it, she would have known exactly how many minutes had passed. "Was the temperature right?"

"For the developer, it was," Tony says. "I don't think it matters for the fixer."

"Hum," Barbara says, returning to feeding Sophie. "Well, it looks to me like it *might* matter."

"It *was* a bit cold maybe," Tony says. "Bloody annoying though. I really thought I was going to flog those."

Barbara loads up Sophie's tiny rose-bud mouth, then puts down the feeding spoon and lifts the sheet so that she can study it more closely. "Ooh, they *are* foggy. Is that a sorting office?"

"Yep. The big one in Bethnal Green. There's no way to get rid of that, is there?"

"The fog? No, I shouldn't think so. Not if it's on the negatives. I suppose you could always go down there and take them again."

"I expect everyone's gone home now," Tony says. "Bloody

annoying. I liked all those undelivered boxes piled behind them."

"Yes. It's good," Barbara says. Then taking her life in her hands, she adds, "If you *did* go back, you could get one of the strikers to actually sit on those parcels in the foreground. Maybe even put a mug of tea in his hand and one of those strike placards at his feet."

"What, you mean stage it?"

"Maybe," Barbara says. "It would make for a good photo, don't you think?"

"Perhaps. Anyway, I don't think I'll have time to go back there now. I've got to take the van up to Manchester, then Liverpool, then Rugby," Tony says.

"But that'll take forever, won't it?"

Tony nods. "It's the postal strike, isn't it," he says. "It's the only way to get stuff around at the moment."

"Any sorting office would do. I'm sure they all have strikers. *And* piles of boxes."

"Yes, I suppose so. I just really liked that one in Bethnal Green. The light was good."

Sophie starts to wave her arms manically, so Barbara hands back the contact sheet and resumes feeding her. "I take it you're going to be late then?" she asks over her shoulder.

"Eight or nine at the earliest," Tony says, already finishing his plate and standing. "Don't bother with tea or anything. I'll grab something at the roadside."

"Well, drive carefully."

"I always do."

In the end, it's almost midnight by the time Tony gets home.

Because Barbara suspects that he's been drinking, she feigns sleep, even snoring lightly for added effect. After a minute or so, Tony, who she can tell is wide awake, whispers, "Barbara?

Are you asleep?" and because he sounds sober and because he sounds *excited*, she pretends to stir from her slumber, stretching and yawning theatrically.

"Hello," she says. "You're home."

"I sold that photo," he says immediately. "I sold the whole roll."

"Which photo?" Barbara asks. "Which roll? Did you go back?" She suddenly remembers that she's supposed to be half asleep, so she throws another yawn into the mix.

"Yes. The one you said about. The strikers on the boxes, drinking tea and that."

"How did you develop them? *Where* did you develop them?"

"I didn't. They bought them on spec. I just gave them the roll straight out of the camera. Just like the agency guys do. I told them what was on them and they took it. Said it was exactly what they wanted. There were definitely some crackers on there, even if I do say so myself."

"That's great news."

"It is," Tony says, proudly. "It must mean they trust me, if they're taking my pictures without even seeing them."

"Yes. I think that's exactly what it means."

Tony stares into her eyes for a moment. His regard seems to hold a question.

"What?" Barbara laughs.

"I know it's late and you're half asleep and everything," Tony says. "But you don't fancy a bit, do you?"

Barbara laughs nervously, both because it's been months since they made love (such things virtually ceased when Jonathan was born and never really picked up again) and because the answer, surprisingly, is yes. She *does* 'fancy a bit'.

By way of an answer, because she could never *say* 'yes' to sex, Barbara leans across the pillow and pecks her husband on the lips.

"Hum," Tony murmurs, shuffling across the bed and sliding one knee over her legs. "Thank God for that then. 'Cos I'm feeling horny as hell."

* * *

Barbara is slowly, methodically, buttering bread. Sophie and Tony are sleeping and Jonathan is eating his breakfast in the dining room whilst reading a picture book. He's hardly a rowdy child but all the same, these moments when the house is quiet are rare and precious, tiny oases in the midst of the screaming and banging that is a home with children. In the middle of the emotional turmoil that is Barbara's life right now, she needs these moments of silence every bit as much as she needs food or drink.

"What you making?" It's Tony's voice and Barbara looks up to see him in the doorway looking sleepy. Her moment is over.

"Sandwiches!" she says. "Are you hungry, sweetheart?" She adds the *sweetheart* in order to soften the sentence. Her tone, she fears, was harsh.

Tony shakes his head. "No, not really," he replies. "Not yet. So what are the sandwiches for?"

Barbara pauses her buttering operation, puts down the knife and turns to face her husband. She has detected something dishonest in his voice and wants to take the time and space to think about what it means. "You know what they're for," she says. "They're for Hyde Park. For the festival thing."

"Yes," Tony says, still sounding fake. "Yeah, about that . . . I thought I might go on my own."

"What?" Barbara asks, then, *"Why?"*

Tony wrinkles his nose. "I'm not sure it will be a good place for kids," he says.

Barbara laughs lightly. "Tony, it's Mary Whitehouse and Cliff Richard! How bad can it be?"

Jonathan has just appeared from the dining room, peering around his father's legs. "Hi Dad," he says, and Tony reaches down and rests a big hand on his blond mop of hair. "What time are we leaving?"

"I . . . We're just discussing that," Barbara tells him. "Go and get your breakfast finished and—"

"I finished."

"Then go and play for a bit. I'll come and get you once we've decided."

Jonathan looks dubious but leaves the room without a word.

"As I was saying," Barbara says, "It's Mary Whit—"

"I know they're supposed to be the moral majority and everything," Tony interrupts. "But they're not actually that nice. There's lots of people they don't like and lots of people who don't like *them*. There might be protests. It might get nasty."

Barbara sighs and lets her shoulders droop. She's been living on her nerves ever since Sophie was born, doubly so since her mother fell ill. She doesn't have any energy reserves available to deal with Tony's (frequent) changes of plan. "Then can we all do something else, please?" she asks. "Can we all just go somewhere as a family? I've made a picnic and everything."

"Look," Tony says. "Why don't you take the kids to a park? Not to *Hyde* Park, obviously but somewhere else. And I'll go take some snaps and then come and join you?"

"One day a week, Tony," Barbara says. "We get to see you one day a week."

"I know. That's why I'll get this out of the way and I'll come join you."

Barbara sighs deeply – a sigh of submission. She simply doesn't have the energy to argue. "Where?" she asks. "When?"

"What about Hackney Marshes? By that kiosk cafe thing."

"Fine. At twelve?"

"Three maybe?"

Barbara glances at the kitchen clock. It's just before nine.

"I've got to get into town and back," Tony pleads. "I need time to take photos too. It's a big event."

"And I have to be at the hospital at five. You know that."

"Two, then. How about two?"

Barbara shakes her head gently, as if to shake away the grain of a bad mood, as if to dislodge this seed of a bad day, already taking root just a few minutes before nine. "Fine," she says. "Just don't be late, OK?"

Tony eats a slice of toast and downs a cup of tea, then (Barbara suspects, more to escape her anger than for any other reason), precipitates himself out of the flat in record time. The second the front door closes behind him, Jonathan reappears. "Dad's gone!" he says.

"I know."

"I thought we was going with him," he complains. "I thought we was going to the park." Jonathan too has learned about Tony's changes of plans and he doesn't like them any more than Barbara does.

"We *were* going to the park," Barbara corrects. "But he's got to do a bit of work first. We're going to meet him on Hackney Marshes instead."

Jonathan pulls a face. "I hate Hackney Marshes," he says.

"You do not! You *like* it there. We can watch all the people playing football."

"I want to go to Hyde Park," he says, sounding stubborn.

"I know. But today, we're going to Hackney Marshes."

"We always go to Hackney Marshes. We *never* go to Hyde Park."

"I know, but—"

"I want to go to Hyde Park," Jonathan whinges, his bottom lip now jutting visibly.

"And so do I!" Barbara snaps, her voice trembling as she loses control. "But we're not going to Hyde Park, we're going to bloody Hackney Marshes. So go and bloody well get dressed! *Jesus!*"

Jonathan glares at her for a second, a look of utter hatred in his eyes, then turns and runs away. Barbara, already regretting losing her temper, sinks into a chair at the yellow formica table and covers her eyes with the palms of her hands. "I'm just so tired," she mumbles.

She stares into the middle distance for a moment, then thinks, *Tony isn't going to come to Hackney Marshes. Of course he isn't. He isn't going to come at all.*

She shakes her head again, then muttering, "Bugger him," she stands. She turns to the doorway and calls out, "Jonathan? *Jonathan?!*" No reply. The boy will be sulking. He's an expert sulker. He's very much her child. "Jonathan," she calls again. "How about *Finsbury* Park?"

Jonathan's face, still glum looking but now ready to be wooed, appears around the bedroom door. "Finsbury Park?" he says. "Why not Hyde Park?"

"It's called a compromise," Barbara says.

"If we do," Jonathan says, getting into the spirit of the negotiation, "Can I take my boat?"

"Yes. As long as you carry it all the way there and all the way back, you can take your boat."

"OK, then," Jonathan says, then, "Mum?"

"Yes?"

"Sophie's really smelly. I think she's done a poo."

* * *

Finsbury Park is, today, a postcard cliché of English summertime. Sunlight dapples the lawns, children run around tree-trunks and young couples lie side-by-side staring at the sky. Barbara is surprised to find herself feeling happy and wonders why she even wanted Tony to come with them in the first place. *Why be so obstinate?* she wonders. Isn't life that much easier when you decide to want what *is* rather than trying to bend life to fit what you want instead?

She lifts Jonathan, whose mood has also transformed, over the railings of the duck pond – she pretends not to notice the dirty looks from the old lady on the bench. She watches as he launches his sailing boat. "Make sure you don't lose it, son," she calls out, and that word, *son*, feels like a blessing today. She feels like a Ladybird book mother with her Ladybird book son, sailing his boat on the lake. "If it goes out to the middle, we'll never get it back," she warns.

"It won't," Jonathan says. "The wind's going the wrong way." And sure enough, because today is, despite inauspicious beginnings, a good day, the boat cuts a graceful arc and returns towards the shore.

Barbara lifts Sophie from the pushchair and crouches around her so that they can throw bread to the ducks together. She hears the woman on the bench tutting, even as Sophie gurgles gorgeously.

Eventually, unable to bear such anarchy any longer, the woman speaks. "Your boy shouldn't be on the other side of the railings. And it says quite clearly not to feed the ducks." She obviously has no idea how unexpected Barbara's happiness is in this moment, nor how precious, but then how could she?

Barbara decides that she will not let this woman spoil her day. "Hello," she replies. "It's a lovely day, isn't it?"

"The park attendant won't be happy if he sees you," the woman says. "He won't be happy at all."

"No," Barbara says, then, "Come on Jonathan. Let's head around that way. It's nicer around there."

Once boats have been sailed and ducks have been fed, and crotchety old women have been ignored and left to their own devices, they head to a spot of semi-shade beneath a poplar tree. Barbara spreads a blanket so that Sophie can crawl around and unpacks the sandwiches.

"Is that one for Dad?" Jonathan asks, pointing at the third parcel.

"It was," Barbara admits, "But he won't be needing it now. We can share it if you're hungry."

"He's not coming?"

"No, he isn't," she says, wondering guiltily if Tony is heading to Hackney Marshes right now.

* * *

At five, they arrive at the hospital. Minnie is sleeping; Glenda is at her bedside.

"How is she?" Barbara whispers, gently squeezing her sister's shoulder.

Glenda glances at Jonathan who is watching them attentively and, by way of reply, almost imperceptibly shakes her head.

"Gran?" Jonathan asks. "Do you want to see my b—"

"Shh!" Barbara admonishes. "She's asleep. You can *see* that she's asleep."

"It's a funny time to sleep," Jonathan replies, lowering his voice. "Is she ill?"

"You know full-well she's ill. She's *very* ill indeed which is why she's sleeping."

"Is she going to die?" he asks.

Barbara is momentarily lost for words.

"Is she?" he asks again.

"Everyone is going to die eventually," Glenda replies quietly, stepping in to save her sister. "No one lives forever. Now, why don't we go down to that little garden? We can talk there without disturbing Gran."

"I did come to see Mum, really," Barbara says. She doesn't really want to talk to Glenda today. She doesn't want to hear about Glenda's new, wonderful boyfriend and she doesn't want to have explain why Tony isn't with her either.

"OK," Glenda says understandingly. "You sit with Mum for a bit and I'll take the kids for a stroll. How's that?"

Barbara glances at her sister and blinks slowly. "Thanks Glen," she says.

Once aunty Glenda has vanished with the children, Barbara takes her seat and reaches for her mother's hand. "Mum?" she says, patting it gently. "Mum?"

Glenda believes that Minnie should be left to sleep whenever she wants, which is pretty much all the time these days, but Barbara wants to make the most of her time with her – *needs* this time with her. The idea that time is suddenly a limited quantity and that it may soon run out is unbearable to her. "Mum?" she says, more loudly and Minnie opens her eyes and turns her head towards her. The whites of her eyes are yellow and her regard is pale and watery. "Barbara?" she croaks.

"How are you feeling today, Mum?"

Minnie works her mouth a little before she manages to speak. "Tired," she finally says.

"Are you in any pain?"

Minnie laughs. It's only a weak laugh but she does actually laugh – her eyes smile – and Barbara can breathe again, because momentarily her mother is back. "You have no idea," Minnie says through the smile.

"Do you want me to get a nurse?"

Minnie shakes her head. "I'm saving that for later," she says. "I'm saving it for the end."

"Saving what?"

"The morphine," Minnie replies. "They say it's bloody lovely."

"Oh *Mum!*"

Minnie is still smiling but there's a sadness in her eyes that's unmistakable. "Where's that 'usband of yours?" she asks.

"Tony? He, um, had to go to work."

Minnie nods and looks enquiringly into her daughter's eyes. "But you're still together?"

"Of course we're still together."

Minnie nods. "Then it all worked out, after all?"

Barbara knows what she means. And yes, by her mother's standards, it's true. It's just that . . . "Yes," she replies. "Yes, Mum. It all worked out just fine."

Tony does not return that evening and he's still not there the next morning when Barbara leaves to walk Jonathan to school. When she gets back home, the recently installed telephone is ringing, and she fumbles with her keys as she struggles to open the door in time. It's the *Mirror* on the line.

"I'm ever so sorry," Barbara tells Tony's manager. "He's been vomiting all night. A stomach bug, I think. I was just about to phone you."

She has just finished the phone call when he appears in the hallway looking as crumpled as a tramp and reeking of beer.

"Where the *hell* have you been?" Barbara asks, more distraught than angry.

"Just . . . don't . . ." Tony says, half raising one hand in a stop sign.

Barbara steps aside as he heads to the lavatory and then

300

again as he returns. He pauses before her. His pupils are dilated, his eyelids droopy. He looks half-dead. Barbara frowns at him.

"I . . ." he says.

"Yes?"

"Look, I . . ."

"Yes?" Barbara asks, struggling to keep the anger from her voice. "You *what?*"

"I dunno. I suppose I just want to say . . ."

"Yes?"

Tony closes his eyes, then wobbles and has to reach out to steady himself on the wall. He hiccups. "Thanks," he finally says. "That's all."

"Thanks? For what?"

"For being so understanding," he slurs. "I don't deserve you."

Barbara glares at him. "But I *don't* understand. I don't understand at all."

Tony stands swaying for a moment and then, with a dismissive wave of one hand, he turns and staggers in the direction of the bedroom. "Forget it then," he says, casting the words over his shoulder.

Once the door to the bedroom has closed behind him, Barbara continues to stand and stare at the empty hallway. "Yes, Mum," she says quietly. "Yes, it all worked out just *fine.*"

* * *

It is the week before Christmas and the forecast is for snow. Barbara can't decide if she hopes for or *does not* hope for snow. She loves snow and yet in almost equal measure she loathes the damned stuff. If it snows, she'll be able to play with Jonathan and Sophie in the tiny shared garden. If it snows enough, they could even build a snowman, their first ever. If it snows, Tony might not be able to get in to work.

He has been doing lots of overtime these past few weeks and Barbara is (finally) starting to miss him. Christmas is nearly here and she feels an urgent need for her husband to be here with her in front of the fire.

The trouble is, of course, that they also need the money that all this overtime brings, so perhaps it's better overall if it doesn't snow. Children cost a fortune to clothe and feed and though Barbara has recently started doing alterations for a local menswear store, it brings in little more than pin money. With inflation running at almost ten per cent, the cost of everything is going through the roof, especially since they introduced decimal currency and all the shopkeepers rounded up their prices.

It's nine p.m., the children are in bed, and Tony is late home again. As she finishes ironing the turn-ups she has just sewn onto the trousers of a very expensive checkered suit, she tries to imagine who would wear such as suit, who could afford such a dandy outfit in these hard times. The suit is pretty much Tony's size and she wonders, briefly, if he'd be game enough to try it on. She would love to see him dressed up like that.

The job finished, she says out loud, "At least that's another ten bob." She forces herself to mentally convert this, then says, "Well, at least that's another fifty pence." She talks to herself more and more these days and feels vaguely concerned about the fact. She folds the ironing board, then, this stowed away, she crosses to the window, looks out at the darkened street and tries not to think about Minnie. Her first Christmas without her mother. Yes, she needs her husband home for Christmas. She has never felt so alone.

A spluttering sound comes from the end of the street and she turns to look, hopeful that it's the noise of Tony's motorbike but it's just an Allegro with a failing exhaust pipe. She's surprised at her mistake. She has come to believe that she can sense Tony's bike from miles away, often before she can even hear it.

The Allegro passes by and right behind it is Tony. He turns toward the house, waves at her and wobbles and, though she's unsure if he can see her through his misty visor or not, she waves back. She crosses to the fireplace and opens the damper and watches as the coals begin to redden. He'll be frozen.

The front door opens, then slams, and Tony appears in the doorway, icy air emanating from his clothes, cooling the room. "I am *so* effing cold," he says, then, "Hello."

"They said it might snow tonight," Barbara says.

Tony pulls off his crash helmet, then removes his jacket and starts to remove the various layers of jumpers beneath. "No doubt about it," he says. "You can smell it in the air." The jumpers removed, he crosses to join Barbara in front of the fireplace. "So how are *you?*" he asks. "How was your day?"

Barbara hates this *how-was-your-day* question. It always feels like a trick, like a *trap* even. For where Tony can say, "I rode to Liverpool and delivered this and then I rode to Derby and delivered that," the only things that Barbara can think of to justify her existence are the endless litany of tiny, mindless tasks that take up her day as a mother. "I walked Jonathan to school, I changed the kids' beds, I did the washing up . . ." These seem, individually, too insignificant to mention, yet together, too numerous to list. And so she always ends up saying, "Oh, nothing much. The usual," or some-such. And then she spends the rest of the evening thinking that Tony has imagined her drinking tea and eating biscuits all day. And, of course, yes, she did that too. And so what?

"You know. The usual chores," she says. "How was your day?"

"Amazing," Tony says, now slipping his arms around her waist and pulling her tight, as if for a waltz.

Barbara frowns. Such displays of enthusiasm are rare in the Marsden household and such displays of affection are even rarer. "What are you after?" she laughs.

"I'm not after anything," Tony replies.

Barbara slides her hands down his back until they are resting on the back pockets of his leather motorcycle trousers. She forces one hand inside a pocket, enjoys, momentarily, the feel of the cold leather hugging his bum. "God, Tony, you're freezing."

"So hug me," he says. "Warm me up."

She pulls him tighter but then shudders with cold. "I can't. It's like hugging an ice-cube," she says apologetically, breaking free. "Maybe you should take a hot bath. I'm worried you'll catch a cold."

Tony pulls a face at this idea, then exaggeratedly sniffs the air. "Is that soup I can smell?" he asks.

"Stew."

"Oh God, you're a marvel. I was dreaming about stew the whole way home."

"I'll fetch it. Stay in front of the fire."

"And then I can tell you my news," Tony says.

Barbara pauses, her hand on the doorknob. "News?"

"Yep," Tony says. "Get my dinner and I'll tell you."

Barbara returns as quickly as she can with Tony's steaming bowl of stew. He has pulled up an armchair and is toasting his hands within inches of the flames.

"You'll get chilblains," she warns.

"I really don't care," Tony replies, then taking the stew, "Aw, fabulous. Thanks."

Barbara pulls the orange vinyl pouffe as close to the fire as she can without risking melting it, then prompts, "So? What's this news?"

"It's *good* news, Babs," Tony says. "It's bloody good news, in fact. It's exactly what we've been waiting for."

They have waited so arduously for so many things in their lives. They have waited for more money, a bigger flat, their first child, and then a sibling for him. But though a little more is always a little better, Barbara can't think what single thing they might be waiting for right now.

"I've got a new job," Tony says, blowing on a spoonful of stew. "Starts after Christmas."

"You have?"

"Staff photographer," Tony says, between mouthfuls. "No more riding parcels around!"

"Really?!"

"Yes. What do you think of that, eh?"

Barbara shakes her head. "I'm amazed. That's brilliant news."

"They were so chuffed with my photos this year, they decided they want me doing it full time."

Barbara wants to ask him if he'll be travelling less. She wants to ask him if he'll be earning more as well. But she knows that such questions would seem calculating and inappropriate. Plus there's something else troubling her and it's taking her a moment to work out how to phrase it in a non-threatening manner. "So, which photos did they like so much?" she finally asks.

"Um, you know . . . the Festival of Light," Tony says. "The mums at the school holding up ten fingers for the decimalisation thing. The kids with the empty milk bottles for *Margaret Thatcher, Milk Snatcher*. Oh, and the postal strike ones. They didn't really say, but I think those are the main ones. Those are the photos people kept patting me on the back about."

Barbara silently pursues her thought process to its ultimate, worrying conclusion and then, despite it, forces a broad grin. "Anyway, that's great news," she says, wincing at her use of the word, *anyway* – a giveaway if ever there was one that certain doubts remain unexpressed.

Thankfully Tony hasn't noticed her *anyway* and so doesn't ask Barbara what she meant by it. Barbara thus escapes having to point out to him what he must already know: that the festival photos he sold were in fact taken by Diane with her new high-powered Nikon zoom lens. That the photos of the kids with their empty milk bottles were, in truth, Phil's (he had failed to sell them to his own newspaper). And that, if the photos depicting decimalisation and the postal strike were his, the ideas for their staging were both *hers*.

But this isn't the moment to point that out. It isn't the moment to point that out *at all*.

2012 – EASTBOURNE, EAST SUSSEX.

"So, Mum," Sophie asks. "What do we think then?"

They are installed in Barbara's lounge. The gas fire is hissing before them and Nut is wandering around trying to decide where he will be the most comfortable. On the coffee table sits Brett's contract, which over the past week Sophie has decided is in fact a small price to pay. The only alternative is really just to cancel everything. But it's immaterial really what Sophie thinks, because she's pretty sure that her mother is going to veto Brett's involvement and sink her boat, right here, right now. She is preparing to abandon ship.

"About what?" Barbara asks. "About Brett, the contract, or the images?"

Sophie shrugs. "Well, they're all kind of linked really, aren't they? But let's start with Brett. You don't like him. Am I right?"

"I don't *dis*like him, Sophie. I just don't see why we have to have a journalist involved at all. I don't trust them. In general, I mean."

"Except when they work for the *Daily Mail*?"

"That's just silly. You know perfectly well what I mean."

"It's not as if Dad was some secret serial killer, is it?" Sophie says. "It's not like Brett's going to find out that he killed Kennedy or anything!"

"You're still being silly."

"But *you* know exactly what *I* mean too."

"There are skeletons in everyone's closets, Sophie. And I

307

just don't want his name sullied to satisfy some journalist's need for print." Sophie rubs her nose and frowns and Barbara suspects that she's on the point of being rumbled. Perhaps she has gone too far.

"Mum," Sophie says. "Are you saying that there's something *specific* hiding in Dad's closet? Something that Brett really *could* find out? Something you haven't perhaps told me?"

Barbara laughs. "And now you're being utterly ridiculous," she says.

"Well then! What's the fuss about?"

"You've said it yourself lots of times. They invent things. They make things up."

"But not about *Dad*. Not about some long-dead, half-forgotten photographer." Barbara looks forlornly into her eyes and Sophie realises that she's been indelicate to say the least. "Sorry, Mum. That came out wrong. I just mean that Brett has no reason to invent anything about Dad. There's nothing to be gained from it. And he is, after all, my boyfriend. He would never do something like that anyway. Not to me."

"I'm sorry to say it, dear, but that's not much of a love-letter he's written you," Barbara points out, nodding at the contract.

"No . . . Well . . ." Sophie swallows with the same difficulty she has been having swallowing Brett's contract. "Business is business, I suppose."

"Can you *really* not just do it without him?"

Sophie sighs sadly. "I *could,*" she says. "But it would have to be some little gallery that no one has heard of, and I'd have to pay for the book to be printed instead of us being paid for it, and the *Times* wouldn't be talking up what a big deal the whole thing is . . . And without all of that, it would be an entirely different proposition. That's what Brett brings to the party."

"I see."

"And if you think about it, Brett's twenty-five per cent is our guarantee that he *won't* do anything to diss Dad. Because he'll want it all to be a success as much as we do."

Barbara nods. "I suppose. And what does Jonathan say? Have you spoken to him about it?"

"He said to do whatever I think is best," Sophie says. "I don't think he's very interested in it all, really. Which is disappointing, frankly."

Having tested the other options – Barbara's lap, next to the fire, the red velvet cushion – Nut now jumps onto Sophie's lap, turns twice and then begins, rattlingly, to purr.

"I liked your choice of images, by the way," Barbara says.

"You did?"

"It was hard for me to look at some of them. Very hard, sometimes. But I think they're a good selection."

"They will look great in a book, won't they?"

"They will."

"We're still a few short, though. I could do with another ten or so."

"Do you think that you'll find them? Because you've pretty much finished going through them all now, haven't you?"

Sophie nods. "I might take some of the rejects and put them in anyway. I know I've asked you this already, but you're really sure, aren't you, that there's nothing else lying around?"

Barbara licks her teeth and then, the decision confirmed, she stands and crosses to the sideboard. She returns with two blue photo-store pouches which she hands to Sophie. "Here," she says. "You're going to be disappointed, but I know how much you wanted to see these so I got them printed."

Sophie looks shocked. "Mum?"

"They're of Paris. But they're very poor."

"They're not! These aren't . . . Are they?"

Barbara nods. "The Pentax tour."

"But I thought you said . . ."

"I just didn't want them to become public. Go on. Have a look."

Sophie tips the cat from her knees – somehow the better to concentrate – and brushes her hair behind one ear. "God!" she says, sliding the wadge of prints from the first pouch. "I knew you wouldn't have destroyed those negatives. I just knew it."

"They're just cheap, normal prints from Tesco," Barbara says. "But you can get enlargements done if you want to."

"Of course. God, this is brilliant, Mum."

"*That*, I rather doubt."

Sophie frowns at the first photo. "Colour!" she says. "And thirty-five millimetre too."

"It was for Pentax," Barbara reminds her. "They dictated everything. That was half the problem."

As Sophie leafs through the first ten or so images, her brow increasingly, furrows. "These look like someone's holiday snaps," she finally comments, flashing a poorly framed image of Notre Dame cathedral at her mother.

"I know."

"And half of them are out of bloody focus."

"Yes, I know."

Sophie continues to work her way through the photos, her expression increasingly distraught. "How can they *all* be out of focus? Was he *drunk* or something?"

"Very probably," Barbara says, then, "But it was the camera mainly. He couldn't get on with it at all."

Sophie snorts. "How hard could it be?" she says. "I mean, look at that!" She holds up a different print – an image of two women sitting in an archetypal Parisian brasserie. The lighting is gorgeous, the bar is elegant and the women are perfect, beautiful, bitchy looking icons of Parisian life. They're even smoking Gitanes, the packaging of which lies between them on the table. Were it not for the fact that the focal point of the photo is on a potted plant in the foreground and everything else is out of focus, it could have been an image taken by Henri Cartier-Bresson.

"If I remember correctly," Barbara explains, attempting to mitigate Tony's posthumous shame, "it was one of the first autofocus cameras ever. Pentax were desperately trying to push it. But your father hated it. He said it drove him crazy."

Sophie nods. "I think I actually remember that," she says. "Did it have loads of batteries in a huge, chunky lens? Did it beep all the time?"

Barbara nods. "Yes, I think that's the one. They discontinued it shortly afterwards."

"He *could* have just switched the bloody autofocus off," Sophie says, feeling angry now. "These are shocking."

"Oh, you know what he was like with technology."

Sophie is flicking through the photos rapidly now. "God Mum," she says. "These really are appalling. There's not *one*."

"And that, love, is why I kept them out of sight. I hope you understand now."

"Too right . . . Jesus. Didn't he take any with his Rolleiflex?"

"No," Barbara says, glancing at her feet. "Not one."

*   *   *

"One *cappucciiiiino!*" the Barista announces. He says it with such flourish, that one might think he had just managed to convert coffee to gold. Which in a way, Sophie realises, is exactly what Starbucks *has* found a way to do. "And one *faaaabulous* double *espresso!!*"

"Thanks," Brett says flatly. Being American, he must be used to such over-the-top service, Sophie figures. He takes his mug and scans the room. It's lunchtime and this is Soho, so

311

the only seats available are those at the dingy end of the room next to the toilets. "Looks like we're over there," Brett says, glumly.

Once they are seated, he smooths his tie then sips his coffee before saying, "So. You wanted to talk?"

"Yes," Sophie says.

"About?"

"I had a rethink," she announces. "We accept your conditions. Well, Mum and I do. Jonathan wants nothing to do with the whole thing."

"You accept my conditions," Brett repeats. "You mean the need for a contract, right?"

"Yes."

"Huh."

"Huh?"

"Don't you think an apology might be in order?"

Sophie shrugs.

"You told me to 'fuck off', Sophie," Brett reminds her. "You said I had a 'stinky ego'."

Sophie snorts at this and, as a result, cappuccino goes up her nose.

"Am I laughing here, Sophie? Do you see me smiling?"

She sighs and gives a little shake of her head. "Anyway, what I was—" she begins.

"Come on Sophie," Brett insists. "Apologise."

Sophie gasps. "Do you have any idea how difficult this is for me, Brett? I mean, just coming here and saying I was wrong? Can't you show a little . . . I don't know . . . *compassion?*"

Now it's Brett who snorts. "I don't think that's really my problem, Sophie. I think you got into this mess all on your lonesome. Now just say 'sorry' and we can move on."

Sophie gasps. "OK! *Sorry* Brett."

"Say it like you mean it."

Sophie laughs again. She can't help herself. "You sound just like my mother! Now just lighten up, will you?"

"You hurt my feelings, Sophie," Brett says.

Sophie notes how often he uses her name when he's being earnest and she notes how much she hates it. It sounds so patronising. "Well, *Brett*," she says. "You hurt my feelings by asking for a contract. Now can we please just forget it?"

Brett shrugs. "So you don't know how to apologise. What's new?"

"Can we?"

"OK. Whatever."

"So, are we OK? Can we go ahead? With the project?"

"I guess," Brett says reluctantly. "But what about Jonathan?"

"It's not like he's going to talk to anyone else. You'll still have exclusivity. He just doesn't want to get involved. He's got a kid on the way and he wants a quiet life, that's all."

"Do you think he'd sign a disclaimer to say that? That he won't talk to anyone else."

"Probably," Sophie says. "But I can personally guarantee that he won't."

"OK," Brett says. "And your mom's onboard now, huh?"

"Just about. I wouldn't want to ask her for much but at least she's not going to throw any spanners in the works. And that at least is something."

"Indeed."

"Hey, look at these," Sophie says, reaching into her bag for the photos. "I finally got them from Mum. We can't use them or anything, but it shows she's changed her mind a bit."

"These are?"

"These are the famous Pentax photos."

"Oh!" Brett says, flipping open the first pouch. "I thought they had all been destroyed."

"That's the official story. But . . ."

"And we can't use them *because?*"

"Have a look."

Brett slides the photos out and leafs quickly through them. "Your *father* took these?"

"Pretty shocking, huh?"

Brett pulls a puzzled expression. "It looks like something went wrong with the camera."

"It was a Pentax ME-F. I looked it up on the net. Their first ever autofocus camera. It was meant to be revolutionary but it was just one big fail, really. The technology wasn't ready and lots of them had technical problems. Dad wasn't the only one who hated them."

"Hum," Brett says. "But I doubt many people failed *quite* so spectacularly."

"No."

"Gee, these are baad!" Brett laughs and Sophie, despite herself, despite that fact that in essence she agrees, starts to feel offended.

"Is there any point in my continuing?" Brett asks.

"Not really," Sophie says, holding out one hand to take the photos back. She slips two from the back of the second wallet and hands them to Brett. "I thought maybe these two," she says. "We're a few images short still and at least these look like the soft-focus was intentional."

"Yeah, I see what you mean," Brett says, doubtfully, "but if you use these, someone will realise that all the others exist too. People will wanna see them all."

"We can just say that we didn't consider them worthy of attention, can't we? Everyone will realise we've made a selection."

"Nah," Brett says. "I say trash 'em."

"*Trash* them?"

"Uh-huh. A famous photographer father is a bigger story than a mediocre one who took some lucky snaps."

"Aw, come on Brett. My dad was *not* a mediocre guy who took some lucky snaps."

"Well, anyone who looks at these will kind of think that he was."

Sophie can sense heat rising. She's starting to feel angry. "Brett, you just can't say that. This is my dad you're talking about."

"Sophie, I'm just saying what I see here."

"You know what? If that's what you really think, then maybe you are better out of this." Sophie stuffs the photographs back into her bag and stands. "Maybe we really should forget the whole thing."

"Sophie!" Brett says. "You're overreacting here."

"Of course I'm bloody overreacting. He was my dad. And he's dead!"

"Hey, I'm sorry. I didn't mean anything, OK?" Brett says, but Sophie is already pulling on her coat. She's knows he's right, but she's stuck and doesn't know how to change direction.

Brett stands and gently touches her arm. "Sophie. I'm apologising here. I'm sorry. Now please, *please* just sit the fuck down." He glances around the room and Sophie, following his regard, now realises that everyone is looking at her. In case of need of a quick exit she keeps her coat on. But she does manage (just) to sit back down.

"Gee!" Brett says.

"I'm sorry. But you just can't say stuff like that about my dad."

"I know this," Brett says. "It's countries and families."

"Countries and families?"

"Sure. People can tell you all kinds of stuff about where they come from. About all the bad things that happened to them. About their home country or their folks or whatever. And they're allowed to tell you that stuff and you're allowed to listen. But you must never, ever agree with them. And definitely don't join in with the trashing."

Sophie runs her fingers through her hair. "Yes," she says. "Yes, that's about the sum of it. It's OK for me to say these are awful. But just leave it to me, OK?"

"Anyways," Brett says. "We agree on one thing. We can't use them."

"Yes," Sophie says. "Yes, we agree on that."

Sophie's phone vibrates, so she pulls it from her pocket and studies the screen. "Oh my God!" she says.

"What's that?"

"Judy's sprogged!"

"Huh!" Brett says.

"It's a boy. Dylan. The poor wee fucker."

"Don't be like that."

"I don't know what's worse," Sophie tells him. "Being called Dylan or having Judy for a mother."

1976 – THE NORFOLK COAST.

"Dad," Jonathan whines. "There's a whole traffic jam stuck behind us now."

Embarrassed, as ever, by Tony's holiday meandering, he is kneeling on the back seat of the Beetle watching the frustrated drivers behind them. Tony only has two driving styles – relaxed and road rage. Personally, Barbara far prefers 'relaxed', but at this moment in time she's unable to come to his defence.

"I'm doing *forty*," Tony says, glancing at the speedometer. "There's nothing wrong with forty."

"Except that the speed limit's *sixty*," Jonathan says.

"It's a limit, Jon, an *upper* limit. It's a maximum, not a minimum. Isn't that right, Barbara?"

Barbara does not answer. She continues to stare out of the side window and Tony drives in silence for a few minutes before he speaks again. "So have you still got the hump with me?" he asks her quietly. "About last night?"

Still Barbara does not answer him.

Sophie, who is seated behind her, shouts (with alarming force) "Beach!"

"Yes, Sophie," Barbara says. "Yes, that's a huge beach."

"I'll take that as a 'yes' then, shall I?" Tony asks.

"Take it any way you want. I'm past caring," Barbara replies.

"*Definitely* a 'yes' then," Tony mumbles.

He did not come home last night and Barbara had been seriously worried. Knowing that they were supposed to be leaving for Norfolk in the early hours, she had been unable to

317

convince herself that this was 'just' one more of Tony's random absences. And when finally, at eight a.m., he had reappeared, revealing that, yes, it *was* just one more of Tony's random absences, she had found herself unable to forgive him. Which is pretty much where she remains still.

"I just don't see what the problem is," Tony is saying now, prompting Barbara to sigh again. "Talk to me!" he says. "We're supposed to be on holiday here. We're supposed to be having fun."

Barbara licks her lips, then speaks quietly, addressing him over her shoulder. "The problem, Tony," she says, "is that I was worried. The *problem* is that I didn't know if you'd be home today or tomorrow, or ever even."

"But I *was* home in time. And we're here now, aren't we?"

"The *problem,*" she continues, "Is that you *still* won't say where you've been."

"I told you. I had a work shoot up north. I stayed over at Phil's."

"And the problem," Barbara says, "is that's simply not true. And we both know it."

"There's another beach," Sophie shouts, pointing again. They have been driving for an hour since lunch and she's getting bored. The car is unbearably hot, doubly so in the rear seats, and having been promised a beach, a beach is what she wants.

"Phone Phil," Tony says. "He'll tell you. He'll back me up."

Barbara turns to face him and raises one hand to paint an imaginary headline across the windscreen. "Man's best drinking buddy confirms dodgy excuse to wife!" she reads. "Shock scoop!"

"You're impossible when you're like this."

"*I'm* impossible?"

"Mum!" Sophie says, now pointing backwards. "What was wrong with *that* beach?"

"Yeah," Jonathan says. "It looked alright to me."

"What was it like?" Tony asks, grateful for the subject change. "I didn't see."

"It was baked solid," Barbara says, fidgeting in the discomfort of her sweaty vinyl seat.

"So we carry on?"

Barbara chews a fingernail and fights with herself. The beach they just passed may not be ideal for Sophie's needs (sandcastles) but it was *absolutely* perfect for Tony's needs, which are for saleable photographic evidence of the 'hottest summer for three hundred years'.

"The next beach won't be far," Tony says, and both Jonathan and Sophie groan.

"Cutting off your nose to spite your face." The phrase, one of Minnie's favourites, pops into Barbara's mind. It happens a lot these days and Barbara wonders if Minnie is somehow present and talking to her, or if it's nothing more than random memories bubbling up from her past. Sometimes she thinks that those two versions of the truth amount to pretty much the same thing – that those who are no longer with us remain with us specifically *through* our memories of them. That memories are perhaps more than just recordings, that they are the actual *essence* of the people we have known, the places we have been, lingering on long after the event, like time travellers, like ghosts.

In this instance Minnie would be right. As a family they need Tony to do well: they need him to take the right photographs and they need him to sell them. And if he isn't going to tell her where he vanishes to – and after thirteen years of marriage, she knows that he isn't – and if she isn't going to leave him – and after thirteen years, she knows that as well – then sabotaging the professional aspect of this trip, which Tony assured her was going, after all, to *pay* for this trip, really doesn't make any sense. It really would be *cutting off her nose to spite her face.*

She turns her body to face him now. She leans in so that only he can hear her. "I hate you right now," she whispers.

Tony glances at her, then back at the road. He frowns. *"What?"* he says.

She leans in and says it again. "Right now, at this instant, I *really* hate you. I just want you to know that."

"Jesus!" Tony exclaims, looking distinctly unsettled.

"But . . ." she adds, more loudly. "You should turn around and go back to that beach."

"What?" Tony says again.

"Go back to that last beach," she repeats, soliciting cheers from both Jonathan and Sophie.

"Why?" Tony asks, suspicious of Barbara's motives, scared that she has perhaps seen a cliff she wants to push him off.

"That beach was amazing," Barbara says. "It's all baked and cracked like crazy paving. And it's covered with semi-naked, bright pink females. It's exactly what you said you were looking for."

Tony glances in the mirror, flicks on an indicator and then pulls into a siding. The tailback of frustrated drivers speeds past, already accelerating to speeds that Jonathan would consider more reasonable now that the *Beetle from Hell* has finally pulled aside.

"Really?" Tony asks. "You're not just winding me up."

"Go back, Dad," Jonathan says.

"Yes, come on," Sophie agrees. "Go back."

Barbara nods and smiles and flutters her eyelashes at him repulsively. "Go back, darling," she says. "You'll see. I meant *everything* I said."

1977 – HACKNEY, LONDON.

Barbara glances at the kitchen clock. "You'd better get a move on," she tells Jonathan. "You're going to be late."

"It doesn't matter," Jonathan says. "It's just P.E."

"It *all* matters."

"I just want to see the dude in his new threads," Jonathan says.

"If you mean your father, you've already seen him in a suit at Phil's wedding," Barbara says, even though she understands entirely. She too is looking forward to seeing Tony in his new suit.

"Yeah, but I've never seen him in a *white* suit," Jonathan says, his voice full of adolescent disdain. "I've never seen him dressed up like a *Bee Gee* before."

"Don't you dare say that to him!" Barbara warns. "He's nervous enough as it is. And it's not white. It's cream."

"He's still gonna look like a Bee Gee," Jonathan says.

"Please! Just go to school will you? You'll see him tonight anyway."

But it's too late. Tony is clomping down the hallway towards them in brand new thick-soled shoes. "Are you sure I have to wear the tie?" he asks Barbara, tugging at his collar.

Everyone pauses to look at him. A moment frozen around him simply because his clothing is different. It's a strange, out-of-time sensation.

"I like it!" Sophie declares. "I think you look lovely, Dad."

Still fiddling with his kipper tie, Tony shoots her a coy grin and a wink. She's very much a daddy's girl and he can always count on her for a feel-good comment when he needs one.

Barbara, who has now crossed the room to meet him, agrees. "You look marvellous," she says, straightening his tie and pushing it a little further into the waistcoat. "You look like a prizewinning photographer."

"I feel like I've been sentenced to death by hanging," Tony says.

"Now you know how it feels, Dad," Jonathan, who has to wear school uniform every day, says. He can't see what the fuss is about.

"I doubt *your* tie gives you much bother. Not the way you wear it around your knees like that."

"Ties are naff anyway," Jonathan says, a smile in his voice. "None of the Bee Gees wear ties."

Barbara shoots Jonathan a glare and he grins defiantly at her.

"Yes, but I'm not in the Bee Gees, am I?" Tony says. "I'm not going on *Top of the Pops*. I'm going on a bleeding arts programme."

"OK," Barbara says. "That's enough. Jon, go to school. Right now! It's almost eight-thirty!"

Jonathan stands, picks up his sports bag and jive-walks across the room to his father. He gives him an exaggerated once-over, then says, "You's the man, Pop," before – humming *Stayin' Alive* in a silly, high voice – he strides, hips swaying, down the hallway.

"Cheeky little git," Tony says, once the front door has closed.

"He's fourteen, Tony. They're all like that at fourteen."

"Will *I* be like that at fourteen?" Sophie asks.

"No," Tony says. "You'll be an angel at fourteen, just like now. You'll be an angel forever." He looks at Barbara again. "It is too much though, isn't it? I should have got the blue one."

"No, really, you look perfect. We watched *Aquarius* together last week. You saw how they were dressed.

Tony feels scared and all of his fear is being focused on the stupid suit. But knowing the cause of his fear isn't enough to actually ease it. He looks at Sophie who is still staring adoringly up at him from the breakfast table. "What do you think, pumpkin?" he asks.

"Can you walk me to school?" she replies. "I want everyone to see how handsome and famous you are." Which is of course the exact perfect thing for her to have said.

"I'd love to, but I can't, sweetheart," Tony says, glancing at his watch. "I've got to be in Wembley by ten."

"Please?"

"We *could* walk her to school and then carry on to Hackney station," Barbara suggests. In truth, she too wants to make the most of Tony today. She too wants to be seen with her husband in the suit, wants to bask in a little of his prizewinning glory.

"Alright," Tony says. "But we'd better get a move on."

Sophie has crossed the room and picked up her father's camera. "Can I take a photo of you?" she asks.

Tony rolls his eyes. "Just the one, then," he says. "Do you remember how?"

"Of course I do," Sophie says, removing the cover.

Once Tony has swept Sophie up in his arms at the school-gates, twirled her around (and at eight years old, this is getting difficult) then released her into the noisy throng, Barbara links her arm through his and they head towards the station.

"I still feel stupid dressed like this," Tony says, despite feeling a little flattered by the admiring glances of passers-by. "I look like I'm going to a wedding. I look like I'm going to *my* bleeding wedding."

"You need to worry less about how you look and think more

about what you're going to say. Because believe me, you'll *look* perfect."

"And what the hell *am* I going to say?" he asks. "You know how I hate all that arty-farty bollocks."

"Well don't say *that*. But really, I'm sure you'll be fine."

"So tell me, Mr Marsden," Tony says in a mocking TV voice. "What is this photo *about?* Which of your deepest desires were you trying to express?"

"Just stop. You'll be *fine!*"

"But they're going to want a load of nonsense," Tony says. "And I'm no good at all that spiel. You know I'm not."

"Tony! Stop it!" Barbara says, squeezing his arm. "You're getting yourself in a tizzy for nothing. You've already won the prize. Everyone already thinks you're the bee's knees. That's why they invited you on."

"It's easy enough for you to say. You're not about to face the Spanish Inquisition on national telly."

"Can't you say they're just photos?" Barbara says. "Say they're photos and they're meant to be looked at, not talked about."

Tony snorts. "Yeah," he says. "Sure. That'll go down well."

* * *

Barbara carries the final dish, a plate of Stilton-stuffed celery, into the dining room. She pushes the devilled eggs to one side and repositions the tray of mini-quiches so that she can fit the celery onto the table. She stands back and appraises the spread, then sighs with satisfaction. It looks perfect.

"Mum, it's playing!" – Jonathan's voice, calling from the lounge.

Next, Sophie appears in the doorway. "Mum!" she says, urgently. "They're playing the tape. Come on!"

Barbara walks through to the lounge, now almost too crowded for her to enter. Neighbours have squashed onto the sofa and Tony's friends from his old photography class are seated cross-legged on the floor. There are new people too, people Tony apparently knows well but who Barbara has never met before: two journalists from the *Mirror*, a painter, a poet, a cook . . . Everyone is drinking. Everyone is smoking. And a vague, sweet smell in the air makes Barbara think that they aren't only smoking cigarettes. Really the place looks like an ashram but Barbara is determined to remain relaxed. She's determined to fit in and have a little fun for once.

Dave, who has brought his Betamax player along, is lying outstretched, and onscreen the generic music to *Aquarius* is playing. Sophie, who knows the words to the theme tune *The Age of Aquarius,* is singing along.

Malcolm is still talking. "Incredible really that that's all on that cartridge thing," he is saying. "When did they show this?"

"Sunday night," Tony says. "Half-past ten."

"And you just recorded it from the telly?"

"Dave did," Tony says.

"Shhh!" Sophie tells them and everyone is glad that she has been the one to silence them.

On screen, Peter Hall is introducing the programme.

Tonight we'll be talking to Steve Leber, the co-producer of a new musical called Beatlemania and Anthony Marsden, who is the first person ever to be named photo journalist of the year twice in a row. But first we have Wolfgang Büld who has made a full length documentary about London's punk movement. Hello Wolfgang!

Hello.

"We could go and get some food maybe," Malcolm says. "I only really want to see our Tony here."

"I can fast forward it to the Tony bit if you want," Dave says, his finger hovering over one of the chrome levers of the video recorder.

"Can you?"

"Of course," Dave says. "You can do all sorts with these." He presses the lever and the on-screen image speeds up.

"That's funny," Sophie says. "I like it when it's faster."

"Can we get one of these, Mum?" Jonathan asks.

"A video recorder? No. They cost a fortune, don't they Dave?"

"This one's rented," Dave says. "But yes, they cost *hundreds* to buy."

"There!" Jonathan, who has been avidly watching the television set, is pointing, and on-screen Tony is wobbling from side to side – gesticulating at triple speed.

Dave rewinds then forward winds repeatedly until, finally finding the right spot, he freezes the image.

"You took your tie off," Jonathan comments.

"It was boiling," Tony says. "The lights . . . I was sweating like a pig."

Barbara sighs. With his shirt collar spread out over the lapels of his three piece suit, he really *does* look like one of the Bee Gees, and that hadn't been the look they'd been aiming for.

"Ready?" Dave asks. Absolute silence falls upon the room. People even stop chewing the peanuts in their mouths.

"It's a shame you don't have a colour set," Malcolm says, prompting another round of shushing noises.

Finally Dave releases the button and the screen is filled with

Tony looking uncomfortable, then a series of his prizewinning photos: a woman on a baked beach, a punk with a mohican climbing onto an Intercity 125 train, a demonstration in front of number 10 Downing Street . . .

We can see from just a few of your photographs that you have an exceptional sense of composition. Did you learn that in a formal setting or is it a natural gift that you have developed?

Barbara, at the rear of the room, sees Sophie grip Jonathan's arm as she waits for her father to reply. She wishes that she too had someone to hold on to. She grips the back of an armchair instead.

It's more . . . natural, really.

A few seconds of silence follow. The interviewer is clearly waiting for Tony to elaborate, and eventually he does.

I mean, I never went to art school or anything. I just like taking photographs.

Splendid! And what's your motivation? Where do you get your *drive?* Take this photo . . .

He flashes the beach photo at the camera.

Is it a comment on modern society? Are all these baked bodies there to tell us something about leisure in the modern sense?

Onscreen, Tony coughs and scratches his neck. He pulls a face as if he is perhaps suffocating. Finally he speaks and everyone in the lounge resumes breathing.

I . . . I . . . Look, I get a bit sick of all this talk about art to be honest. Art, and I mean visual art obviously, well, it's meant to be looked at, isn't it? If people want talk they can listen to the radio or read a book.

Peter Hall is visibly peeved.

Or watch television, ha ha. I'm sure that our viewers are watching in the hope that you'll *talk* to us about your prize-winning photographs, after all.

Yes. But I'm not a television host, am I? I'm a photographer. So I'd rather people just looked at my work. That's the point of photography. It's literal. A camera is, to me, like a butter knife, cutting through reality and saving it in slices for later. What the photo means is whatever the person looking at it thinks it means. Visual art is visual. That's the whole point of it. It's there to be looked at, not to be explained. So why don't *you* look at my photo and tell me what *you* think it's about. That's far more interesting to me than what I think it's about.

Indeed. Well, one thing we can all agree on is that we all enjoy your stunning photographs. So congratulations on your prize.

Thank you.

The camera zooms back onto Peter Hall's face. He looks flustered.

Now long before the punk movement, another musical event took London by storm. Beatlemania. A new musical opening in the West End next week . . .

"You can stop it there," Tony says. "That's it. Some bird had dragged me off the set by then."

Dave presses the button.

"What do you think?" Tony asks. "Did I get away with it?"

"You were brilliant," Malcolm says. "The perfect anti-hero. A man of the people! They're going to *love* you."

* * *

Barbara regretfully leaves the calm of the dining room and forces herself to return to the fray. She feels uncomfortable and self-conscious but holding the plate helps. Having a purpose enables her to forget the mechanics of putting one foot in front of another, enables her to forget, almost, the many challenges involved in breathing.

In the lounge, there are twice as many people as before – strictly standing room only.

Jonathan is playing records on the new music centre (Barbara has told him that he can play anything except the Bee Gees), and people are drinking and shouting above the music. A couple of people are smoking joints and a few are beginning to move their hips to Elton John and Kiki Dee's *Don't Go Breaking My Heart*.

Barbara passes once around the room with her plate of mini-quiches, then returns, like a diver coming up for air, to the safe haven of the dining room where she pours herself a larger than usual glass of sherry and downs it in one. It seems to work for everyone else. Why not her?

When she returns to the lounge, she finds Diane standing in

the doorway. "Wow!" Diane says, almost having to shout to be heard over the music. "This is some party!"

"Yes! I didn't even know you were coming! Celery stick?"

Diane glances at the plate with disdain, as if perhaps Barbara has gone completely mad, which in this instant she perceives that she may well have. "Of course you don't want a celery stick!" she says.

Diane shrugs and takes one from the plate. "Sure," she says. "I'll have a celery stick. Let's go crazy!"

"We haven't seen you for ages."

Diane crunches into the celery, then chews before replying, "No. I'm sorry about that. Things have been . . . you know . . . hard for me."

Barbara nods gently. "I understand," she says. "I understand entirely. It's been a difficult time for everyone."

"Anyway . . ." Diane says, visibly casting around for the next subject. "I *love* your dress! Where did you get that?"

Barbara blushes and looks down at her feet encased in slightly too small but rather smart vinyl boots from the charity shop. "Don't tell anyone," she says, "but I made it. I copied it from one I saw in Carnaby street."

"You didn't do the tie-dye thing yourself, did you?"

Barbara nods. "Uh huh," she says. "The one in the shop was much brighter, all oranges and greens . . . but I wanted something more subtle."

"Well, you look amazing," Diane says. "Really!"

"Thanks," Barbara says, glancing briefly at her feet again. "You're looking very well too. Very tanned and healthy."

"I just got back from California," Diane says. "I'm still jet lagged."

"California?"

"I *loved* it there. I think I want to go and live there to be

330

honest. It's just like in the films. Everyone's groovy and everyone's hip, and *everyone's* stoned. And San Francisco – I just fell in love with the place!"

"Gosh!" Barbara says. "How exciting."

"You wouldn't mind, would you?"

"Mind what?"

"If I really did move there?"

"Me?"

"Both of you?"

"Diane!" Barbara says. "How could we?"

"Good . . . Because I really might. Oh, I saw Tony on TV. It was the night I got back, actually. He did well."

"He did, it's true. We watched earlier on, on a tape recorder thingy."

Diane flicks her hair. "That anti-establishment thing is all the rage in America too. That was a very good move on his part."

"Anti-establishment?"

Diane nods eagerly. "Yes, the whole *I get sick of talking about art* angle. Like he wasn't on an arts programme! I could have died. But it was clever. It worked."

"Actually, *I* thought of that."

"You did?"

"Yes. We were on the way to the train station and Tony was all in a panic about what he was going to say. And I said, 'Just tell them they're photos. Say they're meant to be looked at, not talked about'."

"Well, it was a very good move. People love that stuff. Oh! And here he is! The man of the moment. My, you're looking fierce!"

Barbara turns to see Tony standing beside her. He is indeed looking fierce. But he shakes his head and denies it. "Fierce? Not at all," he says, smiling at Diane, then somehow managing to look completely different when he turns the same frozen smile on Barbara.

He takes Diane by the arm. "Don't stand there on the threshold," he says. "Come and join the party. And tell me about America!"

Diane glances over her shoulder as Tony tugs her away. She winks at Barbara and throws her a parting peace offering. "You really *do* look beautiful in that dress!" she says.

Diane's flattery and the sherry suddenly hit home and as she sashays through the crowd, Barbara feels comfortable in her skin. It's an unusual experience for her and it's a shock to realise just how good that feels – what a relief it is to suddenly have the impression that she's at one with her own body. She generally feels like a tiny, scared child lurking within, trying to pilot some big, alien machine around the room.

"Celery stick?" she offers to the right. "Oh, hello Malcolm! Celery stick? Hello Jenny! How are you?"

"I love the dress!"

"Why, thank you! Celery stick, anyone?"

By the time she reaches the far side of the room, the plate is almost empty, so she turns back towards the kitchen. *The Things We Do For Love* is playing and she feels drunk and perhaps slightly stoned (is it possible to get stoned on other people's smoke?) and Tony is no longer with Diane but with Jules, and 10cc are singing about love. All is right with the world.

"Jules. You know Barbara?" Tony says, grabbing her arm as she passes by. He is shockingly red in the face which is generally a sign that he's getting dangerously drunk.

"Yes," Jules says, smiling benignly. "Of course. Great outfit, Barbara."

"She made it herself," Tony says. "Out of an old bed-sheet! Can you believe that?"

Barbara's smile fades a little. "I actually—"

332

"Babs is terribly creative," Tony interrupts. "She gives me *all* of my best ideas. In fact, I don't think I'd have a clever thought without her. Isn't that right, Babs?"

Barbara opens her mouth to reply but then can't think of anything to say. Nice Tony has vanished and nasty Tony is back. Sophisticated, charming Barbara, so briefly glimpsed, has vanished also, leaving the tiny terrified child back in control, randomly pulling on levers as the vehicle lurches around the room. "Celery stick?" she mutters, stumbling on through the crowd.

Back in the kitchen, she washes the plate before returning to the dining room for another shot of sherry and a handful of cheesy footballs. So what if she *did* make the dress from an old curtain? So what if she did tie-dye it herself? How *dare* he!

At this moment, she is saved, because her favourite song of the moment comes on, Abba's *Money, Money, Money. Damn him!* she thinks. *I will enjoy this party.*

In the lounge, the room has divided into two, those who are drinking at the front, and those who are dancing, crowded around the music centre.

Sophie is spinning around like a dervish, dancing rock-and-roll style with Diane, and Barbara watches them jealously for a moment before she reminds herself that Diane may be leaving soon. Of course she'll want to make the most of the occasion. It's all perfectly normal.

She moves to the edge of the dancers and closes her eyes to shut it all out. She lets her body begin to sway. She likes the way the dress moves around her. She likes the way the music and the floor, filtered through sherry, feel soft and welcoming, like a mattress in the sun. *Money, money, money* . . . She begins to smile. Such an uplifting sound!

Someone speaks to her. "She's such a good dancer!"

She opens her eyes to see Diane dancing in a slow, swaying

333

motion in front of her. With her beautiful straight black hair, she looks like a reed on the seabed, undulating with the tide. "Sophie, you mean?"

Diane nods and smiles some more. "Yes. She's amazing!"

"Oh, I know," Barbara says. "She loves to dance. Yesterday morning, I came in and found her dancing like the Zulus do."

"Like the who?"

Barbara laughs. "Like the Zulus," she repeats, patting a hand against her mouth and turning in a circle whilst stamping one foot in time with the music.

"Oh, how funny!" Diane says.

"I think she saw it on the telly," Barbara says, struggling to intonate – she's definitely tipsy. "I watched her for ages. She went round and around."

"What's all this?" Tony has joined them but is not dancing. Tony never dances, can't dance, in fact. Though Barbara tried in the early days to teach him, it's impossible. He simply has no sense of rhythm.

"Barbara's showing me how the Zulus dance," Diane laughs, gaily.

"Show me."

Barbara shrugs, then laughs and repeats the dance. "I was only explaining what—"

"Ha! That's great. Malcolm!" Tony shouts. "Look at this! Do it again!"

Barbara frowns but repeats the movement one more time. "I was just showing Diane here how Sophie—" she begins again to explain, but Tony, laughing raucously, is staggering away.

"Don't mind him," Diane says. "He's drunk."

"Yes, I know," Barbara replies. But she does mind, not because her little bubble of happiness has been burst, but because she knows that bursting it was Tony's specific purpose in laughing at her like that.

334

Valiantly, so as not to admit defeat, she dances until the end of the song, but her heart is no longer in it. Afterwards, she returns to the dining room where she eats a sausage on a stick and then to the kitchen where she drinks a glass of tap water. But these rooms are busy now, and because all she wants is to be alone, she heads out to the back yard.

With the noise of the party behind her, she breathes in the cold night air and looks at the moon, hanging spectacularly over the neighbour's apple tree.

She sits on a border-wall and forces herself to take long deep breaths until, after what must be at least ten minutes, her jagged breathing returns to normal.

As she stands to return to the house, Sophie runs out followed by Jonathan in hot pursuit. Sophie hides behind Barbara's legs. "Jonathan's trying to lock me in the bedroom," she says breathlessly.

"Dad says she has to go to bed," Jonathan explains. "He says it's getting too rowdy for eight year olds."

Barbara smooths her daughter's hair. "That's probably not such a bad idea. It is almost midnight."

"But I'm fine. I'm not sleepy. I want to dance."

"Look," Barbara says. "How about we dance to one more song and then I'll put you to bed."

Sophie looks up at her. "Two songs?" she says. "No, *three* songs."

"OK, three more songs."

Back in the lounge, the music has stopped. "Where's our disc jockey?" Tony shouts. "Come on lad!"

"I'm on it, Dad, I'm on it," Jonathan replies, forcing his way through the dancers, unexpectedly stranded in a sea of silence.

"Put something African on," Tony says.

Barbara bristles. She knows where this is going already. "*Tony,*" she protests.

335

"African?" Jonathan asks.

"Yeah. Your mum's gonna show us how the Zulus dance, aren't you?"

Half the people in the room now turn to face Barbara. Some of their faces express drunken glee but a few, the women mainly, look sad, compassionate . . . Barbara's not sure which is worse. The compassion probably. Her face begins to burn.

"What should I put on?" Jonathan asks. He still doesn't understand what's happening here.

"Anything," Barbara tells him. "I'm not dancing any more tonight."

Sophie swings on her arm. "Mum!" she whines. "You promised."

"Yeah! Come on Babs!" Tony shouts. "*Everyone* wants to see how the bloody Zulus dance!"

Barbara scans the expectant faces around her, then throws a withering gaze at Tony. But he's too drunk to decode the subtleties of her regard. Or to care. He simply leers back.

"Put the Bee Gees on, then," Barbara tells Jonathan. "Your dad's dressed just right for that."

She glances at Tony, hopeful that her dig, borrowed cruelly from her son, has hit home. But unlike hers, Tony's ego isn't fragile. He is just standing there in his cream suit still laughing at her. She can't even tell if he has heard her or understood the joke.

Stayin' Alive comes on the speakers now and Tony begins to shout and clap. "Bar-bra, Zulu-dance, Bar-bra, Zulu-dance," he chants, and two of his stupid, drunken friends join in.

Barbara pushes Sophie towards the middle of the dance-floor. "Just dance, sweetheart," she says. "I'm off to bed."

Sophie looks adoringly up at her. "But we can do the Zulu dance together," she says.

As Barbara turns to leave the room, a hand reaches out to stop her. It's Jonathan.

"I put it on, Mum," he says.

She forces a smile. "Thanks, son."

"I hate him," he says, shooting a glare at Tony, now whooping it up on the far side of the room. "I hate him so much I could kill him."

"Thanks," Barbara tells him, "but that won't be necessary. Enjoy the party. Good night."

From the bedroom, Barbara listens to the party next door. A part of her regrets her retreat, thinks that she should have stayed behind and fought her corner. But you can't win with a drunkard. Ever. What was it her mother used to say? *Don't wrestle with pigs. You both get covered in shit but only the pig enjoys it.* A pig. That's what he becomes when he drinks. A pig. And yes, in these moments she *does* hate him.

She glances at the tie-dye dress hanging on the handle of the wardrobe and decides that she will never wear it again. The dress is so much more than a dress. It is a symbol of her attempts to change, to please, to fit into Tony's new world.

She had a vision of herself looking and feeling sophisticated in this dress. She saw herself mingling confidently with these people, discussing perhaps the television programme, or Tony's photographs, or maybe even darkroom techniques.

But she has understood, tonight, that though Tony is managing to move into a different world, that's not enough to feed his ego. His sense of advancement requires that he leave her behind as a marker, as something he can point back to so that he can say, "Look how far I have come!"

Art, like some evil mistress, is stealing her husband. But like all men with mistresses, he needs the wife to remain back home. For without a wife, where is the thrill of the mistress?

There comes a thud of someone falling against the partition and Barbara glances nervously across the room as if someone might fall through the wall, fall right into her treacherous thoughts and witness them.

She closes her eyes. The room spins, so she opens them again and focuses on the lampshade hanging above her.

She remembers how small her dreams had been, how honest and practical her ambitions. She came from nothing, from nowhere, from shared beds and outdoor toilets, from bombs and hunger . . . And from there, she had dreamt of little more than a comfortable home and a friendly, reliable man beside her. She wouldn't ask for much from this man, just a regular wage packet, a comfortable silence, a sense of relative safety. And she wouldn't ask for much from life, either: a little money in the gas meter, some food in the larder; perhaps if she was lucky, some hot water from a tap. These were the aspirations of girls of her generation growing up in the East End.

She wanted to escape the grinding poverty of her childhood, that was all. She wanted to raise children who would never know what it felt like to be hungry, who could wash or change their clothes whenever they needed to.

With their music centre and their stocked refrigerator, they have so much more already than she ever dreamed of. But in some way that she can't quite put her finger on, they have so much *less* as well.

2013 – EASTBOURNE, EAST SUSSEX.

Barbara caresses the glossy cover of the book. It's just a proof copy but it looks beautiful. She runs her finger across the raised contour of the letters, like a blind person reading braille. *Anthony Marsden.*

Though she could never explain it to anyone, it seems strange, like a printing error almost, that her name isn't there beside his. It's as if she has been written out of the story, a story which was so very clearly *their* story.

In a way, of course, she let that happen; in a way, she was very much complicit in writing herself out of his life even though she had already abandoned her own in favour of his. It had been – and if only she had realised this earlier – a two-stage trip towards oblivion. But she's not innocent, she knows this. There were specific moments when she retreated instead of advancing, specific forks in the road where she had a choice to assert herself, to put her foot down, to demand some other outcome. But she didn't, did she?

Bit by bit, she stepped out of her own life in favour of his and then bit by bit she let herself get pushed to the sidelines of that life too.

Tony hadn't been a monster all of the time. Much of the time, things had been neutral – they had behaved like a well-oiled machine, like a couple of partners running the business that was their marriage. And aren't most marriages like that most of the time? The good ones, at any rate. Sometimes, perhaps as often as he showed his dark side, he perceived what was happening and tried to make amends. "Do a night class," he would urge her. "Learn to draw." "Let me buy you your own camera!"

But if she did attempt any of these things, it embarrassed him in some way she could never quite understand – some confused emotion stuck halfway between her showing him up by being too good, and her showing him up by being not good enough. Perhaps it was simply that, as a man having grown up in the forties and fifties, his brain struggled to catch up with the times. Yes, there were women all around him doing clever things. But they weren't his *wife*.

And so came the slights, the digs, the good-humoured criticism. With her ego being so fragile, these always hit home with so much more force than any word of encouragement ever could, and that surely wasn't his fault.

So she came to feel embarrassed about herself. She hadn't noticed it happening, it had been so gradual but that had been the end result. She had come to feel ashamed of who she was, of where she came from, of her class, her family, her friends . . .

Her sister, Glenda, would appear on the doorstep, effing and blinding, and Barbara would wince at every word and then wince again as her own accent relapsed when she replied.

Once or twice – it really wasn't more – she had asked Glenda not to swear in front of the children but once or twice was enough. Glenda, who felt perfectly fine about who she was, had no desire to put that confidence at risk.

A memory flashes up of Glenda calling her *Little Miss Lardydar* and Barbara glances out through the bay window at the garden as she tries to remember when this had happened, what had been the cause. Cups and saucers, that was it. Yes, cups and saucers. She had served tea in cups and saucers instead of mugs and Glenda had said, "Ooh, get you, Little Miss Lardydar. Me 'usband's a photographer and I only drink tea from a bone china cup, me." They had laughed at that. But they had both known that it wasn't a joke and they had both understood that they weren't discussing cups and saucers at all. And that, pretty much, had been the end of her relationship with Glenda, or, at the very least, the beginning of the end.

They had phoned for a while. And Barbara had gone (Tony had been working) to Glenda's wedding to Billy the Aussie. But when the news came that she had died, Barbara hadn't even known that she was ill, hadn't even known what continent she was on, in fact. That was how far apart they had let themselves drift.

Glenda wasn't the only mooring point from which Barbara had untied herself. Friends, neighbours, other mothers from the school – none of them ever seemed quite good enough to hold their own around Tony and his friends. Barbara remembers with a shudder, a neighbour (Anne perhaps?), entering the room. Tony and Phil had been discussing modern art and Anne had deigned, had *dared,* to comment. "I don't know nothin' about art," she had said, "but I know what I like. And it ain't piled up bricks."

Funnily enough, that, couched in more intellectual vocabulary, had been pretty much what Tony and Phil had been saying themselves about the pile of bricks that the Tate had so infamously purchased. But Barbara caught the glance between the two men when Anne spoke and had shuddered then as she shudders now, with something akin to shame.

Though she essentially gave up her own friends, Tony's were always very much *his* friends. There were only the vaguest of pretences that they were her friends as well. It was always *shall we go to Tony's place.* It was always *Tony and Barbara,* never Barbara and Tony.

So, lost in the limbo between his friends, who she believed

341

thought themselves too good for her, and hers, who with their casual racism and dismissive attitudes, seemed an embarrassment to her, it had been a lonely life, really. It had been just Barbara and the children and even there, Sophie had grown up to be very much Tony's daughter. And so she struggled to talk to – to measure up to – Sophie, as she had struggled to talk to her husband's friends. Yes, for much of her life it had been her and Jonathan playing second fiddle to clever, arty Sophie and unpredictable Tony.

Barbara's biggest fear, growing up, had been of finding herself alone, but alone is very much how she ended up feeling. It's almost as if putting so much energy into avoiding being alone was the very thing that had made that loneliness manifest.

She caresses her husband's embossed name once again and then sighs and opens the book. And there he is. A full-page, black and white photograph of Tony, taken in 1977. It's a beautiful photograph of a handsome man. She stares into his eyes for a moment. *"Where are you, Tony?"* she murmurs. *"Where are you now?"*

She reads the tiny caption beneath the photo. 'Anthony Marsden. Self portrait. 1977.'

She snorts sourly and turns the page. Because that caption on this photo (a photo she remembers so vividly taking herself) pretty much says it all.

1979 – HACKNEY, LONDON.

Barbara sits on the edge of the creaking bed and pulls on her boots. A gale is blowing outside and the rug beneath her feet lifts and flutters whenever a gust hits the house. It looks like a magic carpet attempting take off.

It was Minnie's parting gift, a secret life-insurance policy, which paid the deposit on the place. There is no doubt that this purchase – a home of their own – was the right thing to have done. Everybody agreed that they needed to stop paying rent, that they had to get "one foot on the housing ladder". But with the mortgage rate at seventeen per cent, they're now stretched to the hilt, and even if the kids do finally have rooms of their own, comfort-wise they've jumped back almost fifteen years.

Barbara zips her second boot then stands and looks in the mirror, cracked during the move. It's lucky she's not superstitious. She looks fine. With the wind, she's going to be cold but once they get there, she'll be *fine*. Yes, she swore she would never wear this dress again but these days it's shoes for the kids or caulk for the windows or fish for tea, or . . . the list goes on. And the money's not there to pay for the half of it. New dresses aren't even *on* the list.

Tonight she will accompany Tony to a private view of his friend Malcolm's work. Barbara has been to a number of these events and she knows what to expect. There will be clever, wild-haired women painters, and wiry, scrious men who went to public school, who inexplicably pause for whole seconds mid-sentence before suddenly gushing out all of their words in a rush. "And Bar'bra," they will say, crisply. "Do (pause) tell-me-a-little-about-yourself. Do (pause) tell-me-how-you-spend-your-days-here-in-fabulous-London."

She has done everything that she can to be excused from this event (apart from feigning illness, an excuse she has overused lately) but Tony keeps insisting that it's *important*, that people will *expect* her to be there. Plus it's supposedly their last chance to see Diane.

Barbara sighs, tugs at the dress (a little tighter than the last time she wore it) and then leaves the relative comfort of the rug to cross the rough floorboards.

On the landing, she pauses to take in the sounds of the new house, the whistling in the eves, a creaking from the attic, the sound of the television set below. A sense of déjà vu swamps her and she struggles to remember a different landing in a different house but she's momentarily unable to place it. Automatically, she glances at the place on the wall where the photo should be. A photo of the royal wedding. Gosh, that was a long time ago. How the years slip by!

She takes a deep breath. She *can* do this. She starts to clomp her way down the uncarpeted stairs.

When she reaches the lounge, she finds the kids and Tony all watching *Grange Hill* – grubby schoolchildren being mean to each other. She can't see the attraction. Tony looks up first. "Ah, there she is!" he says. "You see, you still look great in that dress."

Barbara smiles weakly as Sophie, prompted by Tony's remark, drags her attention from the screen as well. "Oh, wow!" she says, innocently. "It's your dancing dress!"

Barbara smiles and frowns simultaneously. She's not quite sure what Sophie is referring to. "Dancing dress?" she repeats, a physical sensation of dread rising in her chest even as it precedes the comprehension of why.

Sophie nods eagerly. "Yes, that's your special dress. For doing the Zulu dance. *Ouch!*" Jonathan has whacked her across the head. "What was *that* for?" she asks.

"Yeah!" Tony says. "Why are you hitting your sister like that?"

Barbara slips from the room and heads, out of habit, to the kitchen. There's something about the cold surfaces of a kitchen that reassure her at moments like these but this isn't her kitchen, this kitchen is dingy and sad, more in need of decoration than any other room in the house. She takes in the peeling paint and the chipped stone sink and then moves to the dining room but it's not much better there.

The Zulu dance! How can Sophie possibly remember that? She feels miserable – no, hopelessly *utterly* depressed, as if she has been suddenly emptied of every emotion except despair. Nothing, it seems, is ever done; nothing is ever achieved, not definitively. No embarrassment is ever forgotten either. It's all just swimming against the tide, it's all just clawing and grasping and dragging yourself out of the mud, and for nothing. You always find yourself back where you started. She's still (and always will be) uneducated Barbara from the East End, living in a draughty, miserable house, wearing a stupid dress made of curtains.

She feels dizzy. Perhaps she's forgotten to breathe. It happens. She sits on a dining chair and struggles to unzip her boots. They seem, somehow, to be strangling her. She has to get them off, and quickly. The boots cast aside, she silently returns to the bedroom where she locks the door and lies down on the bed.

Soon Tony will come. He will hammer on the door for a while. He'll be concerned and then apologetic, and then he'll move through pleading to anger.

And eventually he will leave, alone.

He will punish her for this by not coming home tonight. And this is absolutely fine by her. Let him go to his damned party alone. And let him stay there forever if need be.

Once the hammering has stopped and the front door has slammed, Barbara changes, then returns downstairs. All she really wants to do is sleep but she can tell from the noises coming from the lounge that the kids have not gone to Anne's as planned, so she needs to get down there and feed them.

She finds them both glued, as ever, to the television. "Anne came," Jonathan tells her. "She was worried that we hadn't come over. She wanted to come up and see you but I said you were sleeping."

"Thanks," Barbara says. "I was, actually."

"Is it my fault you didn't go?" Sophie asks. "Jon says it is."

"No, Sweetie. Nothing's your fault. I just didn't feel very well. Now, I'm going to make some tea and then I want that television switched off, OK?"

"But it's *The Good Life*," Sophie protests.

"They're all repeats anyway. You've seen them all."

"But it's my favourite, Mum."

"OK, well, after *The Good Life* then."

She makes the kids an omelette (she's not hungry herself) and lets them eat it, unusually, in front of the television. She has no energy for such futile battles this evening.

They are just digging in when someone hammers on the front door. Everyone looks up. "Anne maybe?" Jonathan suggests.

Barbara shrugs. "Stay there. Eat your tea," she says. "I'll go." As she stands, there comes another round of banging. She chews her lip nervously. Surely Tony can't be too drunk to find his keys already, can he?

She heads out to the hallway and closes the lounge door behind her. Beyond the door, through the patterned glass, she

346

can see a vague form, too short to be Tony. "Hello?" she calls out, reluctant to open the door. You hear things about what happens to people who open their doors too readily.

A desperate sounding voice replies – a woman's voice. "Tony? *Tony?*"

Barbara opens the door to find Diane, one arm outstretched, prepared for another round of knocking. She's swaying from side to side in the gusty breeze, now tottering backwards and steadying herself against the wall.

Her hair has blown over her eyes but steadying herself *and* brushing her hair away is, in her drunken state, just one challenge too many. She lurches sideways and her hip collides with a pot plant which she fumblingly reaches out to steady. "Is Tony in? Oh! Barbara!" she says. "Is Tony home? He's s'posed to be taking me."

Barbara steps towards Diane and sniffs the air. People say that you can't smell vodka but it's not true, she can smell it from here. "Diane!" she says. "The state of you! Whatever's wrong?"

Diane, suddenly self-aware, attempts to demonstrate her sobriety by standing upright but instead totters forwards then takes a nifty looking square-dance step to the left before collapsing back against the wall again. This, she slithers down until she finds herself, with visible surprise, on the floor. "Where is he?" she asks again.

"Mum? Are you OK?" Jonathan has followed his mother to the door.

"Go back inside. Everyone's fine. And get Sophie away from that window, please," Barbara tells him.

"Tony's gone," she tells Diane, once Jonathan has nodded silently and obeyed. She glances up and down the street. A man opposite, walking a dog, is watching them. "I think we need to get you inside, Diane."

Diane tries to look up at her, then bows her head and pushes her hair aside. "No," she stumbles. "I . . . I want Tony. There's a . . . there's a thing. Tonight. I'm meant to be there. I'm s'posed to go to the thing. We all are."

Barbara crouches down and helps Diane, still fighting with her hair, to brush it behind her ear. "Jesus, Diane," she says. "How much have you had?"

"No mush . . ." Diane says. "Some vodka. Maybe. An' some wine. *Where's Tony?*"

Barbara sighs. "I *told* you. He's *gone*. And he won't be . . ." She lets her voice fade away. Because Diane's chin has dipped to her chest. She looks as if she has fallen asleep.

Barbara rubs one hand across her brow, then mutters, *"Oh God,"* and attempts to lift Diane to standing position. But it's impossible. It's like trying to manoeuvre a huge block of Chivers jelly.

Out of other options, she heads back indoors and beckons from the lounge doorway to Jonathan. "Just stay there, Sophie. Just watch the television. STAY, I said!"

Once the door is closed again, she explains quietly to Jonathan. "I'm really sorry but she's blind drunk. Can you help me get her upstairs? I don't know what else to do."

"Sure Mum," he says with a shrug. He's seen drunk people before. He knows the score.

Together they manage to lift Diane to her feet and slowly but surely, one under each arm, they succeed in hauling her upstairs as well.

"Why are drunks so heavy?" Jonathan asks, once Diane has flopped, with surprising elegance, onto the bed.

"I don't know. The weight of all the beer?"

Jonathan grins at her. He enjoys these little jokes they share sometimes. It makes him feel grown-up. He folds his arms, then looks back at Diane and wrinkles his nose. "I'm never going to get drunk."

Barbara realises, out of the blue, that her son has become a man. It's something in his stance. It's so strange the way you notice these things, as if the change was sudden rather than progressive. "We'll see," she says quietly.

"I *won't*."

"Well good. Now, I'm going to have to stay with Diane a bit to make sure she's alright, OK?"

Jonathan nods.

"So can you go and keep an eye on Sophie for me?"

Another nod.

"And be nice to her, OK? She's your sister and she's only ten. I think you forget that sometimes."

Jonathan pulls a face, suddenly a child again. "Hey, I'm always nice to her. Even if she is a dipstick."

Barbara watches him leave and then turns back to see that Diane has dribbled a little vomit onto her pillow. "Honestly woman!" she says. "Look at the state of you!"

She goes to the bathroom for a towel and then returns to clean up the mess. As she wipes Diane's mouth, she unexpectedly speaks. "Lasangeles," she mumbles. She could be dreaming. "Los Angeles!" she says again, more clearly.

"Yes. You're leaving soon. Tony told me."

"Yesoon," Diane says.

After a pause where she closes her eyes and her head lolls anew, she opens them again and adds, "He won't come. The bastard."

Barbara's hand freezes in mid swipe. *"Who* won't come?"

Diane almost smiles as she struggles to focus on Barbara. "To Los Angeles."

"Who won't come to Los Angeles?" As far as Barbara knows, Diane is single at the moment.

"I love you but you're stupid," Diane says. "You should leave him."

349

Barbara stands sharply and steps backwards, like someone moving away from a snake. She covers her mouth with one trembling hand. She realises that here, in this instant, she can let this thing that's been lurking at the back of her mind surface. She can ask Diane here and now if she wants. With the state that she's in, she can probably even make her reply. She stands there quivering as she hesitates.

"Where's Sophie?" Diane asks, sounding about five. "I want to see Sophie."

Barbara shakes her head. She can't do it. She just can't deal with all the ricochets of finding out, one way or another. What would she do anyway? Leave him because not enough of him was hers? That's like turning off a tap because it's not running fast enough to quench your thirst. She'd end up with nothing, all over again. And what would be the point of that?

"Tomorrow," she says, icily. "You can see her tomorrow when you're sober. And then you can go and live in bloody Los Angeles."

She turns away from the bed but then glances back at Diane, already snoring again, her mouth wide open. People can die if they're sick while asleep. Barbara knows this. She should move Diane onto her side the way she does with Tony, just in case.

She observes her body failing to act. She sees herself *not* do this. She watches as cold-hearted Barbara walks from the room, closing the door behind her.

She thinks, *I am a terrible person*. She glances up at the ceiling. "It's up to you," she says. "You decide."

Back in the lounge, *The Good Life* is on the television. The TV audience are laughing heartily.

2013 – BERMONDSEY, LONDON.

When Sophie arrives at the gallery, she pauses in front of the building and stares at it from a distance. It seems barely possible that her images, next to her father's, will be hanging here by tonight. She taps one foot nervously and wonders if she drank too much coffee this morning. But no, that's not it. She's actually fighting the urge to jump up and down like a ten year old.

It's not the White Cube of old, of course. It's not the fabulous twenties building in the centre of Hoxton that she loved so dearly. *That* White Cube is gone now.

No, this is the new, much larger White Cube in Bermondsey, a vast concrete, Germanic building from the seventies divided into a whole array of galleries. Does being in *one* of the galleries of the *new* White Cube have as much cachet as being in the *old* White Cube? Perhaps not. But it's still one of the most prestigious private galleries in London. It's still one hell of a result.

"Cheers Brett," Sophie says quietly, as she heads across the forecourt to the entrance.

Inside, a pretty, bearded, tattooed hipster in bright yellow chinos and a denim shirt crosses the lobby to meet her. "Sophie?" he says, running a hand through his heavily coiffed hair.

Sophie nods. "You must be Paul, right?"

"That's me. Paul Jelly, at your service," he says. "I'm here to help with the hanging."

"I thought I was here to help *you.*"

"Huh!" Paul Jelly says. "You wish. Come through!"

Sophie follows him past the bookshop (she imagines their

book in the window) and past a couple of current exhibitions, a sculptor, a painter, another sculptor.

As they approach a blanked-out door beyond a sign ('Hanging in Progress') she can barely breathe.

"So," Paul says, pushing open the door. "We're in here. All day!"

"Oh my God!" Sophie exclaims as she steps into the room. She twists her head to take in the bright vastness of the space. "It's huge!"

"It's the biggest one we have," Paul says proudly. "But from the size of the crates, I'd say you'll have no trouble filling it. Am I right?"

"They arrived, then?"

"Sure. They're uncrating now. Come."

He leads her through another door and down a corridor to a delivery area where two more stunningly good looking young men are working. *Oh, to be twenty again!* Sophie thinks.

"Hey guys," Paul says. "This is Sophie. Sophie, Jake and Joe."

Sophie waves. "Hi Jake. Hi Joe."

"Sophie here is the artist," Paul tells them.

"Only of *half* of the works."

"The colour ones, right?" Jake/Joe says.

"Exactly. The others were taken by my father. He only really did black and white."

"I don't suppose they had colour back then, did they?" Joe/Jake says. " 'Cos they're, like, really old, right? Like, before I was born."

Sophie smiles and nods. "Yes, um, some of them are almost as old as me," she says.

It takes all day to hang the exhibition. One by one Jake and Joe uncrate and haul the prints through to the South Gallery, and one by one Paul and Sophie hang them.

352

On the square southern wall, they put a four-metre-high self portrait of her father and, on the opposite northern wall, an identically sized self portrait of Sophie.

Hers is colour, taken in the harsh light of a five-hundred watt studio lamp. It's not a flattering photo by any means and it's certainly not a fashion shot. But it is beautiful. It does, as she had hoped, ooze reality from every wrinkle, humanity from every pore.

Along the side walls, they alternate Tony's sombre news photos with Sophie's brightly coloured images. Grimy children play with a hosepipe in a black and white image and right next to it a joyous little girl flies through the air above a fluorescent green bouncy castle. The famous woman-on-a-beach lies next to row upon row of lobster pink foreigners lined up on a different beach in Benidorm. A grey queue of miserable commuters stand in the London rain waiting for a double-decker bus while, next door, a blurred river of humanity streams down the aggressively modern escalators of Canary Warf.

The space is perfect and the photos look as good as they can but slowly, surely, like the bubbles of a glass of Champagne going flat, Sophie's excitement vanishes into thin air.

With each image hung, a voice in her head becomes a little stronger, a little louder, a little more forceful. With each comment that Paul makes, "Wow I love the colours in that, Sophie," or "Gosh, that's one happy picture," she feels a little less centred.

By the time they hang the final images, a three-by-three matrix of smaller photos, she finds that her self confidence has almost entirely vanished. She feels like an impostor here, like a child playing an adult's game – like a girl playing a boy's game. She feels, when it comes down to it, like a daughter using her father's very real talent as a smokescreen.

For isn't that the truth? Isn't she here merely because she is the *great* Anthony Marsden's daughter? Isn't any interest White Cube may be showing in her little more than contractual? Isn't she simply the price they are having to pay to be allowed to host what everyone *really* wants to see: her dad's pictures?

She regrets her choice of images now. She should have done black and white. She should have chosen images with more clout, with more heft, with more *misery*. It's all too gay (in the old sense, not the Paul Jelly sense of that word). It's all too colourful. It's all too bright and light and downright *jolly*. And as she hangs the final image, she knows exactly what everyone will think: *What a waste. What a shame she's not as good as her father was!*

She walks to the centre of the room now, and sinks onto the hard white bench. She palms her eyes in the hope that when she reopens them, something will have changed, in the hope that when she reopens them, this won't all still be nothing more than a ghastly mistake, perhaps the biggest mistake she has ever made.

Paul – lovely, friendly, supportive Paul – comes and sits beside her. "I think it looks fabulous," he says. "Don't you?"

Sophie un-palms her eyes and looks but it's even worse than before. Her pretensions of grandeur leap from the walls in pyrotechnic colour. She can see nothing else and wants suddenly to cry, to scream, to run amok and rip all her pictures from the walls and stamp on them.

At this precise moment, the door to the gallery opens and Paul stands urgently and heads across the room to turn away this precocious visitor. "We're hanging in here, I'm afraid. You can't come—"

"It's OK, Paul," Sophie says. "He's my boyfriend. Hi Brett."

Brett moves a few feet into the room and performs a double take. "Wow!" he says. "Just . . . like . . . wow!"

"It's cool, huh?" Paul says.

354

"Oh, it's very cool. So you got it all hung, huh?"

"I think it looks great," Paul says. "I'm not sure about Sophie though. I think she's not happy with something."

Brett glances at Sophie with a puzzled expression, then, ever the professional, instead of joining her, he starts to walk around, pausing for a few moments in front of each image pair. When he reaches the far side of the room he looks at the two portraits on the end walls and then, finally, joins Sophie in the middle. "So, what's up?" he asks.

Sophie bites her lip and shakes her head. Brett can see that her eyes are glistening.

"Paul – was it Paul? Yes, Paul. Do you think we could—"

"Sure," Paul says. "I'll give you two some space." He's happy to escape.

Once he has gone, Brett slides onto the bench and puts one arm around Sophie's shoulders. "Is it your dad?" he asks.

Sophie shakes her head and wipes away a tear, then says, with difficulty, "They're just not up to it."

"I'm sorry?"

"My images. They're the best ones I've ever taken but . . . they're still just . . . just girly bubbles of fluff next to Dad's. I tried *so* hard, Brett, but look. Just look."

"I think you're—"

"I want to take all mine out. I *really* want to do that, Brett. Can I? Can I do that?"

Brett laughs at this, genuinely, heartily.

"I'll take that as a 'no' then," Sophie sniffs.

He gives Sophie a squeeze and snorts again. "That's not why I'm laughing, babe. I think your images look awesome."

Sophie glances sideways at him. She starts to cry freely now. She pushes Brett away so that she can fumble in her bag for a tissue. "But they don't Brett," she says through fresh tears. "They look like pretty magazine pieces. And next to Dad's,

355

they look even worse. People are going to think that I'm taking the piss."

Brett rubs her back briefly and then unexpectedly stands. She wonders if he's going to simply walk out. He's not always that good with her moods.

Instead, he parks himself in the middle of the floor and stares at one wall. After about a minute, he turns ninety degrees and studies the next wall. Only when he has finished his three-sixty scan of the room does he turn back to face Sophie, who is by now watching him with all the terror of the executioner's next victim.

"Look, I see what you're saying," Brett says.

Sophie starts to cry again.

"Hey stop. I haven't finished. Gee, Soph! Stop! For God's sake!"

Sophie manages to stem the tears and looks up at him again.

"I see what you're saying but you're wrong. That's what I was gonna to say."

Sophie rubs her nose on the back of her hand. "You *think?*"

Brett nods. "If the world was grey . . ." he says thoughtfully. He glances around the room and then starts again, speaking more slowly. "If the world was black and white and all grime and misery, then you'd be right. But it's not, Soph, it's not like that. It's also colour and life and joy. It's grinning kids on play castles and perfectly contented old-folks with ices. And the juxtaposition that you've created here, between each of your father's images and each of yours, is just so . . . so *joyous,* Soph. That's the only word I can think of. The world moves on and things do get better. It's uplifting. It's brilliant. I wasn't expecting this. But I'm stunned. I'm . . . I'm *moved,* actually. Really. That's it. I'm moved."

Sophie bursts into tears for the third time but these are tears of relief. She stands and drops her bag to the floor and runs into Brett's arms. "God, Brett," she says. "You have no idea what that means to me. I've been feeling so *scared* all day."

Brett hugs her and then pushes her away so that he can stare into her eyes. "You silly, silly girl," he says. "You've done everything you wanted, here. And some. You've got nothing to be scared about. They're gonna be blown away."

"You really think that? You're not just saying?"

Brett shrugs. "Hey, come on. You know me, babe," he says. "When did I ever *just say*."

1982 – HACKNEY, LONDON.

It is Sunday morning. Tony and Sophie are seated at the dining table awaiting the cooked breakfast which Barbara is busy frying.

"Why don't you open it, Dad?" Sophie asks. Sophie, like Barbara, doesn't much like unopened letters but she considers an unopened *parcel* an affront to all humanity.

"I'll open it when I'm good and ready," Tony says, glancing nervously at the package on the sideboard.

"I think Sophie's right," Barbara says, taking her life in her hands. "If you open it today, you can take it to Portsmouth with you."

"Huh!" Tony says. "I'm not going to something as important as Portsmouth with a brand new camera. That's for sure."

The package is from Pentax. It contains a camera, an amazing whole new kind of camera which knows how to focus itself, a camera which calculates its own exposure and sets its own shutter speed. Unfortunately, Tony doesn't much like amazing new things and his tension around the package has been palpable for days.

"*Please* open it," Sophie pleads. "It's been there for years."

"I've told you a million times not to exaggerate," Tony jokes.

"OK, weeks then."

"Days," Tony says. "It came on Saturday."

"It actually came *last* Saturday, so that is more than a week," Barbara comments, from the stove. "Why don't you let Sophie open it? She'll enjoy finding out how it works."

358

An unspoken decision has been made to allow Sophie to follow in her father's footsteps. Barbara did everything in her power to push Jonathan in a different direction. Photography had seemed such a dangerous way to attempt to earn a living back then. It had seemed to offer little more than the promise of yet another generation of hardship. But having saved Jon from the flights and fancies of the art world (he's at college, right now, training to be a quantity surveyor) the world changed. Photography suddenly became important. It became a proper job that could provide a living wage. The brand new kitchen around them, the eggs, the bacon, the mushrooms in the pan, the refrigerator beside her (stacked full) . . . Yes, these are all proof of it.

"OK," Tony says, finally seeing the inevitability of unboxing the camera plus an escape route from the responsibility for making the damned thing work himself. "OK, Soph, go for it. Knock yourself out. Just don't involve me until it works. And don't break it."

"*After* breakfast," Barbara says, heading across the room with the pan.

It is later in the day and the light is fading. They are in the lounge and the new camera is the centre of attention.

"So you just press here," Sophie is explaining. "And point the funny bit in the middle at whatever you want to be in focus. And . . . see . . . It just does it."

The camera lens whizzes in and then whizzes out, and then whizzes in once more before settling down with a happy sounding beep.

Tony groans and takes the camera from his daughter's grasp. He raises it to his eye.

Barbara holds her breath. Tony has a real problem with new technology and this little scene of family unity could dissolve in the blink of an eye into a fit of toddler rage. Things can get thrown. Things can get broken.

They had gone, a few months back, to buy a new car, a Ford Sierra (or 'jelly mould', as Jonathan insisted on calling it). The Beetle, now fifteen years old, had been playing up.

The salesman, a patronising man who told Tony all kinds of technical details about the car (his eyes glazed over) and Barbara all kinds of useful, girly things like where to stash her handbag, had finally handed him the keys for the test drive.

But the controls had been different to the Beetle. The indicators were on the 'wrong' side of the steering column. The reverse gear was in the 'wrong' place. And just a few feet off the forecourt, Tony had swung violently around in the traffic almost killing them all, before driving straight back to the garage.

Barbara and Sophie had then tried as a team to convince him that he'd get used to it. They both liked the Sierra. They were both sick of the unreliable cramped Beetle. So they attempted to calm him down. But eventually when Barbara had, just for a second, in an effort to make him see sense, withheld the keys to the Beetle, Tony had strutted off down the road muttering madly to himself.

"Sometimes, I think Dad's a bit cuckoo," Sophie had commented, daringly.

"Yes," Barbara had replied with meaning. "Me too."

In a way, Barbara understands his pain. Their new video recorder has the capacity to drive *her* to distraction as well. But at least she *tries* to use the damned thing. Even if she does forget to press the record button, or she gets the wrong day, or records the wrong channel, at least she still attempts it from time to time (primarily when Sophie's not there to do so). Tony won't even go near the thing.

Right now, he is peering through the viewfinder of the Pentax and the autofocus is whirring in and out, and in and out, in a way that's setting *everyone's* nerves on edge.

"What are you pointing it at?" Sophie asks, sounding irritated.

"You can see what I'm pointing it at," Tony says. "I'm pointing it over there."

"But the middle bit. What's in the middle bit where the split is?"

"The curtains."

Bzzzzzzz, the lens goes. *Zzzzzzb*, the lens goes.

"That's why," Sophie says. "You have to give it a straight line to focus on. Try the edge of the window frame."

"But what's the point of that?" Tony asks, now aiming it at the television instead. "What if I want to focus on the curtains? What if I have some incredibly strong desire to photograph the bloody curtains?" He lowers the camera from his eye. The lens continues to pfaff around on its own, buzzing like a wasp in a box. "What's it doing now?"

"You have to switch the lens off," Sophie says. "Otherwise it wastes the batt—"

"Well I hate the bloody thing. You can have it."

"Really?" Sophie looks excited.

"Actually, she can't," Barbara points out. She pauses. On reflection, it seems safer to address her daughter than her husband right now. "Sorry Sophie," she continues, "But your dad's been sponsored to take photos with this particular camera. He needs it."

"It is bloody particular if you ask me. I prefer my old Rollei," Tony says.

"Yes, but Rollei aren't sponsoring you."

"I don't care," Tony says. "It's rubbish is what it is." He now chucks it disdainfully at the sofa.

361

"Careful Dad, that's worth hundreds of pounds."

"Not to me it isn't," Tony says, standing. "It's not worth shit-all to me."

"Tony, really!" Barbara protests. But he has gone.

* * *

Two weeks later, a smaller, flatter package from Pentax has been lingering on the sideboard for three full days before Barbara, in exasperation, decides to open it herself.

From the envelope, she pulls a folder, and from the folder, a full page advert printed on glossy photo paper. There's a letter too.

The advert features a full-page black and white photograph of one of the warships in the Falklands task-force setting off. Featuring waving troops and weeping women, swooping seagulls and fluttering flags, it's truly a beautiful photo, one of the best Tony has ever taken, somehow encapsulating all of the dangers and all of the fears involved in Thatcher's new war.

Barbara is surprised. When Tony had failed to show her the photos from his Portsmouth trip, she had assumed that they hadn't worked out. And when he had posted the camera back to Pentax with a rude letter, her fears had been all but confirmed. But this is gorgeous. She feels proud.

Across the top of the advert, the text reads, "The best photographers won't work with any other camera." And at the bottom of the page is an insert of Tony holding the Pentax ME-F, along with a quote that Tony will certainly never have said. *"With the Pentax ME-F taking care of focus and exposure, I can concentrate on what I do best – simply creating beautiful images."*

Barbara turns to the accompanying letter.

Dear Anthony,

Please find enclosed the July advert for the ME-F, which, as you know, is part of a nationwide campaign.

As you are also aware, the 35mm images you supplied were, without exception, unusable, being either over-exposed or out of focus and in many cases both.

After thorough investigation by our technicians, we can confirm that no defects were found in the ME-F you returned and we can only assume that these problems resulted from misuse of the camera by yourself.

If you would like one of our experts to walk you through the features of the ME-F then please don't hesitate to contact us.

In the meantime, for the advert, we have cropped one of your 120mm images taken with the Rolleiflex so that it appears to be from a 35mm camera. Needless to say, this sleight of hand must not be made public under any circumstances.

While this is an acceptable stop-gap solution to an immediate need, I am forced to remind you that our contract specifically states that all photographs supplied must be taken with the ME-F, another verified example of which will be shipped to you shortly.

Failure to respect the terms of the contract will result in cancellation of said contract, including but not limited to all further publications, all future payments, your inclusion in the Pentax Summer Show and cancellation of the slated Pentax/

Anthony Marsden one-man show at the Hayward Gallery.

I trust you will find this motivation enough to get to grips with the excellent camera that is our flagship ME-F.

Yours Faithfully,
Yamada Kuzuyuki.

2013 – BERMONDSEY, LONDON.

Sophie lifts a glass of wine from the table. It is the night of the private view and in less than half an hour people will start to arrive.

"You should maybe slow down on the wine, honey," Brett says.

Sophie pulls a face. "Um, I think I'm old enough to decide for myself how much to drink, Brett."

"You do?"

"God! Stop it. You sound like Jonathan's wife."

Brett shrugs and fiddles with his bow tie. He's wearing evening dress and it suits him. In fact, Sophie can barely believe how stunning he looks. "Whatever," he says.

Much as Sophie hates to be told what to do, she's clever enough to spot when Brett is right. So after one militant gulp of wine, she does, all the same, stop drinking.

Other than Sophie and Brett, only four people are present so far: two eastern European sounding waitresses from the catering company, Sarah Stone of White Cube wafting in and out and a very *Men in Black* security guard. The gallery, freshly cleaned, seems even bigger than usual.

"I wish it would just happen," Sophie says. "I'm so nervous I can barely stand."

Brett reaches out and gently brushes her arm with the back of his hand. "You'll be fine," he says. "Just fine."

"I suppose the *really* big rush will be on Sunday when the centre-spread comes out."

"I think there'll be plenty people tonight, hon. You did invite half of London."

"I hope there aren't *too* many either. That woman at the *Mirror* never got back to me to say how many colleagues she had tracked down. Imagine if they all come!"

"Sophie!" Brett says. "Relax."

"I can't," Sophie says. "I don't know how to. I'm not made that way. Actually, I'm too cold to relax. It's freezing in here. I should have worn more."

Brett attempts to put his arm around Sophie's bare shoulders but because she is so stressed and rigid, this position simply cannot work. "It'll warm up too," he says, dropping his arm to his side. "By the end of the evening, I'll be overheating and you'll be just right. And anyway, even if it doesn't, even if you catch the flu, it'll be worth it. Because you look totally awesome in that dress."

"I hope Mum's dress isn't too similar. Because the way she described it, it sounded exactly the same. Black, strapless, beaded front . . . We better not look like twins."

Brett laughs. "That would be cute."

"It *so* wouldn't, Brett," Sophie says. "But I don't expect a man to understand that."

At one minute past seven, people begin to arrive. The first person through the door is a woman. She's Sophie's mother's age with intense blue eyes and a walking stick. "Hello," she says glancing around nervously as she crosses the expanse of empty floor. She looks like a mouse checking for hidden cats. "I think I'm a bit early."

"Actually, you're right on time!" Sophie says, checking her watch and fixing her warmest grin.

"I'm Janet French," the woman says, wrinkling up her nose. "Are you . . .? You're not *Sophie*, are you?"

366

Sophie nods. "I am."

"I'll bet you don't even remember me," Janet says. "You used to play in our garden. In Lewes. You used to stop in sometimes on your way to Eastbourne."

"Oh, did you have swings in the garden?"

Janet laughs. "Yes, we did. And a big fish pond. You got undressed once and went swimming in it."

Sophie laughs. "Well, I definitely don't remember that." Another group of oldies are arriving now and Sophie glances over Janet's shoulder as she says, "This is Brett, my boyfriend."

"Hi Janet."

"Sorry, but *how* did you know Dad?"

"I was at the *Mirror*," Janet says. "In the early days. When he was still a dispatch rider. Sally Reed contacted me. She seemed to be tracking down all the old crew. I hope that's OK?"

"Absolutely," Sophie says. "I managed to get in touch with Phil. Do you remember him? Yes? Well, he said he'd deal with the *Mirror* crew. And he knows some of Dad's friends from the evening classes he used to do as well, so . . ."

Janet is glancing at the rows of wine glasses. "Do you think I could . . .?" she says, waving one hand over them.

"Of course!" Sophie replies. "That's what they're for."

Once Janet has started, wine in hand, to tour the still shockingly empty room, Sophie leans in to Brett's ear. "I wish Mum would get here," she says. "It's a bit embarrassing when I can't even recognise people." She nods at two grey-haired men who have joined a huddle at the entrance. "I don't know who *they* are either. Unless that's Phil. Actually, it might be. Hang on." She crosses the room to welcome the new arrivals. "Hello!" she says to the man. "Are you Phil by any chance?"

He laughs. "Sophie!" he says. "Gosh, you were this tall the last time I saw you." He makes a chopping gesture with his

367

hand, just above Sophie's waist. "And no. I'm Malcolm. *This* is Phil." He gestures to the man beside him who is so bent over he struggles to look Sophie in the eye.

"Oops," she says, "Sorry! It's been so long."

Strangely, Sophie hadn't imagined quite how old all of her father's friends would be. She had (stupidly she realises) imagined them in stasis since the moment of his death.

She realises now that her *father* would look this old were he still alive today and feels an unexpected surge of grief at his absence, at all those missing years.

"Is Barbara here?" Phil asks, struggling, with his bent back, to look around the room.

"Not yet," Sophie says. "But she should be here soon. Jonathan's bringing her."

Malcolm, who has been scanning the room, now points (with surprising vigour) at one of the photos. "Isn't that the one?" he asks.

Phil turns sideways so that he can peer up at the image. "Yes!" he says. "Ah, thank God! You included it."

Sophie follows the men's gaze. "The shipbuilders?" she asks. "Why that one?"

"Huh," Malcolm says gleefully. "I'll let Phil tell you *that* story."

Phil offers his elbow to Sophie. "Come with me, dear," he says. "And I'll let you in on a little secret."

Sophie takes his arm and shuffles with him across the room to the photo, a huge black and white print of men, suspended on ropes, riveting the panels of a warship.

"Ah, I know," Sophie says. "You're going to tell me that this one got used on the cover of a record, aren't you?"

"No, dear."

"Didn't it? I was sure that—"

"Yes, it was on the record sleeve," Phil says. "Robert Wyatt,

368

I think his name was. But that's not what I was going to tell you."

Sophie catches Brett's eye across the room. He winks at her and she raises one eyebrow and leans in to hear Phil's voice, now little more than a murmur.

"Do you know where it was taken?" Phil asks.

"Scotland somewhere, wasn't it?"

"Yes. Clydeside."

"I think I kind of knew that."

"And guess who never once set foot there?"

"Um . . . not sure. Margaret Thatcher maybe?"

Phil jabs, slightly disconcertingly, at Sophie's chest. "Your father," he says.

"I'm sorry?"

"Tony. Never went to Clydeside. Not once."

Sophie laughs. "He must have gone there at least once."

Phil shakes his head.

"Oh God!" Sophie says. "Don't say someone else took it?"

"Shh! Quietly does it, Sophie. *I* took it, if you really want to know." Phil is unable to hide his pride at this fact.

"But how? It won that prize. They did posters for the record with it. It was all over the place."

"No one knows," Phil says. "And don't worry. No one ever needs to."

"But that's terrible. Why would Dad—?"

"He couldn't get up there for the shoot. He was holed up somewhere, I expect," Phil says. "So I gave him one of mine. We used to trade images quite often back then. It was the way things worked in the papers."

"But it's in the book, Phil. We've got prints of the darned thing for sale in the bookshop. And if you own the copyright—"

Phil pats Sophie's elbow. "Don't worry, Sophie. As far as everyone's concerned, your father took it. And that's just the way it should be. And your father paid me back for that one a long time ago. So there's no account due."

Sophie is staring at the photograph. "God, if I'd known, I would have left it out," she says. "I'm so sorry, Phil."

"I'm so glad you didn't," Phil laughs. "I'm really rather chuffed about it."

Something he said suddenly strikes Sophie as odd. "Phil, what did you mean when you said he was probably 'holed up' somewhere?"

Phil laughs, but his laughter quickly becomes a coughing fit.

"Phil? Are you OK?"

When he eventually stops coughing, he says, "Ah, now *some* things are better left unsaid. And on that note, I could do with a drink."

"Yes," Sophie says, leading him away from the dreaded photo. "After that, so could I. But you have to tell me. I know you will."

Phil laughs again. "Oh really, it's nothing. Your father was quite a character. But then I expect you know that already."

"What was all that about?" Brett asks, the next time his trajectory crosses Sophie's.

"Ugh!" Sophie says. "Don't ask. Something about Dad being a *right character*."

"Huh?"

"Oh, and apparently the shipbuilding photo isn't Dad's at all."

"I'm sorry?"

"Phil reckons *he* took it. He says they traded photos sometimes."

"Wow," Brett says. "And that's a real iconic photo of his."

"Yep. Of course he may be talking bollocks. I'll have to ask Mum."

"Sure," Brett says. "Well there she is. You can ask her now."

Sophie turns to see Barbara just stepping into the gallery. Her eyes scan her mother's dress and she heaves a sigh of relief. Her mother's is longer and fuller and higher cut than hers. It has far less beading too. Other than the fact that it's a black evening dress, there's really not much similarity.

"Mum," she says, when she reaches her. "Thank God you're here. All these people keep coming up to me to say 'hello' and I haven't the foggiest idea who they are."

Barbara, who has moved little more than a yard into the room before freezing, looks pale and anxious.

"Hi Soph," Jonathan says.

"Hi Jon. No Judy?"

"No, she's at home with Dylan. We had a babysitter booked but when push came to shove, she just couldn't leave him."

"And how is Dylan?"

"He's great. Gorgeous. Noisy. You must come out and see him."

"I will. I'm sorry. I've just been so rushed off my feet with all of this."

"Of course. Well, Judy's not that keen on visitors right now anyway, so there's no hurry."

"Well yes, that's what I understood when I called her," Sophie says. "That's a great dress, Mum."

Barbara nods weakly. "Thanks. Yours too."

"Are you OK?"

Another nod. "The photos look, um, nice," she says quietly.

"Well, good." Sophie had hoped for a little more enthusiasm than 'nice'. She glances enquiringly at Jonathan who blinks slowly at her, a blink which means, "*Give her a moment and she'll be fine.*"

"Drink, Mum?" Jonathan asks.

Barbara fiddles with the clasp of her handbag. "Definitely."

"Wine or cava or—"

"Wine, white, please."

Jonathan heads off on the wine mission so Sophie takes Barbara's arm and leads her towards the first of the images. "So, what do you think, Mum?" she asks. "It looks good, huh?"

"Yes," Barbara says, sounding distracted. She glances over her shoulder. "Is that Phil?"

"It is. And the other one's Malcolm."

"Gosh," Barbara says. "How old we all are."

"Well, you've weathered better than they have," Sophie says. But in this moment, she realises that not only had she failed to imagine how old her father's friends would be but she has been refusing to notice how fast her own mother is ageing too. She sees this now. She sees how small and frail Barbara is. "Do you want to go over and meet him? Talk to him, I mean."

"Just let me get my breath, dear. It's a lot to take in."

"The photos, you mean? Or the people?"

"Well, all of it."

Sophie gives her mother's arm a squeeze. "OK. Stay there and I'll go get that drink," she says.

At the drinks table, she finds Jonathan deep in conversation with Brett. "As you know, Brett," Jonathan is saying tersely, "I *don't* want to get involved."

Brett laughs and fiddles with his bow tie. "I'm not interviewing you, man," he says. "I'm just making conversation."

"What's going on?" Sophie asks, reaching for a glass of wine for her mother. "You two aren't arguing, are you?"

"Brett's idea of conversation sounds suspiciously like digging," Jonathan says. "Once a journalist, always a journalist, eh?"

Brett raises the palms of his hands. "Hey, I was only asking why Jon didn't follow in the family way. I'm not wearing a wire or anything."

Sophie shrugs. "You could have, I suppose," she tells Jonathan. "You took good photos."

Jonathan's face contorts as if this is the most ridiculous thing he has heard all year. "I did *not*," he says. "I didn't have the eye. Everyone knew that."

"That's not strictly true. I found some of yours when I was going through Dad's. The three kids on the wall? Do you remember that?"

Jonathan nods but looks puzzled.

"And the one of that bus conductor, smoking. That was yours wasn't it?"

Jonathan nods. "Sure, but you always said I was rubbish."

Sophie grimaces, sips at the glass of wine, remembers that it was destined for Barbara, glances guiltily across the room at her and then, seeing that she's in conversation with Phil, takes another less-guilty sip. "Did I?" she says.

"Yes! Always. Over and over. Every photo I ever took."

"Ooh, sorry 'bout that. That would have been sibling rivalry. I don't think I wanted the competition."

Jonathan looks exasperated; he looks as if this discussion is somehow important to him. Sophie can't for the life of her work out why. "Aw, come on Jon," she says, trying to ease her guilt. "You know what it was like. Mum was always going on about how clever *you* were. How good your school results were. You were always the favourite. I just wanted a little bit of . . . you know . . ." She glances at Brett for help.

"Attention?" he suggests, unhelpfully.

"No! I mean . . ."

"Real estate?" he offers.

"Yeah, kind of. I wanted a corner of the garden for myself. I wanted photography to be *my* thing not yours. That's all."

Jonathan is staring into his glass. He looks like he's about to cry. Sophie catches Brett's eye again and he pulls an 'oops' face.

"Well," Jonathan says, forcibly snapping himself out of it. "Dad never taught me. He taught you. So he must have thought you were better anyway."

"He didn't *teach* me," Sophie says. "He dragged me around with him occasionally. But I don't remember him ever specifically *teaching* me anything."

"He didn't know how."

They turn to see that Barbara has joined them. She reaches across the group for a glass of wine. "Apparently it's self service," she mutters. "Thanks for that, you two."

"Sorry. We got sidetracked," Jonathan says. "Anyway, what do you mean, he didn't know how? Of course he—"

"Oh, he was a *terrible* teacher," Barbara interjects.

"That's true, actually," Sophie agrees. "He used to get annoyed in *seconds*."

"And he was *awful* with anything technical," Barbara says. "Motorbikes, tape recorders, cars . . ."

"Cameras," Sophie adds.

"Oh yes!" Barbara agrees.

"I showed *him* how to use the Pentax. Do you remember that, Mum?"

"I do."

"I must have been, like, five or something."

"More like thirteen, I think."

"Sophie says I was your favourite. Which is why she had to hog Dad all the time," Jonathan says.

"*My* favourite?"

He nods.

"I didn't *quite* say that," Sophie protests.

374

Barbara smiles. "We didn't have *favourites*," she says. "We loved you both equally."

"That's not how it felt," Sophie says. "I was always trying to measure up to whatever miracle Jonathan had just managed."

"Huh!" Jonathan says. "*You* were always the clever one. Clever arty Sophie. Daddy's little girl. You're the one who inherited all of this." He gestures at the exhibition around them.

"I didn't *inherit* this, Jonathan," Sophie says, feeling vaguely outraged. "I *made* this happen. And with no help from you."

"Children!" Barbara exclaims. "Stop it! We loved both of you."

"OK, maybe," Sophie concedes. "But admit it was in different ways. Admit that you had a soft spot for Jon, and Dad had—"

"That's simply not true. We both loved Jonathan. And we both desperately wanted you, too. We would have gone through . . . actually, no, we *did* go through hell to have another child. And when you arrived, we were both so happy we cried. We actually cried."

Sophie shrugs. "Well, it still didn't feel like that."

"That was just you," Barbara says. "Even as a baby, nothing was ever enough, was it Jon?"

Jonathan, who is lost in a traumatic world of parallel could-have-been-a-photographer lives, hasn't been listening. "Sorry?" he says.

"And what does that mean anyway?" Sophie asks. "You went through hell? How?"

Barbara shakes her head sadly. "You kids," she says. "You think everything's so easy. You think things just happen."

"Um, pregnancy? Well, yeah, it's not *that* complicated, Mum."

"Isn't it?" Barbara asks, casting around the room for escape. "Oh Gosh! Is that *Janet?*"

"Yeah," Brett says. "Janet French, apparently. She says Sophie went skinny dipping in her fishpond."

Barbara nods at the memory. "You did! You absolutely did do that. Gosh, it's Janet!" She wanders away. "Hello Janet!"

1983 – HACKNEY, LONDON.

Barbara stirs the pan and swipes onion tears from her eyes with the back of her hand. She glances over at Sophie who, pen-in-hand, is staring from the kitchen window.

"So are you doing your homework there, or just day-dreaming?"

Sophie swivels her head, zombie-style, to face her mother. "Uh?"

"That's my answer," Barbara says. "Get on with it, girl."

"It's maths. I hate maths."

"It's your last week, Sophie. This time next week you'll be on holiday. And a week after that, we'll all be in France. So just bite the bullet and get on with it."

"What does that mean?"

"Bite the bullet?"

"Yeah."

"It means to get on with something you don't like doing."

"I know *that*," Sophie says. "I mean, why do we say *bite the bullet*?"

"I think they used to give soldiers a bullet to bite on when they had to operate on them in the field," Barbara explains. "I think it was to stop them screaming. Now, homework!"

She glances at the kitchen clock. She's feeling nervous. She wants Sophie's homework out of the way before Tony gets home from his meeting with Pentax. She fears tantrums and in a way, cooking lasagne, which requires four different pans on the go, is her way of biting the bullet. It's her way of attempting to think about something else.

Sophie is chewing the end of her pen and staring at the sheet of figures in front of her. "I hate simultaneous equations," she mutters. "There's just no point to them."

"Well," Barbara says, alternately stirring the white sauce and the frying onions. "The sooner you get it over with, the sooner it will *be* over with."

"That's easy enough for you to say," Sophie says. "You don't even know what simultaneous equations are."

Barbara winces at this and slices and dices a red pepper into the frying pan. But she doesn't fight back, because Sophie is entirely right about this. Barbara has absolutely no idea what a simultaneous equation is. To her never-ending shame, she gave up trying to help Sophie with her homework when she was about eight.

"Oh, I get it!" Sophie says. "The answer's forty-two. Of course it is."

By the time a harried-looking Tony arrives, the kitchen is filled with the smell of baking lasagne. He puts his bag down on a chair and plonks a Pentax camera bag onto the sideboard, then crosses the kitchen to the refrigerator. He pulls out a can of beer.

"Hello," Barbara says, wiping her hands upon her apron. "How did it go then?"

"How do you *think* it went?" Tony asks, now pulling off his coat.

"I don't know," Barbara says, blankly.

"Have a guess. Go on. Have a guess," Tony says.

Sophie looks up from her maths homework. "*You* said you don't like the camera and *they* said you have to use it and *you* said you don't want to and they won, which is why you brought it home," she says. "Right?"

A silence ensues as Sophie waits for an answer, as Tony struggles to control his anger and as Barbara prepares to duck for cover.

"Very good," Tony finally says. "If you fail your O levels, you can get a bleeding hut on Eastbourne pier and make a living as a fortune teller."

Barbara bends down to peer into the oven and, knowing that no one will see, raises an eyebrow. Only Sophie can ever get away with cheeking Tony, or telling him the truth for that matter. There's something about her delivery, something about her broad open features, the naivety of her regard, that he simply can't be angry with.

"And what about France?" Barbara asks, quietly. "Did they say anything?"

"I still have to go to bloody France too."

"Well, that's OK," Barbara says. "We'll make a holiday out of it like we said. It'll be lovely. I've always wanted to go abroad."

"I can practise my French," Sophie says. "Bonjour Monsieur. *Je voudrais le ice cream s'il vous plaît.* Can't remember what ice-cream is . . . It's glass or grass or something stupid like that."

"Yes," Tony says, now fumbling in his bag to avoid eye contact. "About that. I'm afraid there's been a change of plan."

Barbara pulls on her oven mitts and bends down to pull the lasagne, which she has decided is baked to perfection, from the oven.

"What change of plan?" Sophie asks.

"They're sending me with, um, an assistant," Tony says, scratching his ear. "Someone to help with all the logistics. Someone who can sort out any problems with the camera."

Barbara carries the lasagne to the kitchen table. "You'll have to put that homework away now," she tells Sophie. "You can finish it afterwards."

"What, someone's coming with us?" Sophie asks, grimacing. "But *I* can help with the camera. You know I can."

"No, he's not coming with *us*," Tony says. "He's coming with *me*. I'm afraid it looks like it's just going to be the two of us now."

"But what about me and Mum?"

Tony shrugs. "Sorry," he says. "But it's work, sweetheart."

"Mum?" Sophie says.

Barbara feels like a wall of glass is forming around her. She feels suddenly very separate from the events in the kitchen, isolated, as if she's perhaps not here at all – as if she's perhaps just watching all of this from above.

"Mum?" Sophie says again. "Tell him."

Barbara picks up the largest kitchen knife and the fish slice, then returns to the table. She looks at the lasagne, steaming so perfectly. It looks like a cookbook illustration. It looks like an idea of a lasagne, just as she is an idea of a photographer's wife. It seems a shame to slice into it, a shame to reveal all those messy layers beneath the topping.

"I haven't been listening, really," she says and it's a lie but also not a lie. For though she has heard the words, they have somehow remained outside the bubble.

"Dad says we're not going to France with him any more," Sophie says. "He's going with some assistant bloke."

Barbara nods. "Is that right?" she says. "Who are you going with now, then?"

"I don't know yet," Tony says. "They haven't told me."

"So you don't know if it's a bloke at all."

Tony catches Barbara's eye, then looks away. He shrugs. "I'm really sorry," he says. "I'll make it up to you both. We'll go away somewhere else later in the summer."

Barbara runs her finger along the blade of the knife. She watches Tony's Adam's apple bobbing up and down and looks at the razor rash around his throat. She senses the weight of the knife in her hand.

"Well, that *is* a shame," she says, turning and slicing the knife through the lasagne in a single, decisive gesture. She watches as the red of the bolognese sauce spills into the pristine white of the béchamel. "That *is* a shame," she says again.

2013 – BERMONDSEY, LONDON.

By eight o'clock, the noise in the echoey gallery is such that everyone is shouting just to be heard, which of course is something of a vicious circle. About fifty people (Brett thinks more) have arrived now. A large group of journalists are yabbering in the middle of the room, various grouplets of Anthony Marsden's peers are dotted around the place, and a widows' club is commiserating in one corner. Only about five individuals are actively looking at the photos.

Though they have sold ten books, not one print has gone yet, but when Sophie asks Sarah Stone about this, she just smiles and says, "Well, it's not that sort of exhibition, is it?" Whatever that means.

Sophie takes a glass of wine from a passing waitress and catches Brett's eye across the room. "What?" she asks him when he reaches her. "It's only my third. And that's since six."

"Didn't say a word, hon," Brett says. "Anyways, no matter how much you drink, you'll never catch up with *her*." He nods towards the crowd of oldies.

"Who?"

"The chick with the wig in the middle. She was blasted when she got here." Sophie moves to the right but still can't see. "Go look," Brett urges. "That hairpiece is priceless. You *need* to see this."

Sophie weaves her way through the crowd to the edge of the circle. Phil, who is closest, steps aside to let her in, then, realising who she is, taps the woman with the wig on one shoulder. She is busy waxing lyrical about a photograph.

"Hey," he tells her. "Look who's here."

The woman turns to face them. She looks haggard almost beyond recognition and much older even than Phil. She looks shrunken, an impression her outsized military coat and badly fitting wig do little to help. But her dark eyes, the curve of her mouth, the snub nose . . . it's still definitely her. "Aunty Diane!" Sophie squeals, crossing the group and wrapping her arms around her, noticing as she does so that beneath the coat there's little more to her than skin and bones. "You came!"

"How could I not?" Diane drawls.

"I didn't know if you'd even got my messages," Sophie says. "I kept sending emails to that bloody website of yours."

"Huh!" Diane says. "Email shemail." She has a vague American accent and the gravelly voice of the chain-smoker but above all, Brett was right – she is utterly sloshed.

"Mum's here," Sophie says, scanning the room. "Did you—?"

"I saw her," Diane says. "She nipped out for some air. Said she'll be back in a minute."

"Oh?" Sophie glances towards the entrance. "Is she OK?"

Diane nods. "Uh-huh. Now," she says, pulling Sophie away from the group. "Tell me about you! I've been looking at your photos. They're *very* good." Diane links her arm through Sophie's in what feels like a very permanent fashion, more, Sophie suspects, to steady herself than for pleasure. "And I *love* your self portrait." She gestures with her free hand at the vast print on the end wall.

"Thanks," Sophie says. "I was scared it was too much."

"No, it's gorgeous."

"And Dad's, too," Sophie nods to the other end of the room. "Did you see? I tried so hard to contact you, Diane. I so wanted your help curating this. I hope you feel I chose the right ones."

383

"It's lovely, Sophie, lovely," Diane says. "Of course, your mother took that one, so the label's wrong but that's OK."

"The self portrait?"

"The *portrait,*" Diane corrects.

"Really?"

"Um. And Phil took the *Shipbuilding* cover shot of course. But you couldn't really leave that one out."

"Yes, he told me that. I wasn't sure whether to believe him. So that's true, then?"

"Oh yes. We often swapped photos. Your father had all the contacts, you see."

"More than you?"

"With the newspapers he did, yes."

"Well, please don't tell anyone," Sophie says. "God, I can't believe you came!"

"All the way from Portland, Oregon, my dear. Fresh off the plane."

"Really. Oh, I'm so happy Diane. I've missed you so much."

"I've missed you too," she says. "More than you'll ever know."

She pauses now in front of an image of Cliff Richard and Mary Whitehouse. "That's one of mine, she says.

"Noo!" Sophie breathes.

Diane nods. "Festival of light," she says, struggling a little to articulate the 's' and the 't'. "Bloody horrible it was . . . All the bigots in one place. Anti-this and anti-that. And I always thought that he was a closet case anyway."

"Is it really yours?" Sophie asks. "Because that's, like, three out of thirty. That's ten per cent that are just *wrong.*"

"Yes. You can tell because it's thirty-five mil'," Diane explains. "Your dad only used one-twenty. That was taken with my big Nikon zoom. God, I loved that lens. I wonder what happened to it."

Sophie groans. "Oh, please just don't tell anyone," she says.

Diane winks and raises a finger to her lips. "Mum's the word," she says.

"Tell me that the others are his, at least?"

Diane quickly scans the walls. "I think so," she says. "Yeah, I reckon you're OK." She steps to the left and then pauses in front of the next image, Sophie's photo of a group of laughing drag queens at a gay pride event. "Now this one, I really like."

"Thanks. It's one of my favourites too."

"They look like they're having such fun and yet . . ."

"I know," Sophie says. "There's a sadness, isn't there? So are you here just for the exhibition? Or do I get to see more of you?"

"No, sadly not."

"Oh. I'd love to see you again. Even if we just have dinner or something."

"Oh sure. I meant I'm not *just* here for the exhibition, sadly."

"Sadly?"

"I'll tell you about it later. But let's just keep things . . . you know . . . fluffy, for now, huh?"

"Oh, you're not ill, are you?"

"No dear. I just get kicks out of wearing silly wigs," Diane says. "Like your drag queens back there."

Sophie slides one arm around her waist. "But you are staying in England for a while?"

"I can't afford the bloody treatment over there, love. So yes. No choice, really."

* * *

Once Barbara's heart has slowed and she feels able to breathe again, she returns to the gallery. She will be polite and friendly to Diane. And then she will ask Jonathan to take her home.

385

When she steps back through the door, she sees that Sophie is with Diane, in fact Sophie has her arm around her. The two of them together is just too much for her to cope with, so she moves to plan B. She skirts around the edge of the gallery until she reaches Jonathan. He's talking to a good looking woman, apparently also from the *Times,* so Barbara lingers and, feeling silly, pretends to study a photograph that she, herself, took.

Eventually, Jonathan introduces the woman to the crazy lingering mother, whereupon she (presumably thinking that meeting the in-laws is a little premature) thankfully drifts away.

"Jon," Barbara says urgently. "Can you take me home, love? I don't feel so well."

"Home?" Jonathan says. "It's not even nine yet."

"I know, but I *do* feel poorly."

"Well, OK, Mum. In a bit," Jonathan says. He's used to Barbara crying wolf. "I just want to chat to a few more people. Diane's here. Have you seen her?" He points across the room and Diane, who happens to be looking their way, now leans in to whisper something to Sophie before breaking away towards them.

"Hello Barbara!" Diane says.

"Hello," Barbara answers with notably less enthusiasm. *Back to plan A,* she thinks. "How are you?"

"About as well as I look," Diane says.

Jonathan, who feels inexplicably unwelcome, coughs and makes his excuses. "I'd better, um, mingle," he says vaguely.

"I'm so happy to see you, Barbara," Diane says.

"Thanks."

"It's a lovely exhibition."

"Thanks."

"Sophie's done an amazing job."

"Yes. She has."

"Is something wrong, Barbara?"

Is something wrong? Barbara repeats the words in her head as she struggles to work out how to reply. What *would* the model of politeness and decorum she decided to be *say* to that? "No. Yes . . ." she mumbles confusedly, then, "Look. Why are you here, Diane?"

Now Diane looks confused. "Here you mean? Or in England."

"Both. Either."

"I'm sick, Barbara," she says. "I'm dying, actually. That's why I wanted to see you."

Barbara nods and manages to both look and *feel* sad at this. The feeling bit is a surprise. Perhaps time does heal. "Is it cancer?"

Diane nods and tugs at a strand of hair. "Hence this monstrosity."

"I didn't notice," Barbara lies. "I'm sorry."

"Well . . . That's what I wanted to say to *you*," Diane says. "That *I'm* sorry."

Barbara laughs lightly. She doesn't choose to do this, it just erupts. "You're *sorry*?"

Diane nods. "I wanted to . . ." But she lets her voice peter out. Barbara is holding one hand up.

"I really can't do this," Barbara says, still unexpectedly smiling. She doesn't feel as if she has full control of her features this evening. "Not here. Not tonight."

"But I . . ."

"In fact, maybe never, Diane. But definitely not here. Definitely not tonight."

"But I know you know," Diane says. "You *always* knew and I—"

"Stop!" Barbara says. The smile has vanished and her voice was louder than she intended. "Please, Diane," she insists. "It's all in the past now."

387

"But . . ."

"It's all so *long* in the past as well. Look around you. Half of the people who were there are dead now. Another ten years, there'll be no one here to even remember. So just . . . just *don't*."

Diane swallows and licks her lips. "OK," she says. "I just thought . . . But OK. God, I'm sobering up. And we can't have that." She turns away and crosses to where a waitress is passing with a tray of drinks.

You didn't cry, Barbara thinks. *You didn't shout. You didn't cause a scene. And now you can just go and forget this ever happened.*

She surveys the room, desperately looking for Jonathan, but it's already too late because Diane is scurrying back towards her carrying not one, but *two* glasses of wine. As protection, Barbara tries to engage a stranger in conversation. But he just nods politely and, no doubt frightened by Diane's other-worldly presence, slides off towards the exit.

Diane thrusts one of the glasses into Barbara's face. "Chink glasses with me," she says.

Barbara doesn't reply but simply shakes her head. She orders her hand not to move one inch towards the offered drink. Diane waves it around some more, almost spilling the contents but again Barbara shakes her head. "No," she says quietly. "I can't do that."

"You said it's all in the past. Just raise a toast with me. To Sophie. Just for that part of the story. That part of our story."

"I can't, Diane," Barbara whispers. "I'm sorry."

"Please," Diane says, still holding out the glass. Her eyes are watering and her bottom lip is trembling, Sue-Ellen style. "I'm not asking for thanks or forgiveness, or anything else. Just raise a glass to Sophie with me and you'll never see me again. I promise."

Her voice is quivering and Barbara can sense her own tears rising, the pressure of them slowly building behind her

388

eyeballs. She feels hot too, senses beads of sweat sprouting on her forehead. To avoid any further drama, she nods quickly and takes the glass from Diane's hand.

"To Sophie," Diane says.

Barbara swallows and wipes a tear from the corner of her eye. "You'll go?"

Diane nods. "I'll go."

"To Sophie then," Barbara whispers.

They clink glasses and Diane downs hers in two hefty sips. "You've done such a good job with her," she says. "You should be proud."

"Thanks," Barbara says, reaching out to steady herself on the wall. The room is spinning a little and the moment, sadly, still doesn't seem to be over.

"You're a saint, Barbara," Diane says. "You know that, right?"

"You can stop now. Please stop." Barbara's eyes dart around the room and she sees that both Phil and Jonathan are watching her concernedly.

Diane is still talking, despite her promise. "I can't believe that she turned out so well," she is saying. "And a photographer as well!"

Barbara's face is swelling. She can feel it doubling in size, she can sense it turning into a vast, hot mass of shame.

"OK," Diane is saying. "Maybe I *shouldn't* have come. But there's no harm done, is there?"

"Please just go," Barbara pleads. "You said you'd go. *Please just go!*"

"I will. But I'm just saying that she's a credit to you both," Diane says, stealing a last glance at Sophie. "And she looks *so* like Tony, it's uncanny."

Barbara gasps. She opens her mouth to speak but manages only a surprising, monotone groan, somewhere between the sound of a bereaved cow with a dead calf and that of a distant fog horn. She shakes her head and watches as, unexpectedly, her fingers release the glass and it falls in slow motion to the floor, where it shatters, wetting her foot.

The perspex bubble is back. It's been years, longer than she can remember, but it's back now and outside it, distorted by it, Jonathan is running towards her shouting something. *"Mum,"* perhaps. Everyone is looking at her. Sixty people have turned to stare. Perhaps they'd like her to dance for them, perhaps she should dance like a Zulu all over again but she can't because her legs are buckling now, even as the room is spinning around her, even as Diane, now fringed with rainbow colours, is covering her mouth and saying, "I'm sorry. I thought you knew. I always thought you knew." And the colours are brighter now, everything is brighter and rainbow edged, and whiteness is seeping in around the edges slowly obliterating the staring faces, the open mouths, the spinning pictures, the twirling ceiling. The brightness, the heavenly whiteness. Thank God for it. It's making all of this go away.

1983 – HACKNEY, LONDON.

It has been a week since the policewoman came to the door. It has been a week since Barbara fell to her knees, since she discovered that at forty-nine she had become a widow. A heart attack, they said. In Paris, they said. The coroner's report would follow. The body too, would follow. Such cruel language, such hard words, but things, even bad things, need to be described.

Since that moment, time has stretched into an endless landscape of nothingness, something way beyond sadness. A feeling that everything is locked outside. A feeling that feelings themselves are beyond reach. Just a void to be got through, just phone calls to funeral parlours and calls to Tony's friends and colleagues, and vain attempts to get Sophie and Jonathan to eat something, eat anything, even though Barbara herself is unable to eat.

But finally the week *has* passed and the body is home. Men, they leave you. Each does it in his own way but they leave you. And sometimes they come back dead.

Sophie slips silently into the lounge. She's wearing black slacks and a black polo neck sweater. Her eyes are puffy from crying.

"You're not wearing the dress," Barbara says, an observation, not a criticism.

Sophie just shakes her head. She crosses the room and sits at Barbara's side. She leans her head on Barbara's shoulder. "I still don't want to go, Mum," she says.

Barbara puts one arm around her. "No one *wants* to go," she says. "But it's good. You'll see. Funerals exist for a reason."

She looks at their reflection together in the curved screen of the television. Mother and daughter in black. Mother and daughter in mourning. As an image, it looks almost like one of those religious paintings. It would make a good photo, she thinks obtusely. But who wants to remember moments such as these?

The door to the lounge opens again and Jonathan enters. He's wearing a grey suit and a grey tie, badly knotted. Barbara makes a mental note to fix it before they leave the house. His complexion is almost the same colour as the tie. "There's a policeman at the door," he says.

Barbara frowns and sighs. She doesn't know why a policeman would come to the house on the day of the funeral but there's probably a reason. There's probably some formality that she has forgotten.

"Shall I show him in?"

She nods. "Yes. Show him in," she whispers.

She removes her arm from Sophie's waist then stands and pulls her dress down. The policeman, barely into his twenties, enters nervously, his hat in one hand. "Mrs Marsden?" he says.

Barbara nods.

"Can I have a word please?"

Barbara manages an approximation of a smile. "Come in."

"In private would be better," the man says.

Sophie glances up at her and then stands. "I'll go," she says.

"You too," Barbara tells Jonathan gently. "Help Anne with the food. I'll call if I need you."

The policeman closes the door behind them. He does this almost silently, as if scared of waking the dead. He pulls an envelope from his pocket. "We got the, um, coroner's report over from the French," he says. "They sent it by fax."

Barbara nods.

"His things are coming later as well," the policeman says.

Another nod. "Yes, I know."

"They sent me because I speak some French. So I can translate it, like. We didn't know if you'd be able to read it otherwise."

"I can't," Barbara says. "But do we have to do this today? The funeral's in two hours." She's trying to hold things together. And unexpected extras like these don't help.

"Oh, no. Not at all," the policeman says, sounding relieved. "I could come back another day, or even translate it and, um, post it to you."

He starts to slide the envelope back into his pocket but Barbara thinks, *What could it possibly say that could be worse than this? What could it possibly say that could bring any more grief? If we do it now, at least the funeral is the end of it all.*

"Wait," she says. "I changed my mind. Let's just get it over with, can we?"

Some emotion sweeps across the policeman's features, like the shadow of a cloud sweeping across a field. Barbara watches it happen and wonders what it means. "If today's the funeral, then it might be better if—"

"Please," Barbara says, sitting back down and patting the sofa beside her. "It'll only take a minute, won't it? And then it's done."

The policeman swallows and wrinkles his brow. "It's . . . not very nice, I'm afraid," he warns. "I had a peek, earlier."

"These things aren't nice," Barbara says.

He sits beside her and she takes the envelope from his hand, then pulls the sheet of fax paper from within. It shows an

393

official form, in French, filled in with a typewriter. Everything's in capitals.

She hands it to him. "So," she says.

The policeman clears his throat. "Are you sure you wouldn't prefer . . .?"

"No," Barbara says. She feels sorry for the policeman. He's little more than Jonathan's age. He's too young for this. She tries to help him out by pointing at the form. "This is when it happened, I suppose?" she says.

The policeman nods. "Yes. One-o-five. In the morning, that is. It's twenty-four hour clock. They always use twenty-four hour clock, the French."

"And this?" Some of the words are jumping off the page at her but she doesn't understand the context, so she assumes that they must just have very different meanings in French.

"Yes, that's the blood analysis," the policeman says. "They did, you know, an autopsy, just in case."

"Was he drunk, then?" Barbara has spotted the word, *alcool*.

The policeman nods gently. "Yes. Alcohol," he says flatly, "and, um, traces of cocaine and heroin."

"Heroin?"

"Yes. 'fraid so."

Barbara struggles to contain inappropriate laughter rising within. She coughs instead. "Tony didn't take heroin," she says. "Or cocaine. He didn't take *any* drugs."

The policeman clears his throat again. "I'm just reading what it says, ma'am."

Barbara snorts. "Then there's some mistake. There's been some mix up."

"I'm afraid that's . . . unlikely," the policeman says hesitantly.

"Heroin? No."

"It's more common than you might realise," the policeman says. "Especially with these arty types."

394

"No. It's just not possible. There's been a mistake. He was a photographer, not a junkie."

"I'm sorry, Mrs Marsden. I was only translating."

Barbara takes a moment to look out of the window, a moment to catch her breath. It's sunny outside and she feels that it should not be. The sunshine seems somehow an affront. It should rain, she thinks, on funeral days.

"Is that what they're saying killed him?" she asks, her voice wobbling strangely. "Did it make him have a heart attack? Because they said a heart attack. Is that right?"

"It says it might have contributed," the man says, pointing at some more French words on the sheet. "With the alcohol and the cocaine. And the, um, exertion."

Barbara chews her cheek. "The exertion," she repeats.

"Yes. He, um, wasn't on his own," the policeman says, clamping his jaw as if he has toothache.

"He wasn't alone?"

The policeman runs his finger across the text and then stops. He nods at the sheet. "I'm sorry," he says.

Barbara looks at his finger. He has a little dirt under the fingernail. And then she looks at the word above the fingernail. It says, 'SEXUEL'. It says, 'RAPPORT SEXUEL'.

Unexpectedly, surprising even herself, she laughs out loud. At first she snorts, then she chuckles and then she cackles like a witch. Tears of laughter start to stream down her cheeks. She knows it's inappropriate but she just can't help herself. "You're trying to tell me that my husband died, drunk and drugged, while he was making love to some hooker?" she says, through the strange wheezy laughter. "Is that it?"

"Mrs Marsden," the policeman says. "I'm sorry but you have to understand, I'm only translating what the French coroner wrote. That's all I'm doing here."

"Oh dear," Barbara says, looking away and wiping her face

on her sleeve. "There's been a mix up my love. He liked a drink but the rest . . . that's not my Tony. That's not Tony at all."

"Maybe," the policeman says, doubtfully. He scans the form. "It's unlikely but you never know . . . the woman, his assistant . . . she was supposed to have . . . you know . . . identified the body, at the coroner's office."

"His assistant?"

He nods and pulls a pocketbook out. "Yeah. A certain Diane Darbott?" he says. "Does that name mean anything to you?"

Barbara continues to laugh, but slowly, over the course of half a minute, the pattern of her laughter changes. It becomes harsher, more raucous, before finally morphing into a spout of uncontrollable sobbing.

"Mrs Marsden?" the young man says. "Mrs Marsden! Please. *Jesus!*"

Eventually, hesitantly, he puts one arm around her shoulders and Barbara, unable to do anything else, shifts her body towards him. She presses her face into the coarse blue material of his uniform and, onto the chest of an unknown twenty-something constable, she lets herself sob.

* * *

The funeral is well attended. That's what people say, isn't it? *Well attended.*

Everyone is there except Diane. Diane who could be back in America or locked in some stinking jail in France. Barbara doesn't know and she doesn't much care. Though if she's honest with herself, she has a vague preference for the latter.

She glides through the proceedings in a daze, listening to people who think they knew him, watching the coffin slide into the floor in a dream of loss. She thanks people on the outside of the bubble for having come. She shrugs when someone asks if Diane 'knows'. "She needs to be informed," the man says. "They were very close."

"I'm *sure* she knows," Barbara replies without flinching.

She's polite and neutral and calm, because this is the only way she knows to get through this. Jonathan, likewise, is stony and grey and self-restrained. Only Sophie cries, uncontrollably. Sophie cries enough for everyone.

Back at the house, Barbara serves perfect little sandwiches and tiny tomato tartlets. She listens to people laughing at stories from Tony's short life and tries not to hate them for owning bits of it she knows nothing about. She's been to funerals before. These things happen.

She eyes the package – his things, delivered in their absence, signed for by a neighbour – and tries to just get through this day without embarrassing herself. Because that could so easily happen. She could lose control and things could get messy. Truths could slip out if emotions run riot and the children must be protected. And that means that she has to bear this secret alone.

Once everyone has gone and leftovers have been wrapped in clingfilm, once the kids have gone to bed and curtains have been drawn, she drags the package to the lounge. She takes a pair of scissors and cuts through the twine.

She rips off the brown paper revealing Tony's suitcase, then breaks the wax police seal and opens the clasps.

First up comes his jumper. His big grey jumper. She sniffs it. She caresses it. She allows herself, unwitnessed, a brief, fond memory. Because of course, it wasn't all bad. Because no matter how he died, there is still loss. There is still, unexpected, unbearable, heartbreaking loss.

Then layer by layer she removes items from the suitcase. There are no surprises, no wafts of perfume, no condoms, no women's knickers . . . .

In the middle she finds his camera, the Pentax, rolled in some trousers and, protected in the Pentax bag, his beloved Rollei. Both have been emptied of their film.

And finally, at the bottom – perhaps someone hoped she'd never find it – is a large envelope stamped *Gendarmerie Nationale*.

In it she finds a series of contact sheets. The French police must have developed his films. She pulls them from the sleeve and notes the negatives languishing at the bottom.

Being contact prints, not enlargements, the images are small but she can still make out their content – blurry facile snapshots of Paris.

A woman, on a bridge (not Diane, thankfully). Two women in a bar, smoking (still not Diane). A dog, a tram, a train . . . The Eiffel Tower in the rain.

And then, at the back, a final sheet of square, black and white images taken with the Rollei – nudes, beautifully photographed. A woman's armpit against a white, crumpled sheet, a blurred shot of long black hair in motion – possibly Diane's – and then Diane, definitely Diane this time, naked, one arm thrown above her head, reclining on a chaise longue. Tony has never, to Barbara's knowledge, photographed nudes before. And she can tell, even from these small prints, that they're beautiful – perhaps, ironically, the best photos he has ever taken.

Despite the fact that her chest feels tight, she continues to work her way through the images. She has to look, just once. It's like all the rest. She has to get it over with. That, as the new head of this family, is her job.

Two hands, overlaid on top of a book; some fingers fiddling with an earring; a headless, generous, hairless nude (too curvy to be Diane) standing in front of a rainy Parisian window, a cigarette smouldering in one hand. Another image of a woman,

Diane again, kneeling before her. The woman still has the cigarette in one hand but is holding the back of Diane's head with the other, actively pulling her in.

Barbara turns away – a reflex, like pulling a hand from the flame. Like pulling herself from the shame.

She sees the fireplace and, still in reflex mode, scoops up the sheets of images and crosses the room to kneel before it. She lights the corner of the first sheet with a match, then slowly piles the others on top. The flames flicker and rise. A smell of burning chemicals fills the air.

She returns for the envelope, then casts it on top.

She wonders where Diane is now. Not that it would help but she'd like to slap her. She'd like to slap her hard, or punch her perhaps. She'd like to hear Diane struggle to justify herself and then push her from a Parisian bridge.

She tries to imagine what Diane would say.

"There were no drugs. They were just photographs. He's an artist," she'd say, as if this excused everything. Or perhaps she'd just deny it all.

"But you didn't even come to his funeral," Barbara would say. "Explain *that*."

She reaches out and snatches the envelope from the flames but it's already smouldering so she tips the negatives onto the carpet before returning the envelope to the grate.

What little power she has over Diane is tied to possessing these negatives, she realises. And with the way their lives have become entwined, Barbara may just need that one day. Sophie, after all, needs to be protected. She shuffles the negatives together and then holding them by the edges – not because she respects their content but because this is how Diane, herself, taught her to hold them – she stands.

She glances back at the prints, now almost entirely consumed, then refills and closes the suitcase before dragging it down to

399

the cellar. She hides it behind Jonathan's old go-kart, then returns to the lounge where only a few smouldering cinders remain.

There. All done. Tomorrow, we can begin pretending that he really was who we all thought he was, she thinks.

2013 – BERMONDSEY, LONDON.

When Barbara comes to, she finds herself in Sarah Stone's swivelling, reclining, office chair. Sophie is holding her hand and Jonathan is peering in at her. She struggles to focus on their faces, then raises one hand to touch the back of her scalp.

"You hit your head on the wall when you fell," Jonathan explains. "You fainted, Mum."

"How do you feel?" Sophie asks.

Barbara blinks repeatedly. "I think I'm OK," she says. "I don't know what came over me. The heat, I think."

"It's exactly twenty-one degrees," Sarah Stone says, perhaps fearing a law-suit. "But we've called for an ambulance, so they'll be able to check you out."

"I don't need an ambulance."

"Better safe than sorry," Jonathan says.

"Really, I'm fine." Barbara attempts to sit up but the sprung chair somehow resists this so she gives up and sinks back into the padded leather.

"Can I get you anything, Mum?"

She shakes her head. "No, I'm *fine*. Really. It was just a little fainting fit. These things happen as you get older."

"You should get back to the exhibition," Jonathan tells Sophie. "I'll stay here with Mum till the ambulance arrives."

"I *don't* need an ambulance!" Barbara says again.

One of the waitresses appears in the doorway. She points vaguely over her shoulder. "Some man," she says.

"Is it the ambulance?"

The girl frowns.

"Is it some kind of doctor?" Sarah paraphrases.

The girl shakes her head. "No. The man . . . he want to buy photograph," she says in a thick Slavic accent.

"Oh, OK. I'll go. Actually, you'd better come too, just in case," she tells Sophie. "If you're sure you're OK, Barbara?"

Barbara waves them away. "I'm *fine!*"

Once she is alone with Jonathan, Barbara beckons at him to come closer, "I need you to do something for me, son. Something important."

"Sure Mum. Anything."

"I need you to make her leave. She has to leave. Don't let her talk to Sophie, OK?"

"Diane?"

"Yes."

"She left already, I think. But why?"

"Please don't ask questions. Just make sure she's gone."

Jonathan stands. He pulls a face. "OK," he says. "If you say so. Will you be OK, or do you—"

"For God's sake. I'm fine!"

"Right. OK. Back in a tick."

"If she's there, just walk her to the door, OK? She's very, very drunk, so anything she says . . ."

"Sure. Fine."

In the corridor outside, Jonathan finds a huddle of Barbara's contemporaries waiting for news. "How is she?" Phil asks.

"She's OK. Um, Phil, do you know, is Diane still here?"

Phil shakes his head. "No, sorry. She left a while back."

"OK," Jonathan says, turning back. "That's fine then."

When Sophie steps back into the gallery, Brett beckons to her, so she and Sarah Stone cross to join him. "This is Jack Miles," Brett says. "He's interested in owning one of these." He points

402

to Tony's photo of a punk boarding a train. "That's doable, right?"

"Oh yes, that's a fabulous photo," Sophie says. "We have some limited edition prints of this one available, don't we Sarah?"

"Sure," Sarah says. "Come with me, Jack, and we can arrange all of that."

"I'd like to chat to you afterwards if that's possible," Jack tells Sophie.

"Of course."

Once Sarah has led him off to the desk in the corner, Brett asks, "So how's your ma?"

"She's OK, I think. She fainted but she seems fine now."

"That was some humdinger she was having with wig-lady," Brett says.

"With Diane?"

Brett shrugs. "If the wig-lady is Diane, then yeah."

"Don't call her that, Brett. What were they arguing about?"

"Beats me. But your ma was bawling at her, and some. She told her to go."

"Really?"

"Uh huh."

Sophie spins on one heel to take in the room.

"If you're looking for her, she's gone," Brett says. "Almost as soon as it happened, in fact."

"How weird."

"She might still be out front, I guess. With the nicotine junkies."

"I'll go check," Sophie says. "I can watch out for the ambulance too."

She walks past the bookshop, crosses the lobby and steps out into the cool night air. The daylight has gone now and the concrete plaza is lit by the orange glow of the street lamps.

A group of people from the exhibition are smoking just outside the door and Sophie suddenly wishes that she still smoked. She pauses, thinking of asking someone for a cigarette but then spots a small huddled figure on the far side of the esplanade. Unsure, initially, if it's a tramp or Diane, she crosses the space as quietly as her heels will allow.

Diane looks up as she approaches. She too is smoking and as Sophie reaches her, she smells the sweet, familiar odour of marijuana.

"Diane? Tell me you're *not* smoking dope in the street?"

"Um," Diane replies. "It helps with the pain. Is she OK?"

"Mum? Yes, pretty much. She fainted. She banged her head too. But I think she's OK. They called an ambulance, just in case."

Diane nods and breathes out smoke. "Good," she says.

Sophie checks the concrete tiles beside Diane. They look relatively clean. She sinks down beside her and leans against the wall. "Are *you* OK? Brett said you two were arguing?"

Diane smiles. "Not really *arguing*."

"He said Mum told you to leave or something?"

"Probably true. She's not my number one fan." Diane takes a deep drag on the joint then offers it to Sophie, who sighs and then capitulates. She takes a hit and it's sweet, the way it should be – high quality grass, not the horrible resin Brett buys – and then as she exhales she says, "Can I ask you something?"

"Sure. Fire away."

"Something personal?"

"Anything," Diane says.

"Did you and Dad ever have, you know . . ."

"Yes?"

"Did you ever have an affair? Because I always somehow thought you did. I always wondered."

Diane laughs, then coughs.

404

"Is that funny?"

"Well, we didn't have an *affair,*" she says.

"You didn't?"

"No. Not an affair."

"Oh. Sorry. I don't know why I thought that. Just a feeling, really."

Diane sighs. "The love of my life, is what he was," she says quietly.

Sophie turns to look at her in astonishment. "I'm sorry?"

"Your father. He was the love of my life," she says again.

"Really?"

"He was an *amazing* guy. Don't sound so surprised."

"But then how come you didn't . . .? Wasn't he . . . I mean, didn't you . . . God. How to put this? Did Dad not like you back? Or was he just very faithful to Mum?"

Diane laughs and coughs again. "Oh, he liked me back plenty, honey."

"Then you *did* have a thing?"

"Yeah. A thing. I suppose you could call it that."

Sophie is suddenly unsure how much more she wants to know. Strange and conflicting feelings are rising up within her, a mixture of outrage on her mother's behalf, disgust at her father's behaviour, and yet, and yet . . . She has always felt drawn to Diane. She's somehow excited, glad even, to learn that her father had a secret, second life. "I knew it," she says. "I knew there had been something between you two. When was that?"

"Sixty-three to eighty-three," Diane says. "Pretty much."

"What, the whole time?!"

Diane nods. "Except seventy-seven. We had a break in seventy-seven."

"What happened in seventy-seven?"

"I got married. It didn't last, though."

"Why not?"

Diane pulls a face. "I was still in love with Tony, I guess."

"And what about Mum? Did she know?"

Diane shrugs. "Barbara? You'd have to ask her. I can't see how she could *not* know but then again . . ."

"I just realised something," Sophie says.

"Yes?"

"You were with him in Paris. When he died? That was you."

"You don't want to know about that, sweetheart."

"But it *was* you, then?"

"Yes. But—"

"Just one thing."

"Really, Sophie. Don't go there. It can only—"

"Just one question," Sophie insists. "It's been driving me insane. The photos I saw, they were awful. Why were they so bad?"

"The photos from Paris?"

Sophie nods. "Yeah. The Pentax shots."

"God, I didn't know they were still around. Barbara told everyone that she had burned them."

"Not the negatives. She kept the negatives. But they were terrible. I couldn't use any of them."

Diane offers her the joint again but Sophie declines this time, so she simply stubs it out on the pavement beside her instead. "I don't know why. Because we were wasted, I expect."

"Really?"

"Really. Even mine were pretty bad. But your father was fighting with that dreadful camera as well. So . . ."

"Was it really that bad?"

"It was pretty lousy. And in Tony's hands, it was a nightmare."

"Why do you say, 'you expect'? Didn't you even see them?"

"The police took the films when he died. Evidence. They got them developed, I think. But I never saw them. I spent three nights in prison, then got expelled. Were there any . . . um . . . black and white ones?" Diane fiddles with a strand of wig. "Any taken perhaps with the Rollei?"

Sophie shakes her head. "Just blurred colour shots of the Eiffel Tower and rubbish like that. So why did you go to prison?"

"Again. It's best not to go there."

"But it wasn't because they suspected—"

"Drugs," Diane interrupts. "We had drugs on us. The French cops didn't seem to like that much. Funny that."

"God," Sophie says. "So he was just too stoned to work properly? Is that the reason?"

"Plus, as I say, the camera was pretty terrible, the light was rubbish – it was grey – and to be honest, with a few lucky exceptions, he just wasn't as good as everyone thought he was."

"Aw, come on. You can't say that. Not about Dad."

"I loved him, Sophie. I loved your father more than anyone I ever loved. But he was no great shakes as a photographer. His real skill was getting everyone else to help him out. Barbara was just as good. Better maybe."

"*Mum?* Don't be daft."

Diane nods. "She took good shots, Barbara did. Including a few that got credited to your father. She was good in the darkroom too. I taught her. Don't look so surprised. Barbara's many things but she's not stupid."

"I always thought she just kind of held Dad back, really," Sophie says. "So this is all a bit weird."

Diane laughs again. "Tony wouldn't have done anything without Barbara," she says. "He was a wild one, your father was. Out of control. Barbara was the only person who could keep his feet on the ground. Well, almost on the ground."

Sophie screws up her features as she struggles to grasp this entirely new vision of her parents' relationship. "You really think so?"

"I know so. She dressed him, fed him, mopped up his puke, took some of his best shots, developed his God-damned photos when he couldn't get them right . . ."

"Wow," Sophie says, still struggling to understand. "I never knew that. She never talks much about him, really."

"Did you even ask her?"

"No," Sophie says thoughtfully. "No, maybe not."

"Barbara's a saint. *Really*. A bloody saint. I don't know how she put up with it all. He was good to me, that's for sure, but as a husband, well, he was a horror, really."

"Don't say that," Sophie says. "Dad was everything to me."

"He was everything to me, too," Diane says. "But that doesn't change the truth. He was a lousy husband and a pretty lousy photographer most of the time. And without Barbara behind him, he wouldn't have . . ." Her voice peters out now and her eyes move to focus on something behind Sophie, something she has spotted lurking in the shadows.

When Sophie turns to look too, Brett steps into the pool of light from the streetlamp. He looks strange, his expression smooth and unreadable. "Brett?" Sophie says.

"So, this is the boyfriend, huh?" Diane asks.

"Yes. Um, how long have you been there, Brett?"

Brett raises his shoulders. "Not long," he says. He points back at the gallery. "The, um, paramedics are here. They came in the side way. You should go."

"Sure," Sophie says. "Can I just get your number, Diane? I'd love to talk about all of this some other time."

"Of course," Diane says. "I'd love to spend more time with you, Sophie."

"You go, honey," Brett tells her. "Your mum's waiting for you. I'll get Diane's details for you."

* * *

Once Barbara has ferociously seen off the ambulance men, Jonathan whisks her off, still protesting, to his place in Surrey.

Feeling a little orphaned, Sophie goes in search of Brett. She could do with a hug and some reassurance.

It's gone ten p.m. now and the crowd in the gallery is dwindling. Even Brett is nowhere to be seen.

Sophie chats briefly to Sarah Stone, who informs her that they have sold fifteen books and nine prints, though only three are hers. She says goodbye to Phil, a goodbye which, considering his age and health, feels final and emotional. And then noting that the remaining people in the room are involved in their own private conversations, Sophie heads back outside to see if she can cadge a cigarette. She's feeling a little over-emotional. Perhaps a forbidden cigarette might calm her nerves.

It's positively cold outside now – a wind has got up – and only a single smoker remains, one of the waitresses.

When Sophie approaches her, she looks concerned. "I am needed inside?" she asks.

Sophie laughs. "No," she says. "I was just wondering if I could scrounge a ciggy?"

"The girls looks confused, then, belatedly understands. "Oh, you want cigarette?" she says. "I'm sorry. Is last one. Here." She proffers her own half-consumed cigarette, which Sophie politely denies.

"I'm supposed to be giving up anyway," she says. "It's just . . . it's been an emotional evening."

409

"Your dead father," the girl says with an abruptness that only lack of vocabulary can excuse.

"Exactly. All his old friends too. Plus the ones who couldn't come because, you know, they died as well. It's a lot to handle."

"Yes," the girl says. "I understand this. My own mother. She die too."

Sophie takes a deep breath of the night air and then shivers. "I'll head back in," she says. "It's too cold for me out here."

"I come too," the girl replies, stubbing out the cigarette on a wall. "Otherwise the agency, they make trouble." Sophie likes the way she rolls the R in trouble and is just about to ask her where she's from when she spots two figures in the distance. "Actually, go in," she tells the girl. "I'm just going to see who that is."

Worried that one of the people in the shadows might be Diane, too stoned to even realise how cold it is, Sophie heads back across the plaza. As she reaches the figures however, she realises that they are in fact Brett and Malcolm.

"Really!" Brett is saying. "That's amazing."

"Yes," Malcolm replies. "That was taken with a high power zoom, whereas Tony, of course, was still using that old twin lens of his." Malcolm spots Sophie at this point and pulls an amusing, embarrassed grimace. "Hello Soph," he says. "I was just telling your chap here all the family secrets."

"Were you indeed?" Sophie replies in a parental voice. "That's very naughty, Malcolm."

"Well, Brett's family now, isn't he?"

"Of course I am," Brett says, chuckling smoothly.

"Anyway, I'd better be going," Malcolm says, spotting a dash of actual reproach in Sophie's eyes. "I was meant to be home an hour ago; your chap here has kept me talking so long, I'm half frozen."

Again, Sophie says goodbye and again, despite promises to

meet up, it feels poignant. It's almost like she's saying goodbye to her father all over again.

As they head back into the exhibition, she asks, "What exactly did Malcolm tell you?"

"Oh, nothing much," Brett says. "The same old stuff. How Phil took the ship pic. How Diane took the festival one. You know, babe."

"Don't you even *think* about using any of that," Sophie says.

Brett chuckles again. "Hey," he says. "It's like the man said. I'm family now."

On their way back in, they cross paths with more stragglers in the process of leaving, so Sophie pauses to say a few more goodbyes. With the end of the private view approaching, she feels even sadder – almost overcome by sadness.

In the gallery, only three visitors remain. "So how long do you need to stay, hon?" Brett asks.

"I need to chat to *that* guy over there," Sophie says, nodding towards the man who purchased a print, the man whose name she has already forgotten, "But then I'm out of here. I'm shattered."

"You want me to wait? So we can share a cab?"

Sophie shakes her head. "Actually," she says, "would you mind very much if I went to Jon's place instead?"

"You're still worried about your ma, huh?"

Sophie shrugs. "A bit. But more, it's just, well . . . I kind of feel we need to be together tonight. As a family. Not only for her but for me too. If that makes any sense."

Brett nods. "Sure. Whatever. You want me to come?"

"No, I don't think so."

"How you gonna get out there, babe?"

"I'll just get a taxi. I'm too tired to think about anything else."

"It'll cost an arm and a leg to get to Surrey."

411

"I'm too tired to care about that either."

"Fair enough," Brett says. "Your call."

"You're sure you don't mind though?"

"No, that works for me too, to be honest. I still have some work to do on Sunday's centre spread."

"I thought that was all done and dusted," Sophie says.

"Oh, it kinda is. But I had a few ideas tonight," Brett says. "Nothing major. Just tweaks. You know how it is."

2013 – GUILDFORD, SURREY.

By the time Sophie gets to Guildford, the entire household is asleep. When she sees the darkened frontage from the taxi, she almost considers returning to London and heading to Brett's rather than waking them. But after all, she texted that she was coming. She can imagine Judy groaning at the announcement, nagging at Jon to come to bed all the same. Yes, it's not her fault if Jonathan has become someone who's asleep by midnight.

She pays the taxi driver and throws stones at the window until a bleary-eyed Jonathan appears at the front door. *They* didn't see the text, he claims. But *they* don't mind either. As long as she doesn't wake Dylan they don't, at any rate.

He fixes her up with sheets and a blanket – their mother is in with Dylan – and then before returning to bed, kisses her on the top of the head like she was five again.

Sophie lies staring at the lounge ceiling and wishes that she *had* gone to Brett's instead. She tries to digest the evening's revelations. That her father had a lifelong mistress. That he was a 'wild one'. That he partied. That he was perhaps – because she can't really believe this one – no great shakes as a photographer. That her mother, who she so long resented, was the rock he apparently leaned upon.

Like some barely remembered identikit photo, she's finding it difficult to picture her father this evening. She's having trouble creating a cohesive feeling about who he really was as well. And with so much of her own identity, both personal and professional, being tied up with his, she has a worrying sensation of not knowing who she is either. Do the questions over his career make her own limited success more or less of an achievement, she wonders. Perhaps they simply make the limited nature of her success more normal, less unexpected? Is she simply a mediocre photographer from mediocre stock?

Does his infidelity to her mother with Diane, who Sophie occasionally wished *was* her mother, make him a better father to her or a worse one?

What to do with all of this new information, as well? Is there even anyone she can discuss it with? With Jonathan perhaps? With her mother? With Brett?

And what about that other strange sensation, lurking at the back of her mind, that feeling that she has missed something, that she has heard and recorded a major clue, yet has no idea what it relates to, nor any idea how to hunt for it.

A noise awakens her and she rolls over to see a dim glow coming from the kitchen. She pulls the sheet around her like a toga then pads across the deep-pile carpet.

"Mum," she says gently, from the doorway.

Barbara, who had been peering into the refrigerator, visibly jumps. "Ooh!" she exhales. "Gosh, I didn't even know you were here."

"I didn't want to go home alone," Sophie says. "Not after all that."

Barbara nods thoughtfully. "Yes. I know what you mean. Dylan woke me."

"Is he awake?"

"No. He just made some gurgling noises but it woke me all the same."

"How come you're in with him?"

Barbara shrugs. "Judy works in mysterious ways, her wonders to perform." She waves a carton at her daughter. "Milk?"

414

Sophie smiles. She literally hasn't drunk a glass of milk since she left home. "OK," she says.

They sit on opposite stools at the fold-out kitchen table. They sip their milk in the dim glow from the counter lights and talk in hushed tones. It feels nice. It feels intimate.

"So, were you happy with it?" Barbara asks.

Sophie nods. "I guess," she says.

"You don't sound too sure."

"I didn't expect it to be so emotional to be honest, Mum. I didn't prepare myself enough for that aspect of the whole thing."

"The worst for me was seeing all his old friends," Barbara admits.

"Phil and Malcolm? And Janet? All that lot?"

"Janet was OK. She was Dave's wife and everything but I always liked her. I always felt like she was my friend too. But the rest of them . . . I never saw them once after the funeral. So that was a bit difficult. That was really hard, actually."

"Why didn't you stay in touch?"

Barbara shrugs. "They were your father's friends, not mine. They wanted to hang out with the big crazy artist, not the big crazy artist's stay-at-home wife."

Sophie nods. Though she can now see how cruel this is, she understands. For most of her childhood she felt pretty much the same way.

"Someone told me that *you* were good with a camera," Sophie says. "In the darkroom too. I don't think I knew that, did I?"

"Oh, I only dabbled, really. Who told you that?"

"It was Diane, actually."

"Really," Barbara says, in a faux-disinterested voice. "Did she, um, say much else?"

"No, not really," Sophie lies, unsure even as she does so, quite why.

415

Barbara nods and sips her milk.

"You don't like her much, do you?" Sophie asks.

Barbara shrugs. "She's OK, I suppose. If you like those arty types."

"There isn't some other reason you don't like her? There wasn't some big falling out?"

Barbara frowns. "Not at all. Anyway, what sort of falling out?"

"I don't know. Just a funny feeling I had."

"No, we were never that close. And she moved to America *years* ago. So we completely lost touch. I didn't even know she was still alive."

"No," Sophie says. "Right."

"Anyway, I think I'm going to have another attempt at sleeping now," Barbara says, standing. "I expect Dylan will have us all awake soon. I'll see you in the morning."

"OK."

"Oh, and well done for the exhibition. I didn't say anything but I thought it was really very good. And I thought your photos were the nicest of all. By a long shot."

"Thanks Mum."

"Night night."

The next morning, it's all, "Dylan this", and, "Dylan that". No one mentions the exhibition once. It's as if it never happened and, after letting Sophie have the briefest of cuddles with her new nephew, Jon and Judy rush off to a meeting with the paediatrician.

After a quiet breakfast, Sophie accompanies her mother to the station. They share a train as far as Clapham Junction where Barbara swaps for the Eastbourne line.

The atmosphere during the journey is strained, as if their inability to discuss the elephant in the room is stealing the

416

oxygen of every other possible subject matter, so Sophie finds herself feeling relieved when their ways finally part.

She is supposed to call into the gallery by lunchtime but as she needs to change, she heads home first.

As she inserts her key in the lock, a queer feeling comes over her. She pauses and sniffs the air like a wild animal as she attempts to work out what strange vibration she is picking up.

She wonders, briefly, if she has been burgled in her absence, and scans the door-jamb for traces of forced entry before, deciding that her nerves must just be jangled, she opens the door and steps inside.

It's there again – the strange feeling. She stands on the threshold and scans the room. Everything looks tidy. Everything looks normal. She closes the door behind her.

She makes a cup of tea and, standing looking out of the window, she sips at it, occasionally glancing back into the room, just in case. The sensation that something is wrong, that the air within the room is perhaps the wrong shape, remains.

Once she has finished her tea, she moves to the bathroom where, still peering through the bubbles for hidden assailants, she showers and washes her hair. The powerful jet from the shower-head washes away the feeling and by the time she steps onto the bathmat she has all but forgotten her strange sense of unease.

She wipes clear a patch of the misted mirror and stares at herself. She looks older this morning. Of course, like most women, she often thinks she looks older than she should. When you're competing with all the Photoshopped beauties on the billboards, it's impossible to feel any other way. But today, she really does look older. It's as if she has moved from one of those categories you see on forms to another. No longer 25-44. Now 44-60 perhaps.

"Nothing a bit of make-up can't fix," she mutters, attempting to force a positive attitude.

She takes the toothbrush from the mug and applies toothpaste. She raises it to her lips. And then she freezes. Because something really *is* wrong.

The mug is empty, that is all.

The mug is empty. And the mug, which generally contains *two* toothbrushes and a razor, should not be empty.

She opens the bathroom cabinet. Brett's shaving foam and aftershave have gone too.

She turns and gently opens the bathroom door again, then peers back out at the lounge and this time she can see what is wrong, this time she can see why the space within the room is distorted. Brett's psychology book has gone. His jumper has vanished. His dope box is missing.

Her heart flutters. She walks, naked, through to the bedroom and opens the wardrobe. Brett's section is empty.

Barely able to breathe now, she attempts to remember their conversation last night, runs it through her mind word by word looking for any tiny hint of conflict. "That's mad," she murmurs.

She returns to the lounge and like a police crime-scene expert, she scans the room anew. It's too tidy. It's too empty. And there in the bowl are Brett's keys. And there on the keyboard is a folded Post-it note.

She crosses to the computer. Sophie, it says, simply. It's folded in two.

She sighs deeply, looks around the room again, then shakes her head and unfolds the slip of paper.

2013 – POWYS, WALES.

Sophie looks out through the spotless windscreen at the rolling countryside beyond. She stares at the pale blue sky, at the rolling hills of green, at this day, somehow familiar, yet entirely unknown, pinned to the cork board of her life forever more. It feels cinematographic, epic even. Some days are like that and you can sense, right from the moment you awaken that they are not going to be like any other day.

She drives well, not too fast and not too slow. She will not add tragedy to this screenplay. She checks the rear-view mirror, indicates and pulls out around the truck. She notes, but tries not to think about, the hundreds of miserable muzzles peeping through the gaps in the crates – tries not to think about the terror of hundreds of imprisoned animals being shipped to a place of destruction. But the thought manifests anyway: why, simply because we can't understand their screams, is this OK? Perhaps she should become vegetarian. Judy would like that.

"You're feeling more comfortable with the car now?" Barbara asks from the passenger seat, interrupting her thoughts.

The manoeuvre successfully accomplished, Sophie pulls back in and cancels the indicators. "Yes. it's fine. It's just the first half an hour, really," she says. "After that, it's just like any other car."

"Good," Barbara says, remembering Tony and the Sierra many years before.

They pass a road sign to Llanwrtyd Wells and Sophie points and says, "Isn't that where I was born?"

"Not quite," Barbara replies. "You were born in Llanelwedd. They're all Llan something or other in Wales. It's probably not that far, though."

"Maybe we could try to find that cottage you stayed in. That could be fun."

"Yes," Barbara says. "I suppose we could, if we could be bothered."

"It's funny, really. I mean, that I haven't been back here since I was born. Not once."

"Oh, I don't know," Barbara says. "I was never a great fan of Wales, myself. We always thought being sent to Wales was some kind of punishment. It was a bit of a family joke."

"You used to threaten *us* with Wales when we were little."

"I don't think *I* did," Barbara says.

"Yes. You did."

"I would have just been joking. It was because of the evacuations during the Blitz. We didn't want to be sent away, and your grandmother said we could stay in London as long as we didn't make a fuss. So any crying or misbehaving, she used to say, 'Watch it, or it'll be The Wales for you my girl'."

"You never told me anything about the Blitz," Sophie says.

"There's not that much to tell. Bombs fell. People died. A *lot* of people died. But *we* survived it all."

"You must have some great stories. The things you saw, the air-raids and all of that."

"I've been trying to forget about it most of my life."

The female voice of the GPS interrupts them. "At the next junction, go, straight on, on A483."

The stuttering interjection over, Sophie glances across at Barbara. "I suppose that's understandable," she says. "And how do you feel about coming to Wales? You don't feel like it's a punishment, do you?"

420

"No, it's beautiful," Barbara says. "And at least it's not raining. All my memories of Wales are of driving rain."

"Yes, we're lucky weather-wise."

"I'm still not convinced this is really necessary though – running away like this."

Sophie raises one eyebrow. "It's just for a few days, Mum. It's just till things cool off."

"All the same."

"There were three journalists outside my flat at seven this morning," she says. "Three. They would have tracked you down by now too. If you *want* to talk to the *Sun*, we can still go back."

"Don't be silly. You know I don't." Barbara fiddles in the glove compartment then offers Sophie a lemon bonbon.

"No thanks," Sophie says. "The sherbet makes me cough. I thought I was going to die after the last one. I almost crashed the car."

"What did it really say on the note?" Barbara asks. The yellow of the bonbons has made her think of Post-it notes.

"I already told you what it said."

"But that can't have been all. You can't stay with someone that long and then just say, 'Sorry.'"

"I told you, Mum," Sophie says again, her voice a little exasperated. "It said, 'Sorry Sophie. This one's a career changer. Forgive me'."

"And nothing more?"

"It was on a bloody Post-it, Mum. There wasn't room for any more."

"There's no need to swear, dear."

"Well . . ."

Barbara twists her mouth. "It's all very . . . I don't know . . ."

"Sordid?"

"Yes. It's a very bad way to behave. But I did say not to trust a journalist. I did warn you."

"Yes, thanks. I was waiting for that one."

"Well, I *did*."

"Yes, Mum. You did," Sophie says, sharply. "So, what?"

After a pause, Barbara asks, softly, "Are you upset? About Brett?"

"I'm furious. You know I am."

"Of course. But I meant more, romantically speaking. About losing him."

Sophie thinks for a moment before replying, "I don't know, to be honest. I keep waiting for it to hit me. Maybe I'm just too angry to be upset."

"Perhaps that'll come later."

"Perhaps it will. Then again, maybe I just didn't really love him like I thought I did," Sophie says.

"That would be a shame."

"I'm not sure," Sophie says. "Would it?"

They drive in silence for ten minutes, both lost in their loss and the scenery, before Barbara asks, "Do you think we'll be able to find a copy? In Wales, I mean."

"Of the *Sunday Times*?"

"Yes."

"Oh, I should think so. They even have electricity by all accounts. *And* telephones!"

"There's no need for sarcasm."

"I was just joking, Mum. But yes. They'll have the *Sunday Times* in Wales. I'm not sure I really want to read it though."

"Nor me," Barbara says. "But I think I'll probably *need* to read it. Before we go back, at any rate."

"I have a feeling it's gonna be pretty bad," Sophie warns.

"If it just says that a few of the shots weren't his, then—"

"The way journalists are," Sophie interrupts, "I doubt *very* much that's all it will say."

"What else do you think it could say?"

Sophie sighs. "I don't know, Mum. You tell me."

Barbara turns back to the side window. "Gosh, Wales is green," she says. "I suppose it's all that rain."

* * *

Barbara makes two cups of tea in the tiny kitchen, then moves through to the lounge of the rented cottage. She puts the cups on the coffee table, then slides onto the settee beside Sophie. "Go on then," she says. "I think I'm as ready as I'll ever be."

Sophie stares at the folded bundle of paper that is the *Sunday Time*s. "Are you sure?" she asks.

Barbara nods. "Yes," she says. "Go on."

Sophie rips off the Cellophane packaging, then extracts the culture supplement from the pile. She flips it over and inhales sharply. There, on the cover, is Barbara's 'self' portrait of her father. "God!" she exclaims.

"Britain's Best Photographer?" the caption reads. *"Or a drunken, womanising fake?"*

"Oh," Barbara says, simply.

When Sophie reaches to turn the page, Barbara puts one hand over hers. "Perhaps you shouldn't read this after all," she says.

"I know, Mum."

"You know?"

Sophie nods. "I *know*. About Diane and Dad."

"Oh. I didn't realise," Barbara says.

"She told me."

"OK then. Go on. Let's see how bad this really is."

Once they have both silently read the four-page spread, Sophie comments, "I can't believe that Brett left me for *this*. What a worm!"

"At least he was nice about *your* work," Barbara says. "At least he said that it's you who has the real talent."

"Who cares?" Sophie says. "He still left me for a single spread in the *Sunday Times*."

"Men do that kind of thing," Barbara says. "At least he left you for a reason. At least it wasn't just on a whim."

"What, this is not just a whim?"

Barbara shrugs. "Well, if it is, it's a pretty mean-spirited whim."

"It says you took the abortion demo photo as well. Is that true?"

Barbara nods. "Yes. Phil must have told him that. He was the only one who knew."

"And what about the others?"

"Oh, the others were his. Don't worry."

"All of them?"

"Well, except the ones I've told you about."

"So, only four of the thirty weren't his, right?"

"Yes. That's right."

"And it says the postal worker shot was staged?"

"Yes. That one was my idea. But your father took the photo. Anyway, there's nothing wrong with staging a photo. You know that. The strike was real enough."

"I suppose. And the summer of seventy-six. I remember, we were on holiday. You told him to take that one too, didn't you?"

"I had good ideas sometimes. That's all."

Sophie sips her tea. "Sure. But why let Dad take all the credit?" she asks. "That's what I can't work out."

Barbara reaches out to close the supplement. "Sorry, but I can't look at that any more," she says. "But in answer to your question, I suppose I just never felt I was in competition with him. That was never my idea of what marriage was. That's not how we were brought up to think."

"What, girls were brought up to be doormats you mean?"

"That's unfair, Sophie. I saw us as a team, that's all."

"But what about Diane? You knew."

"Yes. Of course. I tried not to think about it. I was very good at not thinking about it. But deep down, yes. Of course I knew."

"Did you know she was in Paris with him?"

"Sophie, do we *have* to do this?"

Sophie shakes her head sadly. "I'm only trying to understand, Mum."

Barbara nods and licks her lips. "OK. No, then. I didn't know about Paris until afterwards," she says quietly. "Diane was supposed to be in America, remember. I didn't know until I saw the coroner's report that she wasn't."

"The coroner's report?"

"Diane identified the body. So her name was on the report."

"Oh Mum," Sophie says. "That's awful. Didn't you ever think about leaving him?"

"Of course I did."

"But?"

"I don't know," Barbara says. "Again, it's not how we were brought up. We were taught to make things work. No matter what."

"But he had a *twenty*-year—"

"I *know* what he had, thank you."

"Sorry, Mum, but you know . . . You could have done other things."

"What other things?"

"I don't know. You could have had a whole different life. Didn't you have dreams?"

"Dreams . . ." Barbara laughs. "My mum once told me that dreams are like butterflies. If you catch them, they die."

"Oh, that's a bit depressing."

"But true."

425

Sophie thinks for a while, then says, "I don't think that *is* true. Dreams *can* come true. Sometimes. If you believe in them enough. If you're determined enough."

"Well, I'm glad you think that way. And maybe you're right. Maybe it's a generational thing."

"What is?"

"Having dreams. Or at least, thinking they're possible."

Sophie wrinkles her nose at the logic of this, then says, "Anyway, you didn't want to leave him? Not even once you knew for sure?"

"No. I suppose I thought that he needed her in a way."

"He *needed* her?"

"*We* needed her perhaps. Your father needed a drinking buddy and that was never going to be me. He had a wild streak in him. It was like an illness almost. The pressure would build up, and he'd have to let it out. So in a way it suited me that he went crazy with her instead of me. It kept all of that side of him out of the house. It kept it away from the family."

"I could never have put up with that. I would have killed her. Or him."

"I didn't feel I was in competition with her, really. Or not later on anyway. I had won that battle. Diane did everything she could to get him. But it was me he married, after all. It was me he came back to every night."

"But didn't it hurt you? That must have hurt so much."

"It did. But not as much as it hurt her."

"I still would have killed her," Sophie says.

"Well, I can't honestly say that I *didn't* think about it. But it was complicated, Sophie. It was the sixties and seventies. People were living in threesomes and foursomes and communes ... Everything was changing. Everyone was questioning everything. And Diane was special to me too. For the early years she was, anyway."

426

"You two were friends, then?"

"We were more than friends. She was family."

"A member of family who sleeps with your husband?"

"Yes, well . . . put like that, of course . . ."

"And you fell out . . . when?"

"Paris was the last straw. I thought she was in America by then. I thought it was all over. So Paris hurt. Tony, you know . . . being with her . . . and then not coming back . . . the fact that she saw him last. That hurt more than anything else."

Sophie nods. "I can't even imagine. She said she got married once. For a year. Did you ever meet the guy?"

"Diane? Really? No, I don't know anything about that. She had a boyfriend once. Or so she said. But I don't know anything about a marriage."

"I'm assuming she never had any kids, then?"

Barbara looks away. "I really wouldn't know," she says. "But I doubt it."

"I wonder why."

"I think she was a bit like you. She just never liked them much. She preferred her career."

"It's still kind of unusual for a woman of her generation, isn't it?"

"You're the one who spoke to her, dear, not me," Barbara says, her voice sounding brittle.

"Well, she didn't mention anyone. She sounded very alone."

"That's called karma, dear. It's called *bad* karma."

Sophie stops stroking her mother's shoulder, leans forwards and raises her fingertips to her temples.

"I know it's a lot to take in, dear. But you can't blame people," Barbara tells her. "They do the best they can. And often it's not very good. But it's still the best they could manage."

Sophie shakes her head. "Diane *said* you were a saint."

"I'm afraid that's pretty meaningless coming from the likes of her."

Sophie closes her eyes and continues to rub her brow, prompting Barbara to ask, "Are you OK?"

She shrugs. "I'm not sure." Her phone, which has been buzzing all day, now buzzes again so she swipes it from the table and glances at it, then frowns and taps at the screen. "Huh!" she says.

"More journalists?" Barbara asks.

"There are plenty of those. But no, that one was from White Cube. She says the gallery's gone crazy. They've sold right out of prints. She wants to know if I can bring in some other works."

"Really?"

"That's what it says."

"Any publicity really *is* good publicity," Barbara says.

"Apparently," Sophie says. She puts down the phone and sighs deeply. "Can we go and find that cottage this afternoon? I'd love to see the place."

"Where you were born? I'm not sure I *could* find it," Barbara says. "Why do you want to anyway? It's just a damp little house in the woods."

"I don't know," Sophie says thoughtfully. "I feel weird. It's hard to explain, Mum. But I've been feeling it for days, ever since the exhibition, since before, even. It's like something is missing. It's like there's this one piece of the puzzle that doesn't fit into place."

"What piece? I don't see any puzzle."

"No? Maybe not. I don't know," Sophie says. "Maybe it's me, but it's like ... why didn't you leave him? Why put up with Diane? Why would she come to the exhibition, too? I mean, with the history you have and everything ... And how come we still got to hang out with her when we were little, even though you knew she was sleeping with Dad? I mean, we called her 'aunty' but *you knew*. And she still came to the house. I feel like there's something I've missed. Does that make any sense? I suppose it doesn't to you."

"Well, I didn't know at the beginning." Barbara shrugs. "Anyway, I've explained as best I can. You're probably just a bit in shock. We all are."

"There wasn't some other secret? There's nothing else going to jump out of the closet at me? I mean, say Brett tracks everyone down and interviews them all and everything. And he probably *will* do that. You're not Diane's secret sister or something? That really is everything, is it?"

Barbara fiddles with a box of matches on the coffee table, pushing it around with one finger like a toy car. She senses that Sophie is on the verge of figuring it all out. She thinks that even if she doesn't, then it's true, Brett just might. All he'd have to do would be to get Diane drunk. To get Diane *drunker*. So perhaps she *should* tell her. Even though they all swore that they would never tell anyone, perhaps the time has come.

Tony, Minnie, Glenda . . . they all took that secret to the grave. Only she and Diane remain to tell the story of how their lives got tied together forever. And they swore it should never be told.

"There is something, isn't there?" Sophie says.

Barbara sighs deeply. There's still time, she can still obfuscate here. She could tell her some minor part of the whole thing to put her off the scent. She could tell her about the true contents of the photos from Paris for example. Or she could tell her about the drugs. Either would do the trick.

Then again, she could tell Sophie the one thing that might make sense to her – the one thing that might help her to understand who she is. Because though people these days like

429

to pretend that everything is about how you bring children up, Barbara knows that it isn't. She can see – has always been able to see – just how much of it comes down to genes.

"Mum?" Sophie prompts.

"Well, there is perhaps *one* other thing," Barbara says.

1969 – LLANELWEDD, WALES.

Barbara sits, a blanket wrapped around her shoulders. She watches the door to the cottage. She waits. Beside her the fire sizzles and splutters. The wood is damp. The room is damp. Beyond the door she can hear the rain falling, always falling.

Other than a brief trip to her mother's bedside, she hasn't been out of this horrible house for months. Other than her mother, her sister, Tony and Jon, she hasn't *spoken* to anyone for months. She's on the verge of insanity. She can feel it lingering around her, waiting to take over. But it will soon be over. And it will soon be worth it.

She never wanted anything more than this.

Just after five, the door to the cottage finally opens and Barbara inhales sharply then holds her breath.

Tony stands in the entrance, silhouetted against the dim daylight beyond. Behind him, water falls in sheets from the blocked guttering. He seems hesitant to step into the room.

"Tony?" Barbara says. "What's wrong?"

"Nothing's wrong," he says, then, "It's a girl."

He steps inside and kicks the door closed behind him, then crosses and crouches down beside Barbara.

She leans across and pulls back the swaddling. She inhales sharply. "God, Tony, she's beautiful!" she says, tears unexpectedly welling up.

Tony nods and sniffs. "I know," he says, his voice croaky.

He hands over the baby and Barbara takes her in her arms, fiddling already, to unwrap the blanket.

"She's fine, Barbara," Tony tells her, his voice struggling against the emotion of the moment.

"I know. But I need to see for myself," Barbara replies, lifting the baby free and allowing her blurred vision to roam over every tiny detail of her.

"You see?" Tony says.

"Yes. She's huge compared with Jonathan," Barbara says, swiping at her eyes with the back of one hand.

The child screws up her features and starts to cry, so Barbara stands and crosses the room to wrap her in a new, fresh blanket. She doesn't know why but she needs to do this, she needs to get rid of this other blanket, the blanket that she came in.

"Jonathan was early," Tony reminds her. "Sophie's right on time. Are we still going with Sophie?"

"Yes," Barbara says. "Yes, I think so. Is *she* OK?" She nods towards the second cottage.

"Diane? Yes, she's fine. She's knackered but fine."

"And she's still OK about this? She hasn't changed her mind?"

Tony shakes his head. "No," he says. "Have you?"

"Of course not. Do you need to get back to her?" Barbara asks. She feels an urgent need to be alone with the baby.

"The midwife's still there," Tony says. "So I'm OK for a bit."

"And Jonathan?"

"He won't be back till late. Mrs Llewellyn said she'd bring him back at sunset."

"And you're sure she doesn't know either?"

"No one knows, Barb. No one except us. And the midwife, of course. But she won't say anything. She's paid not to say anything."

Barbara nods gently and rocks the baby at the same time. "I think I should get into bed before Jonathan arrives," she says.

432

"Yes," Tony agrees. "That's a good idea."

"You should go. You should make sure she's OK."

"Alright," Tony says. "If you're sure *you're* OK?"

"Why wouldn't I be?" Barbara replies. "That was the easiest childbirth ever."

By the time Mrs Llewellyn brings Jonathan home, Barbara is in bed without make-up and Sophie is sleeping beside her.

"Come and meet your little sister," she tells him, and Jonathan sidles across the room. "She's very wrinkly," he says, peering in.

"Babies *are* very wrinkly."

"Did I look like that?" he asks, disdainfully.

"Yes," Barbara says. "Yes, you looked exactly like that."

And it's true. They have remarkably similar features. Barbara struggles to push the comparison from her mind. Because the fiction that they have created here, the thing she has pretended to believe, the great untruth they have all, for different reasons, decided to act out, namely that the father of this baby is Diane's ex-boyfriend Richard, requires that she never look for resemblances. Ever.

POSTSCRIPT.
1968 – LAMBETH, LONDON.

Tony struggles to open his eyes. His eyelids seem, in his sleep, to have been pasted shut with some kind of glutinous gunk. He rubs his fists against them, then tries to open them again. The desolation of the room comes slowly into focus.

He works his mouth and then manages to call for Diane but there is no answer.

Still having difficulty focusing, he looks around the room and remembers why he feels so bad. They have been partying for two days. The ash trays are full and the remainders of joints have burned fresh holes in the carpet. Emptied beer bottles lie around. Dirty plates fill the gaps. His jumper, new for Christmas, is lying on the floor in front of him. It is stained with vomit.

In search of Diane, who could still be out for the count, he rolls to the other side. The rest of the room is strewn with rubbish as well: more plates, empty crisp packets, records without sleeves, sleeves without records, three remaining tabs of LSD and a half-smoked joint.

Right next to him is the cover of *The Doors*, one side of which he now remembers they played in a loop for almost twenty-four hours. Diane must have switched off the record player. So she's up and alive then. A few grains of coke are strewn across the record cover and he dabs at them with one finger, then rubs it into his gums. He pulls a face at the bitter, numbing taste of the drug. He could do with a boost this morning. He could do with a bit more of a boost than this. But the only remaining drug is LSD and that won't help him get straight. It won't help at all.

Diane enters the room from the bathroom. She is naked except for a towel wrapped around her middle. Her hair is wet. "Hello, you're back in the land of the living then," she says. She sounds miserable.

"Um," Tony says. "I feel terrible though."

"Me too."

She sits cross-legged in front of him. He can see beneath the towel and he guesses that, knowing Diane, this is intentional. But he feels too rough to care, too hungover and sick and fluey to be interested in any way in anything that she has to offer this morning.

"I've got something to tell you," Diane says, biting her bottom lip in an approximation of cuteness.

"Not now, Di," Tony says. "Whatever it is—"

"I'm pregnant," she announces.

Tony blinks exaggeratedly.

"I am. I'm pregnant," she repeats.

Tony laughs sourly. "You're pulling my plonker," he says.

Diane reaches for a packet of Chesterfield to her right and pulls one out with her lips, then lights it from her Zippo lighter. It wobbles up and down as she speaks. "No, I really am pregnant," she says.

Tony groans, grimaces and finally manages to sit up straight. "You can't be. We were careful."

"I think maybe we weren't one time. When we were out of it."

Tony stares into her eyes and even though he knows that this is true, knows, even, that it wasn't just one time, he says, "I don't think so. It can't be mine."

"It is," Diane says. "There's been no one else."

Tony sniffs, clears his throat, and then pushes the stained jumper away from him. He can smell it from here and it's making him feel queasy. "Are you sure?" he asks.

Diane nods. "Totally," she says.

Tony shakes his head. "Well, how bloody stupid is that?"

"Don't say that. I thought you'd say—"

"What?" Tony interrupts. "Zip-a-dee-doo-dah? What a wonderful day?"

"I don't know. I thought you might be glad."

"Glad?" Tony says, now struggling to control his anger. "Glad?"

"But it's our baby, Tony," Diane says. "It's . . ."

Tony is standing. He's hunting for his missing shoe.

"You're not going?"

"Yes, of course I'm going. I have to work."

"But I just told you something really important. You can't go, babe. I just told you I'm pregnant."

"Just . . . just don't talk to me Diane," Tony says. He pauses and turns to look at her. His face is red. He looks angry. He looks really angry. "I mean, h . . . how?" he splutters. "How the hell could you even think of doing that, Diane? How?"

Diane's eyes are beginning to glisten. "Don't say that, Tony," she says. "You did it too. And we'd be good together. We are good together, you and me. You know we are."

Tony gestures at the room. "Look around you," he spits. "Look at the bleeding mess. This is what you and me would be like together. This is what we are like together. And you want to bring a kid into this? You don't even like kids. Christ!" He taps at the side of his head. "You're out of your mind, woman."

"But you don't love Barbara," Diane says, standing now and letting her towel slip to the floor. "You've never loved her. Not properly. It's me you love. You said so. You told me. That's why I thought maybe . . ."

436

Tony kneels to peer under the sofa. "Where's my shoe?" he asks. "Where is it? And *Barbara*, for your information, is the only decent idea I ever had."

In search of the shoe, he limps to the bathroom where he suddenly realises he needs, urgently, to pee. This done, he returns to the lounge and holds out one hand. "Give me my shoe," he says. "I know you've got it."

Diane, now sitting cross-legged in an armchair, shakes her head. Her expression is cold, calculating. "Not till you tell me you're going to leave her," she says.

"What?" Tony asks, incredulously. "What? Oh, you've hidden my shoe. You win! I'll divorce my bloody wife? You really have lost your marbles, haven't you?"

"You can't expect me to have it on my own," Diane splutters.

"I don't expect you to have it *at all*."

"I can't abort."

"Er, actually, you can. And if you don't give me my shoe, I swear I'll bloody—"

"I'm Catholic," Diane says. "You know that."

"You're *what*?"

"I'm Catholic. I can't abort."

Tony gasps. "You? Catholic?" he says. "That's news to me. It'll be news to the bloody Pope as well. *Catholic?* Honestly!"

Diane starts to cry now. The tears form and tumble down her cheeks and neither does she wipe them away, nor does she turn her face to hide them. She wants Tony to see this. She wants him to share the pain. She wants him to change his mind.

"Don't . . ." Tony says. "Stop crying, Diane. Stop bloody crying. You know I can't stand it when you cry."

But the softening of his voice only encourages her. She lets herself weep ever more freely. And when she reaches the peak of what genuine tears will allow, she adds a few manufactured sobs into the mix. Soon enough, Tony has given up searching for the shoe, which she knows, because she hid it there, is beneath a cushion. Soon, he is kneeling at her side, his forehead pressed to hers, his arms around her shoulders.

Later, when she has cried herself out, when she can no longer even force out *fake* tears, when the last joint has worn off and the alcohol in her system begins to vanish, they talk more reasonably.

"We've been really silly, haven't we?" Diane says.

"Yeah," Tony agrees. "We really have. And you know I can't leave Barbara. You always knew that."

"I don't think I even want you to, to be honest," Diane says. "I don't think I'm made for washing and ironing and mending socks."

"Or bringing up a kid."

Diane sniffs. "Or bringing up a kid," she agrees. "I really *can't* abort, though."

"Honestly Diane. What are *you* gonna do with a kid? You hate bloody kids. You know you do."

"I know. But I can't abort. It's just instinct."

"But think about it. Think about bringing up a little'n on your own. Like I said, look around."

Diane surveys the devastation of the room. The cold light of day is streaming through a gap in the curtains throwing the dirt and jumble of the room into stark relief. She shrugs. "I could clean up my act, maybe?"

"Yeah. Maybe you could. But would you want to? You? Really?"

Diane groans. "I'll get it adopted then," she says.

Tony laughs.

"What?"

"Oh, it's just the irony of it all," he says.

"Irony?"

438

"Yeah. Barbara's banging on about adoption. Because she can't, you know, have any more. And you're the one who gets bloody pregnant."

Diane shrugs. "There's your answer then," she says quietly.

"Where?"

Diane doesn't reply. She simply nods upwards with her chin as if the answer is just behind him.

Tony pinches the bridge of his nose for a moment as he tries to work out what she means, then exhales despairingly and says, "You know, you really need to cut down on the pot, Di. You really, really do."

"But think about it."

"Just *try* to be logical here, OK? I know it's hard but try, just for me. How can you even *imagine* that Barb would go for that?"

"She *might*," Diane says, apparently in all seriousness.

"What, like, 'Hi sweetheart. I got my girlfriend knocked up. Any chance you could bring up her kid?' Something like that?"

"She needn't even know it's yours."

"Of course she'd bloody know it was mine."

"We could say I've got a boyfriend. Think about it. I get a boyfriend, I get pregnant, I tell Barbara. I could get Richard to pretend he's the father or something."

"What, your friend from college?"

"Yes."

"But he's . . . you know . . . one of them, isn't he?"

"Barbara doesn't know that."

"Just stop, Diane. Please stop," Tony says. "You're driving me barmy here."

"I could convince her. I know I could. She really likes me. And she *loves* kids."

Tony stands now and shakes his head. "I'm off," he says. He holds out one hand. "We'll talk about this later but right now give me my shoe. Because if I have to leave barefoot, I swear you'll never see me again. And I really mean that, Diane."

She fidgets to one side and removes the shoe from beneath the cushion. For a moment she holds it out of Tony's grasp. "Just think, Tony," she says again. "Barbara gets the baby she wants and we get to carry on like nothing's happened. It's perfect. For everyone."

Tony lurches now and snatches the shoe from Diane's hand. "Like nothing happened?" he says. "Just get rid of the thing, Diane. I'll pay. But that's the only way here. You're gonna have to get rid of it."

"I'm sorry," Diane says. "But that's my child you're talking about. And it's your child too. It's *our* child. It's half you and half me. Just think about that. Just think about what that means. There's just no way, Tony. There's just no way I could *ever* do that."